The Incumbent

Also by Alton Gansky

Dark Moon
The Prodigy

J.D. Stanton Mysteries

Vanished
A Ship Possessed
Out of Time

The Incumbent

ALTON GANSKY

GRAND RAPIDS, MICHIGAN 49530 USA

ZONDERVAN™

The Incumbent
Copyright © 2004 by Alton L. Gansky

Requests for information should be addressed to:
Zondervan, *Grand Rapids, Michigan 49530*

Library of Congress Cataloging-in-Publication Data

Gansky, Alton.
    The incumbent / Alton Gansky.
        p. cm.
    ISBN 0-310-24958-9 (softcover)
    1. Political campaigns—Fiction.   2. Female friendship—Fiction.   3. Missing
persons—Fiction.   4. Women mayors—Fiction.   5. California—Fiction.
6. Abduction—Fiction.   I. Title.
PS3557.A5195I53   2004
813'.54—dc22

                                                                    2004012892

Interior design by Michelle Espinoza

Printed in the United States of America

04 05 06 07 08 09 10 /❖ DC/ 10 9 8 7 6 5 4 3

The Incumbent

chapter 1

There were five of us, four members of the council and me, Mayor Madison Glenn. I seldom use the name Madison except on legal documents and even then only with reluctance. My father told me it was a good name, "strong, decisive, and majestic." It was my misfortune to be born while my father, a history professor at the University of Santa Barbara, was reading a biography on James Madison. Dad got a good read; I was stuck with the name. I'm thankful that he wasn't reading a bio of Ulysses S. Grant. It took years of gentle nagging, but now even he calls me Maddy.

Santa Rita is the place I call home, as do roughly 125,000 other people. A small city by most standards, it is large enough to provide everything a person needs: hospital, college, nice homes, wide streets, and an eye-popping view. Located on the ocean shore, eighty miles north of Los Angeles and just south of Santa Barbara, Santa Rita sits like a jewel against the usually brown coastal mountains. The azure Pacific waters glitter in the sunlight, cool the city in the day, and provide a warm blanket of air in the evening. Every day is picture-postcard material. To tourists Santa Rita is Eden; to the rest of us it is home.

The Chamber of Commerce promotes our town as "California's Heaven." On most days I agree; on others I can't help but notice that a little hell oozes across our borders.

When I had left my office to make my way to the council chamber, the sun had already set and a slab of gray clouds had rolled in, veiling the stars and moon. An easy drizzle had begun to streak my window, sending sinuous veins of water coursing from header to sill. I hoped this was not an omen.

I've been the city's mayor for two years—two challenging years. I am the town's first elected mayor. Before the election twenty-four months ago, the mayor was selected from sitting council members, as with most cities our size. Last election, however, was different. Candidates ran at large, the first time since 1851, when our town incorporated. It was a hot race, full of contestants, each certain they were the best person for the job and that any other candidate would lead the city into utter ruin and degradation. I won. I don't know how, but when they counted the last ballot, my name was on top. Perhaps it was because I had already served two four-year terms on the council. Or maybe it was because I was the only woman in a contest of six wanna-bes.

Two of the other candidates sat at the bench with me. Larry Wu, an accountant of Chinese descent, had come in third. He was a gracious loser and the least problematic member of the city government. Larry had spent his childhood in Texas and came to Santa Rita when his father's firm transferred him. I'd known Larry for six years but still struggled to reconcile his Asian face with his southern accent.

Jon Adler had also fought hard for the seat. He had money and outspent me on the campaign two-to-one. A lanky attorney, he treated the campaign like the criminal cases he tried before local judges. He attacked the other candidates with the flair and joy of a hunter blasting pheasants out of the sky. He paid little attention to me, assuming I was the dark horse of the group. He shredded poor Larry.

They were able to remain on the council, since their seats were not up for election for another two years. That was two years ago. Both men were once again pressing the flesh, making promises, and leveling accusations.

The chamber was quiet and attendance sparse. When controversial matters are on the agenda, the darkly paneled halls can hold up to 250 agitated, and often loud, citizens. This night was low-key. The agenda was routine, with only one item of business that was close to contentious: an appeal for a conditional use permitfor a local church that wanted to move to a new site. Four people, three men and one woman, sat together close to the aisle. They were whispering to each other. I assumed they represented the church. Across the aisle that bisected the chamber sat Sue Holton, chairperson of the Planning Commission. She was there to speak against the appeal.

Santa Rita has only one newspaper, a daily called the *Register*. They had sent one reporter, who sat three rows back, head in hand. He looked ready to doze. Hard day at the computer, I assumed.

I let my eyes drift to the back wall of the chamber. It faces the concrete plaza and fountain that greets any of the public who make their way to the seat of their city government. The lights of the chamber reflected off the glass, making it difficult to see outside, but I could tell the drizzle had turned to rain. I could also see a man enter the lobby. He paused and brushed the rain from his suit coat as if he could sweep the water away like dust.

I forced my thoughts to the task before me. I am punctilious when it comes to time. Any meeting that starts late is off to a bad start. We were all present and accounted for and thus there was no reason for delay. In one minute, at precisely 7:00, I would call the meeting to order. The agenda for our session was light, and with a little luck we could be done in less than sixty minutes. That was fine with me. I had a double-chocolate brownie waiting on the kitchen counter at home. It had been a demanding day. A double-chocolate brownie was my due.

On the counter before me was a small digital clock with bright red numerals: 6:59 turned to 7:00. As I raised my gavel, the man in the lobby stepped through the back doors of the chamber. In full light I could see it was Bill Webb. He took two steps and raised a hand, mouthing the words, "Hold it." I lowered the small oak mallet.

This had better be important.

Bill Webb was our chief of police and a fixture in the city. He marched to the platform, then sprinted up the few steps to the bench. This was unusual. You don't just dash up the steps to where the council sits—even if you're the police chief.

He leaned over my right shoulder. "I need to speak to you." His breath smelled of peppermint. He had quit smoking the year before and had replaced one oral fixation with another.

"I was about to start the meeting; can't it wait?"

"No."

"What can be so important that it can't—"

"There's been a crime. It involves Lisa Truccoli."

My stomach sank. "What? How?"

"I want to talk to you. Privately. Now."

"Of course." I turned my attention back to the chamber. "The meeting will stand in recess for ten minutes."

"Wait a minute," Jon Adler said. "You can't recess a meeting that hasn't been called to order."

He was being his usual tedious self. I picked up the gavel and smacked it down. "This meeting of the Santa Rita City Council is called to order." I brought the gavel down again. "This meeting will stand in recess for ten minutes."

"But—"

I stood and exited the chamber, Bill Webb on my heels.

T he news was disturbing and Webb was blunt. We were in my office, which is just down the corridor from the chamber. The rain was falling hard, splashing against the window like pebbles.

"We got a call from one of Ms. Truccoli's neighbors, a Mrs. Ramirez, who had returned home from grocery shopping. As she passed the Truccoli residence, she noted the door was open. She thought it odd, especially since it remained open the entire time it took for her to unload the car. When she finished carrying her purchases in, she walked over and knocked on the open door. There was no answer. She went in and found the house empty. That's when she called us."

"And?"

"Just what you'd expect: Dispatch sent a patrol car. The officer investigated and noticed that several things looked out of place, as if there had been a struggle."

"But the house was empty? I mean . . ." The words remained lodged in my throat.

"No corpse was found, if that's what you're getting at."

It was exactly what I meant.

He paused, as if wondering whether to let the next sentence loose. "There was, however, blood."

The acid in my stomach roiled. "Blood?" The word came out as a choked whisper.

"Not much. Very little. Just four drops."

I looked at Chief Webb. He was a stern man whom I had never seen smile. He was fit for a gentleman of fifty-five, with just a slight middle-age paunch over his belt. He stood four inches taller than my own five foot six, and his gray-streaked black hair was combed straight back and held in place by some ancient hair tonic. He was not the kind of man who would use gel. The skin of his face was starting to droop, as if it had grown weary of hanging on to the muscles beneath. The scowl was there. It was always there. I'm convinced he was born with that pinched look: blue eyes narrowed, mouth turned down as if he were in chronic pain. He seemed to be in a perpetual state of emotional constipation. Red highlighted the end of his nose and his cheeks, like a man well acquainted with alcohol, except I had never seen him drink.

Chief Webb and I had history. I was not on his Christmas list and he certainly wasn't on mine.

"Four drops? You found *exactly* four drops of blood?"

"That's right."

"That seems strange."

"It's much stranger than you think." He turned to the window and looked out, staring into the distance. I was just about to ask him for details when he continued. "The drops of blood weren't discovered on the floor or furniture, like you'd expect to find after a struggle. These were on a card—a white card—and they were evenly spaced."

"I don't get it. Could you be less cryptic?"

That made him turn. He eyed me for a moment, as if determining whether I was capable of understanding what he was about to say. "Blood from a fight is never evenly spaced, Madam Mayor. Nor is it perfectly round, as these drops were. Blood splatters and blood streaks, but it never falls in precise drops. These were four perfectly round, evenly spaced spots of blood on a white card . . . like the four corners of a square."

"A card? What kind of card?"

"A business card, Mayor. Your business card."

The phone on my desk buzzed. I jumped. Webb stood like a rock. I snatched up the receiver and barked, "Hello." Dana Thayer, the city clerk, was on the other end.

"It's been fifteen minutes, Mayor. The council is wondering when you'll be returning."

I was five minutes beyond the announced recess time. I was late. "This is going to take some time, Dana. Please inform the council that I won't be in attendance." I hung up before she could respond.

"This is an awkward time," Webb said. I couldn't tell if he was apologizing for the interruption or reveling in it.

"Larry Wu can handle the meeting. That's what deputy mayors are for." I paused, then added, "I suppose you have questions for me."

He nodded. Then—I could hardly believe my eyes—he smiled.

Being mayor—even mayor of a small city like Santa Rita—has certain privileges. Technically, all the powerful people work for you. This means I can stretch the envelope of social courtesy more than most. I was sure Webb would have loved to walk me out of my office, his hand clamped on my elbow, and escort me across the back parking lot and right into the Police Station. What a sight that would have been. Even the dozing reporter from the *Register* would have sat up for that one. "Mayor Taken to Police Station for Questioning," the headline would have read. That would have sold a few extra papers.

I took a seat behind my desk. "Ask your questions." My desk is a wide, cherry wood affair given to me by my husband before his death. It dominates my small and orderly office. Any interview Chief Webb wished to conduct was going to take place on my turf, where I would gain the advantage. The desk is an extension of me, but more importantly, it is an extension of the mayor's office. "Sit down," I said, motioning to a burgundy leather chair opposite the desk. He remained on his feet.

"You knew Ms. Truccoli?"

"I still do know her."

"How do you know her?"

I sighed. "You know the answer to that, Chief. She worked on my campaign."

"This last campaign?" He slipped his hands into the pockets of his pants. Webb dressed with impeccable taste but always in gray. This night he wore a charcoal gray suit, white shirt, and steel-colored tie.

"Yes, and my second city council run. She was treasurer in the last campaign."

"Important position."

"California election law requires every campaign to have a treasurer and demands frequent reports from them. A good campaign must have a great treasurer."

"So she handled the money?"

"She did." I leaned forward. "She was exceptional, organized, focused, and a clear communicator."

"So you had no reason to be unhappy with her?"

"None at all, and let me save you some time, Chief. The books balance perfectly. Nothing missing. Nothing extra. Are you assuming that because my business card was found in her home, I had something to do with her disappearance?"

"These are questions I have to ask, Madam Mayor."

"She would naturally have my card; she worked on the campaign. All my key people had them. There's nothing unusual about that." I was getting defensive and reigned myself in.

Webb stared at me for a moment, his eyes narrowing to slits. I could almost hear his brain chugging. "It's not the card that interests me, Mayor; it's the fact that blood—which for the moment we must assume is Ms. Truccoli's—was found on your card and on your card only."

"You're not suggesting—"

"No, I'm not. It's too contrived ... too obvious."

"So why question me?"

"Because it needs to be done, and I thought better me than Detective West. It's not unusual for the chief of police to talk to the mayor. A homicide detective is another matter."

"You're trying to spare me embarrassment?"

"I'm trying to spare the office embarrassment."

"That's decent of you," I said, making no effort to conceal the sarcasm. "Who is Detective West? I don't think I've met him."

"He's a new man. We got him from San Diego PD. He did homicide work for them."

"He left the big city for us?"

Webb nodded but offered nothing more. As he started to ask another question, his cell phone rang. He removed it from his inside coat pocket. "Webb." He listened, his face a plastic mask of indifference. I would get no information that way. "Give me the name again." More listening. "Hang on." He turned to me. "You know Ms. Truccoli's daughter, Celeste?"

My heart stuttering, I rose to my feet. "Yes. Where is she?"

"At the house. She's upset."

"You think?" I rounded my desk and stepped quickly to a coatrack I kept in the corner, removed my coat, and slung it over my shoulders.

"Where are you going?"

"To Lisa's house. Celeste must be beside herself—she needs a friend."

"We're not done here."

"Wanna bet?" I started for the door.

"I'm going with you. I don't want you contaminating the crime scene."

"Suit yourself."

I turned to see Webb raise the phone to his ear again. "Keep her there." The phone went back in his pocket. "I'll drive," he said. It wasn't a suggestion. "I'll arrange to have your car delivered to your home."

"You don't need to do that."

"Yes, I do."

He didn't explain.

Lisa Truccoli lived in the Shadow Hills area of the city, a community of older but upscale homes on the gentle slope of Shadow Hill. Her house, like all homes in that neighborhood, overlooked the ocean. The sea, under its heavy gray shroud, was dark as India ink.

Rain fell in cold sheets, pelting Webb's city-issued Lincoln Continental. The air was chilly and the breeze stiff. California gets its rain from two sources, depending on the time of year. During the summer months, the rare rainstorm crawls up from the south, first showering Baja Mexico before working its way up the coast. In the winter, storms drop down from Alaska like brakeless freight trains. Those have a sour and chilling impact. This February day a monster was visiting us from the north.

The drive had been easier than expected. The rain had driven most people indoors to warm themselves in the glow of the television. Webb piloted the car over the slick streets with confidence. He said nothing. The chief was puzzled and I couldn't blame him. Our city is large enough to have its share of crime, but abductions and murders are rare, at least when compared with bigger cities.

This crime was an enigma for Webb. It didn't take a psychologist to realize that. While I found him to be annoying and egotistical, he was a good chief of police. I had to hand that to him. I'd never found his work wanting or improper. What he thought of me I could only guess, and I never wasted time worrying about it.

Light from street lamps spilled in through the windshield at regular intervals, like a strobe light in slow motion. With each influx I could see my reflection in the passenger-side window. Staring back was a thirty-eight-year-old woman with shoulder-length brown hair, narrow nose, and weary hazel eyes. My complexion looked pale but that was to be expected. The window was a poor mirror, its impromptu image unintentional. Still, I *felt* pale.

"Why Lisa?" I asked, breaking the silence.

"Don't know. If it's a murder, then it could be many reasons: passion, greed, anger. If it's a kidnapping, it could be profit-motivated. Did . . . does she have money?"

"Some, I suppose. Her ex-husband is an executive in one of the oil companies. He used to work on the offshore drilling rigs. Years ago he started taking night classes in business. He worked his way up."

"So she's divorced."

"He grew tired of family life and went off to find himself; took a twenty-four-year-old receptionist with him so he wouldn't lose his way."

"Conscientious, eh?"

"That would require a conscience. He left Lisa and Celeste . . ." I paused to think. "About four years ago, or so."

"So she was supporting herself?"

"She works as an accountant for a construction company, but I remember her saying that she gets a large alimony payment. I don't think she needs the money; probably just wants to stay busy. I imagine she spends much of her time alone."

"Why's that?"

"Celeste is nineteen and attending the University of Santa Barbara. She's gone a lot. Maybe that's why she works, to pay for her daughter's college."

"Do Ms. Truccoli and her daughter get along?"

"Oh, come on. You can't be implying—"

"I'm not implying anything. I'm asking questions, that's it."

I took a deep breath. I was taking this harder than I realized. "I'm sorry. This has me on edge."

"Do they get along?"

"As far as I know, but I'm not her confidant. We meet for lunch about once a month. I take my key volunteers out from time to time. Good helpers are hard to come by and I want to keep them on my team. A few lunches throughout my term keeps everyone in touch. Last time we met, she was saying how proud she was of Celeste. Still, if there had been problems, I wouldn't have known."

"And the husband?"

"Never met him. They were still married during my last council race but divorced sometime during my term. I'm guessing here, but I think they were at odds long before I met her."

"Do you know where the husband is now?"

"Not specifically. Lisa said something about Texas, along the Gulf, I think."

Webb grunted.

"He might be worth investigating," I said.

"I'll leave that up to Detective West. He's the investigator; I'm just lending a hand." He turned down a street that I recognized as Lisa's. "Ever been here?"

"Once. Lisa held a fund-raiser. I haven't been back since." My stomach knotted and my breath shortened. I had never been to a crime scene before. Worse, I'd never spoken to a young woman whose mother had been abducted—or worse.

Webb directed the car down the narrow residential lane: Dove Street. All the streets in the Shadow Mountain subdivision bore bird names. It fit the quaint houses that lined the roads. Unlike many similar streets in other cities, these had very few trees. Tress block the ocean view, which lowers property value. In Santa Rita the sea is everything.

Built in the mid-sixties, the houses were the developer's idea of a tribute to Frank Lloyd Wright's prairie style. Flat roofs topped every home, with overhangs that extended from the exterior walls farther than seemed right. Unlike Wright's designs, these homes were small and were much less expensive to build. Still, any one of them would have sold for over half a million. A cottage with a view is worth as much as a mansion stuck at the end of an alley.

The community was too pricey for most newcomers, so there was little turnover in the neighborhood. The Truccolis, Lisa had told me, were numbered among the newbies. Her husband, Christopher, had made a good salary on the rigs, and she brought home decent money as an accountant. Through disciplined saving and help from both sets of parents, they had managed to pull off the purchase. I imagine keeping up payments had been a chore, at least until his career took off.

The car came to rest at the west curb. Lights, pushing past gossamer curtains, shone from the few street-side windows, but I could imagine the glow pouring from the much larger ocean-facing panes. A band of yellow tape surrounded the property like a gaudy belt, telling the world that here a peaceful life had been disrupted.

The front door was open and warm light decanted from it, splashing like paint on the small concrete porch. A thin, shallow silhouette appeared between the jambs. Even from the street I could tell it was Celeste. As she walked from the house, raindrops showered her.

I sprang from the car and started down the narrow concrete walk. "Celeste?"

"Go away," she shot back, continuing her march.

"Celeste, it's Maddy, Maddy Glenn. Where are you going?" I met her halfway down the walk. Rain fell in drops the size of raisins, cold raisins that stung the skin.

"Go away." She tried to walk around me. Her head was down; blond hair hung around her young face, shielding it from view.

"No. Not until we talk." I took her by the arms. "Look at me, Celeste. Look at me." She did and I could see the pain. Water streaked her skin—water that had nothing to do with the rain. "Where are you going?"

"I don't know . . . Away."

"Away to where?" I tightened my grip, fearing she would bolt.

"Away from here. I can't stay here. I can't . . . I can't . . ." The sobs came from the deepest place of sorrow, from the abyss of hopelessness. "She's gone. She's dead. I'm alone." Her shoulders began to shake.

I pulled her close, wrapping my arms around her. Her weeping came in waves that pounded the shore of my resolve. The sky seemed to be grieving with the young woman. Water ran down my forehead and face. I could feel my hair sag under the weight of it, and I felt the cold of the wind, but I was determined not to move until Celeste was ready.

chapter 2

I hadn't gone into the house. There was no need. Chief Webb had told me what they found and that was good enough for me. My concern was Celeste. With her father in another state and her mother missing, she was alone. I had decided to take her to my place. I could make her comfortable and relay any information from the police. It was the least I could do.

Celeste had protested at first but without conviction. She was emotionally beat down—a dry leaf in a hot August wind. Who wouldn't be? There are few feelings worse than abject helplessness.

Chief Webb had offered to drive us to my home, but I had insisted on picking up my car. I saw no need in taking an officer off the street just to save the few minutes it would take to drive by City Hall. Once Celeste and I were in my car, I made the thirteen-minute drive to my place.

My home sits on the beach. It is large, spacious, with entirely too many rooms for a woman who lives alone. I never planned to be alone. The house remains my source of comfort. It is a world unto itself. I work hard to make sure the reality of the outside never seeps through the exterior walls. My husband called the place his Fortress of Solitude. He read too many Superman comics as a kid.

Like many houses that line the coast, this one was built in the late seventies, an era when diagonal cedar siding was in. It is three thousand square feet of open space, with one room flowing into another, and only bathrooms and bedrooms constructed for complete privacy. Most of the lower floor is one big room with areas delineated by flooring and counters. Upstairs are four bedrooms, each with their own bathroom. My home office is also there, in what once was a game room. It's an ample space, with large windows that overlook the rolling surf, and small panes facing the street.

The house was my husband's dream. I grew up in much smaller digs and had been content. I'd never known poverty, but my father's salary from the university, and my mother's income as a high school teacher, was not nearly enough to pay for any house on the beach, let alone one this size. My husband's family was a different matter.

I married Peter in my senior year of college. We both attended San Diego State University, where he was a year ahead of me. He had grown up in San Diego. Athletic and intelligent, he excelled in college and even made the baseball team, playing second base. After he took his degree in business, he joined his father's company—Glenn Structural Materials—a manufacturing firm that makes flooring for commercial buildings. "Yup," Peter used to say, "the rich and powerful walk all over our product." His eyes twinkled when he said such things. His eyes always twinkled, and not a day goes by that I wouldn't give up everything for just one more twinkle. Just one.

Eight years ago Peter was in Los Angeles on business. Nothing unusual in that. Most of the company's product went into high-rise buildings. Peter was often on the road. In the last two years of our marriage I filled my time with city council work. It gave me a strong sense of purpose and passed the lonely hours.

At 10:12 that evening the phone rang.

"Mrs. Glenn?" The voice was polite and professional. It melted my strength away like a blowtorch on butter. No call after ten o'clock that begins, "Mrs. Glenn" could be good. This wasn't. A police officer, in succinct but kind words, told me that Peter was gone, the victim of a carjacking gone bad. "He was shot," the officer said. The words pummeled me. I told myself there was no way this could be true, yet I knew it was. I knew before I picked up the phone.

I was a widow at thirty.

The years have muted the pain, but I still hate the ringing of a phone at night.

Peter's company had carried a large life insurance policy on him. The money was enough for me to pay off the house. My father-in-law still ran the company and still paid Peter's salary. All that had changed was the name on the "To:" line. I told him the checks weren't necessary. "Yes, they are," Peter's dad said. "I would have paid him anyway. This way I feel like I'm helping and . . . for the moment it takes to sign the check, I feel as if Peter is still alive."

I've never brought the checks up again.

"Is this okay?" Celeste asked.

I was sitting on the floor of the living room, in front of the fireplace. The blaze warmed my body but could not drive the chill of memory away. Celeste had come down the stairs and was standing on the last step. Damp from the rain, I had shown her my closet and helped her find something comfortable. She was dressed in a blue sweatshirt with a Yale University emblem. I collected college sweatshirts. Why? For the same reason people collect saltshakers. I don't know why, I just do. The sweatshirt was a little large on her. Although we were close to the same height, I still had an inch on her and almost two decades of life.

Celeste wore her body like most nineteen-year-old girls. She had grown into a woman but still retained a bit of a youthful spindle-look. She tugged at the jeans she wore; like the sweatshirt, they were mine. I recognized them. They were the pair that seemed a little too snug lately. She pulled them up again.

"It's great. Do you feel warmer?"

"A little." She lowered her head, as if making eye contact would crack the dam of emotional control she was trying so hard to shore up.

"Come sit down by the fire," I said, patting the floor. "It'll help dry our hair—of course, we'll both end up with a terminal case of the frizzes."

She smiled. Even across the room I could tell it was forced. I've forced many a smile in my day. Celeste crossed the carpeted floor, passed the white leather sofa and the wrought iron end tables, and came to my side. There she crossed her ankles and lowered herself like an elevator until she was seated cross-legged on the floor—a maneuver that would have broken something in me.

We stared at the orange and yellow flames, watching them dance like leprechauns on St. Paddy's day. "I find fires relaxing," I said. "They help me think."

Celeste placed her elbows on her knees, cradled her round face in her hands, and gazed into the fireplace. I could see the light sparkle in her blue eyes.

I wanted to ask questions, but everything I could think of seemed insipid. "How was your day?" seemed inappropriate. I also knew that the police had questioned her thoroughly; she didn't need another round of inquiries from me.

"Will they call if they learn anything?" she asked softly. She had begun rocking.

"Yes, they know to call here."

"The waiting is hard." There was a tremor in her voice. "I don't like waiting."

"Me either. A two-minute egg takes two minutes too long."

She didn't respond for a moment. Then she looked at me. "Do you think she is . . . I mean, do you think my mom is . . ."

I placed a hand on her knee. "I don't know. We still have hope."

"I don't know what I'll do if she's . . . dead." The tears washed over her lids and down her face.

"It's too early to worry about that." My own eyes were starting to swim. "For now, you're welcome to stay with me. I have plenty of room."

"Mom liked . . . likes you." She fixed her eyes on the fire, as if mesmerized by the flame. "She said you were the smartest person she ever met, man or woman."

"I like her. Her good work made my election possible." *Great, I sound like a politician.* "What I mean is, she went above and beyond the call of duty. I always felt comfortable around her. I can't say that about everyone."

"You mean like Chief Webb?"

We exchanged glances. *It couldn't be that obvious.* "What do you mean?"

"Mom said you two don't like each other. How come?"

I hadn't expected that. "It's not that we don't like each other; we just have different views. As mayor, I had to make some hard decisions and he didn't like them."

"Does he want your job?"

I chuckled. "A lot of people want my job, but Chief Webb isn't one of them. He dislikes politicians. He's mad at me for other reasons."

"Like what?"

"Money, for one thing. The Police Department always needs more money."

She nodded. "The police didn't get the money they wanted?"

"Not all of it. The city didn't have the funds. We did what we could."

Celeste continued to rock, then asked, "Could they find my mother better if they had the money?"

The question pierced me. "No, sweetheart. That has nothing to do with this. The money they wanted was going to other things, like new radios and such. The police are doing everything possible to find your mother. They'll ask for help from others if necessary. Chief Webb has a chip on his shoulder when it comes to me, but I've never known him to shirk his duty."

Rocking, rocking, and more rocking.

"Did you hear me, Celeste?"

"Yes."

"Everything is being done that can be done."

"I miss her." She sniffed and ran a hand across her cheek. I leaned back and found the box of Kleenex I keep near the sofa. I handed her one and then took one for myself.

"I know you do," I said. I love words. They're powerful, even life-changing. Now they were as weak as the tissue I held.

"We aren't like other families." Celeste blew her nose. "Most kids my age fight with their parents. Maybe it's because Dad left us, but we never fought, never. All my friends can't wait to move out of their homes; I can never wait to get home. She made it warm and safe. I . . . guess it wasn't so safe after all."

I put my arm around her and pulled her close. My chest tightened. "Do you need to call your dad?" I wondered why I hadn't thought about it before.

"No. The police called him. I doubt he cares."

I started to contradict her, but what did I know? The man did pack up and leave.

"He's in Texas, isn't he?"

"Galveston."

"Do you ever see him?"

"No, and I don't want to. It hurt Mom when he left. She used to cry all the time. I can't forgive him for that."

I nodded. This conversation was doing nothing to ease her distress. "How about some hot chocolate?" She agreed and I struggled to my feet. "Would you rather sit on the sofa?"

She shook her head and returned her gaze to the fire. Watching her sitting on the floor, eyes fixed on something only she could see, flooded my soul with maternal instincts. The sudden force of the emotion surprised me. I wanted to take her in my arms and assure her that everything was fine, that it would all work out. But everything wasn't fine, and there was a good chance none of this would work out. Celeste could be a functional orphan at the age of nineteen. Nineteen was pretty close to adult but still young enough for a girl to need her mother.

I went to the kitchen and poured milk in a saucepan to heat. I could have nuked a couple of cups in the microwave, but this gave me time to think. What was I to do with Celeste? Having her in the house was no problem. There was more than enough room and I would appreciate a little company, but what of the long term?

As I stirred the white liquid, more questions came to mind. Why Lisa? Was it a burglary? Had she brought a stranger home? I knew little of what the crime scene was like, yet had gleaned enough from Webb to know there had been a brief struggle, but not the kind that leaves a room in shambles. And what of the blood? How does that happen? Four drops forming a square. That was certainly premeditated.

Why my card? Surely that was just coincidence. Lisa must have had my card out for some reason, and the attacker or attackers used it to leave their appalling little message.

That was problematic, also. Why bother with such a macabre effort? Not only was it a sick thing to do, it took time. I shuddered to think of where the blood may have come from.

I poured the milk into a pair of mugs and mixed in a few spoon-fuls of Ovaltine. Disturbing images swirled in my mind, like the chocolate in the milk. I tried to evict the mental pictures but they were persistent, digging their heels into my gray matter. An act of unknown violence had been committed against a woman, and as a lifetime member of that lodge, I felt a vicarious terror. And if I felt it, I knew Celeste must be awash in fear. More troubling still was the realization that there was nothing I or anyone could do about it. There was no unwinding the clock. Even if Lisa were found alive and well in the next ten minutes, the events—real and imagined—had already left searing scars in the mind.

I walked back into the living room with the mugs in hand. As I neared, I saw Celeste wiping tears from her face. The sight ripped away what little remained of my shredded detachment. Celeste sat alone on the floor, for the moment more child than adult. No mat-ter how close I sat, no matter how much I tried to infuse my pres-ence into her loneliness, she would still be as lost as a dingy adrift in the middle of the sea.

"I'm sorry," she whispered as I set the mugs on the hearth and retook my place on the floor.

"There's nothing to apologize for."

"I'm trying to be strong."

I put an arm around her. "Stop trying."

Celeste rested her head on my shoulder. She smeared a tear, sniffed, and then plummeted into convulsive sobbing.

A moment later I joined her.

chapter

The morning crept in, the sun oozing through the few residual rain clouds. The normal marine layer of clouds that blankets most evenings and mornings was missing. The sky was azure near the horizon and a deep cobalt blue overhead. The rainstorm had washed the air clean of Southern California pollutants, leaving the sky crisp, as if just created. I had come down from my bedroom, where I spent a restless night fighting the covers and unwanted dreams. When I wasn't asleep, I lay in the dark listening to sounds I was certain were prowlers, ghosts, or some incomprehensible beastie. Several times I awoke to hear Celeste's quiet sobbing in the adjoining guest room.

I stood in the kitchen inhaling the thick, rich aroma of coffee as it trickled from the drip coffeemaker. The smell infused the air, and I found a measure of comfort in the familiar morning perfume. While I waited for the last of the brew to make its way through the basket and into the carafe, I studied the ocean outside my window. It was calm, sending to the shore small rollers that caressed the sand with frothy fingers. The water was blue and gray, reflecting the sky above it.

It was a beautiful sight and promised a gorgeous day. I would have relished it more had there not been so much reality to deal with. The sky had changed, the air had cleared, and another day had been born, as had so many millions before. That was all the same, but the world was different. A woman was gone—a mother, a friend. The new day had not changed that. I had spent the night in a soft, warm bed; I shuddered to think where Lisa Truccoli had spent hers.

A faint padding sound came from behind me. I turned to see Celeste. She wore a pair of my flannel pajamas. Her feet were bare and her face was puffy, eyes swollen and red, betraying the unsettled night she had endured.

"Good morning." I immediately felt stupid. What was good about it?

"Good morning." It was a reflex response and I doubted she even knew she had uttered the words.

"Do you drink coffee?"

She nodded and went to the breakfast nook that adjoined the kitchen, and sat at the small rectangular table in the center of the room.

"Are you hungry? I have some croissants or I could fix some eggs."

"No, thank you."

She needed to eat. Grief was hard work. "I'm going to put some on the table anyway, and some fruit. You can eat whenever you want."

"Okay."

Celeste was a sad figure, the empty shell of a person. At her age she should have been vibrant, filled with energy and unbounded enthusiasm. Someone, by an act of cruelty, had drained her of that, had pirated away her youthful zeal for life. There was a special place in hell for people who did such things. I felt sure of that.

I poured two cups of coffee and placed them on the table, along with evaporated milk, which I use as a substitute for cream. "There's sugar there, too." Returning to the kitchen to retrieve the pastries and fruit, I found some grapes and two oranges. A minute later I sat next to Celeste, stirring my coffee.

"I'd suggest sitting on the deck, but the rain has left all the outdoor furniture wet."

"That's okay." She sipped her coffee. It was black. She screwed up her face at its strong taste.

"You better put something in that. I tend to make coffee strong. Peter liked it that way."

"How did you do it?"

I was puzzled. "You mean the coffee?"

She turned to face me as if I had just asked a profoundly stupid question. "No. Your husband. Mom said he was killed."

"Ah. It wasn't easy. No sense in lying about that."

"How did it happen?"

I told her about the carjacking, trying to remain detached. Detachment was impossible. She was attentive, shifting her gaze from the ocean beyond the French doors to her coffee, which she had now whitened with the Carnation milk.

"Didn't you just want to up and die?"

"Yes, I suppose I did. In my darkest moments I still do. I push on anyway."

"Why?"

"It does no good not to. Besides, Peter would want me to live out my life, just as I would have expected him to if it had been me that day. Sometimes we live for our loved ones whether they're alive ..."

"Or dead."

"We don't know that your mother is dead, Celeste."

"We don't know that she's alive, either."

She had me there.

"Did they get the guy who shot your husband?"

I nodded. "They got him and his partner. There were several witnesses, and my husband's car was distinctive—a yellow BMW Z3 roadster. Are you familiar with the car?"

"It's a fancy sports car, right?"

"That's right. It was a flashy thing and Peter loved it dearly. I sold it after the funeral. I couldn't drive it . . . too many memories. Anyway, the LAPD spotted the car and gave chase. After a high-speed pursuit through city streets, the carjackers finally gave up. Two junkies, both in their early twenties. One struck a deal with the DA. The prosecution charged him with murder-two in exchange for testimony against the man who pulled the trigger. Both are in jail."

"So they're alive and your husband is dead. It doesn't seem fair."

"It's not, Celeste. There are many things in life that are not fair."

"So we just have to accept it? I'm not going to just accept it."

I searched for the right words but found none. I was out of my element. I had no children of my own and I had no experience as a grief counselor.

There was a ring at the front door. My first thought was relief: saved by the proverbial bell. But I was puzzled about who could be on my stoop this early. I had checked the clock when Celeste came downstairs. It said 7:10. Not more than ten minutes could have passed since then. I put a hand on her shoulder, indicating she should stay put. Her face was hopeful as I rose and headed for the door.

The bell rang again.

My hope was that Maria had come early. Maria Rodriquez cleaned house for me once a week. She was a whiz, the best there was. I was glad that this was her day, because she could stay with

Celeste while I went into the office for a few hours. I planned to pump Webb for more information.

My front door has a peephole and I made use of it. On the other side was a man, a stranger. He wore a tie and a suit. I turned the dead bolt, unlocking the door, then put my hand on the doorknob. I paused. Was this Lisa's last action the night before? Did she open the door to a stranger? I removed my hand.

"Who is it?" I called, pulling my terry cloth robe tighter.

"Detective Judson West, Santa Rita police."

I looked back through the peephole. He was holding up a badge in a leather case. Reassured, I opened the door. The man before me was tall, maybe six foot two. His hair was anthracite black with no sign of gray, an enviable trait. Dark eyes peered back at me from his narrow face, and a smile of Hollywood teeth spread above a chiseled chin. His cheeks bore a tan, in usual Southern California fashion. He wore a cerulean-colored shirt with a striped gold tie. On his shoulders hung a sport coat that was a shade darker than the blue of his shirt. His beige pants looked as if they had just come from the tailors, pressed and new.

"Mrs. Glenn?" He corrected himself. "I mean, Mayor Glenn?"

"Yes."

"I wonder if I might have a moment of your time."

Good-looking and polite. I invited him in. "I wasn't expecting anyone this early. You've caught me ..." I looked down at my robe and slippers.

"I apologize." If the awkward moment made him uncomfortable, he didn't show it. "I'm an early riser and I have a busy day. If you want to change, I'd be happy to wait."

"I think I'll do that. First I want to know if you've discovered anything about Lisa."

"Me too," I heard from behind me. Celeste was standing a few feet from the staircase. I started to introduce them but remembered that they must have met the previous night at Lisa's house.

"Miss Truccoli." West nodded.

"Hi." Celeste gave a polite smile, but it was clear there was no happiness there, just eager anticipation. "Do you have any news about my mother?"

The detective's countenance darkened and he shook his head. "I'm afraid not, but we're working hard on the case."

"It will only take me a minute to change," I said. "Can I pour you some coffee?"

"You go ahead. I can wait."

"Well, why don't you wait in the nook? The coffee pot is there if you want to help yourself." I motioned toward the back of the house.

"That sounds good," he said and walked to the eating area.

Celeste started up the stairs and I followed. "What do you feel like wearing today?" I asked as I caught up with her.

She just shrugged and continued taking one step after another. I put an arm around her shoulder. "I'll have Maria wash what you were wearing yesterday. In the meantime I think we can find something comfortable for you."

"That's okay. I'll just wear what I wore last night." She plodded up the steps as if concrete weighted her feet, her brief moment of hope torpedoed.

Ten minutes later we emerged from our respective bedrooms. Celeste was wearing the jeans and Yale sweatshirt she had changed into the night before. I had showered earlier and, not wanting to dress twice, I donned my clothes for the office.

We found West standing in front of the French doors, staring at the gentle surf.

"I'm sorry to keep you waiting," I said.

"No problem." He turned. There was a cup of coffee in his hand, black like his hair. He had taken me up on my offer. "It's my fault for stopping by without calling. I wanted to catch you before you left for the office."

"Have a seat." I motioned to one of the chairs around the table. He did, setting his cup on the glass top, but he first removed a napkin from a holder I keep on the table and put it beneath the cup. A house-trained man; I was amazed. Celeste lowered herself into a chair.

"I wanted to bring you up to date and ask a few questions, if I may."

If I may? He was a police detective; I wasn't sure we had much choice.

"You don't have any news about my mom?" Celeste asked again. "None at all?"

"I'm sorry. Not yet." He looked at her with sad, empathetic eyes. "The good news is that there's no . . . What I mean to say is . . ."

"Body," Celeste blurted.

"Exactly. That gives us a little more hope that she's still alive. Unfortunately, we have very little to go on. Crime techs are dusting the house for fingerprints; we've done a blood scan, and that came up negative. We also—"

"Excuse me," I said. "A blood scan?"

"It's a technique investigators use to find blood that someone may have cleaned up. It's close to impossible to remove all traces of blood. The process involves a chemical spray called Luminol. It glows greenish blue when it contacts blood—even if the blood has been there for years." He offered no more explanation.

I nodded. "I've seen it on television. And you say you found no indication of blood?"

"Just the four drops on the card." He paused, studying me through those dark eyes. "Chief Webb said he told you about that. Is that correct?"

"Yes."

"I don't know about it," Celeste said. Her eyes were wide and there was alarm in her voice. The word *blood* could have that effect.

"I'm sorry, I assumed you knew, since you were in the house," I explained.

"They didn't let me go past the foyer. They made me stand just inside the door."

"We have to be careful with the crime scene," West said. "I know it must have been hard."

"What about the blood? You found blood?"

"Just a little," I said.

"Four drops." West shifted in his seat. He told her about how the drops of blood were arranged on my business card.

"I don't get it," Celeste said.

"Neither do we." He turned to me. "Do you have any idea why someone would put blood on your business card?"

"As I told Chief Webb, many people have my card. Lisa worked on my last two campaigns. I imagine she had several. Whoever did this probably just grabbed what was at hand and that happened to be my card."

West shook his head. "It's a little more complex than that . . . a little more premeditated. We found several other cards on the table where we found yours. There was one for her attorney, one from her business, and a few other miscellaneous cards. They were set to the side, as if someone had dropped them there . . . as if someone had gone through a stack of cards, looking for one in particular."

"My mother kept those kinds of things in the drawer of the china cabinet," Celeste said. "It's near the phone."

"The drawer to the cabinet was partially open when we got there. The cards lay on the dining room table. Have you been in the house, Mayor?"

"Once, but it's been quite a while."

"Then you might remember that the living room opens to the dining area. The table and china hutch are in the dining room. How long has it been since you've visited Ms. Truccoli?"

"It was for a fund-raiser for my mayoral race, so it has to be over two years ago."

He pursed his lips and nodded.

"What's that nod mean?" I was suddenly feeling suspicious.

"It means that we shouldn't find any of your fingerprints."

"What! My fingerprints?"

West raised a steady hand. "We have to follow up on all possibilities, Mayor. That's all. No one is saying you're involved, but if we don't do a complete job, we might overlook something. You wouldn't want that, would you?"

"Of course not."

"Have you ever been fingerprinted?"

"No." I didn't like where this was going. The rational part of my brain understood the need for thoroughness, but another part of me was insulted by the implication. "Well, just my finger for the DMV."

"Just so we can say we did our job, we'll need to take some impressions. It won't take long and you can do it while you're down at City Hall. You are going to your office today, right?"

No, I dressed up for you! I chastised myself. This wasn't personal; it was an investigation. If we had been talking about someone else, I would have been in hearty agreement. "I'll do it this morning."

"Thank you." West let slip a smile. "We'll be sensitive to your ... special public needs."

"What?" Celeste asked. "I don't understand."

"Detective West is saying that he understands what it could do to my career as mayor if word got out that I was being fingerprinted for a criminal case. In politics, being innocent means nothing; appearing above reproach is everything."

"Oh." Poor Celeste was getting a lesson in real-world adult life, much faster than anyone her age should.

I looked at West. He seemed as cool and comfortable as a man discussing the latest Dodgers trade. "So you think whoever did this searched for my card and then placed the drops of blood on it?"

"Yes ma'am, that's what it looks like."

"Why?"

"That's the big question, isn't it? Why abduct Ms. Truccoli? Why leave a calling card on a . . . well, calling card? Why was your card chosen and the others tossed aside?"

I started to tell him that a calling card was not the same as a business card but let it go. In light of things, nothing could be less important. His questions sank deep in my heart. Why indeed? "It doesn't make sense."

"What did Ms. Truccoli do for your campaign?" West lifted his coffee cup to his lips, set it down on the napkin again, then leaned back in his chair as if expecting a lengthy ballad.

"She was the campaign's treasurer—and a good one, I might add."

"She dealt with the money?"

"That's what treasurers do, deal with money."

"How does that work?" His words were soft and smooth, like those of an old-time gentleman feigning interest in his guest's stories, except West's interest was genuine. It was his job to learn as much as possible. I couldn't slight him for that.

I took a moment to formulate my thoughts, then began a quick lesson in campaign funding. "Political campaigns are generally funded by contributions from supporters. These can range from five dollars from the neighbor down the street to corporate contributions which can be upwards of several thousand dollars. Campaign laws control all this. Candidates file reports that become part of public record. The more money that comes in, the more there is to spend on ads, brochures, office expenses, and the like. California campaign regulations require that every campaign committee have a treasurer. That person's name must appear on all advertisements and publicity. Pick up any piece of literature produced by a candidate and you'll see the treasurer's name in the fine print."

"So the money would go to Ms. Truccoli?"

"Actually, it goes into an account, but she was the one who signed the checks."

"Who decides how the money gets spent?"

"I do. In bigger campaigns, that decision is made in consultation with the campaign manager. In some elections, specialists are hired, but that's for the big boys, not small-city politicians like me."

"Who was your campaign manager?"

"Me. This isn't Los Angeles. Campaigns here are small and usually run by volunteers."

West leaned forward, dropping his gaze to the table. I could tell something was on his mind. "I don't mean to imply anything but I must ask this." He glanced at Celeste and then at me. "Is there still money in the bank account, and did Ms. Truccoli still have access to it?"

At first I didn't understand what he was getting at, and then it hit me like a hard slap. "Wait a minute. You're not suggesting she stole money from the war chest?"

"What?" Celeste piped up. "Stole? War chest?"

I turned to her. "*War chest* is term politicians use to describe money saved for the next campaign."

"My mother wouldn't steal anything!" Her voice had jumped an octave, taking on a shrill tone.

Again West raised a hand. "Miss—"

"She wouldn't! You should be trying to find her, not sitting here drinking coffee and accusing her of being a thief."

"Miss Truccoli, as I said—"

"Don't you ever call my mother a thief!" She stood up, pushing her chair back so hard that it toppled over with a crash. "She's not a thief." She made a move toward the living room, then turned on West again. "My mom may be lying in a ditch somewhere, and you don't care—"

"Miss Truccoli!" West snapped with authority, rising to his feet. Just two words, but they were sharp enough to stop Celeste in her tracks.

"What?" Her face was red, her eyes redder, and her mouth pulled into a tight line. The fear and uncertainty had reached volcanic proportions. Outside she was fierce, determined, furious. I knew that inside she was a china doll, cracked by the knowledge that someone had accosted, abducted, and maybe killed her mother.

He set her chair upright and motioned to it. "Sit down." His voice was concrete firm but untainted by anger.

Celeste eyed him hard but he didn't flinch. I was certain he had received a lot of hard looks in his career.

"Please, Celeste," I said. "Sit down."

She plopped down, crossing her arms and clenching her jaw. Tears were seconds away.

West resumed his seat, then leaned forward and spoke with gentleness and the strength of determination. "Right now, as we speak, a great many people are looking for your mother. We've notified other Police Departments, Sheriff Departments, and the

Highway Patrol. We are doing a lot of things you're not seeing. It's important for you to know that."

He paused. Celeste said nothing. A lone tear ran down her right cheek. That said plenty to me.

"I have to ask questions. I have to cover all the bases. For me to determine what happened, I have to look down every dark alley, even if it doesn't lead anywhere. That's what *I* must do. Here's what *you* must do. . . . Are you listening, Celeste?"

Celeste? He had switched to first names.

"Yeah."

"Look at me."

Celeste turned. I followed her gaze and saw that the detective's dispassionate, professional face now wore an expression of concern. "There are some things you must do," he said again. "First, don't give up. I don't know what happened and I don't know how this will turn out, but I do know that hope is helpful. You also have to stop jumping to conclusions when I ask a question. Not every question is an accusation. At this point, a question is just a question. Is that clear?"

Celeste nodded.

"Good." He directed his attention my way. "That goes for you too, Mayor."

I found myself nodding like Celeste. I had to admire the way he handled himself and two edgy women.

"I'm . . . I'm sorry," Celeste murmured.

"It's not a problem; just remember that I'm not the bad guy. I will figure this out." Turning back to me, he repeated his earlier question about Lisa and the bank account.

"Yes, if she wanted to, she could access the account. Technically, the campaign effort is ongoing. I raise money throughout the year. She gives me a report every month."

"How much money is in the account?"

I hesitated. Talking about money with a stranger made me uncomfortable, especially campaign money. "Not much by political standards: thirty thousand or so."

"Who else has access to the money?"

"Me."

"Anyone else?"

"No. The fewer people with access, the safer I feel."

"So only you and Ms. Truccoli can write checks or make withdrawals?" he pressed.

"That's right."

"What about debit cards? Does the account have debit card access?"

I shook my head. "I like checks. They leave a better paper trail. If anyone challenges my campaign financing, I want to be able to withstand a thorough audit."

"But others knew of the account?"

"Yes, dozens of campaign workers. In fact, anyone can figure out that it takes money to run a campaign."

"Yes, but who knew that Ms. Truccoli was the treasurer?"

"In the campaign, my senior volunteers would know. Of course, we sent out tens of thousands of flyers and her name's on every one."

West sighed.

"Do you think somebody kidnapped my mom so they could get at that money?" Celeste asked.

"It's a thought, but I don't know if it's a good one. Mayor, it would be helpful if I could have a list of everyone who worked on your campaign, especially those who had contact with Ms. Truccoli."

"I'll make sure you have it today."

He looked me dead in the eye. "Please don't forget to come by the station and get those fingerprints today, too. Also, would you please check on that bank account? See if there's been any activity. I can get a warrant to do it, but it would be faster if you made the inquiry."

He stated his request as if I had a choice. I was pretty sure I didn't. "I can access the information through my online banking. I'll bring it and the campaign worker list when I come in for my fingerprints."

"That would be great. The sooner the better. I hope to have lab results from the forensic guys soon. They should be able to tell something about the blood. We've gathered hair samples from her hairbrush for DNA testing."

Detective West rose and thanked us for our time. "I may have more questions as the investigation proceeds. If you can think of anything that might be helpful, don't hesitate to call." He pulled a small metal case from his blazer, opened it, and removed two of his business cards, giving one to each of us. "Thank you for the coffee, Mayor." To Celeste he said, "Don't give up hope."

I walked West to the door and closed it behind him. Turning, I saw Celeste standing a few feet behind me. Her expression had hardened and her eyes had narrowed.

"Why was your card chosen from all the rest?"

I was asking myself the same question.

chapter 4

The drive to the office took longer than usual. The quarter-hour trip from my house to downtown Santa Rita seemed to last hours. I was in my silver Lincoln Aviator, weaving my way through the streets. I hit every red light and found myself trapped behind sluggish delivery trucks. No one was in my hurry.

Normally, I use the time to think about what the day will hold, reports I need to read, calls I need to make, and my ever expanding calendar. This morning was different. My thoughts orbited the young woman I had left behind.

It wasn't her question that bothered me. It was the way she asked it. There was more than a hint of suspicion in her voice—it dripped with misgiving, and that worried me. She was as fragile as crystal, emotional, fearful, and too young to have acquired the discretion and wisdom that came with experience. Considering all that had happened, she had the right to be suspicious of everyone—even me.

I thought about how difficult it must have been for her to be staying in the home of someone who was—at least distantly—connected to her mother's disappearance. That was the real burning coal in my belly. Would Celeste be there when I returned home?

We had talked after West left, and I sensed a new wall of separation rising between us. It had ascended the moment she understood that someone had selected my business card, not at random but with forethought, to be the recipient of the morbid message. I half suspected myself.

I had offered Celeste the opportunity to come to the office with me. She declined.

I'd wanted to press the issue but decided to let it go. If she was beginning to suspect me of involvement in whatever happened to Lisa, she might be fearful to get in the car with me. That realization brought a pang of deep regret, partly because I didn't like being the source of more fear in her life, and partly because I worried she would leave ten minutes after I drove off.

It was that last thought that compelled me to reach for my cell phone and call home. One ring. Two. Three. "Come on. Be there." My answering machine picked up. I heard my voice speaking in the third person plural, a single woman's trick. "You've reached the Glenn residence and there is no one here to take your call right now, so if you'll leave your name and number, we'll get back to you. . . ."

"Hello."

"Celeste?"

"Yeah."

"It's Maddy. I was afraid you had left."

"I was getting into the shower." Her tone was the same as when I left.

"Oh, okay. I just wanted to see if you'd like to do lunch later. I could pick you up around eleven-thirty and we could go to the Fish Kettle on the pier."

"I don't know." I could almost see her shrugging.

"Celeste, I'm your friend, not your enemy. You need to believe that."

"Okay." It wasn't okay. Her voice was somber and chilly.

"I'll tell you what: Why don't you invite one of your friends and we'll all go. It'll be my treat."

There was a pause.

"Please. I'm going to the Police Department this morning and I'll see if they've found anything else."

More enduring pause. "Okay."

I said thank you, hit the end button, and then tossed the phone on the passenger seat. That was a step up ... if she was there at eleven-thirty.

Despite the slow drive, I arrived at my office at 8:28—two minutes before my usual start time. Officially, the office doesn't open until nine, but I like to appear a half hour early. It allows me time to settle in and make the mental change from home to office.

My office is located on the first floor of our two-story civic building. The building itself is a modern affair—for the 1950s. White concrete walls make up the bulk of it, with Spanish arches everywhere one could be placed. Across the front of the building runs a colonnade of such arches. The exterior corridor separates them from the large windows of the outer wall—the architect's desire to be faithful to California's Mexican past and still move into the twentieth century. The result was a mixture of the Spanish with a fifties idea of contemporary. The city replaced the old windows with tinted glass, making the building look as if it were wearing sunglasses. A great deal of money went out ten years ago when we updated the structure to new earthquake codes. We are still paying on those bonds.

The grounds are my favorite part, blanketed in lush green grass and bright flowers. Unlike other City Halls, there is no statue in the courtyard. The early fathers were too frugal. Every few years someone raises the question again but receives little support. Very few take notice of their city's government unless we assess a special property tax. That usually brings the good citizens out in force.

I walked through the front doors, heavy golden oak slabs, and into the wide lobby. To my left was the city clerk's office, and to my right the city's building department. My office is down a wide white hall that leads to the back of the building. I moved down the corridor, my shoes tapping on the terrazzo tile. The hallway leads to a reception area, which is split by a low wood rail. On the near side are several chairs and companion end tables upon which rest magazines and the city's latest newsletter. On the other side is a single desk that was manned by a beyond-middle-aged receptionist everyone called Fritzy. Her real name was Judith Fritz, and she had worked for the city almost as long as I'd been alive.

"Hi, Fritzy," I said with a smile. Approaching the half door in the dividing wall, I heard a buzz as she released the lock. Nonemployees require permission to enter the council office area. Politics can bring out the worst in some people. It's best to have at least a token barrier.

"Good morning, Madam Mayor. Right on time as usual, I see." Fritzy's hair was pure gray but her eyebrows indicated she had once been a brunette. A little color from a bottle would have made her look ten years younger, but that never seemed to be an issue with her. I hoped to age with that high level of grace and confidence. She wore a red dress and a wide smile.

"I try. You look good in red."

"Darling, I look great in everything." She winked and I laughed. Fritzy's optimism and humor were legendary.

"Is Randi in?"

"Your darling assistant was in at eight. She came in the back." Fritzy was referring to the back hallway that leads from the rear parking lot to the offices. It allows workers and council members to avoid the front lobby. I frequently make use of it myself, but this morning I parked in the space marked, "Mayor" in the front lot. There is a reserved spot for each person on the council and for the support executives like the city manager and the city attorney. Most prefer to park in the back. Parking out front, they think, is a billboard that says, "Hi, I'm here; come interrupt me."

"Great," I said.

"I just made coffee. Would you like some?"

I said I would and made my way back to my daytime home.

Randi Portman was my personal assistant and a good one. She was sharp, dedicated, and loved public service. There was no doubt she would run for office herself someday, although she always denied it. She seemed content to help me keep my head above the civic waters. I found her at her desk, which is located in a twelve-by-twelve office just outside my more spacious room. She was holding a cup of coffee, cradling the ceramic cup and letting the heat of it warm her hands.

"Cold?" I asked as I crossed the threshold.

"You know me, I'm always cold. They keep the air conditioner on all day and night. Someone should tell maintenance it's February. You could hang meat in here."

It felt fine to me.

Randi was in her mid-twenties, with short red hair parted on the left. Her blue eyes revealed a keen intelligence. She was a whiz with computers, with spelling—which is my weak suit—and with names. She lived and worked with an efficiency that would shame most people and occasionally intimidated me.

Rising from her chair, she set her cup on the desk. "I put several things on your to-do pile. There are also notes about calls you need to make. Councilman Adler left a message on your voice mail. He's upset about last night's meeting. Councilwoman Lawrence left a similar message. Apparently, I missed something. That's what I get for going to a birthday party instead of the council meeting."

"Bring your coffee in here, and I'll explain it to you."

We walked into my office and sat down. Fritzy delivered my coffee, and when she left, I relayed the whole story. Randi absorbed each word. "That's terrible. And the police have no clue as to what happened?"

"None. At least not yet."

I watched Randi's eyes dart around. It was something she did when deep in thought. The cogs were spinning in her head. I let her think.

Randi had been working with me for four years. She was a part-time student at a private college in Westmont, a few miles north of Santa Rita. Like me, she majored in political science.

She was a bundle of high hopes and big dreams and had been encouraging me to run for higher office. I've always maintained that I'm more effective in city government, but will admit that the idea appeals to me. I knew that; I also knew she knew it.

Campaigns could be long. A run for small-town mayor should be well under way a year before the election. A candidate for any higher seat should be running hot and hard at least eighteen months before the primaries. It was not unusual to begin the background work on a campaign two years before election day.

"Is there more?" Randi asked.

I told her about Detective West's visit and his request for fingerprints. Her face remained neutral but her eyes closed, and I knew an atomic bomb had just detonated somewhere in her head.

"They shouldn't ask for that," Randi said through tight lips. "You're the mayor; they should know the effects that might have on your administration."

"They're just doing their job. West said he'd be sensitive to my special circumstances."

"It's Chief Webb I'm worried about. He's still ticked about that funding fiasco of his. You didn't cave to his pressure and now he's got it in for you."

"Maybe, but that changes nothing. I've got to do this."

"I suppose."

"No supposing about it. For me to refuse would be worse than submitting. Imagine what an opponent could do with that. 'Mayor Refuses to Aid Police in Criminal Case.'"

"You're right, of course. Crime and safety are big issues in this district."

"District? You mean the city, don't you?" I paused. "Have you been making plans again?"

Randi blushed. "It's on your desk under the messages and other files, but wait to comment on it until you have time to study it in detail. Okay?"

I eyed her. I trusted Randi but she could be devious. "Okay, but I'm not running for president."

She laughed. "Not yet, anyway. What you just told me explains something." She pointed at my desk. "One of the messages is from Doug Turner."

I groaned. Doug Turner was the crime reporter for the *Register*.

"How could he know?" Randi asked.

I shrugged. "The paper had someone at the meeting last night. Chief Webb walked in and spoke to me. That would arouse suspicion."

"Moron."

"I assume you mean Webb. He could have handled it in a less conspicuous way, but subtlety isn't one of his strong suits. Of course, Turner could have figured it out himself. During the last election, he doubled as a political reporter—one of the benefits of working for a small-city newspaper. He might have remembered Lisa's name."

Randi grunted. She was more than a little peeved.

"It's going to be all right, Randi. Let's not lose sight of who the real victims are: Lisa and Celeste."

"Yes, you're right." She paused, her eyes darting. "Is there anything I can do?"

"I don't want to deal with the press today. Give Mr. Turner a call and tell him I'm booked. Put him off until tomorrow. On second thought, don't use the word *booked*. Also, I promised to take Celeste and a friend to the Fish Kettle. You could make reservations."

"For three, then?"

"Why don't you come along? I could use some help. I remember being that age; it wasn't an easy road."

"Okay. I'll make reservations for four." Randi rose and exited my office, closing the door behind her. A moment later an unladylike word wafted through the closed door. I smiled and glanced at my messages. Since I had returned all my calls before the council meeting the previous night, there were only three demanding a response: one from Councilman Adler, one from Councilwoman Lawrence, and the one I dreaded most, from Doug Turner.

I pushed them all aside. It was still early, and I doubted that any of them would be in their offices. Letting curiosity get the best of me, I put aside a folder on the city budget, the one from the Planning Commission, and the one from the city attorney's office. All could wait until I discovered what Randi had been up to.

A purple file was at the bottom of the stack. Randi and I have a system of colored file folders. Purple meant private or personal. I opened it and read the title page. I was looking at a neatly typeset document with words centered on the page.

MADISON GLENN FOR CONGRESS
A Preliminary Review
by Ms. Randi Portman

I picked up the phone and buzzed her desk. When she answered, I said, "You can't be serious!"

§erious as a heart attack." She begged me again to withhold judgment until I had read everything. I promised and set it aside. I wanted to dig right in, but I knew myself well enough to know that whatever was in that file would overwhelm anything else that needed my attention. I would have to be patient for at least a couple of hours.

I took a few moments to read over the other, more mundane files and made a few notes to myself. This day's schedule was light, as was the rest of the week. No ribbon cuttings, no speaking to senior groups, no personal requests for meetings. It was a relief, considering all that had already happened. The demand on my time varies, like that of an emergency room doctor. Things can be slow one moment, the waiting room jam-packed the next.

I decided to take advantage of the extra time and complete a few unpleasant tasks. It was a personal management technique I learned from my father: Do first the things you least want to do. It was similar to eating one's vegetables before moving on to the fried chicken.

Rising from my desk, I grabbed my handbag and stepped into Randi's office. "See if you can get the minutes of last night's meeting from the clerk. I also need recent bank records on the campaign account."

"How far back?"

"Let's look at the last six months. Better to appear cautious and forthcoming. Go online and download any activity since the last bank statement came in."

"Will do. You headed to Crime Central?" That was Randi's pet phrase for the Police Department.

"Yeah." With a wink I added, "You want me to pick anything up for you?"

"Hmm." She raised a finger to her chin. "They have a nice selection of motorcycle cops. . . . A tall, strapping blond would be nice."

"I didn't know you were into the motorcycle types."

"You'd be surprised at what you don't know about me."

I laughed, said I'd be right back, and headed out the back hall.

The Police Station, a wide affair with an exterior matching that of City Hall, is positioned behind our building. It took only a few minutes to walk across our rear parking area and into the station. One difference between our building and theirs is their employee parking lot, a sea of macadam surrounded by a tall chain-link fence with razor wire on top. The barricade isn't a device to keep people in but to keep thieves out. Five years ago there were several embarrassing auto burglaries from the lot. Nothing gets cops angrier than having a thief trespass on their property, steal things from their cars, and stroll off into the night. Jokes still fly around town.

Inside the Police Station, all similarities with City Hall end. The Planning Commission insisted that the exterior comply with the design regulations, but it had no authority over what happened inside the walls. I always have the feeling I've crossed a time warp when I step through the glass doors of the lobby, leaving behind the architectural style of old Mexico and walking into the twenty-first century.

Stark white tile covers the floor; the ceiling is comprised of narrow bands of polished aluminum interrupted by the occasional recessed incandescent light. White enamel coats the walls. It takes a while to adjust to the brightness. On one wall is a large, framed display of police arm patches from around the country. On the other wall is a plaque bearing the names of the officers of the month. On the same wall is a substantial color photo of Chief Webb, reminiscent of a photo I've seen of a very angry Winston Churchill. As I approached the chief's gruff image, Churchill's words, "Some chicken, some neck" rang in my ears. Webb was Churchill without the humor.

"May I help you?"

A middle-aged male officer was standing behind the counter that divides the lobby from the office area behind. He had gray in his hair and a large belly straining his Sam Browne belt. Three yellow chevrons adorned his sleeve just below the shoulder. Behind him were several desks, most occupied by uniformed women.

"Yes, Sergeant, you can." I gave him my best professional smile.

"Oh, Mayor! I'm sorry, I didn't recognize you at first. I was doing . . ."

"That's all right, Sergeant. I saw that you were busy. Is Detective West in?"

"Yes ma'am. Do you have an appointment to see him?"

My first inclination was to remind him that I didn't need an appointment, but instead I said, "Yes, we have a meeting."

He walked back to his desk, picked up the phone, and dialed a two-digit number. I heard him tell West I was out front. Coming back to the counter, he said, "He'll be right out." Then he leaned forward and lowered his voice. I stepped forward to hear the message he didn't want overhead by others.

"I know the Police Officer's Association backed Adler, which is crazy, since he's a criminal law attorney, but I want you to know I voted for you."

"I appreciate that, Sergeant—" I looked at his nametag— "Sergeant Collins. I'll take all the help I can get."

"My pleasure. My wife was right; you're doing a good job."

"Well, give your wife a hug for me."

"Campaigning, Madam Mayor?"

I turned my eyes to the trim, dark-haired man who had been in my home a little over an hour ago. "Detective West. I hope this is not too early."

He surrendered a little smile. "Touché. Pop the door, Collins. Let's not keep the mayor waiting." The door to my right buzzed. I went to it, turned the knob, and left the civilian area behind. I was now in cop country.

West guided me through the outer office area and through a set of doors that lead to the back of the station. This place is less glitzy, more utilitarian. Gray metal desks fill a large open space. Beige carpet blankets the floor. The air smells of old coffee. To one side of the room is a glass wall, beyond which I could see three people, two women and one man, seated at a U-shaped console. It is the communication room. All 911 calls come here: fire, ambulance, and police. The dispatchers then take over. Detectives and officers use the rest of the room to write reports, interview people, or simply take a break.

I followed West as he negotiated the obstacle course of desks and chairs. We passed through another set of doors and entered a room that is more spartan than the last: gray-painted concrete floor, dull white walls, suspended ceiling, and recessed fluorescent lights. A pair of metal doors leads outside.

On one side is a counter covered in simulated-wood Formica. It looks worn and tired. On the other side is a corridor. When I first came to the council, I received a tour of the facility, so I knew where the hall leads: to small rooms used as holding cells.

"This is where we fingerprint arrestees and take their picture, Madam Mayor," West said, taking the tone of tour guide. He indicated a man standing near the counter. "This is Officer Frank Dell, one of our fingerprint technicians and all-round nice guy. Frank, this is Mayor Madison Glenn."

"Maddy." I extended my hand. His grip was strong and his skin cool.

"Pleased to meet you, Mayor."

"Hey, Frank, why don't you show the mayor what you do?"

Officer Dell looked surprised. "You mean print her and take a mug shot?"

"I think we can skip the mug shot. That's no different than what happens at the DMV." He turned to me. "How about it, Mayor? Want to see what happens to the folks we arrest?"

I saw what he was doing and played along. "That could be interesting."

"After the arrest, this is the first place you'd come. The officer parks just beyond those doors and brings the arrestee in. The person would be handcuffed, of course, generally with his hands behind his back. I don't think we need to cuff you for you to get the idea."

"I appreciate that."

"Now, to fingerprint a suspect, we have to bring his hands forward. If we have some concerns about his behavior, we cuff him again with his hands in front. Frank here knows how to print a man in cuffs, don't you, Frank?"

"Years of experience." Dell pulled a wide white card out of a drawer and placed it in a device attached to the top of the counter.

The device held the card in place. Next to it he set what looked like a large plastic compact case. Inside was a substance that looked like solidified Vaseline.

"After fingerprinting, the officer takes a photo and the prisoner is led down that corridor and put in a holding cell. People who are going to be held longer than a day are taken to a county facility. Drunks are taken to a different place to dry out." He took my hand. "Here, let Frank show you how it's done."

I stepped up to the counter and submitted to the procedure. It made me feel dirty. Officer Dell took my right thumb and rolled it on the pad, then rolled it on the card. The card was divided in several ways. The top portion had several boxes for information like name, date, technician, arresting officer, and more. The bottom had fourteen squares: one for each digit, two larger squares for impressions of all four fingers of each hand together, and two narrow squares for additional thumbprints. Webb wanted to update to a digital system than took prints electronically, but there wasn't room in the budget. It was another bone of contention.

It took less than sixty seconds. Dell pulled the card from its holder and handed it to me. "There you go, Mayor, a souvenir. You want me to autograph it for you?"

"That's all right, Frank," West said with a laugh. "Thanks for the demonstration."

"My pleasure."

I thanked Dell and let West lead me from the room. "Let's go into the conference room," he said softly as we crossed back into the office area. "I'll get you some coffee."

"I'm fine, thanks."

"No, you're not. You want coffee." I started to object but he cut me off. "We don't offer coffee to suspects. Take the coffee and people are less likely to ask questions."

"With cream, please."

A few moments later we sat at a white oak conference table. A half-dozen cheap chairs were sitting at odd angles around it. The conference room adjoins the office area.

"I'll take that." West gently pulled the fingerprint card from my hand. I surrendered it without protest. "I appreciate you taking the time to do this, and doing it so quickly."

"I'm eager to help in any way I can. My aide will bring the bank reports you requested a little later. She's compiling them now."

"As I said before, I'm trying to be thorough. I don't want to cause you any trouble."

"It's too late for that," I said, more harshly than I intended.

"How do you mean?"

"I think Celeste is suspicious of me."

"Understandable. She seems like a sharp young lady."

"Excuse me?"

West realized what he had said. "I don't mean she's right in suspecting you, only that she would naturally have to wonder why the blood was on your card, and so many others were discarded. It's an important question. One we would all like to have answered—including you."

"I'm afraid she'll leave. That's her right, I know. Legally she is an adult. I can't tell her what to do or not to do. I'm just worried about her."

"You think she'll be gone when you get home?"

"Maybe. I'm supposed to have lunch with her. I'll know at eleven-thirty if she's decided to go elsewhere."

West frowned. "It's important that we know where she is."

"If she leaves, I'll let you know."

"Thanks."

"What now?" I felt awkward.

"We keep on keeping on." West took a sip from his cup, then made a face. "Your coffee was better. Anyway, we push on. I'll fill in the information on the card and pass it on to the lab. If your prints don't match those found at the scene, then you're clear. There's a chance a tech will recognize your name, but it's the best I can do."

"Won't you need sample prints from Celeste, too?"

"Maybe. We took prints from other places in the house where it's unlikely perps would go, bathrooms and the like. We should find a large number of her prints in the house, as well as her mother's. We're looking for those that don't fit."

"Do you think you'll find anything?"

"No. Whoever did this was meticulous. I doubt any prints were left behind."

"Then why bother . . . I know, I know, you're just being thorough."

"Exactly." He lowered his eyes, then looked up. "I've been thinking about this whole card thing. The real question is, why you? Why your card? We don't have an answer to that, but one thing we do know: someone wants you involved. Is it a setup? Maybe, but I think it's more. I just don't know what."

"I have no idea, either."

"I think you should be careful whom you trust. Two things connect you to this case: Lisa, the missing person, and your blood-decorated business card. I don't want to alarm you, but you should take measures to assure your safety. Lock your doors, be suspicious. A little paranoia right now wouldn't hurt."

"You can't believe they're after me." I said the words without conviction.

"Who knows? If they wanted you, they would have gone to your place instead of Lisa's. My guess is, they want something *from* you."

"Like what?"

"I'm good at what I do, Mayor, but I'm not that good. We'll know sometime but I need more info. You just be careful—very careful."

chapter 5

I'm back." I breezed by Randi's desk and started for my office door.
"You have company," Randi said quickly. I stopped and looked at
her. "Councilman Adler is here." She made a face and motioned with
her head toward my office. I felt the corner of my mouth turn down.

"Thank you. Did you gather those . . . documents?" I could see
several pages of letter-sized paper on her desk. They were facedown.
Randi was a cautious one.

"Yes, I'm just sorting them now and will bind them for you. How
did your appointment go?"

The last statement was for Adler's benefit. "Fine. I'll fill you in
later." I took a deep breath and plunged into my office with a determination I didn't feel.

Adler was sitting cross-legged in one of the guest chairs in front
of my desk. He remained seated as I entered. He seemed calm, his
thin hands folded in his lap. He said nothing but I knew why he was
there. Adler was a short, thin man who compensated for his lack of
physical stature with a self-serving, aggressive, mean spirit. He
reminded me of one of those dust-mop dogs that yap and growl as
if they can whip a pit bull. Adler was a heel-biter.

I sat behind my desk and leaned back in my chair. "What can I do for you this morning, Councilman?"

"Last night was very unprofessional of you." *Straight to the point.* He offered the slightest of smiles, as if he felt a sudden pride in what he had just said.

I stared at the little man for a moment, showing no emotion. His hair was a weak brown made weaker by an infusion of gray. His eyes were dark and narrow and his skin was pale, as if he had just come over from Siberia. I've heard he is a tiger in the courtroom, but I was pretty sure I could beat him in a fight, and at that moment I was willing to give it a try.

"Aren't you going to say anything?"

I was on edge. I had received the shocking news of a crime against an acquaintance, had taken in an unexpected houseguest, had slept poorly, had endured an early-morning interview by a police detective, and had submitted to fingerprinting. My mood was dark and volatile. I gazed at the weasel for another moment, then asked a question of my own: "Why did I leave?"

"What?"

"Why did I leave?"

"How would I know? You just got up and left, and a quarter hour later the clerk tells us you're not coming back. No explanation. No apology."

"Is that what you want, Jon? An apology?"

"One seems due."

"You're not getting one, but I will accept an apology from you."

He uncrossed his legs. "I don't owe you anything."

I locked eyes with him. "Chief Webb walks in, whispers in my ear, and I have to leave. Did something happen to my parents? My brother? My sister? Was there some pressing police business that I might be able to help with? What was it, Jon?"

"I told you, I don't know."

"Thank you for your concern."

"Did something happen to your—"

"You went to college, didn't you?"

The change of subject took him off guard. "Of course."

"You spent at least three years in law school, Western School of Law, right?"

"Yes, but I don't see what that has to do with our topic of conversation."

"It means that you're probably smart enough to be able to haul your fanny out of my chair and make your way through the doors without help."

He blinked several times.

"That's right, Councilman. I'm kicking you out. Beat it. Now." He didn't move, not from belligerence but from the shock of it. "Maybe I was wrong. Randi!" She was at the door in half a second, with a face as innocent as a newborn's. I would bet a month's salary she had been standing by the door, just out of sight. "Councilman Adler is having trouble finding the door. Would you help him, please?"

"Certainly."

Adler sprang to his feet. "I don't need help. I can't believe you would be this unprofessional."

"You have no idea what professionalism is, Jon. Now leave or I'll ask Randi to slap you around in front of your staff."

His face went white, then reddened like a beefsteak tomato. Spinning on his heels, he bolted from the office, his fists clenched and body rigid, as if he were a walking seizure.

After he was clear of Randi's office, she raised her hands and applauded. "I don't think you know how much I love you," she said, laughing. "What do you think he'll do now?"

"Is Tess in?"

"I think so."

"He'll go there and unload. She'll listen, commiserate, then tell him to leave." I took a deep breath. My heart was thumping. "Were you able to get reservations at the Fish Kettle?"

"You're all set. I told them you'd be there a little before noon. That you gives you time to pick up Celeste. I assume you may have to pick up her friend too."

"You're still coming, right?"

"I wouldn't miss it."

"Great, I could use the support."

"Did they treat you right over at Crime Central?"

I told her the story, then asked about the bank reports.

"They're clean. No withdrawals and only a few deposits, all of which you know about."

"I figured that's how it would be. Package them up and run them over to Detective West. Give them to West and West only. He was there when I left, but I'd give him a call first, just to be sure."

"Will do. Is there anything else?"

"No, I just need a few minutes to cool down. Jon annoys me more than I can say."

"He annoys everyone. You know what his aide calls him?"

"Jane?"

"That's right. She's from the South, you know, and they have a bug down there called a chigger."

"That's like a sand flea or something, right . . . wait, she calls her boss Chigger?"

"Not to his face, but she's been known to use the term around us."

At first I was astonished; then the humor of it landed squarely on my head. A little, annoying, biting bug. That was perfect. I voiced the words: "Councilman Chigger." My indignation washed away with laughter. Randi joined in, raising a hand to her mouth as if she were embarrassed to have shared the story.

The laughter refreshed me.

"Now that you're in a good mood . . ." I noticed she was looking at the files on my desk. I glanced down. The file Randi had given me, the file about a congressional run, was missing.

"He took it!" I said. "The little weasel took it!"

"No, he didn't. Do you think I'd let anyone sit in your office with sensitive files in reach? I have it."

"Whew. Don't do that to me. I'm getting too old for such shocks."

"You're not close to old. You can't even see old from where you are. I'll get the file. Read it. It'll get your mind off things."

I agreed. I could stand to have my mind on something else.

The rest of the morning passed quickly. I had expected a scalding phone call from Adler or Councilwoman Tess Lawrence, his political buddy. To my great relief nothing came. I spent an hour or so reviewing the notes from the meeting I skipped out on, and found only one item of concern: the zoning change requested by the church was denied. The council agreed with the Planning Commission. The vote was three to one against. I felt bad about that. I had planned to support the church, but I doubted my presence would have made a difference.

The other items on my desk took only a few minutes to handle. That left me about ninety minutes to review Randi's proposal. She was good—very good. Before me lay an analysis of demographics, estimated marketing expenditures, possible opponents, and more. The real kicker was something she learned that had yet to reach my ears. Congressman Martin Roth was retiring at the end of this term. There had been the occasional rumor that at the age of sixty-six, he had grown weary of campaigning and Capitol Hill. According to Randi, the rumors were true. She had inside information from a friend who worked in Roth's district office.

Congressman Roth would vacate the office in two years. Once word of this became official, every wannabe politico would come out of the woodwork. Randi was pushing for an early start.

"It is imperative that essential campaign personnel be in position at the time of the congressman's official declaration. An announcement should be made within thirty days of this declaration so as not to appear too opportunistic," her summary read. In short she was saying, "Let's get a jump on things."

I would run as a Republican, the party of which I had long been a member. My standing with various Republican groups was sound, so there was a good chance they would throw their weight, mailing lists, and volunteers my way.

Still, the idea of Congress was hard to swallow. The work would be interesting and meaningful, but the campaign arduous and expensive. The congressional district was larger than the city limits, meaning I would be campaigning in areas where no one knew me. Not an insurmountable problem. Every candidate faced such things.

I had often thought of running for higher office, but always saw it a decade away, and then I saw myself running for state office, like assembly or state senate, never Congress. Still . . .

Randi appeared at my door. "It's eleven-fifteen. If you're going to pick Celeste up at half-past—"

"I'd better get going." I stood and handed her the file. "Lock this away, please."

She took it. "What do you think?"

"Of the file? It's well prepared. You still amaze me. As far as what you're suggesting, well . . . I need time to digest the idea."

"Oh." She sounded sad.

"However, I'm willing to consider it."

Her eyes sparkled and a knowing smile crossed her face. "That's great!"

"Easy, girl. I only said I would consider it."

"That's half the battle."

It was my turn to smile. "You don't know me as well as you think."

"I know you better than you think."

I gathered my bag. "That's probably true. I'll see you at the restaurant. Don't be late. I'm hungry."

"I'll be there with bells on."

"Leave the bells, they distract the other diners."

I exited my office and made my way toward the car. My mind was churning. In less than twenty-four hours I had run the gamut of emotions. My brain had had an aerobic workout that left it weary and longing to shut down—and all this before lunch.

When I pulled up in front of my house, Celeste was standing on the stoop—much to my relief. Seeing me, she walked quickly to the car and got in.

I studied her for a moment. "Ready to eat?"

"Yes. We need to pick up Michele." She told me the address.

"That's not far." I waited a moment before asking, "How are you doing?"

She shrugged. "Okay, I guess."

The girl looked frail, a waif caught in a brutal hurricane of fear and emotion. The skin under her eyes was dark, the rim of her lids still red from crying. She wore the clothes she had on when I took her home: blue jeans, coral tunic, and a pair of white Nikes.

"I assume Maria arrived."

"Yeah, she got here not long after you left. She washed my clothes so I could wear them. She's nice."

I agreed, then pulled the car from the curb. "Have you known Michele long?"

"I'm sorry." I started to repeat myself when she added, "I was rude."

It took a moment for me to catch up. "You mean about this morning?"

"Yeah, I shouldn't have said what I did."

"You didn't say anything wrong."

"I implied it. I mean, you came to my house, you took me in and did nothing but treat me right. When I heard that the blood was on your card, it made me think you had something to do with my mother's disappearance, but that's stupid. Why would you do that? It doesn't make sense."

West was right; Celeste was a sharp young lady. "Thank you. I was afraid you'd leave while I was at the office."

"I know. Turn left here."

Making the turn, I said, "I went to the Police Station and let them fingerprint me. I also sent over the bank records Detective West asked for. They were in perfect order."

"I told him my mother wouldn't steal anything."

"I think he was afraid someone might try to force her to withdraw the money. I suppose they still can."

"Can't you tell the bank to stop any withdrawals?"

This thought had occurred to me while I was in my office. "I suppose, but I don't want to."

"Why?"

"If someone took your mother to get access to that account, I want her to be able to do that. They might let her go if they get the money. It would also give the police some evidence to go on, such as where they made the withdrawal. I gave them permission to monitor the account."

"Oh, but you could loose all your campaign money. Turn right."

"It doesn't matter." I directed the Aviator around a corner. "I can always raise more money. I'd rather have your mother back."

She sniffed. "Me too."

"There's something else I want to talk to you about," I said, trying not to sound too serious. "Detective West thinks I should be careful."

"Careful?"

"You know, about my safety. He thinks that whatever happened to your mother may be directed at me. I don't know if that's true. If it is, why would anyone . . . go to your house instead of mine? But my point is this: I think you should be careful, too."

"I will."

"You know you're welcome to stay with me as long as you like. In fact, I'd like it if you stayed a few days."

"Okay."

A couple turns more led us to a small single-story apartment building that had only eight units.

"Honk the horn. She said she'd be right down."

I did and a moment later a bouncy blond appeared at one of the doors. She waved, then trotted toward us. She was tall and thin, and her hair was pulled back in a ponytail that bobbed with every step. Like Celeste, she wore jeans and Nikes. Above that she wore a hooded green sweatshirt.

Before Michele could reach the car, Celeste was out. They met and embraced, Michele taking her friend in her arms. I waited and was willing to wait a long time. Celeste needed a friend and Michele was her choice. A minute passed before either moved. Finally Celeste pulled away and ran a hand under her eyes, then under her nose. Michele was carrying a small purse with a thin leather strap. She opened it and gave Celeste a tissue. Both came to the car. Michele opened the back door, and I expected Celeste to return to the front seat. Instead she followed her friend into the back.

"Is it okay if I sit back here?"

"Sure, I can be chauffeur, but it's customary to tip."

She laughed politely. "This is Michele. We go to college together. I've known her since middle school."

"Hi, my name is Maddy."

"She's the mayor," Celeste said.

"No way!" Michele exclaimed. "The mayor of what?"

"Mayor of Santa Rita," Celeste said. "How did you get into college?"

"I didn't know."

"That's all right," I interjected. "A lot of people don't know who their mayor is."

"Where are we going?" Michele asked.

"The Fish Kettle," I said. "Is that okay?"

"I love that place. I've only been a couple times but I love it."

"Great," I said. "I know the owner. He'll treat us right."

"Is it just the three of us?"

I could tell Michele was the inquisitive type. "My aide, Randi, is joining us."

"Is he nice?" Michele asked.

"He is a she," I said. "R–A–N–D–I. You'll like her. She's smart and pretty."

"Oh."

"I don't know about you two, but I'm hungry, so buckle up." I pressed the pedal down and pulled away from the curb.

The Santa Rita pier is a quarter-mile-long construction of heavy wood planks and beams. Built in the early sixties, it has endured the decades with grace despite battles with storms and waves. On more than one occasion a storm has undermined portions of the structure, caving in a corner here and there. Each time the city and county have rebuilt it. It is one of the few landmarks of our city and a profound source of pride. The Fish Kettle sits in the middle of the pier.

The restaurant itself looks like a ramshackle fishing shack. The owner paid the architect a lot of money to make the building look a century older than it is. Dark, ocean-stained wood covers the exterior. Streaks of rust run from nails in the siding. A careful eye can see galvanized nails holding the siding in place. The other nails, which have aged and weathered, are there for effect. The roof appears to be made of tar paper, but it too is facade, mere architectural illusion.

The interior is a maritime experience. Walls that are not filled with expansive windows are covered in shiplap siding heavily painted with a dark-blue enamel. Woodcarvings of various species of fish hang from the ceiling and dance in the gentle breeze made by the slowly spinning ceiling fans. The smell of fish cooking hangs heavy in the air. Booths sit around the perimeter wall, and free-standing tables are scattered across the floor like mushrooms on a grass field.

When we walked in at ten minutes to noon, the place was already half full. Soon hungry office workers, laborers, and others would pack the place. At the Fish Kettle a patron can buy a good meal at a reasonable price, but that is only part of the draw. A view of the ocean is available from every table. Atmosphere—the place is loaded with atmosphere.

I had only taken two steps when the owner, Paul Shedd, greeted us. Paul was in his early fifties and had been owner of the restaurant for the last ten years. A former banker, he turned his ledger in for a mass of pots and pans and, according to him, has never been happier. At least his midlife crisis involved changing jobs instead of wives. He was trim and sported the kind of deep tan that made one worry about skin cancer. He kept his salt-and-pepper hair cut close to the scalp. He bounded our way, flashing a smile bright enough to light the room. I've known Paul since he bought the place. He was a favorite of my husband. A deeply spiritual man, he let his faith speak for itself, although on one wall he did put up a large picture of the disciples in a Galilean fishing boat. Jesus is walking on the water nearby. There are days I wish I could do that.

Paul's wife was a winner. She was a few inches shorter than me and round like a barrel. Her eyes were like blue lenses that focused an inner light. She often served as hostess during the dinner hour.

"Madam Mayor," Paul said with a flourish. "We're honored to have you."

"Oh, knock it off, Paul. I eat here at least once a week."

"In that case, you know where the kitchen is. Fix your own lunch."

"It would never measure up to your standards."

He led us to a large booth in the front corner of the restaurant. The sun was high overhead, shinning through a now cloudless sky. The remaining fragments of rain clouds had gone wherever clouds go. The sky was bright and the ocean vivid blue. The air, scrubbed clean by the driving rain, was untainted by smog or haze. California knew how to dress up.

The three of us took our seats, joining Randi, who had beaten us there. I introduced the girls to my aide and they all shook hands. I noticed that Randi let her eyes linger on Celeste a moment or two.

Paul handed us menus and then took our drink orders. I asked
for tea, Randi asked for water with a slice of lemon, and the girls
each requested a Coke. Paul then scurried away. He always scurried.
No wonder he was thin.

The conversation remained light while we perused the menus.
I glanced at the items, which included various seafood dishes and
some traditional lunch fare like hamburgers and sandwiches.

"Get whatever you want, girls; it's my treat," I said as I set my
menu down. Looking at it had been a waste of time. I knew what I
wanted before I left the office.

"Cool," Michele said.

Celeste sat quietly, staring at the menu. I doubted she was at all
hungry.

Paul returned with our drinks and set them down with practiced precision. "Is everybody ready?"

I looked around the table and everyone but Celeste nodded. She
had, however, set her menu down. "I would like a shrimp salad and
a cup of the gumbo," I said, then turned to the others. "I love the
gumbo."

Randi ordered a bowl of clam chowder and Michele asked for
shrimp fettuccine. I looked at Celeste, fearing that she would say
she wasn't hungry. Emotions could be taxing, and she had expended
a lot of emotion over the last eighteen hours. She needed to eat.

"Can I have a hamburger?" she asked. "I don't much care for
fish stuff."

"It'll be a blessing," Paul said and then trotted off.

"He's weird," Michele said with a giggle.

"He's one of the nicest people you will ever meet," I said. "He is
a little weird, though, but only a little. My husband used to go fishing with him."

"Really?" Randi said. "I didn't know that, and I know everything about you."

"You don't know as much as you think, woman. My husband went through a stage, one of those back-to-nature-regain-the-masculine-role things. At least that's how it appeared to me. About once a month he and Paul would go out on a half-day boat. Other businessmen would go with them. Peter used to tell me that he was fishing for business as much as bass or yellowtail or whatever they fish for."

As if on cue, two elderly men walked by our window, fishing poles in hand, and headed toward the distant end of the pier. Others were walking in the opposite direction. The pier is a place of constant activity. Inside, the chatter of the crowd filled the air as thoroughly as the aroma from the kitchen. A mix of humanity occupied the room: men in shirts and ties discussed the day's business next to men in faded jeans and torn work shirts, and mothers with young children sat lost in conversation. Each table or booth was a world unto itself, a galaxy that floated in isolation from all the galaxies around it. There was laughter and there were whispers and at our table there was awkward silence.

Celeste sat with slumped shoulders, staring at the table, shutting out the rest of the world. After Peter's murder, I often felt I stood out like a bride in a red gown. Often I imagined that people were looking at me, pitying me or maybe casting a glare in my direction, like the fishermen on the pier casting their lines into the depths of the ocean. No doubt Celeste felt the same way.

Here we were, doing a perfectly normal thing, in a perfectly normal place, surround by normal people, yet nothing was normal for Celeste. Somewhere, someone was holding her mother, or worse. It was a brutal truth held back by the hope of good news, that somehow it had all been a misunderstanding or a very bad dream. No matter how hard the coals of that hope were stoked, the truth always came crashing in like cold water.

Michele yammered on about different things—friends Celeste knew, school, moving out on her own—but her efforts failed. She was being a good friend, putting on a strong face and attempting to give Celeste something else to think about. I knew from personal experience that never worked. Everything appears trivial in the stark light of tragedy. There was no use avoiding the subject. It was on everyone's mind.

"Celeste," I asked, "do you want to go by your house and pick up some clothing and personal items?"

"I suppose. Will the police let us in?"

"I think so. I'd be happy to check."

"I'll do it," Randi said, pulling a cell phone from her purse. She paused. "Do you know the number?"

I shook my head. Randi entered three numbers, then asked information for a Santa Rita listing.

Turning my attention back to Celeste, I said, "If you're uncomfortable about going in the house, I'd be happy to go for you."

"Me too," Michele said.

"That's okay," Celeste said. "I was in there last night. I can't hide from this."

She was courageous; I had to give her that. "Let's do that right after we eat. Michele can help you pull some things together. How does that sound?"

"Okay, I guess."

My heart ached for her. This young woman of nineteen years appeared to have aged a decade overnight. She looked as if someone had scooped the life out of her.

"Mayor," Randi said. "I have Detective West on the phone. He said the house has been cleared, but he wants to talk to you."

I took the phone. "Hello."

"Mayor, is Celeste with you?"

"She is." Celeste looked up.

"Her father has been looking for her. He wants to talk to his daughter. May I give him your cell phone number?"

"Is he in town?" Celeste cocked her head to the side; she had made the connection.

"No, but he's flying out here. He's at the airport in Galveston now."

I took a deep breath. This was awkward. "Did he leave a number?"

"Yes, he did."

"Why don't you give that to me and I'll pass it on to Celeste. The decision is hers to make."

He agreed and relayed the number while I searched frantically for a pen in my purse. Randi had one at the ready. I jotted the number down, repeating it to make sure I had it right. I said goodbye and handed the phone back to Randi.

"My father?"

"Yes, he's at an airport in Texas. He wants to talk to you."

Her face flushed. "I don't want to talk to him."

"I thought you might say that. That's why I didn't give my number."

"He doesn't care about us. He's been gone for years. He never calls. Why does he want to come out here now?"

"Celeste, the choice is yours. You're over eighteen; you can talk to him or not. This is a . . . an unusual situation. He may just want to make sure you're all right."

She shook her head. "You don't know him like I do."

"True. I told Detective West I'd give you the number. What you do with it is up to you." I pushed the napkin across the table. She stared at it for a few moments, then picked it up, gazing at the scrawled numbers. Then she slowly began to tear it into strips.

That took care of the phone number, but her father was flying to California. He would arrive in a few hours.

What then?

chapter 6

I returned to my office at 1:45, having finished lunch and taken Celeste to her home to pick up clothing. The drive to her house and then to my home had been as solemn as lunch. There was a contagious heaviness that followed Celeste and infected the rest of us. I invited Michele to stay at the house with Celeste and she agreed. We took the time to swing by Michele's place so she could pick up her swimsuit. She was thrilled to exchange a day in her apartment for one in a house on the beach. I made them swear there would be no wild parties, frat boys, or motorcycle gangs. This time when I arrived at the office, I parked in the rear lot.

Randi was already at her desk when I walked in. "Did I miss anything fun?" I asked.

"I don't know about fun, but you missed a call. Celeste's father has telephoned twice."

I had checked my messages at the house when I dropped the girls off and had none. I would have been surprised and upset had someone given my number to Celeste's father. I have a private number, yet another security precaution. There is nothing worse than being awakened at two a.m. by some drunk who wants to talk about the pothole on his street. "Did he leave a message?"

"I told him you were out, but he's an insistent man. He said he'd call every half hour until he got ahold of you."

"Swell. Is he calling from the airport?"

"No, he's calling from the plane. He's already in the air."

"Okay, I'll talk to him when he calls."

"What are you going to say?"

"I have no idea."

I closed the door to my office, sat down, and did nothing. The morning had been grueling in several ways, and now I was facing a phone conversation with a man who was undoubtedly upset. I wasn't looking forward to it. I tried to focus on other matters. I was to give a speech the next week to the Chamber of Commerce, as well as deliver a talk to the Young Republicans. I was also due to have dinner at my parents' home the next evening. I needed to call and bring them up to date, and inform them I'd be bringing company.

Beyond the door I heard the phone ring. I looked at my desk clock. Fifteen minutes had passed, making it two o'clock. I had a feeling Celeste's father was on the phone. Randi's voice came over the intercom: "Mr. Christopher Truccoli. Have fun."

"As if," I replied as surly as possible, then snatched up the phone with an imagined confidence. "This is Mayor Glenn." I tried to sound professional and busy.

"Mayor, this is Christopher Truccoli, Celeste's father." His voice sounded tinny.

"Yes, Mr. Truccoli; I understand you're calling from the plane."

"Can you hear me all right?"

"I hear you fine, sir."

"Good. I want to talk to my daughter."

"She's not here."

"It was my understanding that she was with you."

"Celeste stayed with me last night. I didn't want her to be alone."

"I appreciate that. How is she?"

"She's doing well, considering what she's facing. She's a strong young lady."

"How do I get in contact with her?"

There it was. The question I had hoped wouldn't come. I inhaled and spat out the truth of the matter. "This is awkward for me, sir, but she has made it clear that she doesn't want to speak to you."

"That's crazy; she's my daughter."

"Be that as it may, Mr. Truccoli, the decision is hers, not mine."

"She's staying at your house?"

"For the moment, yes."

"Give me that number; I'll call her there." His voice had slipped up a quarter octave and he was becoming agitated.

"I can't do that."

"You can and you will!"

It was clear that bullying wasn't something new to him. It was time for a different tactic. "Mr. Truccoli, if you're going to speak to me, then you are going to do so with a civil tongue and demeanor. Do you understand?"

"I will speak to you any way I choose." His voice was just a few degrees from shouting. I was glad I wasn't sitting next to him on the airplane.

"No sir, you will not. I'm perfectly capable of hanging up the phone, and trust me, I've hung up on angrier people than you."

"What kind of person are you to come between a father and his daughter, especially at a time like this?"

"I do not stand between you and your daughter. I am merely honoring a young woman's request."

"She's a child."

"She's a legal adult."

"But I'm already on the plane. I'm thirty thousand feet over west Texas."

"That's something over which I have no control."

"Who's your supervisor?" He was shouting. I heard another voice, that of a woman. I couldn't make out everything she said but I did hear, ". . . have to be quiet . . ."

I almost laughed at his question. "My supervisor is the citizenry of Santa Rita." I heard swearing.

"Are you stupid, woman? Don't you know what has happened?"

"I can assure you I am not stupid, and yes, I know what has occurred, as much as can be known at this point."

"So you're not going to give me your number?"

"No sir, I am not."

"How am I supposed to talk to my daughter? You tell me that." I was pretty sure he was grinding his teeth.

"I suggest you get a hotel in the area, and as soon as you get settled, you can call Detective West and tell him where you're staying. I'll ask West to pass that information on to me and I promise to give it to Celeste. What she does with it will be up to her."

There was a momentary pause, then, "Son of a—" The line went dead. I hung up the phone and a moment later Randi opened the door and peeked in.

"I assume you were listening in."

"I thought you might need an ear witness."

"He is one unhappy man."

"I don't think you'll be getting a box of chocolates anytime soon."

"Somehow that's a relief."

Randi laughed. "I'll call West and fill him in."

"Thanks, Randi."

My head began to throb.

Randi buzzed the intercom and announced, "One Mrs. Agnes Anderson for you. She'll tell you I'm right about Congress."

"You didn't tell my mother about that, did you?"

"Of course not, but I will if you want." Even over the intercom I could hear the smile in Randi's voice. She was enjoying herself.

"I'd prefer you didn't. Mom thinks I could be president this time next year if I would just apply myself."

"Hmm. President, eh?"

"Don't get any ideas." I picked up the phone. "Hello, Mother."

"Hi, sweetheart." Mom spoke with lilting, almost musical tones, which was to be expected: she was a first-class musician and teacher. Never quite able to reach the level that would allow her to play viola in a large symphony, she had been content to teach at the local high school. The image of her flashed to mind: tall, thin, short gray hair, large caring eyes, and a mouth more accustomed to smiling than frowning. The gray of her hair, which she used to call "highlights," was dominating, and she no longer hid it under chemical color. I doubted I would follow her example. "I was just calling to see how you are . . . I mean, with all that has happened."

"Happened?"

"About your friend. It was in the papers. Are you okay?"

The newspapers, of course. I had not read the morning edition, something I normally do within minutes of walking through my office door. This day, however, was hardly usual.

"I'm fine, Mom. There's nothing to worry about." Telling my mother not to worry was like telling the ocean not to send waves to the shore. It was a law of nature. Mothers worry; my mother worried at championship levels.

"That's what your father said, but I wanted to be sure. What happened?"

I spent the next five minutes bringing her up to date, leaving out the fingerprinting and the bit about my business card.

"That's horrible."

"We're all waiting to hear from the police. With a little luck, we'll know something soon."

"I hope so. What are you doing for dinner . . . you and Celeste, I mean?"

I hadn't thought about dinner and told her so.

"Well, why don't you two come over tonight? We can push our weekly dinner up a day." I normally had dinner with my parents on Thursdays. One week my mother cooked, the next I treated them to a meal at one of the local eating establishments.

"I suppose we could do that. Let's plan on it, and I'll mention it to Celeste when I get home."

"Great, I'll make an enchilada casserole." Mom was the casserole queen. Fortunately, she was as good a cook as she was a musician. "Is six-thirty okay?"

"That will be great, Mom. Can I bring anything?" I already knew the answer.

"No, I have more time than you do. I'll take care of everything."

I hung up and found myself looking forward to the evening. I might have been just shy of forty, but visiting the home I grew up in always brought a sense of comfort and security. My parents were in their early sixties, but they seemed ageless to me. Spreading gray hair, new wrinkles, widening waddles, meant nothing to me.

Truth was, I could use a few hours with the two people I knew loved me unconditionally.

At 4:50 Randi announced I had another call. This time it was from Detective West. I was just packing my briefcase, throwing in a few files I needed for an upcoming closed-door session of the council, and "the File," as Randi had taken to calling it.

Hoping for new information, I snapped up the phone and said hello.

"This is a courtesy call, Mayor," West said. "Mr. Truccoli was just here and was bending my ear. He's less than pleased with you."

"I gathered that when I spoke to him this afternoon."

"He wants to see his daughter."

"That's not my decision to make, Detective. You know that."

"I do know that and I agree with you. I just thought I'd let you know that he demanded to see the chief. Fortunately, he was gone. Mr. Truccoli demanded Webb's home phone. Well, that didn't fly. Then he wanted to know where the city's offices were."

My heart sank. "And you had to tell him."

"I had to. That's public info. He could have gotten that from the phone book."

"Tell me he's not on his way over here."

"I wish I could. He just charged from the office. You'll be able to recognize him; he's the one with the beet red face."

"Swell."

"I suggest you leave a few minutes early—like right now. Also, I alerted security and sent over a uniformed officer. A security guard should be at your door any moment. Let him walk you to your car."

As if on cue, Randi poked her head through the door, a concerned look on her face. "Security is here," she said softly so as not to be heard over the phone. I nodded and waved her in. A man who couldn't have been more than twenty-five followed her. He wore a white uniform shirt and navy blue slacks. A gold badge hung on his shirt, as did a nametag that read, "Bobby Wallace."

"Security just showed up. Thanks for the heads-up, Detective. I owe you one."

"My pleasure."

"Is there anything new on Lisa?"

"Nothing."

I said thanks again and hung up. I looked at Randi and said, "Gather your stuff, kiddo. Mr. Truccoli is on his way over and he doesn't want to talk about zoning laws."

I didn't have to ask her twice.

"I can take care of this guy," the young security guard said.

"No doubt you can, Bobby, but let's try to avoid a confrontation if possible. Our cars are in the back lot. Let's take the private corridor." I grabbed my briefcase, crossed into Randi's room, then stopped. "If he comes to the offices, then poor Fritzy is going to get an earful. She doesn't need that."

"There's another guard at the front," the security man said. "Detective West demanded it."

"Good for him. Let's go."

We exited the offices, the guard leading the way. We had made it no more than five steps when we heard a loud, angry voice bouncing off the walls. Truccoli had landed. There was no wonder why Celeste didn't want to talk to this guy.

"Go help your partner," I said to the guard.

"I'm supposed to escort you to your car."

"You're supposed to keep Truccoli away from me, at least until he learns to be civil. Since we know he's in the lobby, he can't be in the parking lot. Go help your buddy. That will give us time to get to our cars."

"But—"

"It's a good strategy. Do it."

I started back down the hall, Randi by my side. The guard mumbled something, then marched toward the lobby.

"You gotta love public life," Randi said.

"I'll try to remember that."

I pulled into the driveway of my home, firing two conflicting emotions: relief and worry. I was glad to be home and away from the office, especially away from any chance of bumping into Celeste's father, but I also felt a strong sense of anxiety. I now had to inform Celeste that Daddy Dearest had arrived.

I found the girls sitting on lounge chairs on the deck at the back of the house; each had a glass of tea resting beside her. Michele's glass was nearly drained, Celeste's nearly full. The weather had warmed up nicely after last night's rain, but with the sun now dropping, the air had turned cool. A breeze rolled off the ocean, carrying the sea's salty perfume. The water reflected the golden light of the sun in a long band that looked like a road to the distant horizon. A gull moved past in a slow glide.

"You guys look rested."

Celeste and Michele jumped and let slip gasps of surprise. "Geez," Michele said, "you scared me." She pressed a hand to her chest.

"Me too."

"Sorry. I thought I was noisy enough coming through the front door." Both girls wore two-piece swimsuits. Michele's was a blue-and-white print and far less encumbered with material. Celeste's more modest suit was a satiny green. "Aren't you cold?"

"A little," Celeste replied.

"Well, come on in and let's talk about this evening."

They picked up their glasses and followed me into the dining area. Celeste was last in and closed the door behind her. We sat at the table and I told Celeste I had no new information about her mother, but that I had been in regular contact with the police. She seemed discouraged and I couldn't blame her. I then hit her with the other news. "Your father is in town."

Her eyes widened. "You didn't tell him I was here, did you?"

I shook my head. "He called me from the plane and demanded my home number. I'm not good with demands. I told him you were a big girl and capable of making your own decisions."

She seemed relieved. "I don't want to talk to him."

"I know, but he sure wants to talk to you." I told her about his visit to the Police Department and his arrival at the city offices.

"He's a pain. I don't know what he wants. It's not like he loves Mom or me."

"Was the breakup bitter?"

"He ran off with another woman. That's pretty bitter."

"What a jerk," Michele added.

"He may still be concerned about you. I can't stick up for him. I wouldn't even try. My phone conversation with him is enough to put me off for a good long while. However, he is your father, and maybe your mother's disappearance has brought that home."

"No way. He has never cared about me. Why begin now? Did the police question him?"

I hadn't thought to ask that and said so. "I'm sure they asked a few questions, but with your dad in Galveston and your mother here, I'm not sure there is much of a connection."

"He could have, like, arranged it or something."

That also hadn't occurred to me. "I'm sure the police have thought of that. Anyway, I didn't think you wanted to speak to him, but I needed to let you know he's in town."

"Can he get your number or find out where you live?" Michele asked.

"It's possible but doubtful. My phone number is unlisted. The last thing a mayor needs is a number anyone can call at any time. I suppose he could find out where I live if he is smart enough and persistent enough. I'm not listed in the phone book, but there are ways around that."

"So he could find us here."

"Unlikely but possible."

Celeste's lips tightened and her eyes narrowed.

"On a more positive note, we've been invited over to my parents' house for dinner. How about it?"

"I'm still not hungry," Celeste said.

"I know, but it will get you out for a while and you'll love my parents. Mom is a great cook." I turned to Michele. "You're welcome to come along if you'd like."

"I can't. I promised my mom I'd go someplace with her tonight."

"Okay. Why don't you two change, and we'll drop Michele off on our way to Mom and Dad's."

"What if the police come up with something? How will they get ahold of us?" Celeste asked.

"Detective West has my cell number. He can call that."

She nodded, rose, and moved toward the stairs. Events were moving her against her will. Her mother was missing, she was in a stranger's home, and a father she hated had just touched down in town.

Michele followed Celeste up the stairs. A few minutes later both descended, dressed as they were at lunch. We were out the door and on the road five minutes later.

chapter 7

om must've heard us arrive, because she was standing at the front door waiting for us, her face alight with anticipation. She wore a black tunic V-neck sweater and tan slacks. A simple pair of white deck shoes clad her feet. She looked good. Mom always looked good. "Welcome," she said, more to Celeste than to me. "Come in, come in." She kissed us both on the cheek.

We walked to the house, a simple bungalow-style home in one of the older but nicer neighborhoods. Inside we were awash in the thick, hunger-inducing aroma of enchilada casserole. My stomach did a happy flip. The moment we entered, my father rose from his recliner, cast us a wide smile, and approached.

Closing the door behind me, I said, "Celeste, this is my mother, Agnes Anderson, and my father, Greg."

"Hello," Celeste said timidly.

"Hello," my father bellowed. As a college professor, he had been speaking loudly most of his adult life. He saw no reason to change things at home. Dad was just over six feet tall, still slim but carrying more weight than he did five years ago. He sported a close, neatly trimmed white beard that matched his hair. His eyes sparkled ocean blue and his grin was contagious. A firm man, he was above all else jovial. Laughter was his drink of choice.

"I'm so glad you could join us," Mom said. "Have a seat. Dinner is almost ready. I hope you like Mexican. Maddy sure does. I've seen her out-eat—"

"Mom, you're rambling." I was hoping to avoid any stories from my childhood. Celeste and I walked to the sofa and Dad went back to his easy chair.

"No, I'm not. I'm talking about you."

"That's my point. Can I help you in the kitchen?"

"No, the casserole just needs another ten minutes. Jerry should be here by then." Stunned, I watched her walk into the small kitchen. The house is a forties-style bungalow, which means every area is compartmentalized. The kitchen is enclosed, open to the dining room only by a passageway.

I sighed. Celeste gave me a questioning glance. "Jerry Thomas," I explained. "Dr. Jerry Thomas, actually. I went to high school with him."

"Nice guy," Dad added.

"Mom thinks we're made for each other."

"I never said that," she shouted from the kitchen. "He's a family friend. He and your father play chess. You know that."

I looked at Dad. "Are you planning on playing chess tonight?"

He shrugged and tried to look innocent.

"A doctor, huh?" Celeste said.

"A pediatrician. He has an office on Castillo Avenue."

"Oh."

I had a feeling that had her situation not been so grave, she would have given me a good ribbing.

"He likes to talk history with Greg," Mom said from the kitchen. I remained amazed at how she could carry on a conversation from a different room.

"I wish you had told me, Mom."

"Why? Would you not have come?"

She had me there. It made no difference, really. I also knew that everything she had said was true. Jerry was a friend of the family, he did play chess with my father, and more than once I had endured their long conversation about some historical point. History was Jerry's hobby; it was my father's life.

My parents' living room is small, in keeping with the house. The place where I shared my childhood with my brother and sister is sixteen hundred square feet personalized by nearly four decades of family life. I couldn't imagine my mom and dad living anyplace else.

The doorbell rang. "Get that, will you, Maddy?" Mom directed. "That must be him. Punctual as usual."

I pulled the door open and found Jerry standing there. "Maddy! They didn't tell me you were going to be here."

"That surprises you?" I asked with a smile. Jerry was forty, with sandy blond hair, brown eyes, and wide grin. Like Dad, he had somehow avoided the middle-age spread that was the bane of most men, but I suspected that could change at any time.

"No, not really. I think we've been set up again."

"It's not a setup," Mother shouted.

I laughed a little and then invited him in. Jerry and I dated in high school. There had never been the magic that teenage girls long for. He was polite, fun, and intelligent. The years had been kind to him. His smile was still stunning and genuine, and his character had not dulled with adulthood. He had married after medical school but divorced some years later. His wife apparently demanded more time than her doctor husband could give.

"Come on in," I said, stepping aside. He did and started for the love seat next to the sofa. I took a chance and peeked in the kitchen. "You sure you don't need any help?"

Mother shooed me out. "Go visit with our guests before your father launches into a lecture."

I went back to the living room. "Jerry, this is Celeste Truccoli. Celeste, Dr. Jerry Thomas."

"Hello," Celeste said.

"Hi, it's a pleasure—" He stopped short. I could almost see his neurons sparking as his brain started to make connections. Mom said she had read about the abduction in the newspaper; Jerry must have done the same.

"Truccoli?"

Celeste squirmed. I answered for her. "Yes. It's her mother who is missing. Celeste is staying with me for a while."

"I'm so very sorry. I don't know what to say." I watched as he switched from plain ol' Jerry to Jerry the physician. "How are you holding up?"

It was an honest and heartfelt question. It was also impossible for Celeste to answer. How does one hold up in such situations? She answered with a shrug. Tears were starting to well up again. The poor girl was living on the precipice. Anything and everything pushed her over the edge. Again I answered for her. "Celeste is strong. She's doing everything right. We're remaining hopeful."

"Is there anything I can do? I'll help any way I can."

"There's nothing any of us can do now but wait and pray that the police find her soon ... and healthy." I looked reassuringly at Celeste, then turned to find Mom standing nearby. She was staring at Celeste in a way only mothers could. The look said more than a library full of words.

"Let's gather around the table," she said. "It's time to eat."

Dinner passed with large helpings of the cheese-laden casserole topped with salsa and dollops of sour cream. Celeste ate more than I expected. I was glad to see it, but she left most of her meal on the plate. The conversation was light and covered everything from the weather to my father's classes. The words didn't touch on the questions festering in our minds. For Celeste's sake, we avoided talking about the event she could not ignore. We were ballerinas dancing on eggshells. Despite our good intentions, it was a futile gesture. The shells cracked anyway.

The harder we tried to pretend things were normal, the more obvious the truth became. I caught Celeste's attention and whispered, "We'll go home early."

She nodded and seemed appreciative.

Cherry cobbler followed, which my mother served up in heaping portions. I declined, but she set a plateful of the gooey delight in front of me anyway. It was more than I could eat in two sittings. My mother was nothing if not compulsive. This slight affliction blossomed when she was nervous. Clearly, she was picking up Celeste's discomfort.

I had just put the first taste of the treat in my mouth when my cell phone chimed. Celeste's head snapped around and she stared at me through wide eyes. I excused myself from the table, found my purse, and hurriedly glanced at the small screen on the device. Caller ID told me, "West, Judson" and the phone number. My heart did a somersault.

"Madison Glenn," I said, trying to look calm. Every eye was on me as I held the phone to my ear. I turned my back to those seated at the table so I could focus on West's words. I listened as he spoke softly but firmly. I said I understood and disconnected. My chest muscles tightened and I felt the blood drain from my face. The room spun for a second, then returned to its rightful place. I was holding my breath. I forced a few inhalations. Slowly I turned and faced family and guests.

Celeste broke the silence. "Was it about my mother?"

I shook my head. I was starting to feel numb, distant from reality, like a balloon released in a stiff breeze.

"What, dear?" my mother asked. "Who was it?"

I blinked a few times. "Detective West. There's been another abduction, and . . ." I wasn't sure how to put it. "And it's someone else I know. I'm going over there." I put the phone back in my purse. "Can Celeste stay—"

"Of course," Mom answered before I completed the sentence. Judging from Dad's open mouth, she had beaten him by a slim second.

"I'll pick you up on my way home, Celeste. I'm afraid I have to do this."

She said nothing.

"I'm going with you," Jerry said, jumping to his feet. "I'll drive."

"You don't have to do that."

"No, but I want to. Don't bother arguing. You can let me drive or I'll follow you over. Either way I'm going to be there."

I agreed with a silent nod. Why do men always have to be the ones to drive? Three minutes later I was riding shotgun in Jerry's Ford Excursion.

We got on the 101 and headed north for about five miles. Jerry handled the SUV with precision.

"You going to fill me in?" he asked, his eyes fixed forward, looking beyond the black hood. "All I know is that we're going to Canyon Rim." Canyon Rim is a new subdivision that was built less than five years earlier. It's a gated community with large homes and shared swimming and recreational facilities. "Canyon Rim, the Family Oasis," it bills itself. Three hundred and fifty thousand dollars can get anyone a home with an ocean view.

"Gillespie Street, 1344 Gillespie."

"You said this was another abduction?"

"Yes." I didn't want to face this, didn't want to talk about it.

"Someone you know, you said."

"Yes." I was going to have to talk about it. "How much do you know about Lisa Truccoli's kidnapping?"

"Just what was in the papers, and that wasn't much."

I studied Jerry for a moment. He was a gentle man with a keen mind, attractive in every way. His most winsome attribute was his ability to empathize. That was what made him a good doctor, or so I heard. Having no children, I've never needed his services. I took a deep breath and explained all I knew. I felt as if I had recounted the story every hour of the day. I told him about Lisa's role in my campaign, and the discovery of my bloody business card.

Jerry listened, asking only the occasional question to clarify my sometimes murky descriptions. When I was done, he said, "Wow."

"Wow?"

"I know that's not eloquent, but it's all I can think of to say. This place we're going is also connected to you?"

"The person is. Take the next off ramp." I gazed out the window, watching the terrain zip by as we began to head inland. The 101 bifurcates Santa Rita: coastal communities and businesses to the west, the rest of the city nestled in the hills to the east. Those hills, still green from the winter rains, were lit this night by a waxing gibbous moon. "Poor Lizzy."

"Lizzy?"

"I'm sorry. I don't mean to be opaque. Elizabeth Stout. She was my best friend in college."

"At San Diego State."

"Yes. Peter introduced us during my freshman year. She's from Agora Hills originally. She moved to Santa Rita about ten years ago.

Turn left on Sunset, then make a right on Grove. We're almost there."

"Did the detective say . . . I mean . . . did he mention if . . ." He gave a halfhearted chuckle. "It appears I just suffered a stroke."

He was trying to ask a hard question delicately, but there was no subtle way to approach it. "Detective West didn't say anything about the crime scene, so I don't know if there's blood."

"Isn't it unusual for the police to ask a civilian to come to the scene of a crime?"

"I suppose," I admitted, "but this is all atypical. He said it involved me again, but didn't say how. Maybe because I'm the mayor, I get cut a little extra slack."

"Make's sense, I guess."

"That's it," I said. I didn't have to say anything else. Two patrol cars and one unmarked police car rested near the curb. Jerry parked behind the last car in the queue and I exited. Outside the vehicle I paused, closed my eyes, took a deep breath of sweet night air, and wished I were far away. When I opened my eyes, I found that reality had decided to hang around.

Lizzy's house is a two-story structure that must hover around three thousand square feet. The stucco exterior appeared stark and uninviting in the yellow porch light. The light bar of one patrol car was still on, splashing the house with rotating red and blue splotches.

For the second time in two days, I walked to a house that had harbored a crime.

I'm Maddy Glenn," I said to the officer posted by the front door. As with Lisa's house, the door was wide open. "Detective West asked to see me."

"Who are you?" he asked Jerry.

"He's with me," I said.

The officer frowned, then took one step into the house. "Detective, Maddy Glenn is here."

A second later West appeared, his suit looking as crisp and pressed as it did that morning. "Madam Mayor," he said. "Thank you for coming." He looked at Jerry.

"Dr. Jerry Thomas," I said, "meet Detective Judson West, Santa Rita PD."

They acknowledged each other, but I noticed that West was studying Jerry carefully.

"Jerry is a family friend. He was having dinner with my parents and me when you called."

"Celeste?" West asked.

"She was with us. I left her at my parents' house. I didn't think she needed to see any of this."

"Wise. Come in, but please keep your hands to yourself and watch your step."

We followed West into the house. It was as I remembered it. Clean in a way that only a compulsive organizer could keep it. Lizzy fit that bill. Smart, witty, and aggressive, she was the consummate real estate broker. After learning that a degree in art history was hard to convert into a livable wage, she studied and took the real estate exam, passing it the first time, unlike the bulk of other aspirants. Within five years she had earned her brokers license and opened up shop for herself. She had a knack for placing people in houses and browbeating lending institutions into loaning money to anything that breathed.

Over the years, she and her husband, a civil engineer for the county, had earned enough money to be comfortable. Her only vice was a love for new artists, and her house proves it. Paintings hang from every wall and sculptures rest in nearly every nook.

The foyer is small but opens onto a large living area with a cathedral ceiling. Leather furniture fills the space, which is accented with mahogany end and coffee tables. On the sofa was a man, hunched over, his head buried in his hands. He rocked back and forth like a metronome.

"Leo?" The man didn't look up. I glanced at West.

The detective nodded. "He's taking it hard."

"How else could he take it?" I scurried to Leo's side, sat down on the sofa, and put my arm over his shoulders. He seemed to melt under my touch. I wanted to say something but nothing came to mind, so I just sat there with him for a moment. He never lifted his head.

"Mayor, if you have a moment, please," West whispered.

I rose and Jerry and I followed him to the kitchen. Like the living room, the kitchen was spotless. The tile glowed, it was so clean.

"Here's what we know so far," West said. "Mrs. Stout was alone in her home this afternoon. Sometime after three and before five-thirty, one or more people entered the house, struggled briefly with her, and then removed her from the premises."

"How do you know the time?" Jerry asked.

"Mr. Stout spoke to her on the phone at three. They planned a dinner engagement. He arrived home at five-thirty. He found her missing and he found this." He pointed to a photograph sitting on the counter, just in front of a drip coffeemaker. "Do you recognize the picture?"

I was standing ten or twelve feet from the photo but I could see it clearly enough. It showed Lizzy with her short styled hair framing her round face. We were standing shoulder-to-shoulder next to a wood podium. There was something odd about the picture. "Yes.

Lizzy was president of the Santa Rita Chamber of Commerce last year. I spoke at one of their luncheons. That picture was taken then."

I took two steps closer. An empty wood frame sat to the side. At first I thought something had been spilled on the picture, but then I realized how wrong I was. Mustering courage I didn't feel, I stepped closer. Drops. Rust red drops. Tiny little mounds of viscous fluid had been carefully and strategically placed on the image of Lizzy's face: one drop on each eye and one on her mouth. Three drops. Three tiny drops that hit me like atomic bombs.

I felt sick. Clutching my stomach, I turned away.

Jerry said, "What kind of sick person does this?"

"Good question," West asked. "If we knew that, we could put an end to it all."

My stomach cramped and a burning filled my gut. For a moment I felt as if my knees would buckle. I sucked air, hoping to quell the volcano in my belly.

"You all right, Mayor?" West asked.

"Uh, yeah. Give me a minute."

"Perhaps we should go outside," he suggested, taking my arm. "I can't have you tossing your dinner in here. No offense meant."

"None taken," I squeaked and allowed him to lead me out of the house. I felt like an old lady.

The cool air washed over me in sweet relief. I was angry for being weak, but the picture was the last straw on my camel's aching back.

"Take a few deep breaths," Jerry said. I could feel his hand on my shoulder. "In fact, you better sit down." He guided West and me to his SUV and opened the passenger door. I sat. I breathed. I tried to regain my pride.

"I'm sorry. I don't normally respond this way."

"How often have you faced a situation like this?" West asked. "There's no need to apologize." He and Jerry were standing next to me on the curb.

"I'll take you home," Jerry said.

"Hang on a sec," West countered. "I need to ask a few questions."

"Can't you see she's not up to it?"

West paused before replying. He eyed Jerry hard, then said in a calm but cold voice, "There are two women missing, Doctor. While it may be an uncomfortable inconvenience for the mayor, it is a necessary one. Or would you like to go tell Mr. Stout that we need to hold up the investigation?"

"Of course not," Jerry shot back. "I just think you should show more compassion."

I had to put an end to this. "I'm fine, Jerry. Thanks. Detective West is right. Ask your questions, Detective."

"How do you know Mrs. Stout?"

I explained about being school chums and maintaining a friendship over the years.

"Do you know if she has any enemies?"

"Not Lizzy. She can charm a bear out of its honey. Everyone likes her."

"Has she spoken to you recently about any problems in her life?"

"Problems?"

"Family, business, that sort of thing."

"No. As far as I know, she and Leo have a perfect marriage . . . as perfect as marriage can be, anyway."

"When was the last time you spoke to her?"

I had to think about that. "About two weeks ago, give or take." My stomach settled and I could feel the blood circulating in my head again. I was beginning to feel like I might survive.

"When you spoke to her, did she seem abnormal . . . by that I mean, did she seem stressed, fearful, irritated, or depressed?"

"No." I thought it was time to cut to the chase. "Detective, I know you're trying to cover all the bases, and maybe you're trying to spare me any more shock, but I think I know the real questions you want to ask. Perhaps we should get right to it."

"Okay," he said. "Did Mrs. Stout have any connection to your office or campaigns?"

"Yes. Like Lisa, she worked in my campaigns."

"In what capacity?"

"Lizzy is well connected in the business community and active in the Chamber. As I said earlier, she was president last year. With her connections, we thought it best that she serve as fund-raising chairwoman."

"And that's what she did?"

"Yes, excelled at it. Her people skills are beyond match. She jump-started the campaign with several key fund-raising events."

"So she worked with the money."

"Not like Lisa. Lizzy couldn't write checks and didn't have access to bank records. It wasn't that I didn't trust her; she just had no need to work in those areas."

"Still, it is an interesting tie-in."

"What's it mean?" Jerry asked.

"I have no idea," West replied. "It's a flimsy connection, but it is a connection nonetheless." He paused. "I need to ask another question."

I had anticipated this. "I was at my office until a few minutes before five, which you know, since we spoke on the phone. From there I drove home. Celeste can tell you I arrived at about five-ten or five-fifteen. A little while later we left to drop off Michele and then go to my parents' house for dinner. I arrived there around twenty after six."

"Michele?"

"That's Celeste's friend. They go to college together. She spent the day with Celeste while I was at work."

In the dim moonlight I could see West's eyes narrow. "You arrived home sometime after five but didn't reach your parents' house until nearly six-thirty. What did you do in the meantime?"

"I talked with Celeste and Michele, waited for them to change clothes, drove Michele home, and then drove to my parents'."

"This is insulting," Jerry said. "Maddy is the mayor. That makes her your boss. How can you even think that she might be a party to all this?"

"It's fine, Jerry," I said, cutting West off. "He wouldn't be much of a detective if he didn't ask these questions."

"It's just that—"

"I know, I know. I appreciate it, but I'm not offended."

West showed no sign that Jerry's objections irritated him. I imagined West had seen and heard it all.

"I'm concerned about you," West said to me.

"Why?" Jerry asked. Good ol' Jerry, always eager to help. There was no reining him in.

West said what had already crossed my mind. "Two people closely associated with Mayor Glenn have disappeared. We discovered blood at both sites. Small amount that it is, it is still blood. In each case, at the scene we found something associated with Mayor Glenn. In Lisa Truccoli's case, it was the mayor's business card; here it's a picture of her. This isn't a simple string of break-ins; someone is delivering a message and they don't want it overlooked."

"What message?" Jerry asked.

"That's what we need to find out—and soon." West turned to me. "Do you use an alarm service for your home?" I said I did. "Be sure and turn it on. I'm going to talk to the watch commanders and request that officers patrol your street more often. It's important that you be as careful as possible."

"I will."

"I'm serious. As I said before, you need to develop a healthy paranoia for a while."

A motion behind West caught my eye. I looked over his shoulder and noticed someone walking from the house. It took a moment in the dim light to see that it was Leo. He had something in his hand. He walked stiffly, in a way that made me think of old zombie movies. I motioned toward him and West turned around.

"Mr. Stout," West said. "That's evidence; you can't be carrying it around."

Leo ignored him and held up the picture from the kitchen. Streetlights helped me see the three drops of blood smeared across the photo. Leo must have been rubbing the image of his wife's face. Tears ran down his cheeks.

"Are you responsible for this?" Leo shouted. He shook the picture at me. "Are you, Maddy? Are you responsible for my wife being taken from our home?" His voice was loud and his words hot.

"No, Leo. Of course not. I'm as concerned as you—"

"Why Lizzy?" His voice was breaking. "Why my Lizzy?"

"Let me have the picture, Mr. Stout," West said. He stepped between me and Leo, blocking the grieving husband's advance. "Give it to me." The words were soft but firm.

"I want my wife back. I want her back, do you hear?"

I heard. My heart ached and my eyes were awash in tears. "Leo . . ." It was a sentence with no destination. I didn't know what to say. He was a frightened, sorrowful man, helpless in the face of the horrible facts. I felt sick again.

"Come with me, sir." West took him by the elbow and turned him around. "Let's you and me talk." He walked Leo away from us, and then a few steps later turned. "Take her home, Doc."

Jerry did, but a big part of me stayed behind.

chapter

He didn't mean it, you know." Jerry's words found me gazing out the side window of the Excursion, not seeing anything, wishing I didn't feel anything.

"What?" I asked, reeling in my attention from the dark distance.

"Your friend, Mr. Stint. He didn't mean what he said." We were back on the 101, headed south.

"Stout," I corrected. "Leo Stout. And I know he didn't mean it."

"He's hurt and scared. A man is likely to say anything in that state of mind. I see it all the time."

Jerry was trying to take the sting out of the confrontation, short as it was. I looked at him, his face lit by the dashboard lights. "Pediatrics is a rewarding profession but it isn't all colds and flu. Occasionally, too often for my liking, I have to deliver bad news. Last week I told the parents of a six-year-old boy that he has leukemia. In med school they teach us not to get emotionally involved. Death is the irreducible part of life. It comes to everyone sometime; to some it comes early, and some live a century."

"Leukemia? That's horrible."

"There are treatments that will probably help, but that's not my point. When I sat the parents down in my office and gave them the news, they got mad at me, as if I had given the child the disease. It's called transference and it's common; kill the messenger and all that. The father ripped me up one side and down the other."

"What did you do?"

"I let him vent." He was driving slower than the rest of traffic, something I appreciated. I was in no hurry to get anywhere. "He uttered a lot of nonsense, then broke down. I let him cry for a few moments, and then I discussed the referrals I would need to make and what they needed to do next. Your friend was doing the same thing as that father. He doesn't really blame you, but you're the closest one at hand."

"I know. Still, it was hard to hear."

"How are you feeling?"

"Run over—run over by something big."

"That's how I usually feel when I get chewed out like that." He glanced at me. "You look pale."

That didn't surprise me. I struggled with my next step. I didn't want to go back to my folks' home. Mom was already worried. She would have lots of questions and then would begin to worry more. She was an Olympic-class worrier. If they gave gold medals for anxiety, she would have a drawer full. But there was Celeste to think about. I had promised to pick her up.

"I'm going to make a call." I pulled my cell phone from my purse and punched "memory dial," selected my parents' number, and pushed "send." Two rings later Mom answered. I asked about Celeste.

"She's sleeping on the couch. We turned the television on for her. I did the dishes and came out to find her fast asleep. Poor thing is exhausted. Worry is hard work."

I agreed with her, then asked, "Since she's already asleep, can she spend the night there?"

"Of course. Are you all right?"

"I'm feeling a little worn out myself. Maybe you should put a note on the coffee table for Celeste. That way if she wakes up in the middle of the night, she'll know what happened." Then I switched gears. "Can I talk to Dad?" I had a few things to explain and I wanted to say them to him. He would worry but not to the degree Mom would. A moment later Dad was on the phone. I told him about Lizzy and then said I had decided to go home for the evening. "I'll arrange to pick up my car tomorrow."

"Do you want to stay here? The guest room is available." The guest room was my old bedroom.

"Thanks, but no. I need to sleep in my own bed tonight. I'll be all right." I hesitated, then added, "Be sure to lock things up tight and be careful answering the door. If you have the slimmest doubts about anyone, call the police." I had new fears that my parents might be on the short list for abduction. I couldn't live with the knowledge that something had happened to them because of me.

"I don't think you should stay alone," Dad whispered. I assumed Mom was in earshot.

"I'll be fine, Dad. I don't mind being alone."

"Let me have the phone," Jerry said and held out his hand.

"What?"

He wiggled his finger in a hand-it-over motion. I complied. "Greg, this is Jerry. I'll stay with her tonight."

"You don't have to do that," I said quickly. He ignored me.

"No, it's no trouble. It's my honor. I'll bring her by bright and early in the morning." He listened for a moment. "Don't worry about anything; I'll make sure she's okay."

I smiled, trying to picture gentle Dr. Jerry Thomas fighting off attackers with his rectal thermometers of death. He handed the phone back. "Here, tell your father good night."

I did and then returned the phone to my purse. "You didn't ask to stay at my house."

"What would you have said if I'd asked?"

"I probably would have said no."

"That's why I didn't ask."

"It's unnecessary, you know."

"Is it? If I dropped you off on your doorstep and drove off into the dark, I would spend the rest of the night worrying about you. It's okay, you can trust me. I am a man of old-world gentility."

"You get the couch."

"That's fine with me."

Truth was, I'd put him in the room where Celeste had slept the previous night, but for the moment the threat was all I had. "And you have to make your own coffee in the morning."

"I am man of exquisite education. I can handle coffee making. Just point me at the percolator."

"Percolator? When was the last time you saw a percolator?"

"Okay then, show me the drippy coffeemaker thing."

"I'll make the coffee; you'll break something." I was grateful for the humorous give-and-take. It gave my mind a breather from the darkness that swirled in it. I let a few moments pass before saying, "Thanks for going with me, Jerry. I'm glad you were there."

"I'm afraid I got a little testy with the detective. I tend to be overprotective."

"You were just being gallant."

Jerry laughed loudly, then snorted. "Sir Jerry the Gallant!"

It was good to have company.

Although the clock on the desk in my home office read twenty past midnight, I was wide awake. I had fixed the bed in the guest room, shown Jerry where the bathroom was, laid out some clean towels, and left him to his own purposes. He chose to forego the guest room. "I'll just snooze on the sofa. I don't think anything is going to happen, but I'll be in a better position to hear it down here than I would in the guest room."

It made no difference to me. I had changed into silk pajamas and donned my robe. Despite following my usual evening ritual, I was too keyed up to sleep, so I went into my office. I tried to avoid any thoughts of Lizzy and Lisa. Instead I threw myself into the "Glenn for Congress" file. I read the material again, this time allowing myself to pause and make notes, something I didn't have time to do earlier.

Randi had pulled together a variety of information. The packet contained demographics, district breakdowns, and Republican versus Democratic versus third-party also-rans. Paperclipped together were "Key Issue Concerns," a summary of issues likely to come up in a campaign. There were also financial reports of previous contestants, revealing how much money they spent seeking the congressional seat. It didn't take long for me to realize that I would need to spend three times what I had to win the office of mayor—maybe four times as much. And if there was a strong contender to challenge my run, I could spend far more than that. It would take a lot of fund-raising.

The thought of fund-raising made me think of Lizzy again, and guilt swarmed over me like locusts. Here I was, thinking of my future, when Lizzy and Lisa were ... who knows where? The guilt was misplaced, I knew, but that made no difference. Emotion, especially negative emotion, is immune to logic.

I placed the file aside and turned the page of a yellow legal pad I was using to jot down notes. My mind was spinning like cogs in a sewing machine. A compulsive doodler, I began drawing little meaningless images: swirls, stars, and arrows. That gave way to words. I tore off the doodle-tattooed page and stared at a fresh, blank page.

At the top I wrote, "Lisa and Lizzy." Underneath that I penned, "Similarities." I paused and waited for an epiphany, an inspiration that would give form to the mess of thoughts heaped up in my mind. None came. "Start with the obvious," I told myself. "What do they have in common?"

The only light in the room was the soft glow that poured from the green-shaded banker's light on my desk. The rest of the room was as dark as a sepulcher. The blue ink seemed pale in the light as I wrote the first and most obvious connection: "Me." Under that I wrote, "Campaign." Other ideas came easier: "Professional Women," "Married," "Santa Rita." I even wrote, "Initials." Both had first names that began with the letter *L*. It was a stupid connection, but it was a connection nonetheless. I immediately thought of Superman comics. When I was eight, I developed a short-lived interest in the comic book hero. Truth was, I thought he was dreamy. My father, who as a child had read uncountable issues of comics, told me that the initials L. L. played an important role in the superhero's life. Even his girlfriends had names like Lana Lang and Lois Lane. One of his arch enemies was Lex Luthor, and so on. I asked Dad why that was and he said, "One does not question the wisdom of the comic gods." Then he winked. He didn't know and neither did my husband, who confessed to a love for the adventures of the Man of Steel.

I stopped, then drew a horizontal line across the middle of the page, scribbling, "Differences" just below it. Maybe there was some revelation in what they didn't have in common. The list was small: "Children," "Age," "Neighborhood." I ended up with an orderly but anemic list. The only meaningful connections I could make were the most obvious: both were women, both were married (although Lisa was divorced), and both were connected to me through my campaigns, specifically the money side of them. The differences were no more revealing.

I fell back to doodling—circles, stars, spirals, boxes. Lost in thought, I let my mind percolate on its own. After a few moments I set the pen down, frustrated that I had made no progress. I looked at the pad of paper and saw that my doodles had new neighbors: a box defined by four dots and a triangle formed by three. The picture of Lizzy with the spots of blood over her eyes and mouth flashed like sheet lighting in my mind. Ice water flowed down my spine. Why geometric shapes? Why make them with blood? What would the next one be?

The last thought made my brain seize. The next one? The *next* one! Would there be another abduction? I looked at the dots again. A square and a triangle. Was the answer in their shape or in the number of dots?

I rubbed my eyes. I felt as if I were looking at a handful of jigsaw pieces. How could I put together the puzzle if I didn't have all the pieces? But so far, the pieces came with an abduction. That was a lousy way to get information.

Something else rose to the top of my attention. Aside from the presence of blood, and that amounted to only seven tiny drops, the crime scenes gave no indication of violence or great struggle. West told me about Lisa's house: there was a tiny mess of cards on the table, and one vase was on its side. Not broken, just lying on its side as if it were set that way. Lizzy's was no different. How does an abduction take place and leave so few signs?

It was as if both women had invited their kidnapper into the house. That would mean that Lisa and Lizzy knew their attacker. But who?

My neck ached. The stress was catching up. Weariness finally settled over me and I went to bed, but I didn't go alone. The question, "Why?" followed me into slumber and haunted my dreams.

I don't believe in ghosts. Not in the usual sense. I've never seen gossamer shapes floating through my house, leaving ectoplasm footprints on my carpet. I've never heard the bumps in the night or seen books float across the room. I'm just not a believer. Too pragmatic. Too skeptical. The only immaterial thing I ever believed in is love: the love of my parents and the love Peter showed me every day of our married lives.

In that sense I am haunted. My husband is dead. I know that. I wake up to that ugly truth and it follows me into an empty bed every night. I consider myself fortunate that alcohol has never agreed with me. The few times I tried it in college, I became sick enough to cure my curiosity. Maybe it's genetic. Neither of my parents drink. If I had been prone to the juice, I would have slid down the slimy slope of addiction. The pain was that great.

Still, I tell no one of the dreams that occasionally rise in my sleep-shrouded mind. In the years since Peter's murder, he has come to me once or twice a month. When the sun is long set, when the stars cling to an obsidian sky, when sleep has filled the inside of my skull, he comes. I tell myself it is an illusion; still, he is there.

I've entertained the idea of seeking professional help, of spending time on the couch with some bearded man with a notepad sitting in a chair just out of sight and asking, "And how does that make you feel, Mrs. Glenn?" If that ever got out, my political career would implode. Perhaps that shouldn't matter, but it does.

The dreams should bother me, but they don't. In truth, I've come to enjoy them. A few moments with Peter in a dream are better than no moments at all. It may mean psychological instability but it is my instability and I have grown comfortable with it.

Some of the dreams are cathartic; others pierce the soul. The best illusions are those in which I hold him and he wraps his thick arms around me. If I'm lucky, I wake up still smelling his cologne; if not, he drips through my arms, becoming the nothing I now have, and I awaken to a wet pillow.

This night, I dreamt of him standing in my home office with a plain cardboard box in his hands. I recognized the box. It was the one on the floor of my office closet. It was brown and dusty. It was a box I had avoided over the years. A box I had left untouched since the police gave it to me. I knew what was inside. They told me. Not in detail but in general. At least I think they did. I was not at my best.

"These are his personal effects," the detective had said. I can't remember his name but I can see him standing in the LAPD substation not far from where my husband died. He was a stocky man with a thick face and kind eyes. I can't remember the date. It was two weeks after the murder and one week after the funeral. "We can't release the car yet, since it's evidence in an ongoing trial, but both prosecution and defense have released these to you."

I had taken the box in trembling hands and tried to whip my emotions back into the basement of my mind. I thanked him, went home, walked upstairs, put the box in the closet, and never looked at it again.

Now dream-Peter held it in his dream-hands. He didn't speak. He never speaks in these dreams. He is just there until daylight melts him away. No words are needed. Communication happens through our eyes, through our expressions. He looked sad to me. His eyes met mine; then he looked down at the box.

I hated that box. Everything in it had belonged to him, and they were there when the bullet ripped his life away, killing his body and wounding my soul forever. The lid of the box was where I had left it when it first came to me—pressed down on its cardboard sides. Two things were impossible: throwing away the box and opening it.

Slowly, like the second hand of a clock, he raised the box, offering it to me.

I stood motionless as a marble statue. Didn't he understand? Couldn't he comprehend? Sadness was in that box—ugly, mournful, searing sadness. To open it was to face the murder all over again. To open it was to be reminded that evil wins and goodness dies. To open it would be to face the very thing I had worked so hard to keep out of my mind. Those weren't just his personal effects; they were witnesses to the cruelty. They would not remind me of him as my house did, as photos did; they would remind me of the small bullet hole in the side of his head and the gaping crater it left on the other side. They would conjure up the evil spirit of the men who held life as no more important than a hamburger wrapper, something to be wadded up and thrown away.

Why couldn't dream-Peter understand that?

I looked up from the box and into my husband's eyes. There was silent pleading there, coaxing, encouraging, compelling me to take the box and to open it.

I shook my head.

Peter dissolved.

The box lay where he had stood.

I cursed my cowardice and prayed for sunrise.

chapter 8

The radio alarm came to life at 5:30. The sonorous voice of the announcer slapped me awake. More startling were his words. I have the radio set to a local station that plays adult contemporary music, broken only by commercial spots and twice-hourly news. This was the bottom-of-the-hour presentation. "Another abduction took place late yesterday afternoon when Elizabeth Stout disappeared from her home in Santa Rita—"

I slapped the off button. I had gone to bed with the kidnapping on my mind and now I awoke to it. I swung my feet over the edge of the bed and sat for a moment. My stomach was sour and I was depressed. Not the way I like to wake up. The dream hung in my mind like a foul English fog.

Rising, I wobbled into the bathroom and did what I do every morning. After splashing water on my face, I changed into a pair of shorts and a cotton T-shirt. I then donned a pair of gray and orange Skechers sneakers. I spent the next forty-five minutes on the treadmill. It was normally an invigorating experience, but this morning I struggled with the task. My heart just wasn't in it. Still, I put one foot after another until I had cranked out a quick two miles. I know women who jog every day. Up at dawn and onto the streets, and they do so eagerly. For me exercise is a discipline, one to which I am committed but seldom enjoy. By the end of the walk I was fully awake, and my coursing blood and heavy breathing made me feel more alive.

A shower followed. I love showers as much as I hate exercising. There is something meditative and therapeutic about standing under a stream of warm water. It seems a good place to spend a few hours, something I would have done this morning had I not been afflicted with an incurable case of responsibility and duty, something for which I blame my parents. Reluctantly I got out, toweled off, and used the blow dryer to clear the condensation off my mirror.

The mirror is a prize Peter found at some garage sale. It is oval with gold antiquing around the frame. He loved it and I have grown attached to it over the years. However, the image it reflected this day was that of a different person. The dark hair was there, but it hung down over my shoulders, sodden and heavy. The face that gazed back had dark circles under moist eyes.

"Great. I'm going to have to put my makeup on with a trowel." A bag over my head would have been easier and perhaps more attractive. I began the ritual and when done, felt a little better about myself.

At seven o'clock I emerged from my lair and walked down the stairs into a thick, enticing aroma. I found Jerry sitting at the table in the dining area, a newspaper in his hands. In front of him was a large mug of black coffee.

I made a face. "How can you drink coffee black?"

"It's a guy thing. I prefer a large latte with a double shot of vanilla, but I was afraid you'd think I was a wimp."

"No need to put on airs with me. I wouldn't consider you a wimp, just prudent." I poured myself a cup, dumped in a packet of Equal, and added a splash of evaporated milk.

"How did you sleep?" He carefully folded the section he had been reading and reinserted it into the newspaper. For a moment I expected him to roll up the paper and replace the rubber band.

"Okay, I guess." I took a seat at the table. "Not my best night."

"Restless? I can imagine."

"How about you?"

"Like a log."

"No bad guys coming through the window?"

"If they did, they were quiet. What say we go out for breakfast? We could go over to Hennison's for some eggs Benedict."

"I don't normally eat breakfast, at least not a big breakfast."

"You should make an exception. You're under a great deal of strain. Stress is hard labor. It taxes the body. You need a consistent supply of food to keep going."

"Is that your considered medical opinion?"

"It is. And a little change of scenery will help you cheer up."

"What makes you think I need cheering?"

Jerry leaned over the table and his tone turned serious. "Even I can see that this is starting to wear on you, and it's only been, what, a couple of days? Go to breakfast with me."

"I was planning to go into the office early—"

"Go to breakfast with me."

"Okay, okay. You win. You should have been a salesman."

"I would have made better money."

"Oh, come on, all doctors are rich," I teased.

He shook his head. "I'm in peds." He pronounced it *peeds*. "You're thinking cardiologists and surgeons. A man doesn't go into pediatrics to get rich."

"You're rich in other ways, Jerry. Anything in the paper about Lizzy?"

"A short article. Not much in it. They probably had to squeeze it in at the last moment."

I nodded. "I wish I could do more."

"Like what? There's nothing more you can do." He paused. "I'm still worried about this whole thing . . . about you. I don't like it that you're living alone. I gave it a lot of thought last night. I think you should stay someplace safer."

"Safer than my home?"

"Yes. Lisa and Lizzy were snatched from their homes. Who's to say the same can't happen to you?"

"No, Jerry, I won't go there. I'm not going to let myself be intimidated or to live in fear."

"Fear can be a good thing."

"No, it can't," I snapped. "When Peter was killed, I lived in fear for months. I lay awake at night jumping at every sound. I was sure his killers were going to come after me. It made no sense. He was killed in a carjacking. He was not the target, the car was, but I still felt someone—that elusive, ill-defined someone—would come after me. That was a bad time, Jerry, very bad. I won't go to that dark land again. If someone wants me, then let them come get me."

Jerry stared at me. My tone had been more harsh than I intended, and certainly sharper than anything he had ever heard from me. I felt no pride.

"You need a friend, Maddy. I want to be that friend. You know how I feel about you."

I did know. In high school Jerry had an on-again-off-again crush on me. The passing years and the fact that we both had been married had never changed that. The truth was, his affection had grown. I looked at the man across the table, the man who had insisted on spending the night so he could defend me from anyone wishing me harm, and saw what I had always seen: a sweet, dedicated man of great intelligence and wit. He was handsome, with eyes that glittered when he laughed. His chin was strong and his mouth comfortable with a smile. He had always been supportive, and a single word of encouragement from me would free him to fall headlong into love. I wasn't ready for that.

"Jerry, I'm not ready for any more relationships, especially romantic ones. Maybe I shouldn't be avoiding them but I am. It's me."

"You're not avoiding romantic relationships, Maddy. You're shielding yourself from possible pain. You're acting, or maybe I should say being inactive, because of fear. You're afraid you'll lose another person you love. You know what, Maddy? You're going to. That's the course of life. I will, too. It can't be helped. You need to open yourself to the possibility that another man can love you and that you can love him."

An odd image popped into my mind. It was the image of Detective West. I drove it away. I barely knew the man. It was ridiculous. "I appreciate your concern, Jerry. I appreciate your friendship, but I think it would be best if you left my romantic life to me. After all, it's my life."

There was sadness in his eyes, and the corners of his mouth dropped. "I'm trying to be a part of that life."

I knew that. That truth was in my head and had been there a long time, but hearing it was painful. I felt awash in conflicting emotions, as if I were in a boat being battered by rogue waves. Any woman would be blessed to have a man like Jerry in her life. Why was it so hard for me to see that? I tried to imagine us dating, courting, marrying, but it all seemed wrong, like a pretty shoe that fit badly.

"I know, Jerry. I know." I rose from the table and put my coffee cup in the sink. There were words that should be spoken here, I told myself, but they remained out of reach. "We have to pick up my car at my parents'. I want to check on Celeste, too. Then we can go to Hennison's."

"Okay," he said. His previous enthusiasm had waned. I had just crushed a rose under my feet.

The office was a welcome sight. I arrived later than planned but I was at last there. For me the office is more than a place of work; it's a haven. I have no hobbies and very few outside interests. Politics and family are all that occupy my mind. When I cross the threshold into my inner sanctum, things take on a new meaning. I feel alive with purpose. There are things to do, decisions to make, people to meet. And I love almost every minute of it. Almost. There are days when I would sell the whole thing for a buck and be willing to give change, but those days are few.

Jerry had driven me to my parents' home, where I spent a few minutes with Celeste. She looked frailer than she had the night before. I told her to call at any time and if I wasn't in the office, to call my cell phone. I gave her the number. "What about your dad? Still prefer to avoid him?"

The answer was immediate and definitive: "Yes."

I invited her to join us for breakfast but she had already eaten. Mom had seen to that. I also suggested that she stay with my parents during the day. I didn't tell her I thought it would be safer. She reluctantly agreed. Celeste was a balloon in a hurricane. Things were happening around her, things she could not control.

Breakfast with Jerry had gone well. He didn't push his concerns and I made sure he knew I wasn't upset with him. The eggs Benedict were good and, as Jerry had predicted, I felt revived. I had to admit, breakfast had been a good idea.

After breakfast I drove myself to work.

Randi arrived at her desk just two or three minutes after I plunked down in my leather chair. She was her usual cheerful self. "Did you get much sleep last night?" I assured her that I got enough.

"I have that closed-door, right?" I asked. These council sessions were not public meetings. No official notes were taken and no records kept. It was a time to make plans, assign duties, and air differences. The last item was becoming more common. I had no doubts that I would hear from Adler again. He was never happy unless he was miserable.

"Yes, at ten. I assume you want me there?" Randi took notes for me at such meetings.

"Of course. I need someone to throw her body in front of mine when the knives and guns come out."

"It's nice to be needed."

I snickered. "I want to review the list of our campaign workers again."

"Hearing the call of Washington?"

"No . . . I mean, I don't know. Your report is intriguing. I studied it some last night. I want the list for a different reason. And could you check with the bank again? I want to know about any activity."

"Okay. Anything else?"

I started to answer when Randi's phone buzzed. She excused herself and answered it. From my chair I could see Randi's work area. With the door open I could hear her conversations. After listening for a few moments, she said, "Hang on a sec." She turned and looked at me. "It's Fritzy. There's a reporter out front who wants to talk to you about . . . the incidents."

I'm not fond of reporters. They have a purpose and for the most part do a good work, but they pop up at the worst times, often get facts wrong, and feel their mere presence requires everyone to stop what they're doing and give them their full attention. Still, dealing with them is part of my job, and I didn't want the city thinking I was avoiding the press.

"Which reporter?"

"Turner."

That didn't make me feel any better. But I had some time before the closed-door session. There was no avoiding it. "Okay. Show him in."

Doug Turner was less than fastidious. Every time I saw him, he was dressed nicely, but his clothing never seemed to hang right. Either his shirt was tucked in too tightly, or it bulged around the middle as if the wrinkled cloth were trying to engineer an escape from his pants. This morning he wore black dress pants, a striped, button-down shirt, and an angry-looking red tie. Maybe the tie was angry because it was forced to hang straight while the stripes on the shirt all angled slightly to the man's right. His belt buckle was a good inch and a half off center. I fought the urge to tilt my head to one side to try to even everything up.

Randi had shown the reporter in, and he plunged through the door as if he had been in my office a thousand times before. I rose to greet him, extending a courteous hand. He took it and gave it a shake, holding my hand a few seconds longer than I thought necessary. Once released, I took my seat again and caught myself wiping my palm on my pant leg.

"It's good to see you, Mayor." Turner sat down in one of the two guest chairs in front of my desk.

I smiled and stared at his tanned face, thick eyebrows, and square head. His hair was brown and showed no gray. He was a good ways past his forty-fifth birthday, and I was sure gray hair was someplace on his head, probably camouflaged by some color from a box with the phrase "for men" on the label.

"Sorry to be a little standoffish lately," I said. "Some weeks are a little more constraining than others."

"I imagine." There was a slight smile. He reached into his coat pocket and began to remove something but struggled. The mouth of the pocket choked on Turner's hand and whatever he held. He yanked several times before he freed the reluctant object. A second later he set it on my desk. It was black audiotape recorder.

My stomach tightened. "Is that necessary?"

"You don't want me to make a mistake and misquote you, do you? The days of taking notes by hand are long gone, Mayor. You know that."

I knew that very well. I also knew that a tape recorder was no guarantee that what I said would be rendered faithfully in the next day's newspaper. I reached down and opened the lower of two file drawers on the right of my desk. The wood drawer slid open noiselessly and I quickly found what I was looking for. I retrieved it with much greater ease than had Turner. Holding it in my right hand, I closed the drawer. Like Turner, I set it on the desktop.

"What's that?"

"It's a cassette recorder."

"*You're* going to record this interview?" He seemed wounded. "Don't you trust me?"

"It's not a matter of trust, Mr. Turner. I've been interviewed more times than I can count and I've been misquoted a good third of those times."

"So that's your protection?"

"Oh, I don't think of it as protection. It's just a way to jog my memory should I ever be asked to explain something I've said. Surely you understand."

Turner understood, all right. He frowned, caught himself, then smiled. "I don't recall you using a tape recorder the other times I've interviewed you."

"Let's cut to the chase, Mr. Turner. You're here to ask me questions about the disappearance of two people who have some connection to me, not to quiz me about city ordinances. There is a criminal investigation underway. If you report me as saying something I didn't say, or put what I say in a context that could raise eyebrows, then my life gets much more difficult. If asked what I actually said, I can just play the tape. Think of it as a means of protection for both of us."

He nodded, then let his smile evolve into a grin. "I've always liked you, Mayor. Local politics hasn't always attracted the sharpest knives in the drawer, but you're an exception."

"Thank you ... I think."

"It was a compliment."

The ground rules were set, and I felt a smidge more comfortable, but just a smidge. All I had done with the tape recorder was to maintain dominance during the interview. Reporters, especially Turner, like to put people back on their heels. Once their targets are off balance, they probe with daggerlike questions. I'd learned that early on. I had no intention of tottering on my own heels in my own office.

Turner pressed the record button on his battered device. He then looked at me and raised an eyebrow. I followed suit. With both recorders doing their job, Turner leaned back in the chair, removed a small notepad from the inside pocket of his suit coat, and noisily flipped through a few pages, pausing over each one as if reading it for the first time. Then it began.

"I did some checking. First, I couldn't help but notice that Lisa Truccoli was your treasurer. The second abduction was similar to the first, so I had to ask myself if a connection existed between you and Mrs. Stout. Since you didn't meet with me yesterday, I had a little time to look back at some articles on your campaign and found her name, several times."

I chose to ignore the dig, although several blunt comments flooded my brain. There was no sense in letting him choose the battles. "A great many people voted for me. If you take any five crimes in our city, there's a good chance two of the victims were supporters of my campaign in some way or another. That would be nothing more than simple coincidence."

"We're not talking voters, Mayor. Ms. Truccoli was your treasurer and Mrs. Stout did fund-raising. Isn't that right?"

"It is."

"So then it's safe to assume that these murders—"

"Abductions."

"Yes, of course. So it's safe to assume that these abductions are related to your campaign and therefore to you."

"I would be cautious about assuming anything. The police are looking into that angle, among others."

"Have the police interrogated you?"

"We've spoken but it wasn't an interrogation; it was an interview."

"What did they want to know?"

"You would have to ask them that. I can tell you that the questions were general in nature and that I'm happy to help in any way I can."

"Are you a suspect?"

"In the abductions? No, Mr. Turner, I am not. At least not to my knowledge. The police have been very supportive and open. I have been the same with them."

"What can you tell me about Ms. Truccoli?"

"Not much more than you already know." I briefed him on her relationship to the campaign and on the work she did between election seasons.

"Were you close friends?"

"I knew ... know her fairly well and trust her without reservation."

"What about her family?"

"What about her family?"

"Could you tell me about them?"

I had been afraid he would go there. "I can't add a great deal. My relationship was with Ms. Truccoli, not her family."

"Is she married?"

"I believe she's divorced." In fact, I knew she was divorced, but I didn't want to give Turner more than I had to.

"Children?"

"I know she has a daughter."

"Where's the daughter now?" Turner pushed.

"I understand she's someplace safe."

"Where would that be?"

"You know better than that." I kept the fire out of the words, trying to remain detached.

"Better than what? I'm just asking where the daughter is. You do know where she is, don't you?"

I struggled for a way out of the question. I didn't want to reveal that I knew where Celeste was, let alone that she had been with me. I could think of no slick way to avoid answering, so I took the direct approach. "Do you have another question for me?"

"You didn't answer the last one."

"Well," I said, standing, "if there are no other questions, I'll have Randi—"

"Okay, okay." Turned motioned for me to sit down. "I get the picture."

I lowered myself into the seat.

"How about Mrs. Stout? What can you tell me about her?"

I recounted the basics but offered nothing personal about Lizzy or her family. Turner listened, nodded, grunted, and fiddled with his little notepad.

"Are you connected to the disappearances?" He was blunt. His face remained a passive mask of indifference.

"What do you mean, connected?"

"Do you know more than you're telling?"

"No. Do you?"

He sighed. "Are you frightened?"

"Why would I be frightened?" Was he threatening a harsh, accusative article?

"You're a very smart woman, Madam Mayor. I think you know what I mean."

I said nothing.

He closed the notepad and returned it to his pocket. "Two people close to you have been taken against their will. For all we know, they may be dead—"

"Or alive."

He nodded. "Certainly. Do you think you're in danger?"

Ice water began to run through me. Once again I was forced to face something I didn't want to see. "I have every confidence in the Santa Rita police. While I choose to be very cautious, I am not living in fear."

He pursed his lips, reached forward, and turned off his recorder. I was amazed at my paranoia. Although I had watched him stop the recording, I still studied the device, making sure the record button was no longer depressed and that the spindle inside had stopped moving. Turner looked at me for a moment and again raised an eyebrow, then turned his eyes to my recorder. I turned it off.

"We're off the record now, Mayor. Just so we're clear: I know that Ms. Truccoli's daughter is with you."

The revelation pulled the rug out from beneath me. I answered with a tilt of the head.

"I have no intention of putting that in the article. I'm after the story and I want as much information as I can get, but I will not risk a young girl's life for a few hundred words above the fold."

"I appreciate that."

"The police gave me very little information," he admitted. "I know they found something at each site, but they aren't telling me what. In cases like this, that's to be expected."

"What do you mean?"

He stood. "Kidnappings generally come with demands. Police often hold back clues from the public. It helps them distinguish between crank calls and the real thing. If demands are made, they want something that only the perpetrator can know. I think those clues have something to do with you. Am I right?"

"I can't talk about that."

He picked up his recorder and dropped it back into the reluctant pocket. "Something isn't right here, Mayor. Be careful and take good care of the girl. Whatever is going on isn't over yet."

"How do you know that?"

"Reporter's instinct."

My politician instincts said the same.

chapter 10

I looked up from my desk and saw Randi leaning against the door-jamb. She had several folders in her hand; a wide black computer bag hung from her shoulder. "Have laptop, will travel," I said. "I assume it's time to enter the lions' den."

"Yea, verily." She smiled. "You love these closed-door meetings and you know it."

"And here I've been thinking I hate them. Just goes to show you what I know." A glance at the desk clock told me it was 9:55. The meeting was to start in five minutes, and my compulsion to be punctual kicked into overdrive. Closing the file I had been reading, I rose and started for the door. The file contained the meeting's agenda. The church that had been denied the zoning change and conditional use permit had asked for a second opportunity to present its case to the whole council, meaning me. There was another zoning question on our docket, as well. This one was also an appeal for a second hearing, except the petitioner wasn't a small church trying to broaden its ministry. We had bitterly debated the original request behind closed doors and in the council chamber. It was the most contentious issue we had faced in the last two years, and council divided down the middle. I had cast the deciding vote, and a company named BioMec was denied the zoning change they needed to build a five-story midrise on oceanfront property.

That was one ugly meeting.

Randi followed a step behind me as we exited the office. My stomach tightened with each step and I noticed my apprehension meter pegging on the high side. This was unusual. While I never seek controversy, I also never avoid it. At times I feel shame for those moments when I catch myself enjoying the give-and-take of a heated meeting. However, I never let that guilt get in the way of doing what I think is best for the city.

I stepped into the conference room with two minutes to spare. The room lacks any features worthy of description. Its walls are an uncreative white, the carpet a low-pile, sandy brown, and what few pictures hang on the wall are the same pastoral scenes found in a physician's lobby. The room is a twenty-by-twenty-foot affair, too small for the mayor, four council members, the city clerk, the city attorney, and a staff member for each.

Dominating the room is a bulky, square conference table covered with a simulated-wood veneer that suggests maple but has trouble carrying off the impersonation. Stains from coffee cups and soda cans were still present from the last meeting. I made a mental note to have Randi call a janitor and point out the oversight.

Fred Markham, the city attorney, sat in his usual spot at the foot of the table, as he called it. As mayor, I would be moderating the meeting from the table's head. Fred was one of my favorite people. He was easy to deal with, straightforward in his communication, careful in his words, deliberate in his work, and as contentious as a monk. A graduate of UCLA Law School, he had a mind that was sharp and hungry. When occasion demanded that I visit his office, I frequently found books and magazines that surprised me. On my last visit I noticed a copy of Steven Hawking's latest book on his desk.

"Good morning, Counselor," I said.

"Good morning, Mayor." He rose from his seat. I always found this quaint. He was the only man I knew who held on to social customs that had died a generation before. I also appreciated the gesture more than I let on.

Fred was a man of thirty-eight years. His white hair made him look a decade and a half older. His face was handsome but always seemed a little puffy, as if he were having an allergic reaction to shellfish. Maybe he was just allergic to politicians.

"How's the family, Fred?" I took my seat and spread out my files and notepad.

"Fine. Judy wants to go back to school and Jason is thinking of taking up tennis. He just learned that tennis stars make a lot of money."

I laughed. Jason was his sixteen-year-old son. "What does your wife want to study?"

"Law." He chuckled and shook his head.

"Can't talk any sense into her, eh?"

"I've tried, but her mother was a big Perry Mason fan."

"Just don't let her con you into doing her homework."

The door swung open and a stream of people poured in like an impromptu parade. Leading the pack was the city clerk, Dana Thayer, a severe-looking woman with black hair combed back over her ears, and a pair of reading glasses hanging from a silver chain around her neck. A city employee for twenty years, she was no-nonsense, humorless, and organized to the point of being frightening.

Councilman Wu followed her. He saw me and smiled. Wu was impossible not to like. When the election results had rolled in and I learned that I was to be the city's first full-time mayor, I felt conflicting emotions: joy that all the hard work had paid off, and guilt that I had to beat a man like Wu. If I hadn't been running for the office, I would have voted for him.

Titus Overstreet was the quiet councilman, although not a man without opinion and conviction. He stood a slender six foot two and looked to be in good enough shape to trot the floorboards of the basketball court he had dominated in high school. He'd been a hero in those days but lacked skill and, or so I'm told, the aggressive nature to make it very far in college ball. Six two was a good height for high school ball, but he was just too short to play at a major university. He was wise enough to realize that while still a teenager and directed his efforts to his education. He held an MBA in marketing and owned a public relations business in the city. As usual, he was dressed to the nines in gray suit and black, collarless shirt. He looked as if he had just stepped from the cover of *Ebony*. A dazzling white smile beamed from his black face. I returned it with a nod.

The room cooled as if it were about to ice over. Intellectually, I knew that the entrance of a human could not dramatically change the room temperature, but wherever Tess Lawrence went, an arctic chill seemed to follow. She was a glacier in pantyhose. Whereas the others strolled into the room, she marched. I expected to see a display of goose-stepping any moment. She was a stern-looking woman with bleached white hair, perpetually narrow eyes, and a tense expression that gave the impression of terminal indigestion. Tess was not affected by stress but she was a carrier.

Her lapdog, Jon Adler, trailed her. I had an urge to rise, cross the room, and give him a resounding slap. I don't know why, but it seemed like such a satisfying action. It was an urge I had to suppress frequently.

Aides filed in and took their places in chairs along the wall, ready to pass a note, run an errand, deliver coffee, or answer a question beyond the knowledge of their bosses.

"Good morning, everyone," I said with as much formality as I could muster. "It's straight-up ten o'clock, so let's get things under way. The clerk will note the time."

Since the meeting was technically off the record, there would be no formal minutes taken other than noting that the conference took place and listing those in attendance.

"I assume we all have our agendas, so let's begin with the first item—"

"Let's start with something else," Adler said. "I think you owe the whole council an explanation and an apology."

"Jon, we went over this in my office."

"I'm not the whole council, and not to put too fine a point on it: you were very rude to me."

I wondered what he would look like with my pen shoved up his nose. "The explanation is simple, and everyone in this room who reads a newspaper knows why I had to leave the meeting. I'm sorry if Lisa Truccoli's abduction has inconvenienced you."

"This isn't about me—"

"This is about you, Mayor," Tess Lawrence said. "It's about your connection to two disappearances."

I had wondered when she would wade in.

"Exactly," Jon added. Good lapdog.

"What are you insinuating?" Larry Wu asked in his soft Texas accent.

"I insinuate nothing," Tess said. "I simply feel that we on the council have a right to know what is going on. A lot of people in the building are a little nervous about the mayor."

"A lot?" I asked. "How many?"

"I don't know exactly—"

"No? Well, how many have come to you and expressed their concerns?"

"Again, I don't know exactly." Tess was starting to backpedal.

"Name one," I demanded in even tones.

"It was told to me in confidence."

"You're not a priest, Tess. Name one person other than Jon who has come to you expressing concerns about me, and I'll personally go to them and assure them there is nothing to worry about."

"I can't do that."

"I don't imagine you can." I had much more to say, but to do so really would have given people something to worry about. I set my jaw but continued to stare innocently at the now fuming councilwoman.

"You two are out of line," Titus interjected smoothly. "The mayor has enough on her plate without you adding your paranoia."

"Is that a fact," Jon snapped. "I might have expected such a comment from you. You two are like dogs, one following the other with his nose firmly planted—"

Titus's head snapped around and he raised a single finger. His face darkened two shades. "Don't finish it," he said with words hot enough to melt steel.

Jon slid back in his chair and blinked rapidly. I could almost hear his pounding heart. He started to say something but his mouth would not cooperate. He did manage to get a weak "Um" out.

I should have calmed everyone down, taken control, diffused the situation, but I wanted to see Jon squirm a few moments more. Larry did it for me. "Is there any news about the investigation?" he asked with genuine concern. Of all the people on the council, Larry had the biggest heart.

I shook my head. "No. The police are doing everything they can, but nothing has come up yet." I paused. As much as I disliked Jon and Tess, they were right about one thing: the council needed information about the investigation. I filled them in about most things, keeping to myself the details about my business card and the photo. Those particulars had not been in the news reports, and I assumed the police were keeping that to themselves for the moment.

"Is there anything we can do?" Titus asked.

"Not that I can think of. I wish there were. I wish there were more that I could do."

"Just let us know," Larry said. "We're here for you."

By that he meant himself and maybe Titus. I thanked him and tried to return the meeting to the agenda. I was just about to bring up the first item of business again when I heard something just beyond the closed conference room door.

"Where is . . ." The muffled words sounded angry. It was a man's voice.

". . . in there . . . meeting." A woman's voice. A familiar woman's voice. It took a second for me to realize it was Fritzy. She sounded disturbed.

"Sir, you cannot go in there." The words were clearer and sounded closer.

"Get away, woman—"

The door exploded open, swinging around fully on its hinges until it smacked into the wall with a resounding bang. The sudden invasion glued us to our seats. No one moved.

In the doorway stood an angry man, his face red and puffy. The color spread from his chin up and over his bald head. What little hair he had ran neatly from ear to ear in a brown band. His eyes were wild. He wore a white golf shirt, jeans, and sneakers.

"Which one of you is Mayor Glenn?" Drops of spittle flew from his mouth like ejecta from a volcano. No one moved or spoke. The shock had paralyzed us. "Glenn. Mayor Glenn. Which one of you is Mayor Glenn?"

Jon pointed my way. What a hero.

I stood. "I'm Mayor Glenn and we're in the middle of a meeting." I could see Fritzy standing behind the man, her hands raised to her mouth. She was beyond scared; she was terrified. The angry, broad-shouldered man with clenched fist and red face was enough to frighten anyone. Women her age don't need that kind of scare in their lives. I shot a slight nod her way, hoping she would divine my silent intent. She blinked twice and scampered off.

"We have business," he snapped.

When in doubt, I reasoned, be assertive. "You will lower your voice before you speak to me," I commanded as if in control. "Who are you?"

"Where is my daughter?" That explained it. Christopher Truccoli, Celeste's absent father. He was not absent now. "I asked you a question, woman."

"That's enough," Titus said, shooting up from his chair. I had never appreciated Titus more. He was the tallest and most fit man in the room, apart from Truccoli.

"Out of my way," Truccoli spat and started around the table, pushing by Titus as if he weren't there. Titus took a step back, then rebounded quickly, seizing the man's left arm. I couldn't have anticipated it and Titus didn't see it coming. Truccoli spun and brought a thick fist up into Titus's belly. I could hear the air rush from his lungs and saw his knees shake, then give way. He dropped to the floor.

Truccoli turned in my direction. Aides scampered out of the way. "You will tell me where Celeste is." I backed up. He seemed to grow in size with each step. He raised a finger and stabbed the air. "Tell me!"

I felt something brush past my shoulder, something unexpected. It was Larry Wu. He interposed his body between me and Truccoli. "Back off," Larry commanded.

"Out of my—"

Larry was on the move. He lowered his head and charged, burying his shoulder into Truccoli's gut. The men careened into the side wall. My heart bounced around in my chest as if trying to find a way out.

Truccoli grabbed a fistful of hair on the back of Larry's head and pulled back savagely. He raised a fist, ready to bring it down like a meteor.

"Stop!" I screamed.

Just as the fist began its brutal plunge, it was deflected. Titus was up again, and the look on his face said he was taking no prisoners. He plowed into both men and they tumbled to the floor, a mass of legs and arms. Obscenities filled the room, some from Truccoli and others from Titus.

They wrestled and struggled for a half minute that clicked past like eons. A movement at the door caught my attention. It was the young security officer.

"Whoa," he said, then started for the heaving pile of men. He pulled a set of chrome handcuffs from his belt but couldn't hold Truccoli's wrist steady long enough to clamp the metal ring into place. "Hold him still."

Titus grunted. "What do you think we're trying to do?"

Another movement at the door. I expected to see another security officer but it was Detective West. He assessed the situation in less than a second, then casually walked to the scuffle. He put a hand on the guard, who was still trying to work the cuffs. "Here, let me give it a try."

The guard yielded and West reached for Truccoli's hand that was clamped around Titus's neck. I expected him to begin wrestling for control like the security guard, but West took a different approach: he seized the attacker's little finger and bent it back.

A howl filled the room.

"Relax or it gets worse."

Truccoli began to struggle again and West gave a solid yank. Truccoli froze in place.

"Let go of the councilmen," West said calmly, still applying pressure.

"Okay, okay—just don't break my finger."

I'll admit, a part of me was hoping West would do exactly that. Larry and Titus freed themselves from the human knot, stood and brushed themselves off. I saw them make eye contact and they communicated something in a way only guys can. I assumed it was an unspoken thanks.

The sound of running feet echoed from the corridor. A half dozen police officers poured into the room. There is an advantage to having the Police Station just across the parking lot.

"I've got it," West said as he removed a pair of handcuffs from his belt. With a precision that must have come from years of practice, he locked the first cuff in place. "On your stomach," he ordered.

Truccoli refused and West gave the cuff a sharp twist. I saw the metal dig into the angry man's flesh. Another cry of pain. "You're breaking my wrist!"

"I said, on your stomach."

This time Truccoli was quick to comply. A few seconds later he was cuffed and being led from the room by the guys in uniform.

"Is everyone all right?" West asked.

"Titus took a punch," I said.

The councilman waved me off. "I've had worse."

"Anyone need an ambulance?" West asked. No one did. "Okay, I'll need to get statements from everyone, but first I want to get Mr. Truccoli booked."

"How long can you hold him?" I wondered.

"Not long. We've got him for assault and battery, and I'll see what else I can tag on to that."

"This is the kind of problem we're talking about," Jon said. He was still seated and I could see his hands shaking. "You've brought violence into City Hall."

"Not yet I haven't," I mumbled. Louder I said, "Thanks for your help."

I looked around the room; it was filled with frightened aides and staff. It took a moment before I noticed that Tess was gone. "Where's Councilwoman Lawrence?"

"She left when things got fun," Randi said. I nodded and found I couldn't blame her. I turned to Fred Markham. "I'm not sure what legal gymnastics we need to do here, Fred, but I think a restraining order might be useful. Will you check into that?"

"With pleasure." He looked pale.

I took a deep breath. "We all owe Larry and Titus a great big thank-you, as well as Detective West and the rest of the Santa Rita Police Department." Everyone but Adler applauded. "We will reschedule this meeting for the near future. As for now, the meeting is adjourned."

I waited for the others to leave before I returned to my office, took my chair, and spent the next ten minutes holding back tears and trying not to vomit.

chapter 11

The problem with violence is that its effects last long after the event. I sat in my comfortable chair, behind my comfortable desk in my comfortable office, feeling like a tomato that had just been dropped in a blender. The blades of shock and fear were still spinning, churning my guts and ripping at the few strands of composure I had left.

I felt cold. I felt hot. I felt sick and faint. I had denied it, of course. When West asked if I was hurt, I told him the truth sugared with a lie. "I'm fine. Really, I'm fine. No worries."

He'd studied me for seconds that seemed like hours, then nodded. He didn't believe me. Why should he? I didn't believe myself. West asked a few questions, praised Larry and Titus, then started for the door.

"What are you going to do with Truccoli?" I asked. It was a shallow question with a deep need. What I wanted to hear was that he would be locked in some dark, rat-infested jail, but the small part of my mind that was still acquainted with logic knew better.

"I'm going to have a long, long talk with him."

That had been thirty minutes before and my heart still flipped and fluttered, ricocheting off my rib cage. No matter how I tried to ignore the fear, it refused to be denied. Tears kept rising in my eyes and I kept forcing them back. Just when I thought I had won the battle, the image of Christopher Truccoli marching toward me rose in my mind like a demon summoned by some ancient necromancer. I could see his red face and hear his spittle-laced demands. My ears were filled with the sound of air punched from Titus's lungs.

I had to shake this. I had to quench the fire before it fanned into a blaze beyond anyone's control. I had been through a worse conflagration, I told myself. I had endured the tragic loss of my husband. Truccoli's antics were nothing in comparison. All I had to do was keep it in perspective.

The tears attempted another getaway.

"I brought you some coffee," Randi said as she strode into the office. She was carrying a mug with the city's seal on it. Smoothly she set it on my desk.

"I didn't ask for coffee."

"I know. I brought it anyway." She sat in one of the guest chairs.

I took a sip. "Yuck! It's cold. You brought me a cup of cold coffee?"

"Yeah. You're too upset to have caffeine right now."

"Then why bother bringing it?"

"I had to bring something."

"Why?"

"I don't know." Small red veins tinted her eyes. Like me, she was teetering on the edge of tears. "I was feeling alone out there. I can't concentrate."

She began to shake. I'd known Randi for years and she had always struck me as unflappable, but at this moment she was as frail as an old china cup.

"Randi, you never need an excuse to come talk to me. You know that."

"Yeah, I know. I'm just not thinking straight. That chump has shaken me and I hate myself for allowing him to."

"I'm a little off myself—okay, I've been shaking like a leaf for the last fifteen minutes. At least I don't feel like I'm going to hurl my breakfast anymore."

She nodded and stared at the floor. "If I went over to the jail and shot him, do you think the police would mind?"

"Yeah, they might," I said with a tiny laugh. "They're kinda fussy about such things."

Randi buried her face in her hands. Her shoulders shook and my heart broke. I got up and closed the door. Stepping to her side, I placed a hand on her shoulder and guided her to her feet. She kept her head down.

"I'm . . . I'm sorry. I hate crying."

"I know," I said, then took her in my arms.

I lost the battle with my tears.

What followed was five minutes of wet therapy, a psychological scrubbing that came by shedding a river of tears. I wasn't sure who was holding whom, nor did I care. "Tears are like vomiting," my mother used to say. "The process isn't much fun but things seem better when it's all over."

She was right; crude but right. While I didn't feel good, I felt as if something nasty had passed from me.

I released Randi and handed her a tissue from the box on my desk. We began the ritual nose-blowing and eye-dabbing that follows every communal cry.

"Thanks," she said.

"It's a small price to pay for cold coffee."

"Starbucks has made millions off it." She laughed. I joined her. It was a laughter that came from relief, not from joy.

A soft knocking came from the door. We looked at each other, then hurriedly tried to pull ourselves together. I quickstepped to my place behind the desk and Randi opened the door. I wasn't sure who I was expecting, but it certainly wasn't the man who stood across the threshold.

"Chief Webb," I croaked. Crying was hard on the voice. I cleared my throat. "Please come in."

"Thank you. Am I interrupting?"

"No. We're just a little traumatized by what happened. Please have a seat. Can Randi get you something, water, coffee—" I glanced at Randi—"*hot* coffee?"

Webb's eyes narrowed. I assumed he knew he was on the outside of an inside joke. "No, thank you. I won't be here long." He sat down.

Randi removed the mug from my desk, then excused herself.

"West tells me you're unharmed," Webb said the moment she was gone. "True?"

"No physical harm. Thanks to Titus ... Councilmen Overstreet and Wu. They really came through."

"So I hear." He fidgeted, something I had never seen him do. "I'm glad to hear it."

A quivering silence filled the void between us.

Something needed saying. "Your officers were great. They got here fast and took charge, especially Detective West. The whole thing seemed old hat to him."

"He's been around the block a few times. I imagine he's seen it all. Big-city cops usually have."

"Well, I'm thankful for his work and that of the other officers. I should send cookies."

"No need," Webb said, holding up his hand. "It's their job."

"Perhaps, but knights in shinning badges deserve something, even if it's just baked goods."

"Suit yourself."

More silence. More fidgeting.

"How can I help you, Chief?"

"I'm here . . . to apologize." He shuffled his feet. "It shouldn't have happened."

"You're not responsible for Truccoli's actions."

He tilted his head and frowned. "Truccoli was pretty hot when he first got into town. West tells me he called you from the plane while flying in. When you refused to tell him where his daughter was, he got really steamed. He must have saved it all up on the flight, because he bent West's ear but good, and when he didn't get any satisfaction, he insisted on seeing me. I was gone at the time, but he came back."

"You actually met with him?" I was astonished. Webb was chief of police. He didn't have to meet with any citizen just because the person demanded it. Truccoli didn't even live in the state.

"I was hoping to calm him. We don't need someone kicking up dust while we're trying to run an investigation. Besides, it was his wife—ex-wife—who was taken. I owed him that much."

"Why do I have this feeling that things didn't go smoothly?"

"It could have gone better. He started soft and easy. Maybe he was trying a different approach. I told him what we knew about the case and he asked a few questions. Then he turned the conversation to his daughter. He wanted to know what you had done to her."

"Done *to* her?"

"That's how he put it. I said as far as I knew, you hadn't done anything to her. I then reminded him that his daughter is a legal adult. That set him off. He went ballistic. The man has a real temper."

"You think? Then what happened? I assume you ripped him but good."

He shook his head. "Nah. I just removed my handcuffs from my belt. He sorta calmed down, then stormed from my office. That was yesterday. One of our officers caught him at Ms. Truccoli's home. The officer didn't know who he was, so he put a few questions to him. After all, the man was at a crime scene. We had released the scene, so he wasn't tampering with evidence, and he claimed to be on the deed. I had someone check on that today. He lied."

"He's a real piece of work." My stomach soured again. "I still don't see the need for an apology."

"You and I don't get along very well, Mayor. We don't see eye to eye, and I doubt we ever will. I didn't vote for you and I won't vote for you next time. But you are mayor and that fact alone demands some respect from me. I should have seen this coming. It's only natural that someone in Truccoli's state of mind would come to the city building looking for you. I didn't see it. Maybe I didn't want to see it. Whatever the reason, I let him slip through the cracks. For that I am sorry."

I didn't know how to feel or what to think. In one way the chief of police had just insulted me; in another way he had paid me a compliment. Not knowing what else to say, I uttered, "Thank you, Chief."

"There's something else. West told me that Mrs. Stout, like Lisa Truccoli, has a connection to your campaign. He also thinks you might be in some danger."

"He mentioned that."

"Did he mention your parents?"

My spine chilled. "What about my parents?"

"When you won the election two years ago, the paper carried an article about what made your campaign so successful. In the article you thanked several workers, including Truccoli and Stout and—"

"And my parents," I murmured. That must have been where Doug Turner made the connection. For all I knew, he may have written the article. I couldn't remember. My nerves were already on edge; this pushed me to the brink. "Do you really think . . ."

"There's no way to know, but I would suggest that they take some precautions. I don't have the manpower to assign an officer to everyone who worked on your campaign. I wish I did."

The ice water that had chilled my spine suddenly turned hot. Webb and I had knocked heads on several issues since I came to the city council, but the real wedge between us was the city budget. I'm tightfisted with other people's money, especially when that money is taxed out of their wallets and purses. Webb had asked for a substantial bump in his budget. He wanted more squad cars, better computers, and enough money to hire ten more officers. If he had gotten his way, his budget would have swollen by forty percent, and those dollars would have had to come from some other department. I fought against it. In the end he got a three percent increase and I got a political enemy.

Hornets of angry thoughts swarmed in my mind and apparently it showed. Webb raised his hands. "This has nothing to do with our problems, Mayor. I'm just telling you the facts. I have only so many men and too many square miles to protect."

"And so you thought you'd come over and rub that in my face." My jaw tightened like a vise. "You're here instead of Detective West so you can see my reaction. Is that it? You're here to make a point and you're using my fear and family to do it."

"No." He snapped the word loud and hard. His eyes flashed and his face grew red. "You're wrong. That is *not* why I'm here. I'm here because the chief of police owes his mayor the truth, no matter how much she dislikes him. I am not an evil man, Mayor. I am not nearly as low as you think I am."

His words stung me. Webb had always been a good cop. He was opinionated and at times blunt to the point of rudeness, but I had never known him to be mean-spirited. I worked my lips in frustration and drummed my fingers on my desk. Misplaced anger filled me and it wanted a new target. None was in sight. Words stayed just out of reach, too ethereal to grasp. I felt like a cat chasing reflections on a wall. I pawed at the words but they just kept moving away from me.

Webb bailed me out. He cleared his throat, then said in much softer tones, "I've approved of Detective West's decision to have patrols stepped up in the area around your house. That will continue, but you should think about taking a couple safety measures yourself."

"Like what?" I finally managed to say.

"If it were me, I'd move my parents into my home for a few days, until we get a solid lead of some kind. It's no guarantee of safety, but at least you'll know where everyone is. Better yet, you have siblings, don't you?"

"A brother and a sister."

"You and your parents could move in with one of them."

I shook my head. "I can't do that. They live too far away for me to commute to the office. I doubt my parents would even consider it. My brother and sister have small children in the home. My parents won't take danger to their grandkids."

"Then you're back to your house. Have your folks move in for a bit and hire some private security."

I nodded. There was wisdom in his words. I didn't like it, my parents would hate it, but Webb was right. "I'll see what I can do."

Webb rose. "Good. I'm sorry my visit upset you." He started to leave.

"Chief?" He stopped and turned. "Thanks."

He nodded once and left, closing the door behind him. In the silent, empty office, I felt alone, adrift in rising seas. I picked up the phone and dialed my parents' number.

I couldn't take the office anymore. The morning had been emotionally grueling as well as physically taxing. I had been untouched by Christopher Truccoli, but the stress and tension were beating me up in their own way. Dealing with Doug Turner early that morning, being accosted by Truccoli, then meeting with Webb, had left me feeling as if I were in the eleventh round of a ten-round fight.

I buzzed Randi. "Let's get out of here." She agreed without hesitation.

A few minutes later we were riding in Randi's yellow Volkswagen Beetle. When I left for college, my father bought me a VW bug. It was old but in great condition and I loved it more than any car I've ever owned. Other than a similarity in shape, Randi's Beetle was nothing like what I drove two decades before. Hers was heavier, solid, and far more comfortable. The engine was larger and the suspension rivaled that of luxury cars. "Corners on rails," she had bragged the day she got it. She'd insisted on popping the hood and showing me how the large engine was crammed into the front of the car. The front! Could it be a true Beetle?

Hers was a convertible and she had the top down before she pulled from the parking stall. The day had warmed and the sun had evicted any remaining clouds. The air was sweet, perfumed with salt from the sea and with Southern California desert plants. I leaned my head back and let the breeze knot my hair and the sun toast my face. It felt wonderful, California catharsis. For me sunshine cures everything.

Randi, normally cautious in everything she did, especially driving, took corners faster than she should have and left stoplights as if in a drag race. I said nothing. I didn't care. I was out of the office and that was all that mattered.

"I suggest we go eat things that will make us fat," Randi said. "Indulgence is the vice of the noble."

"I'm impressed. What great philosopher said that?"

"Me. I just made it up."

"And here I'm wasting your talents making you work in an office when you could be writing greeting cards."

Randi laughed and turned onto the freeway. "The sacrifices I make for our city. I want Mexican. So do you."

"I do?"

"Yes, you do. You want two ground-beef enchiladas, chips, salsa, and the biggest bowl of guacamole they make."

"Do you have a place in mind?" I asked, my eyes still closed and my face still turned skyward. "Or were you planning on driving until we bumped into a restaurant?"

"I know a great place in San Diego."

"Me too, but that's two hours away. How about something closer?"

"San Diego is nice this time of year."

"I know. I went to college there, remember? Closer."

"Okay, Tiny Titos it is. I'll take the next exit. We'll be there in five minutes."

"I've never been there."

"It's just what we need."

"You weren't really thinking of driving to San Diego, were you?" I sat up and looked at her. Her short red hair snapped in the breeze and her blue eyes sparkled. Gone was the red that had foretold the coming tears. She smiled and beaming white teeth that I had more than once wished were mine shone in the bright sunlight. She said nothing.

Ten minutes later we were walking into an out-of-the-way Mexican restaurant. Thick white plaster covered the walls, which proudly showed off their cracks as if they were battle scars. We had a choice of eating in a courtyard festooned with cheap plastic tables and green and red picnic umbrellas with the names of Mexican beers emblazoned on them or dining in the dark interior of the restaurant. We chose the former. I'd had all the confining rooms I wanted for the day.

A young Hispanic man with what was obviously his first mustache seated us next to a bubbling fountain. A naked plaster cherub held a small pot out of which water poured into the fountain's basin. The sound was soothing. Exterior speakers released soft recorded music from a mariachi band.

We fussed with our hair, trying to force the knots out and make our manes hang as they were supposed to. I gave up. Randi, whose hair is half the length of mine, made a better job of it.

A few minutes later a waiter showed up. He was an older man and much more adept at mustache growing. He took our drink orders, called us "amigas," and disappeared.

We filled the next few minutes with small talk but I knew it wouldn't last. I couldn't pretend that all was well with the world. I doubted Randi could, either. Sooner or later the conversation would swing around to the very thing we were trying to avoid.

The waiter was back. It was just 11:30 and the lunch crowd had not arrived. At the moment we were the only two customers in the courtyard. As the waiter set up a small folding table, the young man who seated us joined him. He brought a stone bowl, two large avocados, salt, cilantro, lime, and a large knife, and then disappeared into the bowels of the restaurant.

Wordlessly the waiter cut the first avocado in half and removed the large pit by smacking the sharp edge of the knife into it and twisting. The golf ball–sized seed popped free. What followed was high drama. He scooped out the green, pasty contents of the avocados and plopped it down in the stone bowl, mashed it and mixed in the other ingredients, bathed it in a shower of lime juice, sprinkled on some salt, and then set the dish before us. Instant guacamole, and my stomach immediately became impatient. A basket of chips was set on the table and I had a scoop of glorious green goop before the waiter had picked up his little table.

The morning had been rough and I needed this moment of heaven. After two or three minutes of dipping, eating, and moaning, I was starting to unwind. "Can we stay here forever?" I asked.

"Fine by me, but we might get bored. Or they might make us do the dishes."

"Party pooper."

"You feel like talking about Chief Webb?"

"No, but I will." I filled her in on the meeting, leaving nothing out.

"You really said that to him? You said he was rubbing the budget issue in your face?"

"I'm afraid I did. I think I hurt his feelings. In retrospect, I may have been overreacting."

"I don't think Webb has feelings to hurt."

"Everyone has feelings; some people are just hard to figure out."

"Don't go soft on him now," Randi said, shoveling another guacamole-laden chip into her mouth. "He's not your friend and I doubt he ever will be."

"He's still a good cop, one who takes his job seriously. He doesn't have to be my friend to do that. I expect him to respect my office even if he can't wring out any respect for me. I suppose I owe him the same courtesy."

"You're far more generous than I. So are you going to follow his advice about your parents?"

I nodded and sipped my tea. "I called them as soon as he left. They balked at the idea. They tend to be a little stubborn. Maybe that's where I get it. Anyway, I talked, cajoled, and finally pleaded. They're going to my place this afternoon."

"So you whined them into submission."

"I wouldn't put it that way. They're doing it as a favor for me. That was the only approach that worked. I told them I'd sleep better with them and Celeste in the house."

"Speaking of Celeste, what are you going to do with her?"

"What do you mean?"

Randi paused, as if sorting through her words. "Is she going to stay with you? If so, how long?"

I shrugged. "I don't mind her staying with me. I kind of like it. It makes me feel like I'm doing something to help Lisa. As for how long—I don't know. Certainly until we know something about her mother. One thing is for sure: she shouldn't go with that mental-case father of hers."

"Amen to that. That man has a temper and too few brains to control it."

The waiter returned and we ordered our meals. I chose two ground-beef enchiladas, one in green sauce and the other in red. It was going to be more than I usually eat, but I didn't care. Randi went with a wet burrito—basically an enchilada on steroids.

"Getting back to your parents, do you think they're in danger?"

"I don't know. I doubt it. Webb's contention is that Lisa and Lizzy were part of my campaign. Since my parents were also involved, they might be targets. I'm still not convinced that my campaign is the common factor."

"You think it's just coincidence?"

"I'm having trouble seeing it any other way."

She raised an eyebrow.

"What?"

She shrugged but said nothing.

"Spill it, girl."

Randi pursed her lips. "I think you don't see it because you don't want to see it. Personally, I can't see it any other way."

"Why?" I knew where she was going and I dreaded it.

"Could all this be a coincidence? Perhaps, but I sure wouldn't bet money on it. I certainly wouldn't bet my life. I think you know this. You've taken some precautions, including insisting that your parents spend the next few days at your house. Two women, both associated with you, have been abducted. And not abducted off the streets but from their homes—homes which are across town from each other. You're not dealing with a neighborhood nut case. Everything you've told me says this guy is methodical. He works with a plan. If he were a rapist, then . . . well, you know. If he were a murderer, there would be bodies. If he were just a burglar, he wouldn't take hostages."

"Still—"

"Hang on. There's more. Did you tell me your card was found with four drops of blood on it and that the drops formed a square?"

"Yes."

"And that in Lizzy Stout's case, there was a picture with three drops of blood on it?"

"Yes, one over each eye and one over the mouth."

Randi shook her head. "That is not random behavior. You don't break into someone's house, subdue the occupant, then say, 'Gee, what else can I do? I know; I'll put four drops of blood on a business card.' It's too premeditated, too rational in an irrational way, if you know what I mean."

"I get it." None of this was new. Those very thoughts had bounced around in my brain like Ping-Pong balls, but hearing them voiced by Randi gave me the chills. "I just don't know what it means."

"It means you need to do what you do best: be proactive. Sitting around waiting for this guy to make his next move isn't going to cut it."

"If there is a next move." It was a weak rebuttal. "The bad guy has to know that the police are on the case. That should scare him off."

Again Randi shook her head. "No. I'm sorry, Mayor, but you're avoiding the hard truth. The abductor doesn't care about the police. He's baiting them. He's leaving a message."

"What message?"

"I have no idea, but the sooner that gets figured out, the sooner the clown will be caught."

One reason Randi worked for me was her honesty. Somewhere between being brutally blunt and being insipidly diplomatic was a realm of honest expression untainted by selfish motive. Randi lived in that land.

She had addressed issues that had already occurred to me, but she put them into perspective. More importantly, she forced me to see the urgency. My history professor father had once opined, "The problem with politicians, Maddy, is that they surround themselves with smart people, then are too stupid to listen to them." It was now my turn to decide if I would listen.

The waiter brought our meals on too-hot-to-touch plates, and we set ourselves to the delicious business of consuming our orders. The food was a treat to my mouth but it sat heavy in my stomach, perhaps because my belly was full of fear. Randi was right. It was time to face the truth.

Not wanting to taint our meal, we shifted our conversation from abductions to other topics. We covered the weather, movies, books, and men. Since neither of us was involved in a relationship, the last topic was short-lived. To my surprise, Randi didn't bring up the research she had done on the congressional run. I was glad.

Thirty minutes later we were leaning back in our chairs and making the well-known noises of the stuffed. The waiter cleared our plates. We left the courtyard of Tiny Titos just as it was beginning to fill with hungry lunch-goers. The early meal had been perfect; I was feeling revived and my nerves had returned to their normal functions.

"To the office, James," I said with a flourish, "and don't spare the horses."

"James? Do I look like a James?"

"Okay, how about Jamie. Don't spare the horses, Jamie. Nah, it doesn't sound right."

"Just fasten your seat belt," Randi said with a crooked smile.

"I'll have to let it out. I'm bigger now than I was."

"I have an extension in the backseat."

"Hey, I'm not the one who ate the monster burrito. That thing was huge."

"If I eat many more of those, I'll need my own zip code."

She checked for traffic, then pulled away from the curb. I leaned back and soaked up more sun and enjoyed the caress of the wind that flowed through the convertible. "That was great. Thanks for being up front with me."

"No problem. You've always been a straight shooter with me. I figure I owe you that much, and . . ."

"And what?" I prompted, my head against the headrest, my eyes closed.

She didn't answer.

I turned to her and saw that she was shifting her eyes between the rearview mirror and the road ahead. He face was drawn.

"What?" I sat up straight in the seat and started to turn to see what had captured Randi's attention.

"Don't," she snapped. "Use the mirror on your door. Do you see that van? The blue one?"

I cut my eyes to the passenger-side mirror. "Yeah, I see it."

"It looks familiar. I think I saw it when we were driving up here." Her voice was strained.

"You think it's following us?"

"Maybe, or maybe I'm just getting paranoid."

"Paranoid people face danger, too," I said, trying to sound philosophical. "Take the next right."

"That's not the way to the freeway."

"Exactly. Let's see if he follows. If he does, make another turn, then another. If he's following us, we'll know."

Randi did as I instructed, making a slow right turn onto a residential street. Manicured lawns dressed up small but immaculate houses. She drove on, glancing in her rearview mirror. I fixed my eyes on the side mirror. I saw the van slow at the corner and then continue on.

She sighed. "I must be getting jumpy. I was sure that guy was following us."

"He might be. If he is and if he knows the town, then our turn would have been unexpected. He slowed down for a moment. If he had turned with us, he would have given himself away. I don't suppose you got his license number."

"No, I was too busy watching him."

"I didn't, either." Looking at the mirror again, I added, "These passenger-side mirrors are designed to give a wide-angle view. I could see the van easily enough but not the license plate."

"I'm not sure there was a front plate." Randi frowned, then shook her head. "I just don't know. What do we do now?"

"Take a different way to the freeway. If we see him again, I'll call the cops on my cell phone."

"This has been one wacky day," Randi said.

She had that right.

chapter  12

Back in the office, I spent the afternoon trying to focus on work. It was an uphill battle. There were things to do, people to call, decisions to make, and none of it was happening. Christopher Truccoli's mad-dog attack kept playing through my mind.

I rang Larry Wu to see how he was feeling. His aide informed me that he had left for the day. I couldn't blame him. A quick call to Titus's office revealed the same thing.

I had much to thank these men for, but words seemed inadequate. After a little thought, I composed a letter to each, promising to treat them and their wives to a steak-and-lobster dinner. It was the least I could do.

I studied my calendar, doing my best to forget about Truccoli. My job is normally the most effective therapy available. Usually I can lose myself in zoning considerations, speaking engagements, and the general business of running the city. Usually.

The phone rang and Randi answered it. She put the caller on hold, leaned back in her chair so she could see through the doorway. "It's Fred Markham."

I snapped up the receiver. "Good afternoon, Mr. City Attorney."

"Hi. I wanted to give you an update on the restraining order. I was able to pull a few strings, and a restraining order will be issued before day's end. I've informed Detective West that it's coming, and he said he'd pass the information on to Mr. Truccoli."

"I appreciate this, Fred," I said, telling myself I should feel relieved.

"That's the good news. I was able to get the order for you but I can't get one for Celeste. As you know, I represent the city but I can't represent you as an individual. Since the attack took place on city property and was directed against city employees, I was able to get the order without any conflict of interest. You might want to talk to your young charge about getting a similar order. The best way to do that is for her to hire an attorney, but I have to tell you, it's going to be a bit of a fight."

"Why is that?"

He sighed and a moment passed before he replied. He was choosing his words carefully. "Maddy, her mother is missing. Truccoli is her closest relative. A judge is going to take that into consideration."

"But she's nineteen, an adult, and she has made it clear that she doesn't want to see him."

"I know this, but Truccoli's violence was directed toward you, not his daughter. She will need to show some viable need for a restraining order."

"She's at my house. The restraining order you obtained for me will keep Truccoli away from my house, right?"

"Theoretically. He could defy the order. People do it all the time. All it does is give the police a ready excuse to arrest him."

"But he can't come near me or my house."

"Right."

"So if Celeste is in my house, the order protects her."

"No, it protects you, but since Truccoli is forbidden to approach you, the function is the same. Once she leaves the house, it's a whole different matter."

"So you think she should get her own restraining order, but it may be difficult to do. Is that what you're saying?"

"That's pretty much it."

"How long will Truccoli be locked up?" I asked, hoping to hear the word *weeks* in the answer.

"Not long, Maddy. I spoke to West about it and he confirmed what I assumed to be the case. He's entitled to appear before a judge within forty-eight hours of his arrest, but he'll be out long before that. Police are charging him with two counts of assault. He has no prior arrests, no outstanding warrants; he doesn't even have a parking ticket. He'll go before a local bail officer, who will set bail: something between seven thousand and ten thousand dollars. Since there are no prior aggravating factors, he could be out as soon as he comes up with the money."

"Meaning what? He could be out in a few hours?" That thought made me sick.

"Exactly. West said he'd hold him as long as is reasonable but his hands are tied. My guess is that he'll be out by suppertime."

"Swell."

"Do you know if he has money?" Fred asked. "Will he be able to come up with the bail?"

"As I understand it, he's an exec in one of the major oil companies. I don't think a few grand is going to hurt him. I wouldn't be surprised if he's carrying several credit cards with limits over that."

"Pity. I'd like to have seen him spend a couple nights in jail."

"I'd like to see him just disappear."

Fred grunted his agreement, said goodbye, and hung up.

I glanced up and saw Randi at the door.

"You look like you swallowed a lemon," she noted.

"I wish. It would be a whole lot easier to stomach. Christopher Truccoli will probably be out of jail by early evening." I filled her in on the rest of the conversation.

"You gonna call about private security, like Webb suggested?"

I thought about it. It seemed unfair. I had done nothing wrong but take in a young woman whose mother was the victim of a crime. Now a man who could be the poster child for anger management was hounding me. "Yes. It's the wisest thing to do."

"It's also the expensive thing to do. They're not going to come cheap."

"Can't be helped," I said, then quipped, "I'm sure it's tax deductible."

"I have an idea. Why don't I call the company that provides security guards for the city? Once they find out it's for you, I bet they'll give you a good rate."

It was a good idea but a politically dangerous one. "Be careful. If they give away too much, it can come back and haunt me during an election. You know, 'Mayor Receives Personal Favors from City Contractors.' That sort of thing. In fact, we'd better run the contract by the city attorney to determine possible conflict of interest."

"Will do," Randi said cheerfully and disappeared.

I leaned back in my chair and wondered why the righteous suffered.

It was ten minutes past five when I lowered the automatic garage door and stepped into the house. Heavenly smells greeted me, aromas that reminded me of my childhood. I didn't need to ask to know that Mom was in the kitchen making plain ingredients into something memorable, like an alchemist turning lead into gold. I inhaled deeply and immediately knew everything that was going on in the kitchen. A meat loaf was simmering in a Crock-Pot filled with hunks of carrots and potatoes. The oven was hosting homemade rolls and the stovetop was warming gravy. This was the meal Mom made to cheer me up. A thick slice of dense meat loaf covered in catsup, potatoes awash in thick brown gravy, and butter-laden rolls could cure anything. Since my teenage years, I'd been convinced that our country could convert any enemy into an ally if we could just get them to try my mother's cooking.

Mixing with the aroma of food was the sound of MTV music. Celeste sat on the leather sofa, her eyes fixed on my Panasonic television. She seemed frozen in place, not by the images and music, I suspected, but by stress, that Gorgonian monster which can suck the life out of the heartiest people and turn them to stone. Next to her was Michele. I assumed that my parents had picked her up.

I set my purse on the small table next to the door, kicked off my shoes, and walked to Celeste. "How are you doing?" She looked pale.

"Okay, I guess." She shrugged. I put a hand on her shoulder and gave it a squeeze. "I asked your mom if Michele could come over. She said it was all right."

"It is. Hi, Michele."

Her head moved in beat with the music, her ponytail swaying in rhythm. "Hey."

"Who's that on the television?"

"Tinkertown," Michele said. "They're new. The lead guitarist is a solid-gold babe."

I smiled, glad they hadn't settled for admiring mere sterling-silver babes. "I'm going to say hi to my parents, then change clothes. These pantyhose are cutting me in half."

"Okay," Celeste said. "I don't suppose . . ."

I shook my head. "No news, yet." Choosing not to discuss her father until after I changed, I strode through the living room and into the dining area, where I found my father seated at the table drinking tea and reading. He rose and gave me a hug. It felt good. No matter how old I got, a hug from Dad seemed to imbue me with strength and the sense that all is right with the world.

"Welcome home, kiddo."

"Hi, Dad. Whatcha reading?"

"A biography of Chester Alan Arthur."

One more biography I'm grateful he wasn't reading when I was born. *Mayor Chesty Glenn.* I shuddered.

"Your mother has moved into the kitchen, as you can tell." He took his seat again. "Thank you."

"For what?"

"She thinks you're stressed out, and that means I get to eat things she won't let me eat otherwise. Act depressed; maybe we'll get ice cream with our peach cobbler."

I went into the kitchen. Mom was bent over, her face staring into the oven and her fanny directed at me.

"That's a fine way to greet your daughter," I said. "Point that thing in a different direction." She quickly closed the door and turned. I gave her a swift buss on the cheek. She was wearing the only apron I own, a birthday gift from Randi. The words "That's Mayor Cook to You" adorned the front.

"Daughters are not allowed to talk about their mothers' rear ends." She gave me hug. "How was your day?"

"You've probably already guessed. I'll fill you in after I change. Just tell me dinner is going to be on the table soon."

"Fifteen minutes. Didn't you eat lunch?"

"Oh, I ate lunch, all right. I ate too much. I have no right to be hungry, but I'm sure I'll manage to get a few bites down." I studied the kitchen. It gleamed. My mother was fastidious in many ways. She cleaned as she cooked. On the stove a pot simmered. I lifted the lid. Asparagus. It was just getting better and better.

"Put that down," Mom snapped. "And get out of the kitchen. You're throwing my rhythm off."

"Surely there's something I can do to help."

"Go get comfortable. Leave the rest to me."

"Aye, aye, Captain." I snapped a salute and turned to leave. At the edge of the kitchen I paused. "You're the best, Mom. You know that, don't you?"

"That's what I keep telling people."

I smiled and went upstairs.

Changing into a denim jumpsuit, I hung up my office clothes and slung my evil pantyhose onto the floor of the closet. My mother's tidiness gene had skipped a generation. I'd just reached the top of the stairs when the phone rang. "I've got it up here," I called to the others. Trotting down the hall and into my office, I snapped up the receiver. It was the owner of Atlas Security, Jim Lynch. I gazed at the ocean through the large windows. The sun was starting its slow descent to the blue horizon. The thick layer of clouds was late for its nightly appointment with the shore. The setting sun painted a gilded strip on the undulating sea.

Lynch had called to inform me that a man from his office would be on site at seven o'clock and that another guard would relieve him by one a.m.

"The first guard is Tom Wilson," Lynch said. "He's big, he's black, and he's the nicest guy you'd ever want to meet. He's also one of the sharpest employees on my payroll. I hope to keep him for a long time. He will come to the door and introduce himself. He'll be wearing the same-style uniform our people wear at City Hall, and he'll show his ID.

"Since Tom's relief won't arrive until the wee hours, he won't be checking in with you, unless you really want him to." I said I didn't. "Just so you know, his name is Allen Rodriguez. He's about four inches shorter than Tom and about twenty-five pounds lighter. He's also one of our best. You know why I'm telling you this?"

"Because if anyone else shows up in a uniform but doesn't match your description, I'll know he's not from you. Right?"

"Exactly. Your aide seemed . . . concerned."

"Actually, I feel a little silly. This was Chief Webb's idea."

"It's a good one. I have enough details to know that I want my best men on the job. There's something else you should know. The guards will be obvious. That's the goal. They will stand out front and walk around the house, and they'll be driving our patrol cars with our company name and emblem on the door. We want it known that the grounds are guarded."

"I understand."

"I hope this all works out for you," Lynch said. "I'll have a courier bring a contract to your office tomorrow."

"Remember, the city isn't hiring you; I am. So put my name on the contract."

"I think the city should pay for it, but I'm no politician. Tom Wilson will bring a private contract. Just sign it and let me do the rest."

I agreed and hung up.

Placing my hands behind my back, I began to pace the large room, my bare feet cushioned by the plush carpet. How quickly things can change. In just a few days I had gone from my organized, day-to-day routine, loving my job, to being attacked at work and having guards placed outside my house. The world is a nutty place.

I took a deep breath and walked to the narrow street-side windows. The house cast a long, dark shadow as the sun set behind it.

The street on which I live is a quiet lane, narrow and well maintained. Little traffic passes down it. I wondered where the guard would park.

D inner was every bit as good as I expected. Even Celeste ate more than she had in the last two days. That's the way it was with my mother's cooking. It was food therapy, pure and simple. It couldn't solve a problem, but for a short time it could make you forget it.

At my mother's prompting, I related the day's events. I tried to downplay the incident with Truccoli in the conference room, but there was no way to dilute it completely. My preference would have been to avoid the topic completely, but that would have been irresponsible. My parents had a right to know and more importantly, so did Celeste. The mood at the table darkened as I told the story. My father's face hardened and he chewed his food as if punishing it. I expected that. Like most fathers, he was extremely protective of his children.

Celeste was angry, too. "You see? You see? That's why I don't want to see him. He's nuts. He left us. He left Mom. He left me, and now he comes back to make things worse. I won't see him. I won't." She started to rise but I placed a hand on her shoulder.

"You don't have to," I reminded her. "You're no longer a minor. You make your own decisions."

"But what if he causes more trouble for you?"

"Then he'll end up in jail again. I've taken some extra precautions." I explained about the restraining order and the guards.

"Wise," Dad said, "but irritating. One shouldn't have to have security guards posted on the front doorstep." He stabbed another piece of meat loaf as if it were about to attack him.

"So when does Celeste's dad get out of the joint?" Michele asked.

"As soon as he posts bail. He may be out already."

Her face darkened. "Will he, like, come here or anything?"

"I doubt he knows where I live. Besides, we'll have a guard out front, the police have stepped up patrols in the area, and the house has a great alarm system."

"So we're going to be okay?" Celeste asked.

"Yeah," I replied with a smile. "We're going to be okay. We're as safe as we can be anyplace."

Mom stood. "Well, I think it's time for peach cobbler. Anyone want ice cream with it?"

Dad cast me a quick glance, then winked. "I'd love some, dear," he said sweetly.

The doorbell rang. Mom turned to answer it.

"No, Mom. Let me get it," I said, springing from my seat. "I was told the guard would check in once he arrived. It's probably him."

At the door, I peeked through the peephole. A large man with a black face stood on the other side. He held up a leather folder with what looked like an identification card. The curved lens of the peephole made it impossible to read. I could see that he wore the same white shirt and dark pants as the private guards at City Hall.

Just to be safe, I asked, "Who is it?"

"Mayor Glenn?" His voice was deep and resonant. It seemed to vibrate the door. "My name is Tom Wilson. I'm with Atlas Security. Mr. Lynch should have called to tell you of my posting."

I turned off the alarm and undid the locks on the door. Before I could turn the handle, my father was by my side. He said nothing, but he wasn't going to let his darling daughter open the door by herself.

"Ma'am," Wilson said. He seemed even larger when not seen through the peephole. His face was round and smooth. He smiled, showing a straight row of white teeth. His eyes shone with intelligence.

"I just wanted you to know I was here. I parked my car in your drive-way. Did Mr. Lynch explain everything?"

I said he had and thanked him for coming. I then asked if he had eaten. He said yes but thanked me for the offer. Just as I was ready to close the door, a car pulled up and parked in front of the house. Wilson saw my gaze shift and he turned. A man exited a dark sedan.

"You know him?" I could see the big guard tense.

"Yes. It's Detective West."

"He doesn't look very happy," Wilson observed.

"No, he doesn't."

Someone dropped a hot coal in my belly.

chapter 13

I ushered West in and introduced him to everyone. He was polite, even offering a slight bow when he shook my mother's hand. This evening West had exchanged his suit for a black T-shirt and gray slacks. A gold, shield-shaped badge, nestled snugly in a black leather holder just to the left of his belt buckle, gleamed in the dining room light. A smooth, padded holster rode high on his right hip.

My eyes lingered on him and for a moment I was certain everyone in the room had noticed my fixation. Without the suit coat, I could see the round muscles of his arms. The shirt lay against a table-flat stomach. The room warmed and I wondered if the heater had kicked on.

Pulling my eyes away from West, I let them drift to Celeste, who still sat at the dining room table. Her face was white as marble and her eyes red and wide.

"I'm sorry to break in on dinner," the detective said. His voice was casual and his face relaxed, but I felt there was news pressing against his resolve like water against an earthen dam.

"Have you eaten?" my mother asked. "We have plenty. I could fix you a plate."

"No, thank you, Mrs. Glenn."

"How about a plate to go? I do make a mean meat loaf, even if I do say so—"

"Mom," I said gently, touching her arm. "I think Detective West has brought us some news."

"It's about my mother, isn't it?" Celeste blurted. Fear was a pressure cooker. It worked fast and hot. I was surprised she had held out for the three minutes West had been in my home.

"No," he said with a slow shake of his head. He stared at her for a moment. "We're still working very hard to find her. I'm afraid the only good news I have on that front is from SI."

"SI?" Dad asked.

"Scientific Investigations," West explained. "They're the people who come in and examine the scene for evidence."

"Like the TV shows," Mom said.

"Exactly," West replied. "Different police organizations call them by different names. Crime Scene Investigation is a popular one. They all reduce down to some alphabet soup. Bottom line is, they do the same work."

"What did they find?" I asked.

"It's what they didn't find. They examined the house top to bottom and found no signs of blood—other than what we found on your business card. Nor did they find any evidence for . . ." He lowered his head in thought. "There was no evidence that would make us think the attack was sexual in nature."

Body fluids.

I looked at Celeste. She was motionless but I got the impression she was a balloon stretched to bursting. One more puff of air and her thin, taut membrane would rend.

"If you're not here about Lisa, then you must be here about Lizzy."

A cloud passed over his face. "I wonder if I might have a minute of your time—alone."

I had to try twice before I could force the word "Certainly" out of my throat.

"Why can't we hear?" Celeste asked.

West didn't answer; he just turned and walked to the living room. "Let's use my office," I said and started for the stairs. I walked up the treads quickly. I could hear West behind me. I moved with a confidence I didn't feel, as if we were going upstairs to chat about some real estate deal. Inside I was melting like a candle in a forest fire. I hoped I had enough steel in my spine to hear whatever West had to say without morphing into a quivering jellyfish.

"This is nice," he said as he stepped into the room. "The whole house is nice."

Small talk before the hammer fell. Like the dentist saying, "This might pinch a little," before he plunged the big-bore needle into sensitive pink gums.

"It was my husband's favorite room," I replied, helping shoulder the illusion of professionalism a few minutes longer. "There used to be a pool table up here."

"I bet that was a bear to carry up the stairs."

"I don't think the delivery men voted for me."

He chuckled politely, just enough to meet the need. Then he took a deep breath, narrowed his eyes, and donned whatever psychological armor policemen have for times like this. "Perhaps you should sit down."

I didn't like that. "I'm better on my feet."

He frowned. "There's been another abduction. I checked the campaign information you gave me. You know him."

"Him?"

"Him," West reiterated. "Allen Dayton. On the campaign papers you provided me, you had him listed as a consultant."

I decided West was right: I did need to sit down. I moved to my office chair and motioned for him to sit in a side chair I use for reading. "He's one of the principals of Dayton, Holliman, and Associates. They're out of Santa Barbara, although they work all over the country."

"What do they do?"

"They advise. They, um . . ." I forced myself to focus before I completely lost my ability to speak. "Campaigning can be tricky. To do it right, you need a good candidate and great information. Dayton, Holliman, and Associates provides full-scale campaign support. They'll run the whole thing if you want them to."

"Is that what you did?"

I shook my head. "I'm too hands-on. The idea of releasing my campaign to someone else didn't sit well. I wanted to call my own shots."

"So . . ."

"I retained them to coordinate my direct mail, polling— although at this level there isn't much polling—and demographics."

"By demographics you mean who lives where and what their income is?"

"It's more than that. It's important to know where the voters are, what precincts have the higher voter turnout, and how they vote. That way, a campaign with limited funds can target phone banks, direct mail, and such things to areas where people are likely to vote. Allen's company keeps a huge database on these facts. They have all the western states covered and can get information on any district in the country. But they do more than gather information; they process it. It helps the candidate know what issues are hot and what to stay away from."

"And they did this for you?"

"Yes. I retained them six months before the election. They did the basic work, then consulted throughout my campaign."

"Pretty pricey?"

"It can be," I admitted. "Since I ran my own campaign, it wasn't too bad. I think I paid them ten thousand dollars over the six months they worked with me."

"How well did you know Mr. Dayton?"

"Where?"

The sudden change of direction confused him.

"From where was Allen abducted?"

"He has a home just north of Santa Barbara. He disappeared from there. We don't know when. The Santa Barbara police have jurisdiction, but they called us since it so closely matched our two situations. All the surrounding Police Departments are kept appraised of our investigation."

"When you say closely matched, you mean what?"

West knew what I was getting at. He inhaled deeply. "We found a folder. It had your name on it."

"What kind of folder?"

"It was taken into evidence, so I wasn't able to look at everything it contained. Once the forensic boys are done working their magic, I'll be able to go through it in detail."

"But you saw enough to link it to me. Right?"

He nodded, then crossed his legs. "True. It was a standard manila folder, letter size. A label with your name was pasted to the tab. At first I thought it might be from the kidnapper, but the top page and the one that followed it indicated it was from your office."

"I haven't sent Allen anything in over a year, maybe eighteen months. It must have been an old file."

"I don't think so," West said. "It was dated last week. Actually, the title sheet surprised me. I didn't know you were thinking of running for Congress."

A wrecking ball crashed into the walls of my mind. How did Allen Dayton get that file? I spun in my chair and yanked open the lower file drawer. I keep my active files in two drawers in my desk. The right-hand drawer is where I keep the miscellaneous ones. It was there, the file Randi had given me two days before. I didn't know whether to feel relieved or worried. I decided on relieved. At least no one had broken into the house and stolen the file. If that had been the case, my sense of security would have dissolved like a sugar cube in hot water.

"Did it look like this?" I handed him the folder.

He studied its exterior, opened it, and examined the first few pages. "Best I can tell, it was identical. How many of these files exist?"

"Until tonight I thought that was the only one. My assistant, Randi, gave it to me just a few days ago. The whole Congress thing is her idea."

"So you're not thinking of running for higher office?"

"I didn't say that. I have no immediate plans, but Randi learned that Congressman Roth is retiring. She took it upon herself to investigate the possibility of my taking a stab at the seat."

"So you didn't send it to Mr. Dayton?"

"Like I said, I haven't had contact with him for a year or more. Randi must have sent it to him. You want me to call her?"

"No, I may need to ask her a few questions and I'd rather do that in person. May I stop by your office tomorrow morning?"

It was a chivalrous gesture. He was investigating several crimes; he didn't need my permission to talk to Randi. I said, "Of course," then asked the question that was really on my mind. "Was there . . . you know."

"Blood? Yes. But just like the first two cases, only a tiny amount." He held up two fingers.

"Two drops of blood?"

West nodded. "They were placed dead center on the outside of the manila folder, one above the other." He paused, then added, "I've been talking to a criminal psychologist. I worked with him in San Diego. He doesn't think the blood drops are geometric. You know, four drops formed a square, three drops an inverted triangle, and now two drops a line. He thinks—"

"It's a countdown." The coal in my belly fanned to flame. "The abductor is counting backward: four, three, and now two."

"You're very perceptive." The compliment was wasted. I felt no pride in the realization.

"I'm next. Four, three, two, me."

"We don't know that. We're just guessing that the blood drops are a countdown. It could be something else."

"Like what?" I jumped to my feet and began to pace the floor.

West said nothing.

"You don't have another suggestion, do you? Of course not. The countdown thing makes the most sense."

"You may not be the one he's after."

"Of course I am. Lisa was my treasurer, Lizzy did fund-raising, and Allen was my consultant. They're all associated with me. We can flush the coincidence idea."

"I'm not flushing anything. You need to sit down."

"I'm too agitated to sit." I continued pacing. "No wonder you wanted to talk to me privately."

"That is only one reason," West said softly. "Please sit down."

I didn't like the tone in his voice, and liked even less the look on his face. I took my seat.

He pursed his lips, studied his hands, and lowered the leg he had crossed a few moments before. Then he leaned forward and spoke in firm but gentle tones. "There's no easy way to do this—"

"Just say it!"

"We found Elizabeth Stout."

"That's great. Right? I mean . . ." I began to shake. "What do you mean, you found her?"

"She's dead, Mayor. Her husband identified her body thirty minutes ago."

I wasn't sure I could tolerate hearing more. Everything—my strength, my resolve—drained from me. I was Jell-O in the summer sun. I couldn't look at West, couldn't raise my eyes from the spot on the rug to which they had attached themselves. My skin felt cold and damp, my palms slick with perspiration. My heart didn't thump; it fluttered like a drummer trying to find the beat to strange music. My mind began to barricade itself from the truth I had just heard. I could almost hear heavy doors slamming shut in its desperate effort to deny access to the penetrating, burning reality.

"I'm sorry to have to tell you," West said. "I spent a half hour trying to find some way of breaking it to you that would have made the news easier to hear. I couldn't think of anything."

I nodded and started to speak. Nothing came out.

West put a hand on my knee. "This doesn't mean the others are dead. We're still investigating. There's a good chance Lisa Truccoli is still alive."

"Do you really believe that?"

His brief pause said more than his words. "It's a reasonable belief."

"But the reverse may be true."

"Yes. We have to consider that possibility."

The phone rang. Before it could ring again, a distant voice from the first floor shouted, "I'll get it." Mom was on the job.

"Where?"

"Where what?"

I found the strength to lift my head and stare into the eyes of the man who brought the news of death into my house. "Where did you find Lizzy's body?"

"Perhaps we should save the details until you've had time to adjust to the news."

"No," I insisted. "My imagination can come up with things worse than reality. Let's just get it over with."

He broke eye contact and stared over my shoulder for a moment. He had been around the police business long enough to anticipate the question, but I doubted that made it any easier. He sighed and leaned back in his chair. "The pier—under the pier, actually. A jogger caught a glimpse of her as he was running by. That was close to sunset."

"No one saw anything earlier? How can that be?"

He cleared his throat, then let loose with the facts. "She was tied to the pier during low tide. She wouldn't have been visible until the tide went out again."

The image was awful. I could see poor Lizzy strapped to the rough wood supports, trying to free herself before the water drowned the life from her. "You mean . . . you mean he strapped her to a pylon and left her there to drown?"

I was surprised to see West shake his head. "We think she was dead before the tide came in."

"How can you tell that?"

"I can't with certainty, but . . ." I could see him considering his words. "The wood supports for the pier are covered with mollusks—the California mussel, to be exact. They attach themselves to objects like the posts of a pier. Colonies of them cluster from the sea bottom to the high-tide mark. As you probably know, they have a hard, blue-black shell."

"I know what a mussel is," I said. "What does that have to do with Lizzy?"

"Mrs. Stout was tied with her back to the column. If she were alive and struggling when the water rose, there should be bruises and cuts where she rubbed against the sharp edges of the mussel shells. I didn't see that. Most likely, she was dead before she was tied up."

"That means the killer would have had to carry her body to the spot where you found her."

"Not necessarily. It's possible that he made her walk to the spot, then killed her there."

"This is sickening."

"Hopefully, we'll know more when the autopsy is done."

"Hopefully?"

West frowned. "Our killer is a smart one. Evidence is going to be hard to come by at the crime scene. He or they walked through sand, so footprints are out of the question. The body was submerged for hours, compromising evidence. Since her body was covered in cool salt water, determining time of death by body temperature is going to be difficult."

The nightmare was getting darker and more lurid. "What am I supposed to tell Celeste? She's a smart kid. Just because it was Lizzy's body that was found and not her mother's doesn't mean Lisa won't be next. Celeste will know that. This is going to tear her apart."

"She may be stronger than you realize. There's no way to control what she will think or imagine. The best you can do is be honest and be there for her."

"I suppose."

"Do you want me to tell her?"

It was a nice gesture and I wanted more than anything to say yes. "No. I'll do it." I rose from the chair again, wobbled, then found my footing.

West stood also. "Before you go, I need to ask: Do you have any idea why someone would have it in for you?"

"It really is about me, isn't it? I've been trying so hard to convince myself otherwise." I tried to come up with a reason why somebody would go to such an extent to hurt me. "I can't think of a single thing. You don't work in politics without ticking off a lot of people. There are always those who think you're a crook because you're a politician—perhaps not without reason—but I can't think of any cause so pressing that someone would abduct and kill over it."

I led West back down the stairs. My steps were slow as I tried to think of what I would say. I knew that my parents, Celeste, and Michele were waiting and would expect some explanation. Dread dogged me.

Voices came through the front door. I couldn't make out the conversation but it didn't sound all that pleasant.

"Oh, that must be Dr. Thomas." I looked over the banister and saw my mother scurrying toward the front door.

"Wait!" West demanded. Mom stopped midstep and turned toward him. West pushed by me. "Stay here," he said and trotted down the steps.

"You called Jerry?" I asked my mother.

"Of course not, dear. He called here. That was him a few minutes ago. I think he called from his car."

West placed a hand on the door and peered through the peephole. He then unlatched the door and flung it open. I was far enough down the stairs to see the security guard planted on the front stoop, his hand pressed against Jerry's chest. Jerry's face was red and his jaw tight; his hands were balled into fists.

"Is there a problem here?" West snapped as he stepped beside the security guard.

"Who are you . . ." Jerry's eyes traced West's form, lingering on his gun and badge. "Oh . . . it's you. I'm here to see Maddy. I called."

"It's my fault," Mom said. "I forgot to tell the guard. I'm sorry, Jerry."

"It's all right," I said to the guard, finishing my descent. "He's a family friend." The guard lowered his hand and West turned toward me. The tension had yet to leave his face. He stepped aside to let Jerry through, then followed him in.

"It really is my fault, officer," Mom said. "I didn't think to tell the guard. I should have let you know, too, Maddy, but you were upstairs with the detective and I didn't want to interrupt."

Jerry tossed a glance at West. West just nodded. Turning his attention to me, he said, "I'll be on my way. It's going to be a long night and I need to get back to it."

"Thank you," I said and shook his hand.

"I wish—"

"I know. I'll be in touch."

He walked through the open door and gave the guard a pat on the shoulder. "Good job, pal. Keep up the good work."

I then apologized to the security guard and promised better communication. Shutting the door, I walked back to the dining area.

"What was he doing here?" Jerry asked as he followed a step behind.

I ignored the question. My mind stumbled under the Herculean task before me. There was no good way to deliver bad news.

chapter 14

I arrived at City Hall thirty minutes late and parked in the back lot. It was full, just the way I wanted it. I had also taken a different route to work, adding a good ten miles to the trip.

My eyes skittered around the property and the building. I saw no one. I didn't feel any more comfortable.

I exited my car as if it were on fire. I kept my head up and my eyes moving. Only after I was in the building and the steel security door shut behind me did I relax. After two deep breaths I started for my office.

Last night seemed like a dream—a horrible nightmare that not even the passing of years could erase. West had left, Jerry had entered, his face chiseled with concern. I led him into the dining area, where the others still sat at the table, in front of them crumbs of peach cobbler and melting vanilla bean ice cream.

Dad was staring at me. He was reading me like he read his biographies. I stood erect, wearing a pasted-on mask of confidence, having approached with my patented "I'm still in charge" gait. My father wasn't buying it. "What happened?"

"Detective West brought some news. Some bad news." I took a deep breath. "It seems . . . it seems . . . they, um . . ." The tears broke through like Huns attacking a village. I couldn't talk. I couldn't move. All I could manage was standing, weeping, and wiping mucus from my nose.

It took nearly five minutes to compose myself. I looked up from the Kleenex my mother had given me and found five pairs of tear-filled eyes staring back at me. I inhaled deeply and then spilled the news as fast as I could. I knew of no other way to do it. My guts were a Gordian knot so tightly tied that I was sure I would live with it for the rest of my life. When I was done, there were more tears.

Celeste had been my biggest concern. Surely she would assume that Lizzy's death meant her mother was dead or soon to be so. To my astonishment, she held up better than I thought possible. Her eyes were red, her face was puffy, and her lips were pulled back against her teeth. I searched for words to say to her. I considered, "Honey, this doesn't mean your mother is dead." It was true; it was also unrealistic. I percolated a few other statements and tossed them all. Instead I reached across the table and took her hand. It was all I could think to do.

The night was lousy. I slept poorly and I know everyone else did, too. Jerry refused to leave, inviting himself to stay the night, arguing that one guard outside and one inside made more sense. I wanted to dispute the point, but he was right, and I was glad to have another man in the house.

I rose at five a.m., skipped my treadmill torture, and went downstairs. Surprisingly, Dad and Mom were sitting around the table having coffee with Jerry. We exchanged greetings, then discussed the day. Dad said he would cancel his classes and stay with the girls. Jerry suggested I stay home from work, but I laid down the law. There were things I wanted to do; I wasn't going to be put off. After

I finished my coffee, I told them, "I'm going to go shower and steal all the hot water." I did just that, then headed for City Hall.

"Good morning, Mayor," Randi said as I approached her desk. "I was starting to get a little worried."

"We need to talk," I snapped. "Please come into my office." I didn't wait to see the expression on her face. I dropped my purse in the large desk drawer and took my seat. Randi showed up a second later, a pad of paper in her hand. "Please close the door."

She did, then asked if something was wrong. I made her sit. "The file you prepared in anticipation of my running for Congress— did you show that to anyone else?"

"No," she shot back, and then hedged. "I mean, no one around here."

I raised an eyebrow.

"I made a copy and gave it to Allen Dayton, but I swore him to secrecy. I just wanted a professional opinion of my work, and he was willing to give it pro bono."

I felt a frown. "Pro bono means for the public good, Randi, not the private good."

"You get my point. It didn't cost us anything."

"He's missing."

She sat like a stone. "Missing?"

"Detective West came by the house last night. That was just one bombshell he dropped on me."

"What's that have to do with the file I gave him?"

I told her. She swallowed hard. "Oh, that's horrible."

"It gets worse." I filled her in about Lizzy. My emotions were raw and just a millimeter below the surface. I had to fight hard not to fall back into a weeping mass of mayor.

Randi raised a hand to her mouth. I gave her a few moments, then asked, "Do I have any appointments today?"

"A few. Two this morning, three this afternoon."

"Cancel them all. I have other plans. First, I need the number for the county coroner. I would like to have that right away. Then I plan on making a visit to the Police Station."

"Why do you need the coroner's number?"

"I'm inviting myself to an autopsy."

"You're not serious."

"Please get the number."

She rose and started to exit. "Just a second," I said. She turned. "Randi, you are the best assistant anyone could ever ask for. Beyond that, you're my friend. This thing about the file isn't going to change that, but I want your word that you will never do anything like this behind my back again."

"You have my word." She was on the verge of tears.

One minute later she stepped back into the office with a piece of paper. It was the phone number I'd requested. The phone was in my hand before the paper hit my desk.

The line rang twice and then a woman with a sweet voice said, "County coroner's office."

"This is Mayor Maddy Glenn," I said firmly. "I would like to speak to Mr. McKee, please." She put me on hold. As in many counties in California, our county coroner was an elected official. His work was primarily administrative. Trained medical examiners did the actual autopsies.

"Mayor Glenn," McKee said cordially. "What brings about this honor?"

"I need a favor."

I'm heading over to the Police Station," I said to Randi. "I'm going with you." She rose from her chair.

"Thanks, but no. Someone needs to man the phones."

"You shouldn't go alone. At least take a security guard with you."

I started to object, but she was right. I agreed and she placed the call. A minute later the young guard who had thrown himself into the mix when Christopher Truccoli went ballistic was standing outside the office door. I smiled at him. "Let's go, Kojak."

"Who?"

"Kojak. You know. On TV . . . Never mind. Kids!" I left the office and was soon walking across the sea of asphalt that separates City Hall from the Police Station. I walked briskly but the guard kept up easily. I watched for any movement that was out of the ordinary. To my relief I saw none.

Overhead the sun poured down through a cloudless sky. A slight wind caressed my face. I should have been praising the beauty of the day but couldn't. Death destroys so many things.

Inside the station, I thanked the guard and sent him packing.

"You don't want me to wait for you?"

"No. I'll call if I need you."

His brow wrinkled and then he left. The officer I had met before was at his station behind the counter. He recognized me and asked what he could do to help. I told him I wanted to see Detective West. He escorted me to West's office. The office is small, drab, and devoid of art. West sat behind the metal desk. A plastic bottle of orange juice was to his right, dripping with condensation.

"Mayor," he said with surprise. "What are you doing here?"

"I understand Lizzy's autopsy is going to be performed today?"

"Yes. Considering the nature of the crimes, I asked that she be put at the top of the list."

"I'm going with you."

"Where?"

"The coroner's office, of course."

"You want to witness the autopsy? Are you nuts? Have you ever been to an autopsy? It's not pretty. It's worse if you know the person."

"I can take it."

He shook his head. "With all due respect, Mayor, this isn't television. An autopsy looks bad, smells bad, it even sounds bad. Why would you want to do this?"

"I want to know as much as I can and I don't want to wait for a report."

He sighed and leaned back in his chair. "Well, I'm sorry, Mayor. You're a private citizen, and that means you need special permission from the coroner himself."

I had started to say something when a woman in plain clothes stepped into the room. I assumed she was one of the secretaries. "This just came for you, Detective. It's from the coroner's office." She handed him a fax. He read it. Set it down and rubbed his eyes.

"You are clever, I'll give you that."

"I try to plan ahead," I said with a smirk.

"I can't talk you out of this?"

"No."

The expression on his face made it clear that he wasn't used to having someone manipulate him. "I hope you brought a helmet."

"A helmet? For what?"

"For when you faint and your head bounces off the floor."

"I may surprise you."

"I doubt it. I've seen it before." He got up. "Let's go and get this over with." He stepped from the office and I followed close behind. I began to wonder about the helmet.

The Santa Rita County Coroner's Office was a ten-minute drive from City Hall. As West steered the unmarked police car, our conversation was minimal. He didn't want me along and I didn't want to explain any further why I was there. Truthfully, I'm not sure I could have. Somehow I felt I owed Lizzy that much. I also wanted details. It's a fault in my personality, and I've driven more than one person crazy by asking for more information than they had. West had been open, holding nothing back; at least that I could tell. Still, details were coming my way in bits and pieces. I suppose that's how it is in murder cases. Nonetheless, I needed to do something, I needed to be involved. I was committed to that.

That commitment began to waver the moment I entered the building where the autopsy would soon take place. It is a fairly modern stitching together of glass and concrete. Neatly trimmed grass and flowers cover the grounds. Two flagpoles stretch toward the sky, one displaying the Stars and Stripes, the other the California bear on a field of white. It seemed such a pleasant place, but my mind could not escape the nagging truth of what lay inside.

West flashed his badge at the receptionist and introduced me, then led me through a door and down a hall that reminded me of a hospital corridor. There was something in the air, an odd mix of institutional building, floor wax, and chemicals.

"Ever been here?" he asked. His dress shoes squeaked on the highly polished sand-colored linoleum. The noise, echoing off the high-gloss, pale green walls, was unnerving.

"Can't say that I have."

"I doubt you'll want to come back." It was a blunt comment but offered without anger.

We passed office doors and an employee lunchroom. I tried to imagine medical examiners, assistants, and secretaries gathered around talking sports and eating tuna sandwiches while a dozen corpses lay a short distance away. At the end of the corridor is another hall, forming a T. West turned right and I followed. He stopped suddenly.

"One of the MEs should give you a tour, but just so you know, these doors—" he pointed to a double set of metal doors to our left—"lead to the foyer where the bodies are logged in. Just beyond is the refrigeration unit. Want to see it?"

"No, thanks."

"Okay." He turned. Another pair of doors, matching those across the hall, were before us. "This is it. I don't know how many autopsies are under way, so if you're going to change your mind, now would be the time."

I shook my head, but the temptation to leave was almost overwhelming.

"Tallyho." West plunged through the doors. I steeled myself and followed.

The autopsy room is bright, its illumination provided by overhead fluorescent lights. Four metal tables stand perpendicular to the wall. Each table butts up to a square metal sink. The floor is the same light-brown linoleum but the walls are white. To one side of the room is a set of shelves that holds scores of small jars filled with fluid and containing things I don't want to know about.

"Hey, Doc," West said as he strolled in. Clearly he had been in such places many times before.

A tall man with a completely bald head and a thick yellow mustache turned. "Ah, Detective West, hero of Santa Rita." He was standing next to the closest table, on which was a body covered with a thin white sheet. The tall man's eyes were a bright blue, and his easy smile revealed crooked teeth colored by too many years of smoking. "I see you brought a guest. Detectives are getting prettier every year."

"She's not with the department. This is Maddy Glenn, mayor of Santa Rita. Mayor, this is Dr. Donald Egan."

I said I was pleased to meet him. He studied me for a second. "It's a pleasure to meet you, too. Forgive me, but—"

"She's been cleared," West explained. He pulled the fax from his pocket and handed it to Egan, who studied it and frowned. Then he shrugged. He gave the paper back to West.

"You staying for the whole thing?" he asked West.

"No, just the gross and maybe a little more."

"Okay, let's rock and roll." Egan snatched the sheet off the form on the table.

It was Lizzy. She was naked and I felt embarrassed for her. She lay on her back, gazing at the acoustic tiles on the ceiling through unblinking eyes covered with a white film. Her skin was blue and her mouth was parted as if she were about to speak. Her hair was a mess of tangles. In death she looked alien and barely recognizable. I felt my breath catch.

Egan folded the sheet and set it to one side. He then took a small tape recorder and pushed a button. I expected to see a microphone hanging from the ceiling, like on television shows, but there was none. Maybe the bigger cities and counties have the high-tech stuff. Here things seemed simple and awkward.

Egan began to speak, first stating the date. "Autopsy begins at nine-o-six and is being conducted by Dr. Donald Egan, Assistant Medical Examiner, County of Santa Rita. In attendance are Detective Jerry West—"

"Judson West," West corrected. "Jerry West was a basketball player."

"Correction," Egan said without missing a beat, "Detective *Judson* West of the Santa Rita City Police Department. Also in attendance is Mayor Maddy Glenn of Santa Rita City. Autopsy is being performed in compliance with mandates of the state of California and at the request of the Santa Rita Police, Robbery and Homicide division. Subject is Elizabeth Stout, a female Caucasian, forty-six years of age and weighing one hundred and forty-five pounds. Positive identification was made by her husband. Subject was found in a situation suggestive of homicide. An active investigation is under way. All limbs, fingers, and toes are present. No tattoos, no obvious sign of drug abuse. On cursory examination, cause of death is not apparent."

He began to touch her and I again felt great embarrassment on her behalf. First he pressed on different areas of her skull, then bent over to peer at her hair. "No indication of trauma to the head; no sign of blood in the hair." He lifted her head and moved it from side to side, spoke about levity and cervical spine being intact. I felt my face flush and I was beginning to get hot. Egan looked at her eyes, in her ears and her nose and her mouth. He paid special attention to her neck. "No signs of strangulation." He returned to her mouth and pointed out change in the texture of the skin.

"Tape," he said to West, who stood on the other side of the table. I remained several steps back. "She was gagged and for some time, I would say. It looks like her skin developed a rash from the tape. Some tests might reveal the type of tape."

"There was no tape on her mouth when we found her," West said. "It's another reason we think she was dead before being tied to the pier."

"Logical. I checked the sinus for water and didn't find any. I'll see what fluids we have in the lungs in a few minutes, but I'm betting she didn't drown."

Egan continued his exam, poking and pushing and taking samples with swabs on long, thin wooden sticks, like giant Q-Tips. He worked his way down her body and my embarrassment grew. It all lacked dignity. Lizzy was a proud woman. The thought of lying naked on a steel table while two men examined every inch of her body would have mortified her.

"No obvious signs of rape," Egan said. "But I'll take samples."

He did.

"I'm especially interested in seeing her back," West said. "I would like your opinion."

"Fine with me. Help me roll her over."

West donned some latex gloves and helped pull Lizzy onto her side. I could see her back from where I stood. It was darker than the rest of her body.

"The blood pooling is interesting," Egan said. "She was seated when you found her?"

"Yeah. A rope held her back against the post under the pier."

Egan looked at me and explained, "When someone dies, the blood moves to the lowest parts of the body and settles into the tissues. If she was killed in a seated position, the blood should have settled into the buttocks. That tissue can hold a lot of blood. But I'm seeing a more even distribution. I'd say she was supine when she died."

"What do you make of the marks?" West asked.

I watched Egan bend over and place his face near Lizzy's back. He blocked my view with his body. I was strangely grateful. He stood up and while holding her body in position, reached for a magnifying glass. Then he returned his attention to the wounds. Seconds oozed by as Egan studied each injury, tilting his head from side to side. I wondered how a man could do this work every day. He set the glass down and began probing each cut with his finger.

"Hmm. They're not deep, but then I didn't expect they would be. You told me on the phone that you saw these wounds at the crime scene and thought they were caused by mussel shells?"

"That's right."

"I'd say you're correct. What's odd is that they're relatively smooth and shallow. None of the wounds are ragged, which would indicate tearing."

"So she didn't fight against the rope or the rising water. I figure the tide action pressed her against the mussels repeatedly, developing the gashes we see. If she had been alive at the time . . ."

"She would have struggled to free herself, even panicking as the water continued to rise. Her back should be shredded but it's not."

"More proof she died elsewhere."

"That gets my vote. Hold her up while I take some shots." Egan removed a digital camera from the nearby counter and started snapping pictures of Lizzy's back. Then, with West's help, he lowered the body to its original position. I kept waiting for Lizzy to protest, but I knew she never would. It's odd how the mind continues to deny truth even in the presence of undeniable facts. Egan recited his findings for the recorder, continuing in the same dispassionate tone.

"Okay," he said to West. "If she didn't die at the scene, then she was killed elsewhere. That's your problem. My problem is discovering how she died. There are no marks around the neck to indicate strangling. The skull is whole and undamaged, so blunt force to the head is out. I find no bruises on her body, beyond that left by the rope which held her to the pier, and some ligature marks around the wrists and feet, indicating forced restraint. If she had been beaten, I would expect more bruising." He placed a gloved hand on either side of Lizzy's rib cage and worked his fingers around. "No fractured ribs. I don't think she was abused by her captors."

"Any guesses?"

"In the absence of gunshot wounds, knife wounds, evidence of beating, bludgeoning, or strangulation, I'd guess suffocation by something like a plastic bag, or maybe poison." He paused and bent over Lizzy's face again. "Usually forced suffocation causes capillary breakdown around the face, especially the mouth and nose. I don't see that." He began searching her body again but he seemed to focus on her arms. He pulled at the skin on her shoulder. "Bingo!"

"What?" West said.

Egan reached for the magnifying glass again. "Take a look at this." West rounded the metal table. Egan put a finger on Lizzy's shoulder, then handed the glass to West. "Looks like an injection mark. Could be a bite. After a night in the water, it's hard to tell."

"I see that. It's high on the arm, not likely to be self-inflicted." West turned to me. "Was Mrs. Stout a diabetic?"

My first attempt at words came out like a croak. I cleared my throat and said, "Not that I know of."

"Diabetics don't shoot insulin into their arm," Egan said. "Usually they insert the needle in the thigh. It could be nothing more than a flu shot. We won't know until the toxicology report comes back. I've already sent the blood in."

"When do we find out?" West wondered.

"I put a rush on it. Of course, everyone puts a rush on these things. I let them know that other lives might be in danger. That should get it on the top of the list. With any luck, I'll be calling you this afternoon."

"That would be great." West handed the glass back to Egan, who set it on the counter. He then stepped to one side, where a metal tray was resting on a wheeled cart, and pulled the cart close. I had paid it no notice when I first came in, because I could barely take my eyes off Lizzy's form. Now I took more notice than I wanted. The oblong tray held several scalpels, and tools that looked more suited for the garden than for a medical procedure. I had to remind myself that this was no medical procedure. There was nothing curative about it.

Egan snatched up a large scalpel, placed his index finger on the back of the blade, and positioned it just south of Lizzy's left collarbone. My blood chilled and my stomach roiled. I wanted to close my eyes, but I had told West I could take it. Now I had serious doubts.

West grabbed Egan's wrist. "Hang on a sec, Doc." The detective studied me for a moment. I tried to appear calm and strong. "You need to leave, Mayor. You do not need to see this. Lizzy was your friend. The last thing you need is the image of her autopsy burned into your brain."

"I'm fine."

"No, you're not. Dr. Egan is about to cut open someone you know, and that's the easy part. It gets worse from there. Trust me on this, Mayor. I've been to more of these than I can count and I still can't sleep at night. You need to go. Wait in the waiting room."

"But—"

"No. No buts or pulling rank. You can order the chief to fire me if you want, but I'd much rather explain why I kicked you out than why I let you stay until you tossed your cookies or passed out. Go. Get out."

There was nothing harsh in his voice, no anger in his words, but the determination was unmistakable.

"He's right, Mayor," Egan added. "Truth is, you're making me nervous."

I shook my head, turned, and exited without a word. I was ashamed at the relief I felt. Thirty steps later I was seated in the lobby, having placed myself under the closest air-conditioning vent. I felt hot on the outside and frozen on the inside. It was all I could do to hold down breakfast.

I picked up a *People* magazine and tried to lose myself in the lives of the famous, but the only image my mind would allow was that of Lizzy strapped to the pier, the water covering her lifeless body.

West emerged a half hour later. "Ready to go?"

"Done already?"

"Dr. Egan is still working, but I've seen all I need to. Now I wait for his report."

I rose from my seat and walked with him into the parking lot. After a few moments I said, "You can be pretty bossy, you know."

"It's a character flaw."

"Thanks."

He opened the car door for me and waited until I was safely in before closing it. One minute later we exited the lot and headed back to City Hall.

"Did you learn anything new?"

He shook his head. "The real evidence will probably be in the blood."

I hoped he was right.

chapter 16

"Let me ask you something," West said as he pulled the car onto the freeway.

"Sure." I was glad to be out of the coroner's building. I wanted to shake the image of Lizzy on the table, which seemed to be flash-burned into my brain.

"Was Mrs. Stout a . . . difficult woman?" He made a face. Apparently, the words failed him.

"Difficult?"

"Bad word choice." He drove in the far right lane, slower than the rest of the traffic. "What I mean is, was she headstrong, determined?"

"Oh, she was that, all right, and some more. She was a savvy businesswoman and didn't take guff off anyone. At the same time she was kind and considerate. Still, if she had an opinion, it was destined to see the light of day."

West pressed the issue. "If someone had threatened her, how do you think she would have responded?"

"I don't know. I imagine she wouldn't have taken it lying down. I once saw her chew the ear off some guy who suggested that her commission was too high. It was at a Chamber of Commerce meeting. The man left knowing how the cow ate the cabbage."

"How the what did what?"

"Something my grandmother used to say. It means she let the man know how things were. I don't have details; I wasn't party to the discussion—just in earshot."

"I see." West fell silent.

"Oh no, you don't. Don't clam up now. Why ask such an odd question?"

He sighed. "Just thinking. Why is Mrs. Stout dead? She was taken second, not first. I would have guessed that if our abductor were a murderer—"

"If? Of course he is."

"You want to hear this or not?"

"Yes."

"Then let me finish before passing judgment. I'm just thinking out loud. I go back to the question: Why did we find Mrs. Stout first? Serial criminals work with some degree of logic—granted, it's twisted logic, but it's still there. Lisa Truccoli was abducted first, then Mrs. Stout. It's possible we just haven't found Ms. Truccoli's body yet, but somehow that seems too simple an explanation."

"You're thinking that maybe Lizzy made too much of a fuss or was too hard to handle."

"Yeah, but it's just conjecture." His eyes darted to the rearview mirror, lingered, then returned to the road ahead. "There have been other serial abductions, but they usually involve young women who are kidnapped and kept as sex slaves."

"That's an image I don't need." It was a sickening thought.

"It's beyond horrible, but my point is that our women are middle-aged businesswomen, not the type associated with those kinds of cases. To make things more complex, the third person abducted was a man. Add to that the one thing we really know: they're all associated with you."

"I'm not following."

"Your friend wasn't beaten and so far there's no evidence of a sexual crime. Why is she dead? There are no visible signs of murder except an injection mark in the shoulder—if it's an injection mark. Everything is so clean: the places where the abductions took place and now Elizabeth Stout's body. I'm thinking that her death may have been unintentional."

"What!" This was too much to take in. "She was tied to a pier and left in the rising tide."

"*After* she was dead. That's important. It also tells us the perpetrator is still in the area, which means his captives can't be too far away. I doubt he would cart a dead body up and down the freeway."

"But how does that make Lizzy's murder accidental?"

"Unintentional, not accidental. It's too early to tell. The blood work will tell us more, but I can't help wondering—and that's all I'm doing here, wondering—if the abductor was trying to sedate Stout, who may have been giving him grief, and overdid it. Then he unloaded her body."

"Why put her in the ocean, tied to the pier?"

"The water's colder than the air; he's probably thinking that it would make it difficult to assess the time of death. He's partly right, but the forensics folks and the medical examiner are sharp people. They know how to adjust the calculations. Putting her in the ocean also makes it very difficult to gather clues. This guy is a thinker."

"It sounds like you admire him."

He looked at me and frowned. "Not admire, Mayor. I respect his intelligence. If I don't, he'll outthink me and everyone else on the case. I have to get into his head. This is part of the process." His eyes went back to the rearview mirror and lingered longer this time.

"What?" I asked and started to turn.

"Sit still. I think we have company. A blue van has been behind us and has had plenty of opportunity to pass."

"Oh no. A blue van followed Randi and me yesterday."

"You might have told me."

"I'm sorry. When you came over last night and gave me the news about Lizzy and Allen, I was overwhelmed."

"Fix your lipstick," he said flatly.

"What? Now?"

"There's a mirror on the back of the visor. Lower it and pretend to fix your lipstick. Tell me if the van behind us looks like the one you saw."

Pulling down the visor, I touched my lips and fussed with my hair. I could see the van in the mirror. "It's the same one."

"Interesting." The corner of his mouth rose slightly and his eyes narrowed. He pulled out his cell phone, dialed a number, and asked for the watch commander.

"Chet, it's Judson. I have Mayor Glenn in the car with me. I think someone is following us. I need two patrol cars." He gave our location and direction, then fell silent. He glanced at me. "He's having dispatch put out the call. In a minute we'll know how soon they can be here."

"You're going to stop the van?"

"That's the plan. I want to talk to the driver and—" West turned his attention back to the phone. "Yeah, I'm here." He listened. "Great. Make it a felony stop, okay?"

"Felony stop?"

"It simply means we're going to be more cautious."

"How come you didn't use the radio?"

"It might alert the driver. I'm guessing he doesn't know he's following a detective's car."

Almost on cue, the radio came to life and I heard the dispatcher send out the call and give our location. A few minutes later the radio revealed that two patrol cars had just pulled behind the van. West kept the cell phone to his ear. I heard him say, "Good. Light 'em up." He switched off the phone and set it on the seat. "Okay, Mayor, here's what is about to happen. The patrol cars are going to turn on their lights. If the guy in the van is smart, he'll pull over; if he runs, the units will give chase."

"We will, too, right?"

"We'll follow but I'm not putting your life at risk. It's the patrol officers' job to run him down."

In the passenger-side mirror I could see one of the black and white cars. Suddenly its lights went on. I turned to see the driver's response. The sun reflected off the windshield, obscuring his face, but I could see his head snapping back and forth. Then he slammed a hand against the steering wheel and moved to the shoulder of the road, slowed, and stopped.

West also pulled over. A second later he said, "Stay here," then threw his door open. He had drawn his gun before his feet hit the pavement. Immediately he took charge.

"Driver, turn off the vehicle!" West pointed his gun at the van's windshield. "Driver, throw the keys out the window." I watched as the man lowered the driver's-side window and tossed a set of keys to the asphalt. "Driver, put your hands outside the window." The man who had been following us took direction well. West gave one command at a time in a loud don't-make-me-shoot-you voice. Seconds later the driver was facedown on the shoulder and two uniformed officers were cuffing him. It was like an episode of *Cops*.

I left the car and walked toward the crowd of four men. I wanted to know who had been dogging my steps. The man in cuffs, who by this time had been pulled to his feet, was large, with a thick neck and a round, very unhappy face. He looked Hawaiian. He wore jeans and a T-shirt that read, "Bounty Hunters Do It for Money." Swell.

"I can explain, officers," the man said.

"That's good, because that is exactly what you're going to do." West was hot.

One of the officers pulled the man's wallet from the back pocket of his jeans and handed it to West.

"My name is Melvin Horn. I'm a private investigator. My ID is in the wallet."

"Why are you following us, Mr. Horn?" West asked. He rifled through the wallet. At the back he found the PI license.

"I was following the Mayor."

"Who's your client?"

"I can't reveal that. That's privileged information." Horn tried to sound cocky but was having trouble pulling it off.

"I'm investigating a serial abduction and murder case," West said. "You may think you're a private detective protecting your client, but you look like a suspect to me. Do you know what obstruction of justice is?"

"Yeah. But I ain't obstructing justice." The big man shuffled his feet. "I don't have to answer any questions. You can ask me for my driver's license and registration and that's it." He grimaced. "These cuffs are a little tight."

"Like I said, you look an awful lot like a suspect to me. Let's see, I can hold you for a day or so before your arraignment, and then you could post bond—assuming no one loses the paperwork. You have some cash stored away for bail? The mayor is under police protection, and since you won't tell me who your client is, I have to assume you don't have one. That makes me think you might be a danger to her."

"Okay, okay. I was hired by Christopher Truccoli to follow the mayor."

"Why?"

"To see if the guy's daughter was with her, then let him know."

"Did you tell him?"

"Not yet. I was going to follow you a little farther, then call him."

"Good," West said sharply. "Tell him I take exception to being followed, especially by someone as lousy at it as you. Clear?"

"Yes."

"Is there anything in the van I should know about?"

The man hedged. "I know how this works, you know. If I say no, you'll say, 'Then you don't mind if I take a look.' If I say yes, you'll have grounds to search it anyway."

"Very perceptive. Now answer the question."

"There's a 9mm Glock in the glove compartment," Horn admitted. "There's also a .25 caliber handgun under the driver's seat. I'm licensed to carry a weapon."

"You had better hope so. How about drugs? Any controlled substances in the vehicle?"

"No, and you're free to search."

"I'll let the officers do that. Just in case you don't know, there's a restraining order against your client. You might want to make sure he knows that."

"He has a right to see his daughter," Horn objected.

"Not when that daughter is an adult and refuses to see him. Your client is digging a hole for himself, and he may just pull you down with him." West removed a business card from the wallet. "This yours?"

"You can see my name on it."

"So I can, so I can. Mind if I have it?"

Horn lowered his head and sighed. "No. Take it."

"Thanks." West handed the wallet to one of the officers. "Make sure his licenses are up to date, both the PI and the weapons. Check for wants and warrants. Oh, if you find anything worth booking him for, let me know. I might want to talk to him again."

West took me by the arm and led me back to the car. "I thought I told you to stay put."

"I want to know who's hunting me. Besides, you had the cuffs on him." He opened my door and I took my seat. Then he got in, started the car, and pulled back onto the freeway.

"This case is bad enough without Truccoli messing things up," West said. "I can't figure his sudden interest in his daughter. From what I've learned, he's shown no concern for her since he bailed on the family. Why does he care now?"

"I don't know. Guilt, maybe." I shook my head. "I'm not sure he's all that balanced."

"He's not crazy. He's driven, but by what?"

"Maybe it's not what but whom. His new wife could be pushing him."

"I don't think he pushes all that easy. I put the pressure to him and it hasn't slowed him down much."

"Will you let me know what the medical examiner says about the blood work?" I asked, changing the subject. I'd had all the talk of Truccoli I wanted.

"I will. It'll probably be tomorrow. For now, I'm taking you back to your office."

"It seems there should be more than what we're doing. I know you're doing your best; I just wish there were something else. Can't the FBI help?"

"Not unless we have evidence that one of the abductees was moved across state lines. You should know that there is more going on than you see. In fact, I left the autopsy early to make it back in time for a task force meeting . . ." He had the look of a man who realized he had just made a big mistake.

"A task force?"

"With cases like this, it's customary to bring in other law enforcement agencies: Sheriff's Department, Highway Patrol, other municipal agencies, even parole officers who might pick up something from their charges."

"When is this meeting?"

He let a few seconds tick by before answering. "Eleven o'clock."

"At your office."

He nodded. "In the conference room."

"I see."

He saw, too.

It was barely 10:30 when I set my fanny down in my office chair. My stomach was a mess from my stint in the autopsy room and then churned up even more by the confrontation with Horn. This day had started off badly and I feared that darker clouds were on the horizon.

I placed my elbows on the desk and rested my head in my hands. I had not slept well in two days, and the emotional toll was building. I felt like an earthen dam ready to give way. I wanted answers and the more I searched for them, the more questions I found.

"How'd it go?"

I looked up and saw Randi standing in the doorway. Her office had been empty when I first entered. I'd assumed she was in the rest room. "Hard. I don't want to talk about it." My words were harsher than I intended. I was still angry about her sending the file to Dayton.

Her head drooped a little. "Here are your messages." She set several pieces of pink paper on my desk. I looked them over. My depression deepened.

"Doug Turner wants to talk to you again," Randi said. "He knows about Lizzy."

"There's nothing I can tell him. I don't want to meet with him."

"He . . ."

"What?"

"Don't kill me. I don't know how, but he knows about the file."

"The congressional campaign file that you prepared? How is that possible?"

"Like I said, I don't know. I certainly didn't give it to him."

"I didn't say you did."

"Yeah, well, I still feel guilty. I have more bad news. You agreed to speak to the Young Republicans at Santa Rita High."

"What?" I looked at my calendar. There it was. I had forgotten. "When?" I asked even as I read the time.

"Eleven-thirty. I should have reminded you yesterday, but with everything—"

"No, it's not your fault; I can read my own calendar. I should have checked it." *There goes the task force meeting, Swell.* I explained about wanting to go to the meeting with West.

"You want me to cancel?"

"No. It's important that I fulfill my duties. This has been in the works for some time and it's too late for them to get a replacement."

"What about Turner?"

"I suppose I should speak to him, if for no other reason than to find out how he came to know about the file." I slammed my hand down on the desk. "The harder I try to get control, the more chaotic things become!"

"I wish I could do more for you." Randi looked crestfallen.

"Close the door." She did. I motioned for her to have a seat. It was time to mend fences. I began by bringing her up to date. I told her about the autopsy and about the private investigator hired to track my movements. I also filled her in on all that West had said.

She shook her head slowly. "We go through life hearing and reading about crimes against people we don't know but give it little thought. When it's this close to home, I can't think of anything else."

"Me either. I don't sleep well and I've lost my concentration, today's speech being evidence of that. I can't believe how completely I forgot it." I paused to gather my thoughts. "Okay, what are we going to do about Turner? You said he knows about the file. That doesn't mean he's actually seen it, right?"

"I can't say for sure, but there are only three copies of that file. You have one, I have another, and Allen Dayton had the third."

"Two drops of blood were found on the file cover. That would render it evidence. The cops wouldn't turn that over to Turner. At best, he merely knows of the file's existence."

"That's my guess. I suppose he could have found out about it by interviewing some of the police."

"Perhaps. Maybe I should agree to an interview." It was an idea, although I doubted it would lead anywhere. Perhaps I could persuade Turner to keep quiet about the whole thing. "Call him and tell him my schedule is full, but that I could meet him at the coffee shop near the high school."

"The Brewed Bean?"

"That's the one. I'll meet him at twelve-thirty. Don't tell him about the Young Republican thing. I'd rather he not be there. He might want to ask some of his questions publicly."

"He may already know about it. The school sometimes publishes these things."

"If so, then there's nothing I can do about it, but I don't see any reason why we should be the ones to inform him."

"Got it."

"Go with me, Randi. After we meet with Turner, we can grab some lunch."

She smiled. "I'd love to."

Fences mended.

"Okay, now get out of here; I have to come up with a speech in the next twenty minutes."

The speech went well, although I had to wing it. In front of me had been the fresh faces of the high school's Young Republicans. The office of mayor was technically a nonpartisan position, but everyone knew of my affiliation.

I strode into the meeting place as if I owned it, and had thirty seconds to spare. Randi was close behind. The club met in the cafeteria. Folding doors on tracks in the ceiling were pulled shut, separating us from the rest of the large, sterile-looking room. Despite the sound-dampening doors, I could hear the bang of pots and pans, and the constant chatter of workers. Lunch had begun, and several of the students in our meeting had trays with plates of hamburgers and potato chips.

Only twenty students had shown and I felt disappointment. Government and politics is my passion; I expect others to share it. It's an unrealistic expectation. A teacher who served as the club's sponsor called everyone to order, then introduced me. He was a tall, thin man with dwindling hair.

I stepped to the area designated as the front and readied myself for the presentation. Just as I did, Doug Turner walked in. I tried not to frown but was only partially successful. He made eye contact with me, then raised his hands as if surrendering. He mouthed the word *relax*. I hoped he was as good as his unspoken word.

I spent ten minutes discussing the importance of city government and how I became interested in politics. I followed with five minutes on the issues our city faced. That left fifteen minutes for questions before a bell would ring, sending them all back to classes. Fortunately, the questions were benign. My greatest fear was that someone would ask about Truccoli's attack and the abductions of Lisa and Lizzy. Lizzy's death and Dayton's disappearance had yet to make the papers, but I suspected they would be in the morning issue.

I fielded about fifteen questions, then turned it over to the instructor. The kids were nice enough to applaud and only one fell asleep. Not bad. True to his word, Turner had made no inquiries. A few moments later the room was nearly empty. I exchanged pleasantries with the teacher.

Randi stepped next to me and we watched Turner approach. He had spent a few minutes with a young man, one of the students who had been listening to my impromptu presentation. He was the only one taking notes.

"I thought our meeting was for twelve-thirty at the Brewed Bean." I was trying to sound sweet but professional.

"It is," he said with a slight smile. "I should have mentioned when you called that I was going to be here."

"You're not obligated to tell me your schedule." *But it would have been nice.*

"I had two other calls going when your office called. I just forgot to mention it. I don't want you thinking I was trying to ambush you—not that I'm above that." He laughed. "My nephew attends here. That's who you saw me talking to. He works for the school paper and I serve as a consultant." He scratched quotation marks in the air as he said *consultant.* Turner looked at his watch. "Is it all right if we go ahead and meet? By the time we get to the coffee shop, we'll only be about ten minutes early."

"That's fine with me."

Randi and I made our way back to the car. The day was bright, the sky a silky blue and the air warm as a blanket. Freshly cut grass sweetened the breeze. Looking up, I saw a distant airplane sailing through the air, destined for some unknown location. I wished I were on it.

The Brewed Bean is a Starbucks knockoff. They even use the same green color scheme. While their decor is far from original, they make great coffee. Randi and I arrived a few seconds before Turner. "Why do you suppose he didn't ask you any questions?" she wondered.

"I don't know. He could have really put me on the spot and made himself look good in the eyes of his nephew. Maybe he's saving it all up to unload on me now."

We got in line. The place was hopping and the line long but it moved quickly. Turner took his place behind us. To make small talk, I asked about his nephew. He sang the boy's praises but I remember little of what he said. My mind was trying to anticipate the questions he would ask and the answers I would give.

I reached the front of the line and offered to buy the reporter's coffee. "No, thanks," he said. "I don't want it said that I was bought off by a double latte. I'm scrupulous about such things."

"Scrupulous?" I placed my order, buying myself a chai tea and Randi a blended coffee. "Not a word you hear every day."

"Not from a reporter's mouth, anyway," Turner said.

"The same could be said for most politicians."

The place was crowded but we found a round table on the patio in front of the shop. We settled in. I was glad to be outside. Lately I had been breathing only the air found in my car, house, or office. Sparrows hopped around on the concrete, hoping for crumbs from some pastry.

"That was a good speech," Turner said.

"Thank you." I decided to take the offensive. "How did you know about the file?"

"I'm an investigative reporter; I investigate." He saw that the answer didn't appease me. "I've been following the police radio traffic. I was at the scene where Allen Dayton was abducted. I must have broken fifteen speed laws getting to Santa Barbara, and you know how the traffic bottlenecks as you get into town."

"One of the police officers told you about the file?"

Turner sipped his coffee. "Yes, but not one of yours. It was a Santa Barbara guy. A uniformed cop. He was the first one on the scene and saw the file."

"And he opened it?" Randi asked.

"Nah, at least I doubt it. The file had a label on it with the mayor's name and the word *Congress*. Since our mayor is, well, our mayor, I have to ask why that word would appear on a folder. Why is that, Mayor? Thinking of moving up in the world?"

Here's where I had to be careful. "I have not filed to run for any other office. My job keeps me plenty busy."

Turner laughed. "Why is it that every time politicians are thinking of running for higher office, they deny it when asked? It's like they're ashamed of wanting to do more for the community. Are you planning on running, Mayor?"

"I have no such plans at the moment." I was sounding evasive and I hated it.

"But there is a file, and Allen Dayton is . . . was . . . a political consultant, right?"

"There is a file but I didn't prepare it. I only recently became aware of it." Keep the answers short, I reminded myself. Politicians get into trouble by saying too much.

"If you didn't prepare it, then who did?"

"It is not unusual for concerned citizens to encourage someone to run for office."

"You're being evasive."

"And you're being invasive. All I am willing to tell you is that I neither prepared the file nor called for its preparation. Its existence came as a surprise to me."

"Could Dayton have made it?"

"I suppose. That's what he does for a living." The word *living* struck me hard. Was he still living? "I'm not saying that he did."

"Do you have knowledge that he didn't prepare it?"

I sipped my tea to buy a few seconds. "What is the point of all this?"

"I'll take that as a yes." He paused. "I'm worried about you, Mayor, and you know why. Congress or no congress, something is happening around you, and I'm afraid it's all going to fall down around your ears."

"I appreciate your concern, but we have good people on it."

"I'm sure you do, but I'm still worried. It doesn't take a savant to know you're right in the middle of this and you don't know why. Do you know why?"

"No," I admitted.

"Neither do I. I'm betting the police don't, either. I want you to know that I'll help any way I can. I have to report the news—that's my job and my passion—but that doesn't mean I write off the people who matter." He set down his cup. "Do you have a comment to make about Allen Dayton's abduction?"

"Only that I hope he is well and returned home soon."

"Does Dayton have family?"

"Not that I know of. He once told me that his wife died a few years before. I think she died of Lupus. He said they had no children."

Turner rose. "Thanks for the meeting, Madam Mayor. Be careful." He started to leave, then stopped and returned his attention to me. "For what it's worth, if you run for Congress, I'll vote for you."

He walked away.

chapter 10

hat was far less painful than I thought it would be." Randi raised the straw of her iced drink to her lips. "I thought you handled him well."

"I think he handled me, Randi." I watched Turner enter his car and drive off. My eyes tracked to another man seated in a truck. His red Ford pickup faced us. It looked new. The man's features were narrow and drawn. When our eyes met, he quickly looked away. An alarm began to sound in my brain.

". . . in the paper?"

"I'm sorry, what did you say?"

"I asked if you thought you might be reading about your congressional campaign in tomorrow's paper. You think he'll write something?"

"I don't know—and there is no congressional campaign. I've made no decisions."

"Why didn't you tell him I was the one who prepared the report? It wouldn't have bothered me."

"Because then he would have started pressing you for information. He has a job to do and I don't fault him for doing it, but his work is making things more difficult for me, for us. The less he knows right now, the better."

A movement caught my attention. The man was exiting his truck. He did so leisurely—too leisurely, it seemed to me. He was thin and wore jeans that covered his cowboy boots. His hair was light and short. An unzipped LA Dodgers windbreaker covered his dark-blue shirt.

"Let's move inside," I said, then rose.

"Why? It's nice here."

I didn't answer; I just went back into the shop, knowing Randi would be close behind. Inside there was still a crowd of people. Some stood in line waiting to order, some waited impatiently for their coffee, and some sat in light wood chairs at matching round tables. I was hoping there was safety in numbers.

"What's the matter with you?" Randi whispered in my ear. She was standing just behind me and to my right.

I saw an empty table in the back of the room. "Over there." The place had only one exit. If someone was going to nab me, they were going to have to do it in front of other people and drag me across the shop. But that didn't make sense: a public kidnapping? Still, I was in no mood to take chances.

"You're freakin' me out."

We sat down and rested our drinks on the table. I turned to see the man in cowboy boots saunter in. "I think that man has been watching us."

"The skinny-faced wrangler?"

"Yeah, him."

He looked around, spied us, and moved our way.

"Brazen, isn't he," Randi said.

As he approached, I could see a day's growth of stubble on his chin. "You're Madison Glenn, aren't you?"

"Who wants to know?" Randi demanded.

The man reached inside his windbreaker and I tensed, waiting for the gun to appear. Instead of shiny steel a leather case emerged. He opened it to reveal a picture ID. "My name is Ned Blair; I'm a private detective."

I looked at the identification. It appeared to be real. Two encounters with PIs in one day. It was more than I could fathom. "What do you want?"

"May I sit down?" He reached for a chair.

"No," Randi snapped. "This is a private meeting." She surprised me.

"Fine," Blair shot back. "I'm trying to be decent about this."

"About what?" I asked.

"I was retained to deliver a message." He looked tired. "Mr. Christopher Truccoli wants to speak to his daughter. He wants you to arrange it."

"I already know what he wants. The decision is not mine and he knows it. I've explained it to him, the police explained it to him, now you can explain it. There's a restraining order leveled against Mr. Truccoli. I don't want to see him."

"He made me aware of the restraining order. That's why I'm here and he is not."

"The message has been delivered; now take off," Randi said.

"Aren't you a testy one." He turned back to me. "Mrs. Glenn—"

"Mayor Glenn," Randi corrected.

Blair sighed. "Mayor Glenn, a man has a right to speak to his daughter. You stand in the way of a simple, well-understood privilege."

"I've already told you, the decision is not mine. The girl is nineteen. She has the legal right to see or not see whomever she likes."

"Got it, pal?" Randi said. "Now buzz off."

His eyes narrowed. "This doesn't concern you."

"I hate guys like you," Randi snapped. "You stroll up to two women and think you can intimidate us. Well, you can't. We're not buying it. Bullying women is out, Galahad, now take a hike. And find a razor. The stubble look died in the eighties."

"I don't know who you are, lady, but I've had my fill of you."

"You know where the door is. Don't let it hit you in the butt on the way out."

I stole a glance at Randi. Her jaw was set like a vice and there was a red tint to her face. She was hot, really hot, something I had never seen. I was afraid she would explode and that if she did, it wouldn't be pretty.

"Why don't you shut your pretty yap—"

"Is there a problem here?" It was a new voice, deep and resonant, as if someone had turned up the bass in the room. I snapped my head around and saw a thick-necked man in paint-splattered coveralls approaching. He was six inches shorter than Blair and pudgy around the middle, but something in his eyes told me there was more behind the soft exterior. He stepped to within inches of the now red-faced PI, his head tilted back to make eye contact.

"Mind your own business," Blair said.

"I'd rather mind yours." The painter smiled and I felt a chill. Behind him, I saw a frightened-looking employee at the counter pick up the phone. *Good girl. Call the police.*

"You're interfering with my work," Blair growled. "I'm a private detective—"

"And you're interfering with my coffee break." I didn't think it was possible but the painter moved forward. "You wanna pick on someone? Pick on me, Sherlock. Or do you prefer frightening women?"

"What? You wanna go?" Blair's hands tightened into fists. They seemed to be familiar with the position.

"Um, guys . . ." I stood, backing to the wall. This wasn't going well, and I didn't want to be in the middle of it. "Everyone take a deep breath and—"

Blair struck the painter on the chin, spinning him around, but he didn't go down. Instead he staggered back, touched his chin, then grinned. The smile lowered the temperature in the room. He spoke in an icy tone. "There are only three things in the world I love: my wife, my work, and a good fight." He sprang forward with surprising agility. Blair raised a fist, but before he could launch it, he had a bellyful of the painter's head, driving him backward as if he had been hit by a speeding car.

I heard a grunt from the painter, a curse from the PI, and a scream from Randi.

The two men crash-landed on her. The chair she was sitting on shattered and the three fell to the floor.

"Stop it!" I shouted.

They paid no attention. Fists flew, elbows jabbed, and scorching epithets filled the air.

"Get off me!" Randi pleaded.

I grabbed the painter and pulled with all my strength, but it was like trying to move a sack of bricks. The two were intertwined. The painter fired a fist at the face of Blair, who moved his head out of the way. The blow caught Randi in the sternum; she coughed out a hard breath.

"You're hurting her!" I cried as loudly as I could. I looked at the other patrons. They were backing away. A mother hurried her children out of the shop. Two young men smiled and seemed to be enjoying the show.

"Someone help us!"

No one did. I stepped around the grappling men and tried to pull Randi from beneath their bulk. She was grimacing.

"Move!" a voice shouted.

I turned to see two men in uniforms pressing through the crowd.

"I said move!" An officer pushed one of the patrons aside.

More fists flew, more punches landed. Randi writhed in agony.

"Break it up," the first officer said. He didn't wait for compliance. Seizing the painter by the collar, he did what I couldn't; he not only pulled him off Blair, he yanked the shorter man upright. The painter raised a fist, ready to send it into the officer's face, then stopped short.

"Whoa." He dropped his arm. "Sorry, Officer. I thought—"

"Shut up." The officer spun him around and pulled him to the front of the coffee shop. "Hands on the counter—spread 'em."

"But I'm the good guy." A moment later he was in handcuffs.

"On your belly," the second officer ordered Blair, still struggling with him. "Stop resisting."

"You ain't got no right. I was just doing my job."

"Roll over, pal, or the pepper spray comes out."

The struggle ended.

I dropped to my knees and bent over Randi. Tears rolled down her cheeks. Her breath came in ragged sobs. "My ankle. I think it's broken."

Turning to the first officer, I said, "We need an ambulance."

"I'll decide that," he replied, then looked at me. His expression said he recognized me. "Yes ma'am." He raised his radio to his mouth.

"Try to lie still," I told Randi. "Help is on the way."

"I'm sorry. I'm so sorry."

"There's nothing for you to be sorry about," I said, but I knew what she was getting at. "You didn't do anything wrong."

"I didn't do anything right.... I was just ... just trying ..." Sobs swallowed her words. I sat on the floor and stroked her hair. I felt helpless.

I was feeling that way a lot.

I arrived at the hospital an hour after Randi. The police needed a report and I was the one to give it to them. I explained about Blair and the painter who came to our "rescue." They asked me a thousand questions and I answered as fast as I could, wanting to get to the hospital. I referred them to Detective West. "He can give you all the background that led to this."

"In some ways you're lucky, Mayor," the lead officer said. "I've arrested Blair before. He's got a real bad temper. He's been in the slammer for assault several times."

"It's a wonder he has a PI license," I replied.

"That was revoked some time ago. He keeps working anyway. Some people don't worry about credentials, if you know what I mean."

I did know. Christopher Truccoli was one such person.

The drive to the hospital was agonizing. I felt guilty because Randi had been hurt, and I didn't understand why. I was as much a victim as she, but she was the one injured. I was feeling like the reincarnation of Typhoid Mary. People I counted as friends were being damaged and destroyed. My own family had to move in with me for security reasons. Lizzy Stout was dead, Lisa Truccoli was still missing, and her distraught daughter was living with me and being hounded by her estranged father. Allen Dayton was gone and now Randi was in the hospital. Being associated with Mayor Maddy Glenn was becoming a dangerous occupation.

Pacific Horizon Hospital is a four-story building on the east side of the freeway, nestled in the side of a gentle hill. It has a fine reputation, is well staffed, and sticks out like a sore thumb. In a city where most of the buildings pay homage to mission-style architecture, PHH is a glass-and-concrete monstrosity with all the character of a cardboard box. That is the exterior. Inside, bright colors decorate the walls and artwork hangs everywhere. Despite the joyful interior design, however, it is still a hospital. The smell, the intense activity, the rooms, the doors—everything says medical institution.

I parked in the visitor lot, walked briskly through the automated glass doors that opened into the emergency room, and marched to a window in one of the interior walls. A sign hung over it: "Emergency Check-In."

"My name is Maddy Glenn," I said to a well-padded middle-aged woman in green scrubs. "My assistant was just brought in by ambulance. I would like to see her."

"Her name?" the woman asked without making eye contact. I wondered how many times a day she went through this routine.

"Randi Portman—that's Randi with an *i.*"

She turned to her computer and typed in a name, then nodded. "Yes, I see her name. She's in the back."

"Do I go through this door?" I asked, motioning to a large metal door to the left of the window.

"No ma'am. Visitors are not allowed in the ER."

I hadn't planned on this. "Look, I'm very concerned about her. I would like to be by her side."

The woman shook her head. "I'm sorry, it's hospital rules. We're unusually busy today. The ER has been closed to everyone except patients and immediate family."

Frustration bubbled in me. It was time to pull out my title. "As I said, I am Maddy Glenn—Mayor Maddy Glenn."

"Really?" She smiled. "You're mayor of Santa Rita?"

I blinked in disbelief. By now I should be used to the fact that less than half of the voting population can name the members of their city council. "Yes, I'm mayor of Santa Rita. May I come back?"

"No exceptions, Mayor. Rules are rules. You understand."

"No, I don't. I just want to be near my friend. I'm not going to cause any problems or get in the way."

"If the hospital makes an exception for you, then it will have to make exceptions for everyone."

I considered just marching through the door, doubting they would throw me out on my ear. But then again . . .

"You can have a seat in the waiting room. I'll let you know when you can see her."

I frowned but held my tongue. I'm sure the hospital had rules for a reason, and it was selfish of me to expect special treatment. Still, I felt I had a right to a measure of selfishness. I turned my back to the nurse and glanced around the waiting room. Impatient patients filled half the vinyl seats. I wondered how many viruses and bacteria made their home on the surface of those chairs.

I found a seat in the corner, where I could see the resolute nurse. Three chairs down was a toddler with mucus drying on his upper lip. A man in his forties held a bloody handkerchief to the palm of his left hand. He caught me looking at him and smiled. "Band saw. It's just a nick. The price I pay for new kitchen cabinets." I nodded and smiled back. I didn't want to hear more. A grand-mother-type sat in the opposite corner holding a crying child. The kid's face was red, and she appeared to have been crying for some time. The lady gazed into space, oblivious to the caterwauling.

I pulled my cell phone from my purse and called the office. Fritzy answered cheerfully and I brought her up to date. She asked what she could do and I told her to take messages.

"Councilwoman Tess and Councilman Adler mentioned that they wanted to talk to you," she said. "They asked me to tell them if you called."

"I'm too drained for that now." I was glad I hadn't shared my cell phone number with them. Only family and certain friends have it. I prefer to keep office calls in the office.

"What shall I tell them?"

"The truth, Fritzy. They can do with it whatever they want." I said goodbye and pressed the end button. Returning the phone to my purse, I settled in for an exasperating wait. Weariness settled over me like fog over the ocean. I was spent. What I wanted most was an hour in the tub, surrounded by hot water and scented candles. I closed my eyes and took several cleansing breaths. When I opened them, I saw a man in a white coat stroll through the entry doors of the ER. It took a second for my clouded mind to recognize him. He walked with his head down, as if looking for a lost quarter.

"Jerry!"

He stopped and turned toward me, then smiled. I stood as he approached.

"What are you doing here?" I asked.

He laughed. "I'm a doctor, remember? One of my patients had surgery this morning. I'm here checking up on the tyke."

I felt foolish. "Of course. I'm not thinking clearly." I rubbed my eyes.

"The important question is, what are you doing here? Are you ill?" He motioned for me to sit and joined me, taking my hand.

"No, I'm fine. It's Randi; she was hurt."

"How? What happened?"

I told the story in a voice just above a whisper and hated every moment of it. To tell it was to live it again.

"Are you okay?"

"Yes, I'm fine. Tired, worn out, but okay. I'm also a little confused. I've never seen Randi that confrontational before. She seemed like a different person."

Jerry let his gaze slip back to the floor. I wondered what he saw. "Did something happen between the two of you?"

"What do you mean?"

"Did you have a fight, exchange words or something?"

"No—well, I was pretty rough on her about contacting Allen Dayton without my permission, but we didn't argue."

"But she took it personally?"

"She's a very conscientious worker."

Jerry nodded. "Randi may have been compensating. She disappointed you with the Dayton thing, and she may have been unconsciously trying to make it up to you by defending you."

The fog lifted a little. "Of course, that must be it." Randi had never done anything to cause me to question her loyalty. The whole affair with Dayton could be written off as youthful enthusiasm. I shook my head, beginning to feel guilty.

"I'm just guessing here but I've seen it before. In a sense, her exaggerated behavior is a compliment."

"They won't let me back to see her."

"That's not unusual. The ER is hard enough to navigate without nonessentials clogging the aisles. This hospital is pretty strict."

"Could you check on her?"

"I can do better than that. Come on." He stood. I sat, puzzled. "You coming or not?"

"But—"

"As long as you're with me, things will be fine." He extended his hand and I took it, rising from the chair. His hand was smooth but strong. It felt good and supportive. He led me to the door next to the admissions window, opened it, and went in as if he were walking into his own home. The matronly nurse spun in her chair, then stood. She saw Jerry and it was enough for her to hold her tongue. "We'll just be a moment," Jerry said with authority.

"Bay four," the nurse said. "Doctor Knowles is there now." She nodded toward the back of the large room.

The ER is a large rectangle. The bays the nurse referred to have light-blue curtains that hang from thin chains attached to ceiling rails. Several of the bays were closed off by the drapes. Bay four was open. A stout man with red hair stood next to a bed. His white coat seemed too small for his wide shoulders. Randi lay on the bed, her left leg elevated. She waved as she saw us approaching. The doctor turned to face us.

"Hey, Jerry. You're a long way from peds."

"Ted," Jerry said with a nod. "I'm just checking on a couple things. Have you met our esteemed mayor?"

"Never had the pleasure. Ted Knowles." He offered his hand and I shook it.

"Maddy Glenn."

"Isn't the patient supposed to be the center of attention?" Randi asked with a weak smile. "If not, I'm leaving."

"No, you're not," Dr. Knowles said. "I'm keeping you overnight for observation."

"How is she, doctor?" I asked.

"Hey, now," Randi said. "Let's not start talking like I'm not here."

"Sorry. How are you feeling?"

Randi turned to Knowles. "How am I feeling, Doc?"

He laughed a little. "I was just getting ready to explain that. The good news is, you're going to be fine; the bad news is that you won't be roller-skating anytime soon. You have a radial fracture of the distal tibia and a pretty banged-up knee."

"Banged-up knee?" Randi said. "Is that doctor talk?"

"Impressive, eh? You have some bruising around the patella and some swelling. That will pass in a few days. The X-rays show no permanent damage. The ankle will take longer. You also have a slight concussion. That's why I'm keeping you overnight. I'm sending you over to casting. They'll fit you with a really stylish new boot."

"Oh, swell," Randi groaned. "Do you know what that will do to my tan?"

"You shouldn't be tanning anyway," Knowles said. "It wrinkles the skin, and then there's that whole skin cancer thing."

"Now I feel better. At least I won't have to mess with pantyhose. How long will I need a cast?"

"Six weeks or so. A short time in a young life."

"I don't feel young. I do feel foolish, however."

I stepped forward and took her hand. "I'll be here when they take you to your room. Is there anything I can get for you?"

"You don't need to do that. You need to get back to the office."

"I've already called Fritzy. She's taking care of the calls and schedule until I get back. There's nothing to worry about."

"I've already been replaced." She squeezed my hand, then spoke in choked words. "I'm sorry. Really I am."

"I know." I fought back a fresh batch of tears.

chapter 17

I hadn't gone straight home from the office. I needed some time to myself. The dream of Peter, the image of Lizzy's body on the autopsy table as Detective West and the medical examiner discussed her demise in cold, emotionless terms, the encounter with Turner, Randi's work behind my back, and her injury in the coffee shop confrontation—all of it ate at me. I was an emotional mess and I didn't want others to know it. If I had made the short drive from office to home without some decompression time, my mother would have sensed my pain before I cleared the front door. Age had stolen nothing from her motherly intuition.

When I drove from the lot, I'd had no particular destination in mind. I was looking for the illusive nowhere, a place where I was not mayor, not employer, not daughter, not friend, and not target. I wanted precious moments of anonymity. Somehow I ended up on the pier.

Maybe I'd driven there because it was a public place but not usually crowded. Maybe I wanted to watch the sunset over the distant horizon. Maybe it was because they had found Lizzy's body below the very deck upon which I stood. That was it. I had come to say I was sorry, to apologize to a woman who died because of her connection to me.

I'd parked in the lot and strolled along the creosote-soaked boards that make up the decking. They are black-brown and worn from years of foot traffic. Heavy spikes hold the planks in place. I walked as if carrying cement on my shoulders, my head down, my eyes fixed to the surface. Each step took me farther over the water. I could see between the planks; small gaps allow water to drain off during rainstorms. Below, blue water was turning green and becoming capped with white foam as waves churned their way through the support posts.

I wondered which post they had found Lizzy tied to. The thought chilled my soul and filled me with the heat of nausea. I continued toward the pier's terminus. My feet felt weighted, as if heavy mud were accumulating on my shoes. A chilly wind skipped off the ocean, and the waves rose and rolled in beat with the breeze. I felt goose bumps pop up on my flesh. I kept my head down to shield my face from the wind and to avoid making eye contact. I passed the Fish Kettle but paid it little mind. My appetite was dead.

I reached the end of the pier and leaned against the wide wood rail. The weather has worked the wood over, like a boxer pounding a body bag until it is misshapen and taped to hold its guts in. The grain of the dark wood has risen in response to years of direct sunlight, ocean spray, and wind, leaving the surface rough to the touch. Several carved initials and a few obscenities mar the rail. I've never understood the latter. I can appreciate why someone would feel compelled to etch the initials of their great love into the soft wood, but scratching offensive words seems a waste of time, merely concrete and public proof that one has nothing better to say.

The edge of the rail also has a string of V-shaped grooves notched into its edge. Those I understand. Local fishermen notch the wood so their poles won't slide to one side when they lean them against the railing. It is still defacement, but at least it serves a logical purpose. I felt an awful lot like that rail—battered and carved up.

Overhead, white gulls circled and studied me with practiced eyes. Seeing I carried no bait that might serve as an easy meal, they moved on. The air was thick with salt, and the sky shifted hues from blue to slate gray. The sun dipped to the edge of the horizon, yielding the sky to the press of night.

"I never get used to it."

The voice startled me. I turned and saw Paul Shedd two steps away, wearing a waiter's apron. He smiled. "The sunset, I mean. I never get used to it and I pray that I won't. I don't like taking things for granted, especially creation."

"Hi, Paul," I said, trying to sound normal. I failed. He glanced at my face, then stepped forward and leaned his arms on the rail, his face toward the undulating ocean.

"I come here when the work gets to me," he said as if we had been talking for the last half hour. "I love the Fish Kettle. Buying it and leaving the banking world is one of the best things I've ever done. Still, it gets to me from time to time and I need some fresh air. This is the best place for it."

I turned my gaze to the water. "Working over the ocean has its advantages."

He nodded but said nothing.

I started to tell him I was in no mood for company or conversation, but I didn't. I'm not sure why. I came here to be alone and now I had company. I couldn't bring myself to protest.

"I'm sorry you're going through so much," he finally uttered.

How could he know what I was going through? It took a moment for me to realize that the local paper had carried a short article about the abductions. It took another moment for me to make another connection: Paul Shedd owned the Fish Kettle, a restaurant smack in the middle of the pier. There was a good chance he had seen the police recover Lizzy's body.

I nodded. "It's been a strange journey ..." I needed to correct myself. "It *is* a strange journey."

"I can't even imagine." The conversation paused, and then he surprised me. "I owe you an apology." His voice was tight, as if he had to push the words out. He rubbed his hands together as though trying to remove a stubborn spot.

"An apology? I can't think why."

"I may have wronged you, but there was no way for you to know that." He let his eyes drift down to the darkening water. The breeze picked up. It felt colder. "How long has it been since Peter left us?"

Left us? That was an odd phrase. It sounded like Peter's death had been a choice. "I can never decide if it was an eternity ago or the week past. It seems like a long time, but it hurts like yesterday." That was more than I wanted to reveal. I chastised myself. "Eight years ago."

"Eight long years. I can't believe I let that much time pass."

Another odd phrase. "I don't understand. Time passes whether we want it to or not."

"When your husband was killed," he said as if he hadn't heard me, "I promised myself I would talk to you when the time was right. I just never knew when that was ... I mean, with his murder, the investigation, your campaign and service ... Well, the time never seemed to come. I don't know how many times I've started to approach you in the restaurant, but something always seemed to hold me back or you were surrounded by others."

"I'm afraid you're losing me, Paul."

He took a deep breath. "Some people are gifted at this sort of thing, but I'm not. I never know how to start."

"Okay, Paul, now you're being cryptic and to be honest, I'm in no mood for games."

He turned to face me. "I don't mean to be cryptic and I'm certainly not playing a game." He frowned and looked at his feet for a moment. "You know Peter and I used to go fishing together with some other businessmen."

"He used to look forward to those times."

"Did he ever talk about it with you?"

I shook my head. "What's to talk about? Men get together, go fishing, drink beer, and then lie about what they caught. It's something on the Y chromosome."

He laughed lightly. "I suppose that's true, at least in part. We didn't drink any beer, and none of us were good enough liars to make a believable story."

"Okay, then what?"

"I'm a man of faith, Mayor. I don't know if you know that."

"I figured that out. You don't hide it very well."

He smiled. "That's a compliment. At least I'm going to take it as one. What you can't know, if Peter didn't tell you, was that those fishing trips involved more than bait, hooks, and lines. It was a Bible study at sea."

"A Bible study?"

"Yes. A group of local businessmen from the area meet once a month for fellowship, Bible study, and prayer. We also get together at other times to enjoy each other's company and talk about the Lord. For a while we used to rent a half-day boat, have a study on the way out to sea, fish, and then have another study on the way back. We haven't done that for the last couple of years, but I'd love to do it again."

"What does this have to do with Peter? He wasn't much of a . . . Bible man." That was a dumb way of putting it, but Paul seemed to understand.

"It wasn't unusual for some of us to bring along friends and acquaintances, people who we thought might like the spiritual and intellectual stimulation of the study. I asked your husband one day when he was lunching at the restaurant. I was up front with him about what we did and told him who all went along. I hate it when Christians get sneaky about such things. Ambush evangelism is wrong in so many ways. I think Peter went along to meet some of the other businessmen. A couple of them were getting ready to put up new buildings. I think he saw an opportunity to make a couple of sales."

It was my turn to smile. Peter and his father had built a thriving construction materials business, and much of that was due to Peter's natural sales ability. He loved selling. "So you were trying to evangelize him and he was trying to evangelize you."

"That's pretty much the way it was. As it turned out, your husband did make a few sales, but he kept coming back for the fishing trips."

"I know he enjoyed them. I thought it was odd; he was never much of an outdoorsman."

That brought a chortle out of Paul. "Yeah, that's true. His first trip out he spent most of his time chumming instead of fishing."

"Chumming? Oh, you mean—"

"Tossing his cookies. He was pretty seasick. I was sure we'd never see him again. I was wrong. He got pretty good about keeping his lunch down."

"That's my man." I noticed I was speaking in the present tense. "He was determined if nothing else." Again the conversation lulled, and Paul seemed preoccupied with whipping up some new anxiety. "I don't see the need for the apology, Paul."

He bit his lower lip. "Did you ... I mean, I gave ..." He stumbled to a stop, then tried again. "The last time I saw Peter was the day he went to LA, the day he was killed. He had come by the Fish Kettle that morning. He caught me in the kitchen working on the clam chowder. We weren't due to open for another two hours, but he got my attention by rapping on one of the windows with a quarter. That's an annoying sound."

"I imagine." I was intrigued. If nothing else, the story took my mind away from my present troubles for a while.

"Of course I let him in. He said he had something to share with me. I poured us a couple cups of coffee and we sat down. He told me about his trip to LA and then made some other small talk. Then he said it."

"Said what?"

"He said he had made the decision. I wasn't surprised. I had been watching him change over the months."

It was true. The last few months of Peter's life, he had seemed a little different, but not in an identifiable way, not in a way I could describe. He seemed . . . contemplative, puzzled, as if he were trying to untie some densely wound knot. A couple times I asked if he was okay and he said, "Yes, just thinking."

"The decision?" I prompted, but I had a good idea where this was going.

Paul nodded. "He gave his life to Christ. Do you know what that means?"

"It's that born-again stuff."

"That's one way to put it. As we studied the Bible together, Peter began to feel a need for a relationship with his Creator. That's often how it starts: realizing that something is missing and we need more. It is my belief—no, that's a bad start. The Bible teaches that sin separates God and humans. This is a problem for God. God is love, but he is also just. So he desires to forgive, but at the same time he must also punish sin. Jesus was the solution. Jesus took our sins upon himself. He became our sacrifice and paid the price for our disobedience. He did that on the cross."

"Wait a minute." I raised my hand. "The last thing I need is a sermon."

"I'm not trying to preach, Mayor. Really, I'm not. Like I said, some people are gifted in this, but I'm not one of them."

"What are you getting at?"

He ran a hand through his hair and turned his back to the setting sun. "I'm trying to tell you about a change in Peter's life. A change he told me about the day he died." He sighed; then his face lit up. "Look that way," he said, nodding toward the parking lot at the other end of the pier. I did. "What do you see?"

"Um . . . the shore? The parking lot? Is that what you mean?"

"Exactly. How would you get from here to there if this pier didn't exist?"

"If the pier didn't exist, I wouldn't be standing here."

"I understand that."

I knew where he was headed. "You're saying that Jesus is the pier?"

"Yes. Or bridge or whatever illustration you want to use. Your husband came to understand that. Not quickly. Not easily. But he did."

"He never talked to me about a religious conversion."

"He never had the chance, Mayor. He told me he had made up his mind before he left the house to go to LA. You had already gone to the office."

That could be true, I thought. I often left before Peter. He was a slow riser. "Still, I should have picked up on something. Why didn't he tell me he was thinking about religion?"

Paul shook his head. "Not religion, Mayor. Not denominations. We're talking about a commitment of faith. Church is extremely important. Jesus founded the church. He died for the church. It is the only institution he started. But faith comes by hearing, and

---

hearing by the Word of God. It's an individual decision. Peter's faith was new. I doubt he could have explained it to you, but I know he was going to."

"How do you know that?" This was all news to me. I didn't know what to think, didn't know how to process this. I'm not sure I welcomed the revelation. I had enough on my emotional plate to fill a platter. I felt close to dropping everything.

"He told me, Mayor. He told me the day he died. Hours before the murder, he sat in my restaurant and told me he had made a personal decision to follow Christ. He was going to talk to you when he got back. He never got back. And that's why I owe you an apology. I should have told you. I should have told you eight years ago, but I didn't. I thought maybe you found it." His eyes glistened.

"You're being cryptic again, Paul. Found what?"

"I just assumed it would be in his things." I thought of the box. I thought of the dream.

"It's all right, Paul. It's all right. What should I have found?"

"A Bible. Every year I buy a new Bible and read it, marking my favorite passages and making comments in the margin. Then I pray that God would let me give it to someone who might benefit from it. When I heard your husband's great news, I gave him the Bible I was working on. It seemed the perfect thing to do. He took it with him. I just assumed you would have it."

"I may." I explained about the cardboard box. "I've never looked inside. Never. I can't. And if you're asking for it back—"

"No, no, please, Mayor, no. I don't want it back. I want you to have it. And I want you to have the knowledge of Peter's decision."

"Why tell me now?" I felt a new heaviness.

"Because of . . . you know . . . all you're going through. I just thought you should know. And when I saw you walk by the restaurant, I knew the time had come."

I looked down the pier and watched as people strolled along its boards. Fishermen left, only to be replaced by those who preferred to dip a line after dark. I watched people enter and leave the Fish Kettle, all of them supported by the pier. *Jesus as a pier.* That was a new one on me. For some reason I felt angry. Someone knew something about my husband that I didn't. That seemed wrong. And then ... then there was the truth of the matter, the truth that Paul had avoided.

"I appreciate what you've said, Paul, but I can't forget that God allowed evil men to kill my husband. What kind of God allows that?" He looked crestfallen, and guilt settled over me like night descending upon the ocean. The wind blew colder. I excused myself and started back down the pier.

"The same kind of God who allows evil men to kill his Son," I heard him say. I kept walking but one other comment floated through the salt air. "Sometimes the righteous die so that others can live."

I left Paul behind me. I left the sea and the wind and the gulls behind me, wishing I had not taken this side trip.

I slipped into the hot water, lowering my body inch by inch. At first it stung my skin, but the tingling pain soon gave way to pleasure as the fluid covered me. I leaned back and let the water tickle my chin. I had wanted this. I needed this. I deserved this. Reclining in the large tub of my master bath was not a luxury; it was mental and physical therapy. I lay there with just my knees above the surface. The lights were off, leaving only the half-dozen scented candles around the tub to illuminate the room. I watched their light dance on the walls and ceiling, flickering ballerinas.

I closed my eyes and tried to shut out the events of the last few days. Worry is an irresistible force, and no matter how I chastened myself, I continued to see the fight in the coffee shop and the tortured look on Randi's face as she crumpled to the floor, two grown men falling on her like bags of wet sand.

None of this is fair. Randi shouldn't be in the hospital, my parents shouldn't be downstairs preparing dinner because it's unsafe to stay in their own home; it's unfair for Celeste to spend each moment of the last week worried about her mother, and Lizzy certainly shouldn't be dead.

I felt responsible. It was nonsense, but feelings are unreasoning things. I tried to blank my mind but the ghosts kept haunting. The best I could do was ignore them and try to lose myself in the satin water and the fruity scent of the candles. My unexpected meeting with Paul Shedd whipped around in my brain. His tone had been so serious, his expression so heartfelt, his anxiety so palpable. The news was too slippery for me. I didn't know how to deal with it, how to hold on to it. It was mercury in the palm of my hand. If I didn't mess with it, I could let it puddle, but if I tried to grasp it, it would run through my fingers.

So what if Peter had a religious experience? What difference did that make? That was eight years ago. He was still dead. I thought of the cardboard box in my closet and what might be in it. I surmised most of its contents: Peter's wallet, his keys, his business card case, and the electronic PDA he carried for business. I also knew their condition, and that was one of the biggest reasons the box remained closed.

During the sentencing phase of the murder trial, the prosecution painted a graphic and garish picture of the events, describing the condition of my husband's body. He pulled no punches and laid out the sickening scene like a passage from a Stephen King novel. I don't know how many times he used the word *blood*. There were more than personal possessions in that box. My husband's lifeblood was in there as well. I'd had to pay a fortune to have his car cleaned so I could sell it. I couldn't bring myself to look upon the blood and the violence that put it there. If that made me weak, then so be it.

Noises of life reverberated up from the lower floor. I could hear the television, which my father was watching. When I came in, it was on the History Channel. If Dad had his way, every TV would have its tuner welded to that station.

Celeste had been in the kitchen with Mom, trying to be a help. My mother worked alone. I had been shooed out of her kitchen more times than I can count. This evening Mom said nothing to Celeste. She always considered work the best tonic for any emotional ill.

The hot water was working its magic, its warmth seeping through my pores. My body was sore, my back ached, my neck felt petrified. I felt some shame. My pains were from tension, Randi's from physical abuse. Slowly the tight muscles relinquished their bulldog grip. It was a good feeling, a great feeling, and I did my best to fall into its embrace.

Eyes closed, I willed my hyperactive mind to slow. It finally settled. A moment's peace. It was as rich as chocolate and more welcome.

A soft knock snapped me out of my blissful nothingness.

"What now?" I whispered. I spent a second wondering what would happen if I ignored the intrusion. Only Mom would knock on my bathroom door. "What is it, Mother?"

A deeper voice than I expected answered. "It's Detective West. Um . . . your mother was up to her elbows in the kitchen. . . . She said you were upstairs and sent me up. . . . I didn't mean to . . . I mean . . ."

Annoyance melted under the heat of concern. West wouldn't come by unless he had something important. "I'll be out in a minute—make that five minutes."

"I'll wait downstairs. . . . I mean, of course I'll wait downstairs."

He sounded flustered. Not used to knocking on a lady's bathroom door. "That would be best."

I popped the stopper and rose from the tub. Water cascaded off my body like a heavy rain. I felt an odd embarrassment knowing that West had stood outside the door a moment before. More nonsense. I slipped from the tub, toweled off, and dressed in a pair of jeans and one of my husband's old dress shirts. I often wore his shirts when I felt depressed or ill at ease.

I trotted downstairs barefoot and found West seated at the dining room table, a cup of coffee before him. Also seated there were my father and Celeste. Mother stepped from behind the kitchen counter. "Will you stay for dinner, Detective West? We have plenty of pork chops and I've made gravy for the mashed potatoes."

"Not the best meal for the ol' ticker," Dad added, "but it's a great way to go."

"No, thank you. I appreciate the offer, but I have a deskful of paperwork to do."

"Are you sure?" Mom pressed. "Jerry will be joining us. The more the merrier."

"He is?" I said. This was news to me.

"Didn't I tell you? He called a few minutes before you got home. He wanted to know how you were doing after all the excitement. I guess I forgot. I do that a lot lately."

I took a seat at the end of the table. "He saw me at the hospital. I was fine then—"

"Hospital?" West said. "You were in the hospital?"

I shook my head. "Not in the way you mean. My assistant, Randi, was hurt. I was visiting her." I related the events at the coffee shop, noticing that I was speaking of them as if they were part of my usual routine. I could tell West wasn't buying the act. He pressed his lips into a line.

"You still with us, Detective?" I asked.

His head snapped up. "Yes. I have some news about Mrs. Stout. The blood tests came back. We're a little surprised."

"Surprised?" I looked at Celeste. She sat in sober silence.

"Yes. Her death may have been accidental."

"She was tied to the pier," I said. "That doesn't happen by accident."

"I'm not saying a crime wasn't committed. Obviously one has— several, actually. But the autopsy and toxicology report show something different, unexpected."

"How did Lizzy die?" I asked bluntly. It was time to get to the point.

"Anaphylactic shock."

No one spoke. The pork chops sizzled in the kitchen.

"What's that?" Celeste asked.

"It's an allergic reaction to a substance."

"She died of allergies?"

West shook his head. "She died because she was extremely allergic to something. Anaphylaxis is an extreme response to a substance. For example, some people are allergic to shellfish or nuts. The most common problem is with insects."

"When I was teaching," Mom said, "I had a student who was allergic to bee stings. He carried a little medical kit with a syringe in case he was ever stung."

"Exactly. Lizzy died of something similar." West paused, as if trying to convince himself of the statement he was about to make. "She died of an ant bite."

He let the absurd announcement sink in, then continued. "We almost missed it. There was tissue-swelling from the time she spent submerged, and the mussels on the pier damaged her back. After the blood work came, Dr. Egan reexamined her body. He found a bite just below the right shoulder blade. There was one on the shoulder too. Remember, we thought it might be an injection mark?"

"You're saying she wasn't murdered?" my father asked.

"Not directly, but the abductor will be charged with murder anyway. Even an accidental death is considered murder if it happens during or because of a felonious act. This doesn't change anything in our investigation, but I promised to keep you posted."

I didn't know what to make of his revelation. An ant! It was unbelievable. "You're saying a bug killed Lizzy?"

"Not just any bug. Most likely it was a red imported fire ant."

"I've heard of those," Dad said. "They came from South America, right?"

West leaned back in his chair. He looked tired. "The Scientific Investigation detective contacted an entomologist for me. The ants were introduced to our country in the 1930s. They've been spreading ever since. I'm told their bite is vicious. Perhaps I should say their sting. The entomologist told me that these fire ants bite with their mandibles but then sting their victims with a stinger in their abdomen. They can sting more than one time. For most of us it would be painful, but Mrs. Stout was allergic to insect bites. I spoke to her husband. She'd had problems before, but apparently she was especially susceptible to this particular venom."

"Why don't I feel any better?" I asked.

"There's only one reason to feel any better about all this," West suggested. "Since Mrs. Stout was not intentionally killed, there is hope that, well—"

"That my mother is still alive," Celeste said.

Mom put a hand on her shoulder. "We can hope and pray."

"What now?" I asked.

"Things continue on," West replied. "We continue our aggressive investigation. We continue the search."

My head was beginning to ache again. The thought of something as small as a red ant killing an acquaintance of mine seemed fictional. Did such things happen in real life? The answer was obvious but it didn't satisfy.

"How is Leo doing?" I wondered.

West shook his head. "Not good. He's taking this very hard, and who can blame him. I spoke to him before coming here. He took the news without emotion but looked like he was going to melt right in front of me. He said he was going to stay with his sister in Thousand Oaks. He gave me the address and phone number. I think he just wants to get out of the house. Too many memories and all that."

"Seems wise," Dad said. Mom agreed.

"He knew how susceptible she was to ant bites?" I asked. I didn't want to go further, but West picked up on my thoughts.

"You're wondering if he could be the murderer."

"I don't know what to think anymore. Too much has happened. I'm not at my best. It's wrong for me to even entertain such a thought."

"No, it isn't," West said. "We're investigating him. We investigate every possibility. My gut, however, tells me he's nothing more than a heartbroken husband."

I nodded but said nothing. I was feeling rung out again.

Silence hovered over the table for a few moments, and then West stood. "I must be going. Thank you for the invitation to dinner."

"You won't reconsider?" Mom asked.

He smiled and shook his head. "No, I really must get back to the office."

"I'll walk you to the door," I said, rising.

"No need, I can—"

"I want to see my father."

The words were so soft, it took me a moment to realize what I was hearing and who it was that said it. "What was that, Celeste?"

Celeste sat unmoving, her eyes directed at the table.

"I want to see my father," she repeated louder.

The doorbell rang.

"That must be Jerry," Mom said cheerfully.

chapter 10

After her announcement, Celeste had gone to the guest room and refused to come out. Mom, who could talk a lobster into boiling water for a swim, was able to convince her to take the plate of food she had prepared. It took a while and several requests but Celeste agreed to meet with me. She refused to talk about her reasons for the sudden change but she was resolute in her decision. I used all my interpersonal and negotiating skills trying to convince her to let me set up the meeting, suggesting that Detective West should make the contact and that the meeting should take place in City Hall. If I couldn't control the decision, I could at least attempt to control the venue. Celeste agreed quickly enough. I left worried.

The next day I rose early and, foregoing my usual workout, went downstairs and made coffee. The morning passed slowly. I went to the office, arranged for the conference room, alerted security, and placed a call to West. I learned that Truccoli had agreed to the ten o'clock meeting time I'd requested. *Decent of him.* West also said he would send an officer over just in case things went sour. I thanked him, returned a few calls, reviewed the next council agenda, and did anything that would help keep my mind off the pending reunion.

I could think of no reason why Celeste would change her mind. From the moment of her mother's disappearance, she had insisted that she wanted nothing to do with her father. The anger I had seen in her eyes and heard in her voice was genuine. Why request to see the beast now? No explanations surfaced in the dark waters of my mind.

At nine-thirty I left the office and made my way to the car. Security, who had remained alert since the second abduction and tense since Truccoli's last visit, insisted that a guard escort me from the office to my vehicle. I didn't argue.

Ten minutes later I had Celeste in my car, and we made our way back to City Hall. When I arrived, the security guard was waiting for me. He was leaning against Jon Adler's car and smoking a cigarette. I considered telling him he shouldn't lean against a councilman's car but then tossed the idea. *He can slice Adler's tires for all I care.*

"We'll meet in here," I told Celeste as we exited the private elevator used by council members and staff and entered the conference room. "Are you sure you want to do this?"

"Yes."

I started to press her for a reason but stopped. "I can still stay, can't I?"

She nodded.

I led her to the head of the table and let her sit. Placing a hand on her shoulder, I said, "I'm here for you. I'll be right behind you. If you want the meeting to end, just say so. Okay?"

"Yeah, okay."

She looked like a steel spring too-long wound. Something was going to give.

The phone buzzed and I picked up. "Yes." It was Fritzy. I listened, thanked her, hung up, and took a deep breath. "He's here." I didn't think it possible but Celeste tensed all the more.

It would only take a minute for Fritzy to lead Truccoli from her desk in the lobby to the conference room. Not that he needed leading; he had been here before. That time, however, he had left in handcuffs. The image brought me a moment's pleasure.

The door opened and I saw Fritzy come in and stand to the side. Two men filled the entry: Truccoli and a stranger in a dark suit. *Lawyer.*

"Madam Mayor, Mr. Truccoli is here for his meeting." Fritzy tended toward the formal when nervous.

"Thank you, Ms. Fritz."

"Can I get anyone something to drink—"

"No. We're fine."

The two men entered. I made eye contact with Truccoli and felt a strong urge to look away. I rejected the desire. We were on my turf; I refused to give away that advantage, little as it was.

"Madam Mayor," the stranger said. He was a short man with ruddy skin, dark eyes, and thick brown hair. He carried a calfskin briefcase. On his wrist was a Rolex. "My name is Matt Stover of Stover, Richman, and Newcomb, Attorneys at Law. I'm here in my capacity as counsel to Mr. Truccoli. Thank you for meeting with us."

I gave a polite nod.

Truccoli stood just at the foot of the table. He was wearing a dark-blue polo shirt and tan pants. He appeared calm, even friendly. The sight of him made my gut twist. He turned his eyes from me and looked at Celeste. At first his face showed no expression; then a slight smile pushed up the corners of his mouth.

"We appreciate this meeting," Stover said, stepping to the table. "I know there has been some tension between you and Mr. Truccoli, but there is no need for this to be an adversarial gathering." He pulled out a chair, set his briefcase on the table, and began to seat himself. Then he noted I was still standing. To his credit, he remained on his feet. Someone had instilled manners and a sense of protocol in the man. "Should we sit?"

"I'm fine," I said.

He pursed his lips, then folded his hands in front of him. "Mr. Truccoli would like to express—"

"Celeste," Truccoli said, his smile now Cheshire cat wide. If only he would have disappeared as quickly. "Celeste, I've missed you." He held out his arms and approached her.

"Don't touch me," she snapped. "Don't you dare touch me." I could see her eyes puddle and her jaw set tight.

"But, baby, it's been a long time and we've been through so much together."

"Long time is right! Too long. And we haven't been through anything together. You've been gone. No calls. No letters. Nothing."

"I came as fast as I could, sweetheart. I hopped the first plane out of town and came to Santa Rita. I came to be with you."

"As far as I'm concerned, you can hop the next plane out. I don't need you. You didn't need Mom, you didn't need me, and now I don't need you."

"Miss Truccoli," Stover said, "if you'll give your father a chance, I'm sure—"

"He doesn't deserve a chance."

Truccoli's smile melted and his eyes hardened like stone. My mouth went dry. I was simultaneously proud of Celeste and frightened for her. Her words and the power with which she fired them were surprising.

"Listen, baby, your mother and I had our problems. Things didn't work out and we went our separate ways. This tragedy should pull us together. I want to be here for you."

"I don't want you!" Celeste shouted, her voice rebounding off the walls. I flinched and Truccoli blinked hard. "As far as I'm concerned, you are just one tragedy in my life. What has happened ... is happening to Mom is another."

Truccoli's spine stiffened and his mouth drew tight. I had seen this look on his face before and I didn't like it.

Silence fell in a suffocating blanket. Stover cleared his throat. "I'm confused, Miss Truccoli; why did you ask for this meeting if you didn't want to see your father?"

Celeste turned her burning gaze from Truccoli to the attorney. "To tell him to leave me alone, to tell him to leave Maddy alone. Because of him Randi got hurt."

"That was an accident," Truccoli countered. He must have heard about the scuffle in the coffee shop when he sprang his PI from jail.

"Was it an accident when you attacked Maddy right here in this room? Was it an accident that some guy was following her and the police had to arrest him? Go away. Don't call me. Don't write me. I don't want to see you. I hate you. I hated you before and I hate you more now!"

Tears began to run. I squeezed her shoulder. She sniffed and ran a hand under her nose.

"This is your fault," Truccoli said, glaring at me. The room froze over.

"Actually," I replied, "it's your fault."

"Shut up! I don't need you to tell me how to be a father."

"Someone needs to." I knew the comment wouldn't help, but I'd had enough bile building up in me over the last few days that I had to let some of it go. Truccoli was a deserving target.

Stover spoke up. "Settle down, Chris. Let's everyone settle down. Emotions will get us nowhere." He turned to me. "Mayor, please, you're not helping."

"This is all because of you," Truccoli said. "I know what the police have found. I know that my wife's disappearance is connected to you and so are the others. Now you want to take my daughter away from me."

"She didn't take me away from you," Celeste protested. "You threw me away when I was little. I wasn't good enough for you. Mom wasn't good enough for you. You dumped us. Maddy took me in. She gave me a place to stay and has asked for nothing."

If Truccoli heard Celeste, he gave no sign of it; he was fixated on me. I felt myself flush. For a moment I thought I would ignite under the heat of his stare.

"You poisoned her mind, didn't you? You turned her against her own father—against me, her own flesh and blood."

"Apparently, you did that all by yourself—"

He lunged at me, arms out, hands twisted into claws. I heard a roar rumble from his throat. My heart seized and I backpedaled, pulling one of the chairs in front of me. Truccoli didn't see it. He hit hard, lost his balance, and plummeted to the floor.

Celeste screamed.

Truccoli grabbed his shin, then filled the air with obscenities. "You stupid—"

"Mr. Truccoli, that is enough!" Stover shouted.

Staggering to his feet, Truccoli reset himself. "I'll make you pay for this. Take my daughter away from me, will you?"

He started forward. I stepped between him and Celeste and steeled myself for what was to come.

The door to the conference room sprang open and two security guards and a uniformed police officer rushed in. A guard, Bobby, was first in. What he lacked in physical presence, he made up for with enthusiasm. Truccoli charged again but the guard cut him off, flinging himself at my attacker. Both tumbled to the ground in a heap of arms and legs. A half second later the cop was on the pile. "Stop resisting," he ordered. "Stop resisting."

"She took my daughter!" Truccoli struggled. "She took my daughter from me."

The officer played no games. He placed a knee on the back of Truccoli's neck, reached for his cuffs, and with the help of the guard cuffed him. Yanking him to his feet, he spun Truccoli around. "It's over, pal."

"She hit me with a chair," Truccoli complained. "My attorney saw it. You should be arresting the stupid little—"

The officer shoved Truccoli hard against the wall. "You had better think before you finish that statement." Then he turned to me. "You okay?"

"Yes, thank you."

He looked at Celeste. "How about you, young lady? Are you all right?"

Celeste nodded. I put my arm around her.

"I'm suing," Truccoli spat. "I'm suing this Podunk town for all it has and I'm suing you, Mayor. Do you hear that?" He directed his gaze at the attorney. "We're going to sue them, Stover. I want the paperwork drawn up today. Do you hear? Today!"

"Let's take a walk, mister," the officer said. Taking Truccoli by the elbow, he led him from the room. The guards went with them.

I looked at Stover, who watched his client being marched off in handcuffs. "It sounds like you have some paperwork to do."

He offered a weak smile and shook his head. "I should have gone to med school, like my brother." He reached into his coat pocket, extracted a small silver case, and removed a business card from it. "If he brings suit, give me a call. I'll be happy to serve as a witness for your side." He picked up his briefcase. "I need to go tell him to find a new attorney." With a pause, he added, "I'm sorry about this, Mayor. Had I known, I would never have hooked up with the cretin." Nodding politely, he left.

With everyone gone, I put an arm around Celeste and pulled her close. She was shaking. "You are full of surprises, girl," I said softly. "You are one gutsy chick."

She tittered, then gave me a hug. Then she broke into sobs, her shoulders shuddering. The sadness was deep, erupting like pent-up lava. Her breathing came in ragged waves and for a moment I thought she would collapse.

I held her tight and stroked her hair. My nose filled with mucus, my face felt hot, and then something in my soul tore in a ragged edge. Tears began to flow and breathing became difficult. We were two women separated by age but identical in need. The pressure had become too much, the crushing concern and fear was, at least for the moment, winning—and I didn't care.

Moments passed and the boiling sobs soon settled into eye rubbing, nose wiping, sniveling. I took a deep breath. "Whew. I've needed to do that for a long time."

"Me too."

I took a step back and held Celeste at arm's distance. Her own weeping had calmed. I smiled, then noticed something out of the corner of my eye. Turning, I saw Jon Adler and Tess Lawrence standing at the door. Both were frowning and Adler was shaking his head.

"We need to talk," Tess said flatly.

Sixty minutes later I sat in my office reviewing a long list of telephone calls waiting for my attention. I had tried to send Celeste home, offering to have one of the security guards drive her. She'd had a different idea.

"I'm tired of just hanging around the house. All I do is watch TV and talk to Michele on the phone. Your parents are great, but . . ."

"I understand."

"Can't I stay here with you? I mean, Randi's out, so maybe I could sit in her office and answer the phone or file or something. I took a couple of business classes in high school and another one in college. I can't replace her but I can do something."

I studied her for a moment. She was right. If it were me confined to the house, I would have lost my mind long ago. Besides, I liked being around her. "I think I can find something for you to do."

The arresting officer had come back and asked a few questions for his report. I had also, after spending a quarter hour in the rest room touching up makeup and hiding from the world, sought out the young guard who had executed the NFL tackle on my behalf. I promised a pizza for him and his pals, and a letter of thanks to his boss. He was appreciative, but no more than I was for his heroic effort.

It felt good to have my fanny in the leather seat of my desk chair. Better than good; it felt normal. It seemed odd to look out the door of my office and see Celeste in Randi's chair. According to a message left with Fritzy, the hospital was going to release Randi today, and I had promised to pick her up. That would be a joy. Still, work went on, and with my assistant out for the next few days, my workload had doubled.

"What are you doing here?" a voice said. I looked up and saw Tess and Jon standing in front of Randi's desk, staring down at Celeste. The brusque question took her aback.

"I'm . . . I'm helping Mayor Glenn."

"You're not an employee," Tess stated.

I rose from my desk and went to the door. "Last I heard, my office operations were my responsibility." Tess's head swiveled. Her expression beamed her irritation. "Celeste has offered to do volunteer work for the city. You're for volunteerism, aren't you, Tess? At least you said you were in your last campaign."

"I told you earlier that we need to talk. I've been waiting over an hour to hear from you."

I shrugged. "Must have slipped my mind. I've been preoccupied with health and welfare—mine."

"That's what we want to talk about," Tess said in her best terse voice. "When can we meet?"

"You're here now; come in and have a seat. You don't mind meeting in my office, do you?"

"Of course not."

"What about you, Jon? I don't think I've ever seen you this quiet. Tess got your tongue?" I was being more testy than needed, but either one alone was more than I could take; having both of them bully their way into my office made my already bad mood worse.

"I agree we should meet."

I bet. You agree with whatever Tess tells you to agree with. "Well, apologize to Miss Truccoli, then come on in. Should I send for coffee?"

"Apologize?" Tess said. "I have no intention of . . ." She took a deep breath, turned to Celeste. "I'm sorry if I came off a little harsh." She didn't wait for Celeste to reply. She and Jon followed me back into the office. I closed the door behind them, motioned for them to sit, and then took my place behind my wide desk, wishing it were wider.

"What's eating you now, Tess?" I picked up a piece of paper from my desk. It was an unimportant document, but I didn't want to make eye contact with the shrew sitting opposite me. I tried to look nonchalant.

"At times you speak crudely," Tess said. "Do you think that is suitable for the city's highest representative?"

"A mayor should speak so as to be understood. Are you having trouble understanding me?"

"No."

"Let's get to it, folks. It's already been a long day."

"Very well, then," Tess said. "We feel that your involvement in these disappearances, and the continuing violent dealings you've been having with that young lady's father, is distracting you from city business, and that your mind is not on the job as it should be. You show signs of preoccupation."

"Preoccupation? Really. Let's see, two of my friends and a former political consultant are missing. One has shown up dead, strapped to the deep end of a pier. Twice I've been attacked in the conference room. The situation has forced me to post a guard at my house. The police drive by my home every hour. My family has moved in with me for their own safety. What in all of that could be distracting me?"

"You're arguing our point."

"Am I? Thank you for pointing that out. What is it you're suggesting?"

"We think you should step aside and let someone who is more focused take the reins of leadership," Tess said without a blink. I almost admired her gall.

"Someone? Have anybody in mind?"

"Well . . . There are a few obvious choices."

"Odd," I said, doing my best to sound naïve, "none come to mind. Of course, there's Ned Boese, the planning commissioner. He has a good head on his shoulders and has yet to show a single fiber of opportunism. Most people on the council think highly of him."

Jon snorted.

"I'm sorry, Jon, I missed that comment. Could you repeat it?" I leaned back in the chair.

"We weren't thinking of Ned Boese," he said.

"Somehow I knew that."

"You're making light of this," Tess said. "I think you'll find that we have more than adequate support on this in the council."

"Do you? Well, let me just test the waters." I hit the speaker-phone button on my telephone and dialed two numbers. There was a ring.

"Councilman Titus Overstreet's office."

"Hi, Susie. It's Maddy. Is Titus in?"

"Yes, Mayor. One moment, please."

A few seconds later Overstreet was on the line. "Hello. I just heard about what happened. Are you all right?"

"Fine. A little shaken but I'll be fine, Titus. As you can tell, I have you on speakerphone."

"Yeah, I picked up on that. What's up?"

"Jon and Tess are in my office." Jon squirmed and Tess blinked rapidly several times. "They think I should pass the mantle of mayoral leadership on to someone else."

"What? Why would they suggest that?"

"Apparently, I'm too distracted." He mumbled something I couldn't make out but I sensed it might make a longshoreman blush. "They tell me they have the support of much of the council."

"Nonsense. They haven't talked to me. What are you guys trying to pull?" I could hear the heat in his voice. "Send them my way, Mayor. I have some counsel I'd like to give them. Better yet, I'll be there in two minutes."

The color drained from Tess's face. I took pity on her. "No need, Titus," I said. "I'm just taking a straw poll."

"Well, let me give you my straw in clear terms: I'm with you. I stand with you without reservation. Did you hear that, Jon, Tess? You try speaking in my name again, I'm gonna be all over you like ugly on an ape. Sure you don't want me to come over, Mayor? I can bring a Girl Scout to work Jon over."

I fought back a laugh. "No need, Titus. Thanks for your support. I'll talk to you later." I disconnected but not before another colorful metaphor seeped through the speaker. "Okay, let's give Larry Wu a jingle."

"No need," Tess said. "We all know Larry's in your pocket."

"Larry thinks for himself. He's in no one's pocket. Not yours. Not mine." I leaned forward and lowered my voice. "I have no inclination, no intention, of stepping down, stepping back, or stepping away from the likes of you. If you want my office, you're going to have to earn it in the next election. You beat me fair and square, then you can have it. The day that happens is the day I leave the city."

"For Washington, you mean?" Jon asked with a slight smile. I burned the smile from his face with a gaze.

"Explain yourself."

"You haven't read this morning's paper?" Tess said. "You should keep up on current events. Front-page article, just below the fold. It seems that the police found a folder at Allen Dayton's home—a folder containing plans for a congressional campaign. Your name was on that file."

Turner. He finally ran the article.

chapter 10

The brief comfort I felt from being in the office had been sucked out of me by Jon and Tess. I tried to put them out of my mind but my brain wouldn't let go. Their words buzzed around my head like black flies. I was angry and I hate being angry. It's a self-destructive emotion.

"You look ready to chew nails."

I turned my attention from the road ahead and gave Randi a quick glance. She raised an eyebrow. We were five minutes from the hospital and on the freeway to her home.

"It shows?"

"Not much—okay, I'm lying."

"Sorry. I drifted back to something that happened this morning."

"And that was . . ."

"Nothing, really." I gave her another glance. She wasn't buying it.

"Dish it. I've just spent the night and most of the morning in the hospital and am bored out of my skull." She shifted in the car seat, her face twisting with the pain.

"How's the foot?"

"It hurts. My back hurts. My head hurts, and you're trying to change the subject."

I laughed, then launched into a recounting of Jon and Tess's visit. Randi listened in silence but I could tell she was beginning to fume.

"That's it. We're going to the office. I'm gonna beat someone with my crutches."

"Tell her about what happened before," Celeste said. She was sitting in the back.

Randi looked at me. "Before?"

I didn't want to relive that too, but resistance was futile, so I gave the *Reader's Digest* version of Christopher Truccoli's actions.

Randi shook her head and then shifted again in her seat. Sitting in the car was making her discomfort worse. "I'll say one thing: hangin' with you ain't dull."

I pulled off the freeway and made my way up the hill to the Paseo Grande district. Randi rented a one-bedroom condo with an "almost view" of the ocean.

"So you've taken over my job, Celeste. Moving in on me, are you?"

Celeste snickered. It was the first sign of humor I had seen from her since her mother disappeared. "Not really. I just sit at the desk and wait for the phone to ring. There's not much else for me to do. I don't know the files and stuff."

"Well, hang around, kid. I'll show you the ropes. Sometimes I need the help. My boss is a slave driver."

"Are you asking to walk the rest of the way home?" I joked.

"I meant it in the kindest way possible."

I parked in one of the handicapped spaces close to the front entrance, then came around to help Randi out. Although not seriously hurt, she had enough pain to last her for a good long while. Celeste exited and carried the crutches that had been with her in the backseat. I wished I had borrowed a wheelchair from the hospital.

"Should I throw you over my shoulder?"

"Lovely as that would be, I had better stick with the sticks."

Randi's condo was on the third floor of the four-story building. We entered the foyer and made our way to the elevator. Each step was slow and painful for Randi. The crutches kept her from putting weight on her ankle, but they aggravated her sore muscles.

"I suppose I deserve this," she said in the elevator. "It was my mouth that got me in trouble. It does that more times than I care to admit."

"No need to apologize," I said. "It's been a rough week for everyone."

"Yeah, but I made it worse. Now I can't even do my job. The doctor wants me to take a week off. I'll give it a day, maybe two."

"You'll give it whatever it takes. Take the time off. Your job isn't going anywhere."

"Maybe," Celeste said.

"Step closer, kid. I want to hit you."

We laughed lightly, like people at a funeral. A quip spoken, a joke told, a funny remembrance recalled and mourners share a pressure-relieving chuckle, but it is nothing more than a lone beam of light in a sky of dark clouds.

Randi lived two doors down from the elevator and she led the way. "The key is in my purse." I was carrying both her bag and mine. I fumbled for a moment, then handed her the key chain, a small ring with only four keys on it. I recognized one as the key to our offices.

Inside, Randi worked her way to a sofa that was out of style by ten years, and eased herself onto the well-worn cushions. Setting the crutches on the floor, she struggled to lie down and raise her foot to rest it on the arm of the sofa. I helped her get as comfortable as possible.

"This is my first time here," I said, looking around. There was no art on the pale white walls; the furnishings were few and dated. A few books and magazines rested on a battered coffee table.

"You'll have to forgive the mess. The maid doesn't come till Friday."

"The place looks fine," I said. Randi tried to reposition herself. "Can I get you something?"

"A pillow for my foot. There's one at the end of the couch."

I found the small throw pillow and gently raised Randi's foot. The plaster cast covered the ankle, leaving her toes exposed. As easily as I could, I lowered her leg to the center of the pillow. Something caught my eye.

"What's this?"

Randi drew her head up to see what I was looking at. "The red spots on my big toe? It's a bite. An ant bit me. Three times, to be exact. Hurt like crazy. I crushed the little bugger."

I caught the look on Celeste's face.

"I don't recall you mentioning it," I said.

"That's because I'm embarrassed about it."

"I don't understand."

"It happened when I took the file to Allen Dayton. He has a nice porch off his home office. We met out there over iced tea. I was wearing sandals. That's when the little monster got me. That man has a real ant problem. You should see his backyard."

After dropping Celeste off at home, I made another trip to Police Headquarters. Randi's revelation about her ant bite probably meant nothing. There had to be billions of ants in our region—red, black, and otherwise. Still, Randi had described the bites as extremely painful, and hadn't West said that red imported fire ants were known for their vicious bites and stings? It was the stinging. That's what he said; the ants had a stinger in their abdomen. He also said they could sting more than once, and Randi had three marks on her toe.

It could be coincidence but it nagged at me like a dripping faucet. Bells were going off.

I parked and marched into the building. The desk officer recognized me. "Good morning, Mayor." He looked at his watch. "Yup, still morning, but not for long. Almost lunchtime and I'm—"

"I'd like to see Detective West, please."

"I'm sorry, Mayor, but he left about half an hour ago."

"Do you know where he went?"

"No ma'am. Is there a problem I can help with?"

I let slip a frown. "No. Thanks." I had turned to leave when an idea hit me. "How about Chief Webb? Is he in?"

"Yes ma'am. Let me tell him you're here."

A few moments later I was shown to Webb's office. My uniformed escort left and I approached the large desk.

"Thank you for seeing me without an appointment, Chief."

He nodded slightly, studied me for a moment, then offered me a seat. Two leather chairs sit opposite his desk. I took the one on the right. His office is wide, too wide for its depth. I felt as if I were sitting in a bowling lane. On the walls are photos of Webb in his younger days: a shot of him when he graduated from the academy, a formal photo of him in uniform, and a large image of him with right hand raised as he took the oath of office.

"You're the city's mayor; you don't need an appointment. I hear you've had a busy couple of days—a coffee shop brawl and another run-in with Truccoli. You seem to be courting danger."

"Not courting, Chief, pursued." I wasn't sure I liked his tone or his implication. "I was minding my own business in the coffee shop. It was Truccoli's thug who started things."

"And the conference room today. What happened there?"

"Truccoli went ballistic and charged me." Webb frowned, "What? What's that look for?"

"It means nothing, Mayor. How can I help you?"

"No, no, wait a minute. You've got something on your mind. What is it?"

"It doesn't matter. You didn't come here to see what was on my mind."

"Spill it, Chief. You may not like me all that much but we do serve the same city."

He frowned again, sighed, and raised his beefy hands. "You're too involved in this case. You're making things hard on us and endangering others."

That was sharp. "I've done nothing to interfere with the investigation and I have done nothing to endanger anyone."

His face reddened. "Where did your assistant spend last night? I'll tell you where—in the hospital. Where was Lisa Truccoli's daughter today? In a room with a man who has shown signs of instability and violence. Truccoli already attacked you once in that room, and then you allow him to do it again."

"That was not my choice. Celeste insisted on seeing her father. I did my best to talk her out of it but it was her choice. She's an adult."

"And you're a more experienced adult. You being there in that room was the match in the powder keg. You should have handled it differently—better, with planning and foresight. You showed none of those qualities."

"You're out of line, Chief."

"You asked; I didn't offer."

"I've done everything I can to keep Truccoli away from me and those with me—including Celeste."

I was surprised to see him laugh. The guffaw came from nowhere and returned there a moment later. "You set up the meeting and then stood in the room with him. It's hard to enforce a restraining order when the complainant invites the abuser over for tea."

"It wasn't tea; it was a response to Celeste's request. I was there to make sure she was safe. I took precautions. You know that."

"If Truccoli comes by your house tonight and we arrest him for breaking the restraining order, his lawyer will argue that you waived the order by inviting him to meet with you in City Hall. We're trying to do a job here and you're handcuffing us."

"West doesn't seem to mind."

"*Detective* West is new to our force and you are, indirectly, his boss. He has extended you every courtesy you're due and well beyond that."

My heart began to pound. Webb had always been in the opposite camp from mine. If I told him the sky was blue, he'd argue the point. I sat in silence, choosing not to fuel the fire. Time ticked by, neither of us wanting to break the reprieve. Finally I said, "I came by to pass on some information that may be helpful. I was going to speak to Detective West but he's not here. Do you want to hear it or should I wait?"

"I'll relay the info."

Don't want me coming by again, eh? I told him about the ant stings on Randi's toe and where she got them.

"Ants?"

"Yes, ants. West . . . Detective West said that Lizzy died because of a reaction to an ant bite . . . or sting. Those kinds of ants sting."

Webb closed his eyes.

"It's not just the ant," I insisted. "It's where Randi was stung. She was at Dayton's house when she was bitten. Doesn't it strike you as odd?"

"I'll admit it's interesting, but that's all. So what? So Ms. Portman visits Dayton and she takes it on the toe from a fire ant. Later
Lizzy Stout is found dead and we come to learn that she died of an
extreme allergic reaction to ant venom. Does that mean Mrs. Stout
was at Mr. Dayton's home? Does it mean that some ant made the
journey from Dayton's home to wherever he and Lisa Truccoli are
being held, if they are being held? Are you trying to show they are
all somehow connected? We know they are. They're all connected
to you. We don't need an ant to tell us that."

"But . . ." I was uncertain what to say.

"But what?"

"I don't know. It just seemed important."

"Mayor, please, please let us run the investigation." He stood,
signaling that my welcome had worn thin. "I will, however, pass on
your theory to Detective West."

"Thank you, Chief." I tried to feel as courteous as I sounded. I
started for the door.

"Mayor." His voice was softer but still tainted with disgust. "You
should know that Mr. Truccoli posted bail. He left the jail about fifteen minutes before you arrived."

"I'm not surprised."

"My point is, you should be careful."

Webb was a royal pain. While I could understand his concern, it
was misguided. He was painting me as a nuisance, even a hin-
drance to the investigation, and while he maintained his formal
airs, his approach was disrespectful. Politics is not for the thin-
skinned. I had developed a tolerance to ridicule, innuendo, and out-
right attack—but it still hurt. People like Jon and Tess were easy
to dismiss; they were overtly self-serving. The thing that bothered

me most about Webb was ethics. He was not narcissistic. His job was his life and he was dedicated to police work. I had never known him to commit anything close to an impropriety. But he was a bulldog about things he believed in, and once he decided that something was right or wrong, there was no changing him. His thoughts and beliefs set like concrete. At times he was maddeningly unreasonable.

There was a time when such a confrontation would have put me back on my heels. That had changed over the last few years. Maybe it was dealing with my husband's murder that steeled my spine; maybe it was the years of living on my own; maybe it was the truth that nothing gets done backing up. Whatever it was, resolve was now part and parcel of my constitution.

On occasion that was a bad thing.

This was such an occasion. I should have marched from the Police Station to my office and left it at that, but I didn't. I couldn't. There was something about Randi's ant stings and Lizzy's death from a similar sting. I didn't know what the connection was but it bothered me. Perhaps I was fabricating the relationship; perhaps I only wanted there to be a connection. None of that mattered. If Webb wasn't going to take it seriously, then I would.

Minutes later I was back on the freeway and headed north. Once again I settled in the far right lane to let speedier cars pass. My mind bubbled like my mother's old coffee percolator and there was no turning it off. I knew where I was headed but wasn't in a hurry to get there. I needed time to organize my thoughts before I arrived. I drove in silence, pushing Webb's words to the back of my mind and trying to focus on what I was about to do.

It had been well over a day since Allen disappeared; I hoped the police were finished with the house. I reminded myself that I was leaving my city and that although my title might bring polite conversation from the Santa Barbara County Sheriff's Department, it would garner little more. The sheriff's leadership flowchart did not connect to mine.

The drive went smoothly until I hit the city limits. Then the typical Santa Barbara bottleneck slowed me down. The blue ocean on my left sparkled under an intense sun that sat like royalty in a cloudless sky. Hills covered in native shrub and grass framed my right. That's where the beauty stopped. In front of and behind me was a coagulated mass of cars, creeping along the clogged asphalt artery. I sighed and summoned my patience.

It took thirty minutes longer than I had planned for me to pull in front of Allen Dayton's wide home. Two years had passed since I last set foot on the property. For all other meetings we met in my campaign office. His firm had a central office in Santa Barbara, but Allen had once told me he preferred working out of the office in his home. "Less interruptions and I can watch *M*A*S*H** reruns at lunch."

The only indication that a police investigation had taken place there was a small remnant of yellow tape stuck to the frame of the front door, compliments of a less than conscientious policeman.

I parked in the driveway and worked my way toward the side of the house to my left. The police would have locked the front door but that was fine with me. I didn't want to go into the house. I was interested in the backyard. Hoping not to appear guilty, I looked around. The neighborhood was quiet. A breeze through the cottonwood trees made the only noise. The house appeared normal, as it should have. Still, I had expected that it would look different, as if it could convey through its wood siding, stucco, and red-tile roof the crime that had been committed inside.

At the front edge of the garage was a redwood fence with a narrow gate. An uncertainty stabbed me. What if the gate was locked? How would I get in? The image of me climbing the fence didn't sit well. It's hard to look as if you belong when doing burglar gymnastics.

Taking a deep breath, I strolled to the gate as if I had done it a hundred times before, and found a simple, self-closing metal latch. It looked identical to the one on my own gate. *Form follows function. How many different kind of latches can there be?* To my relief, there was no lock on the gate. I pushed up the latch and pressed through the gate, closing it quietly behind me.

The side yard was narrow. To my right was the stucco garage wall, to the left the redwood fence. Three large plastic trash cans were set snug against the fence. Their lids were askew and an odious aroma was crawling out. The neighbors would be complaining about that soon. I wondered if the police dug through the cans looking for clues, then left the lids just resting on top.

A concrete walk led to the backyard. I followed it.

Something hit the fence with a bang. I choked off an involuntary scream and leaped back. It hit the fence again, this time with a cacophony of yapping. Through the slats of the fence, I could see a dog the size and shape of a dust mop, with a little black nose and wet round eyes, protesting my presence. It shook, either from delight or irritation.

I laughed at myself and moved on, hoping the owner didn't feel compelled to investigate the commotion.

The backyard was deep and wide by Southern California standards. Next to the house was an open patio with expensive-looking yellow outdoor furniture. A barbecue as wide as a small car sat to one side. *What is it about men and barbecues?* A flat roof hung above the Spanish-tile floor. There was no house behind the lot, just an expansive canyon. Between the back fence and the porch was a plaza of thick grass in need of a trim. It was a beautiful backyard.

It was the grass that intrigued me. What I was looking for would be in the lawn. I stepped from concrete to the thick pile of turf. I looked down at my feet. I was wearing a pair of bone-colored business pumps, the kind that professional women prefer: pretty enough to say footwear matters but plain enough to be understated. They were great for work, but I was skeptical about their efficacy in the garden—and around ants.

Most people have some form of paranoia, something that sets their teeth on edge. Some people despise snakes. My irrational fear is bugs. I hate bugs. I'm a bug bigot. Always have been and always will be. As far as I'm concerned, they're just minute monsters. Of course, some bugs are worse than others. Ants don't generally bring a terror response, but I still don't like them. I noticed my pulse quickening as I took another step on the grass, feeling the blades surrender to my weight.

If there are ants, then there should be ant mounds. I raised my eyes and looked the lawn over more closely. A brown pile of dirt rose above the grass. It wasn't alone. Two others were in the planter that ran along the back fence.

"There you are," I said, sounding more nonchalant than I felt. I approached the closest mound and bent over to study it. A wave of revulsion ran through me. My bug bigotry was working overtime. These mounds looked different than others I had seen before. They were larger and more flat. I could see the inhabitants wandering around, working feverishly at something.

The ants were about a quarter of an inch in length. Some were smaller, others a little larger. They weren't truly red, not as I'd expected. There was a brown tint to them. I wondered how such small things could inflict such great pain, and how the little amount of venom in their bodies could have killed Lizzy. I reminded myself that she was allergic to insect venom. Still, while larger than other ants, they weren't all that big.

The dog began yapping again. I ignored it, hoping it would go away.

"I wouldn't stand there, lady."

I jumped a foot and trod backward, spinning to see the unexpected visitor.

"Wha—what?"

"Didn't mean to scare you. Please step back on the concrete patio." He was short, round, and red-faced and was wearing a brown workingman's uniform. On his head was a brown baseball cap with the words "Stewart Extermination." I did as he said.

He walked over. "You don't want to mess with those buggers. They have no sense of humor. *Solenopsis invicta.* That's their scientific name. The last part means 'invincible.' Scientists named them that because the little monsters are so aggressive."

"You're here to exterminate them?" I tried to quiet my heart.

He nodded. "Name is Danny Stewart. Me and my brother own and operate Stewart Extermination. We're subcontractors to the California Department of Food and Agriculture. Actually, I'm going to plant some traps. The traps have a food substance that attracts the ants which they take into the nest and share. It kills them underground."

"Why not just spray them?" I was hoping he wouldn't ask what I was doing there.

"Not good enough. You see those mounds? That's one nest, not three. The state wants these guys gone, and the only way to do that is to introduce IGRs and MIs into the nest."

I looked at him blankly.

"Insect growth regulators and metabolic inhibitors. It's important to kill them all, including the queen. These guys don't belong here and they're not our friends. They came to the U.S. in the 1930s and have infested the Southwest. Now they're starting to work in

California. Been in the state for a few years and making headway. There may be as many as half a million ants under this lawn. If you had disturbed the nest, they would have come boiling out of there like lava from a volcano, all over your lovely feet. Not a pretty sight."

"And you get called out to deal with them?"

"Yup. Usually it's the homeowner. Don't get many calls from the police."

"I don't imagine you do."

"I read about what happened to Mr. Dayton. It's a shame. If we was talkin' any other kind of insect, then we might have just let things go, but like I said, the state wants them all dead before they become too big a problem to handle." He paused and turned his attention from the dirt mounds to me. "I don't believe I caught your name."

I smiled and held out my hand. "Maddy. It's a pleasure to meet you. I suppose I also owe you a thank-you."

"Naw. You didn't know. Most people don't. You a friend of—"

"I was just curious," I said, short-circuiting his question. "How big a problem is this in California?" I felt somewhat embarrassed. I was willing to bet that information from the state or at least the county came through my office and I ignored it.

"Depends where you live. We've had only a few infestations but the number is growing. Other states have it worse; some haven't seen the problem yet. People don't recognize the need until someone gets hurt, and the nests grow and new nests start. Right now I wouldn't put any money on winning the battle. If you ask me, bugs are gonna take over the world. Long after humans are gone, these guys will be around, making life miserable for other living things."

"But how do they spread? Does someone have to transport them from place to place? I mean, like on fruit or something?"

He shook his big round head. "They fly. Some of them have wings. The winged males swarm out of the nest, usually after a rain and when the sun is shining. Pretty soon winged females join them in the air. Probably following a pheromone trail. They mate while in flight. Pretty neat trick, eh?" He winked at me. I offered a courtesy smile. "After that, the males fall to the ground and die. That's gratitude for ya." He laughed at his little joke. "At some point the females land, strip off their wings, and begin a new nest. The fertilized females are now queens. Each queen lays her first batch of eggs and then tends them until maturity. After that, all she has to do is lay around the house producing eggs for the other ants to care for. Then it starts all over again."

"Amazing."

"Yeah, it kinda is. Too bad they're such vicious varmints."

"You've given me quite an education," I said. Then I thanked him and hustled out of the backyard before he started asking more questions. As I approached the side yard, the dust-mop Cujo hit the fence and started yapping again.

A few moments later I was in my car, backing out of the drive. I saw a brown van parked at the curb, the name of Stewart's business stenciled on the side. I cranked the wheel, shifted from reverse to drive, and, peering through the passenger-side window, gave Allen Dayton's house one more look. A beautiful home was now a monument to a tragedy. I let my eyes trace the property, then started to drive off.

Something seemed wrong—there was something I was overlooking. It happens to me occasionally. My subconscious sees something my thinking mind misses. It drives me crazy, like trying to remember the name of an actor not seen for a few years. I had just removed my foot from the brake when it hit me. Looking at the side yard, I changed my focus from Allen's home to the house with the hairy yapper. I rolled down the window and could hear the muted yipping of the small dog.

It wasn't the dog that was calling to me. It was something else, something that was different. I looked up from the fence to the roof of the house. There it was: a small, rectangular metal box just under the eave. It was pointing at my car. From its perch at the edge of the garage, it could see the house's driveway, the front street, and—if it could be moved—the front yard of Allen's home.

I looked at the other end of the garage and found another camera. That made two on the front of the garage. I pulled forward a little so I could see the home's entry. Sure enough, there was a camera near the front porch.

I pulled the SUV to the curb, got out, went to the front door, and rang the bell. Nothing. I waited a few moments, then started to press the bell again. Before I did, I looked up and noticed that an entryway camera was gazing at me. Before, it had stared at the street. I smiled and waved. I reached for the bell, then jumped when a woman's voice said, "No need to ring again." It came from a speaker somewhere overhead. "Who are you?"

I looked around, trying to find a place to direct my reply. Finding none, I just spoke into the air. "My name is Maddy Glenn." Nothing for several moments. "Hello?"

"The mayor of Santa Rita is named Madison Glenn. Did you know that?" the metallic voice said.

"I did know that. I am she."

"Look at the camera, please."

I did.

"You look like her, all right."

"As I said, I am Madison Glenn. I wonder if we might talk for a moment. Face-to-face, I mean."

A second later the door opened and I was staring at one of the most beautiful women I've ever seen. I had to look down to make eye contact. Her wheelchair made it necessary.

chapter 20

The woman stared at me. Her blond hair hung to her shoulders in supple waves and her blue eyes were bright but unblinking. Her alabaster skin was pure and smooth. Her naturally full lips were unadorned by lipstick. In fact, she wore no makeup at all, yet she seemed to glow. I felt old and hag ugly.

My eyes drifted down from her face. There was a slight droop in her shoulders and one hand, her left, was thin and twisted. The muscles in the arm were flaccid and the skin hung loosely, like adult clothes on a child. Her right arm looked healthy and strong. She wore an ivory shell top that looked as if it had once hung on the rack of an expensive store. She also had on a pair of jet black stretch pants—nothing to button or buckle. They draped over thin legs. Her feet were bare.

"You really are Madison Glenn." There was depth, a resonance, in her voice that sounded familiar. Her words came easy, as if practiced.

"Um, yes, I am." Why had I suddenly gone inarticulate? I refocused. "Not many people recognize a small-city mayor on sight."

"Nonsense. Many in the know think you're an up-and-comer."

There was something familiar about the woman but recognition stayed just out of reach. "I'm sorry to bother you—"

"Where are my manners?" She gave a smile of dazzling, professionally maintained white teeth. "Come in."

I thanked her and followed her as she backed the wheelchair away from the door. The chair was narrow and had a sleek appearance to it, unlike most wheelchairs I had seen. She operated it with a joystick on the right armrest. She moved with such fluid motions that it was obvious she had been motoring the thing for some time.

"Let's sit in the dining room." She led the way. "Can I fix you some tea, or maybe you'd like a cold drink?"

"Just water." I started to offer my help but caught myself. "I am sorry to bother you." I took a seat at the dining table, a contemporary blend of black tubing and smoked glass.

"No bother, Mayor; I don't get many visitors anymore. The chair makes them uncomfortable—my chair, I mean." She wheeled into the kitchen, opened one of the lower cabinets, and removed two glass tumblers. "You sure you don't want something else? I have lemonade. Fresh-made, not store-bought."

"That sounds wonderful."

She set the glasses on the marble counter. It took a moment but I realized the counters were lower than normal. It made sense for a woman in her situation. She must have had the kitchen redone to accommodate her ... I wasn't sure what word to use. *Handicap* seemed too harsh and cold.

Her house had an open floor plan, which is so common in Southern California. From the dining room I could see into not only the kitchen but also the wide living room, where two brown leather sofas faced a coffee table that sat upon a narrow pedestal, seeming to float above the floor. The sofas looked unused. A stone-and-wood-trimmed fireplace dominated the far wall.

The woman approached and set two glasses of lemonade on the table. She made two trips to do it. I took a sip of the sweet fluid. Tasty pulp clung to the inside of the tumbler. It was delicious and I said so. She moved closer to the table. It wasn't until then that I realized one of the chairs in the dining room set was missing, leaving a place for her to park her wheelchair. The table must have been custom-made, because it was a little low for me and a little high for her, a compromise.

She took a sip from her glass, then laughed lightly. "I just realized. I haven't introduced myself. I'm Natalie Sanders. You can call me Nat. That was my professional name."

Suddenly I remembered. She *was* familiar and now I knew why.

"It's coming back to you, isn't it? I've changed in many ways since the accident, but my face remains the same. It confuses people all the time."

"Channel 3 News. You were the anchor for the News 3 team. You were on the air for a long time. I used to watch you every evening."

"Ah, so you were the one." She gave another flash of that winning smile.

"If memory serves, you were the most watched anchor in the LA market."

"That's what the Nielsens said, but I never put much stock in such things."

Details began to trickle back into my mind. Four or five years ago there had been an accident: a news van had lost control and rolled down an embankment.

"You're trying to remember the particulars." I wondered if she were psychic. "I can see it in people's face. It's been long enough since the event that most folks have trouble remembering what they heard."

"Auto accident, wasn't it?"

She nodded and her eyes shifted, as if she no longer saw the present but the distant past. "Ironic in a way—I mean, you being here and all. We were on our way to do a remote broadcast at Election Central in downtown LA. It was something new for us. Usually we just sent reporters and cut away to them as election results came in. That was six years ago. You, if I recall correctly, won your second term to council."

I was amazed. "That's right. Why would a famous news anchor in one of the largest markets in the country know about a small-time politician like me?"

"I cut my reporter's teeth on local elections," she said, using her good arm to raise the glass to her lips. "I got to where I could remember details and names quickly. It's mandatory in the news biz. And as I said, talk has been that you're an up-and-comer."

I wanted to press that comment more but she continued with her story.

"My car was in the shop, so I chose to ride with the camera crew. It was early afternoon—results wouldn't start coming in until after eight—but we needed to set up and I had interviews to arrange. Broadcasting from a makeshift set isn't easy and the details can trip you up. I'm a detail person and hands-on, so I went in early. One of the crew left his lunch at home and wanted to swing by and get it. No problem, really; we had lots of time. He lived up one of the canyon streets in LA. Coming back down the hill, the passenger-side front tire blew. My driver overcorrected, and the van flipped a couple of times and went over the guardrail. They tell me it was a hundred-and-fifty-foot roll down the hill. When I came to, I was in the ER. I don't remember much of the next few hours, but when all was said and done, my back was broken, much of my spinal cord was severed, and I became the lovely creature you see before you today."

"You're still lovely."

"Thank you, but I'm not what I once was." She paused. "I wasn't married. Lots of dates, but I loved my career too much to get involved in a relationship. My parents died a few years before the accident. So it was just me—is just me."

"No other family?"

"I was an only child, something I enjoyed." She looked at me. "No need to feel sorry for me. I have always been a loner. I like living alone. I like what I do. A nurse comes in every day to check on me and I have a housecleaner to tidy up. The insurance money was substantial. I get by."

"You mentioned that you like what you do. May I ask what that is?"

"I'm a researcher. I provide a service to reporters and others who have a need for quick information. I do a lot online and through connections I've made over the years."

"I don't understand."

"Okay, let's say you work for a newspaper and you need some background information on, say, a new biotech firm. More specifically, on the firm's CEO and her past. I find that information using the Internet, several databases I subscribe to, and a lot of hard work. There's more to it than that but you get the idea. I also do research for novelists and nonfiction writers. It keeps me busy."

"You might be a good person to know."

"I'm a great person to know. Would you like more lemonade?"

"No, thank you. But I wonder if I might ask you a question."

"Sure. You want to know about the video cameras. Right?"

"It's nosy of me, I know."

"Ease up on yourself. I have been, and at heart remain, a reporter. Curiosity is part of my nature. I admire it in people."

"I wish others did." My mind shot back to my confrontation with Chief Webb.

"The cameras are my way of keeping track of the outside world. I don't go out much. I'm uncomfortable in crowds and, to be truthful, a little paranoid. I haven't always been, but something else was injured in the accident—my confidence. In my home I feel safe. Outside I feel vulnerable. So I experience the world vicariously. The television, newsmagazines, radio, and newspaper bring me the world. My video system brings me my neighborhood."

"So you can see everything that goes on in front of your house?"

"In front, around the sides, out in back. I can see pretty much three hundred and sixty degrees." She paused and studied me. "I'm not a voyeur, mind you. I don't and can't peek into people's windows. It's a convenience, really. Answering the door takes me from my work and it also takes more effort for me than most. Besides, I've grown weary of the shocked and pitied look I see every time I open the door."

I felt awash in guilt. "I imagine it's difficult."

"Not difficult, awkward. And yes, you had that look, but it's okay. I just don't want to put up with it every time the Jehovah's Witnesses want me to read the latest issue of *Watchtower* or the Mormons want to lead me in a Bible study."

I nodded.

"You're wondering about my next-door neighbor, aren't you?"

"Yes. I imagine the police have talked to you—"

"No one has spoken to me."

I was aghast. "I would have thought they'd have come by. I mean, you live next door. You might have witnessed something."

"I wasn't here when Dayton disappeared. I found out about it while I was in the hospital. I had been there a week. I just got home this morning."

"I hope it wasn't serious."

"It's always serious with me," she stated without emotion. "My plumbing doesn't work like it used to, if you get my meaning. The catheter led to an infection. I waited longer than I should have to deal with it. I was on a project. Long story short, I was admitted for a weeklong treatment of antibiotics."

"I'm sorry."

"Don't be. I'm fine now."

"So you weren't around when Allen was abducted?"

"No, but I may still have what you want." I gave her a quizzical look. She smiled. "Let me show you something."

Nat activated the wheelchair, backed away from the table, then started down a hall off the foyer. The hall seemed narrow when filled with the wheelchair, but it was wide enough to allow her to move without scraping the walls. Photos lined the hall, as in many homes, except these were not of family, vacations, and graduations; they were images of Nat seated behind a desk looking at a television camera, or holding a mic in the face of someone famous. I recognized California's senators, several congressmen, and a few athletes.

She turned left through a wide doorway. It was the master bedroom, or what would be the master bedroom in most homes. This room had no bed. What it did have was a host of electronics. Near a wide set of French doors was a long rosewood table upon which sat a laptop computer. Next to it was a flat-screen monitor hooked up to another computer. Both were running. The rest of the work center contained neatly stacked editions of newspapers and newsmagazines. A large mahogany desk sat center in the room, underneath a futuristic-looking ceiling fan.

On the opposite wall was a media center that looked as if it had been pulled intact from a television studio. I counted six small TV monitors. Two were tuned to television news networks: CNN and MSNBC. Through the others I could see both side yards and the back and front yards. The monitors flickered from one image to the next.

"This is where I spend my waking hours. Everything I need is here. Well, almost everything. My computers are hooked up to the Internet through a satellite system, and to the other computers in the house."

"You have more computers?"

"Almost every room has at least one computer. I have them networked. There's even one in the kitchen—attached to the refrigerator. I just wish I could teach it to cook."

"I'm impressed."

"What you're interested in is over here." She moved to the media center. As I stepped closer, I could see that below the monitors were several wide but thin black electronic devices that reminded me of VCRs. "I record everything. The images from the cameras play on these monitors. As you can see, every five seconds the system switches between cameras. The system records the day onto hard drives, the kind you get in entertainment systems that allow you to pause live programs. Such devices don't really pause the action; they just record in real time until you return. With a push of a button, the image begins to play again right from the stopped position. What they're really doing is playing back what was just recorded, while continuing to record the live feed."

"I see," I said, not certain I did.

"When I went into the hospital, I set up the system to record what happened while I was gone. I have a dog. She's in the backyard."

"We've met."

"I know. I was watching you." That gave me the chills. "I had someone come in and check on Lucy and feed her. The kid I hired was supposed to play with her at least a half hour a day. I'm glad to say that he did. Lucky for him. In a sense, I used the system like a 'nanny camera.'"

"You mean, like parents who secretly tape-record their babysitters."

"Exactly. Lucy is important to me."

"So you got back from the hospital today—"

"About nine this morning. They sprang me early. I think they needed the bed."

"But you watched a week's worth of video since this morning? How is that possible?"

"I don't watch it in real time," she explained. "I watch it in fast forward. It's something you learn in the television business. I don't need to see the grass grow. I just need to know if the boy I hired came over and fed and watered Lucy. I did the same for the other views. You learn to look for what doesn't fit. I was getting ready to clear the hard drives when you showed up. I watched you instead."

"So you have a week's worth of neighborhood goings-on."

"Not much going on, though. It's a pretty boring place."

I gave that some thought. "Can you find a particular date?"

"I know where you're headed. When do the police think Mr. Dayton disappeared?"

I told her and we scanned the video. A moment later I said, "I need to make a call."

It was there on the tape: Allen Dayton leaving his home—alone.

chapter 21

Nat and I watched it several times while we waited for Detective West to make his way north to join us. He arrived forty-five minutes later, apparently having had less trouble with traffic than I did. He pulled up in front of Nat's house and I greeted him at the door. We exchanged pleasantries, to which he added, "You're getting around today. I understand you paid the chief a visit."

"I was looking for you. Is he still mad?"

"You could say that. Don't expect any flowers."

"Maybe this will put me back on his good side." Not that I cared. I showed West to the back room and introduced him to Nat. It took five minutes to lay out why I was there, what I was doing at Dayton's, how I came to knock on Nat's door, and what we had seen on the video. Then we showed the footage.

We played it several times without comment. West was enthralled. He asked Nat to play it forward. She did, the image sped up, and the movement of plants and trees in the wind took on a jerky, surreal motion. The camera, which, Nat explained, recorded a frame every few seconds, caught a clear view of the front of Allen Dayton's house. The shadows lengthened and the sunlight faded. No Dayton.

"You see the problem," I said.

"Yeah, Dayton leaves and doesn't return. And he leaves alone."

"But the blood on the file folder indicates that the abduction took place inside the house."

"Correct."

"So what does that mean?" I asked. "Did Allen somehow make his way back into the house without Nat's cameras seeing him? If so, when did the abductor arrive? None of this makes sense."

"It will. In time it will. Obviously, we are missing something. When we learn what that is, the pieces will begin to fall together." He turned to Nat. "Ms. Sanders—"

"I know, I know. You want the videodisks."

"Actually, the Santa Barbara police have jurisdiction in this area. We'll have to call them. Can you make copies?"

"Yes. It will take some time, because video eats up a lot of disk space, but I can do it."

"I would appreciate it. You've been very helpful."

"I'll get started."

"This might be important, Mayor," West said. "Only time will tell. Still, I think it might be best if you left. Chief Webb might not appreciate your presence."

"Does he have to know?"

"He's on his way. Your call generated some interest. He wants to know what you've found, but I suspect he also wants to know what you're doing snooping around, especially right after your little confrontation."

"I've done nothing wrong."

"I agree, but you'll never convince Chief Webb of that, and if it's all the same to you, I'd prefer not to have to separate you two. I've got police work to do."

I agreed to leave, but with reluctance I didn't hide. Thanking Nat, I excused myself and walked from the house. My mind was an avalanche of confusion. Nothing had made sense before, and it all made even less sense now. I walked to the car with my head down. I was angry. I was baffled. I was frustrated. I know Webb thought I was an interfering nuisance, but sitting idle has never been my way.

Swinging the SUV's door open, I plopped down in the driver's seat, fastened my safety belt, and pulled away. I drove faster than necessary and I caught myself chewing a fingernail. Dayton was gone. That was obvious. He had not returned to the house, and the campaign file was on his desk with the drops of blood. The pattern was consistent. But why, then, did the video show him walking leisurely from his house, never to return? If he was abducted elsewhere, how did the file come to have the two drops of blood on it? Nat's cameras didn't show anyone approaching or entering the house. I supposed it was possible that an intruder could have come over the back fence, crossed the rear yard, made entrance through the French doors, and then planted the file, or at least the blood.

While possible, it didn't seem likely, and such an act would have left signs of forced entry. It was nuts.

I arrived at the freeway five minutes after leaving Nat's home. The traffic was thick but flowing. *At least one good thing.* I pulled into the middle lane and settled into freeway speeds. It was time to get back to the office and get some work done, if I could. Concentration was becoming more difficult. It is hard to focus on the mundane when you may be the next one abducted in a string of kidnappings.

Video images, fire ants, blood drops, a brokenhearted daughter, murder, and more tap-danced in my head. How could life be turned upside down so quickly?

I merged with the southbound traffic, happy in the knowledge that I would have at least half an hour of solitude. Perhaps that would be enough time for the mental maelstrom to calm to mere hurricane status.

A chill ran up my neck and I released it with a shiver. Odd. I shook my head at my foolishness and checked the rearview mirror—

I jumped and my lungs seized. A face was staring back—a face in the mirror. Christopher Truccoli was in my car.

"Wha–what do you want?" I shouted, trying to sound fierce.

"Take it easy, lady. You know what I want. I want my daughter. You're going to take me to her." His words were flat but hot with threat.

"Get out of my car."

"That would be a little difficult on the freeway, Mayor. Just take me to Celeste and do it right now."

"And if I don't?" It was all bluster.

His eyes darkened and his face hardened. He looked like a man who had just lost touch with reality.

"No more games, Mayor. Take me to your home."

"No."

"I think you will." He looked behind him. Satisfied that no one was following, he said, "Your options are limited."

"Are they?"

"*Yes!*" His voice was so loud I thought the windows would crack. "It is my right! I will not be denied! I will not be put off by a woman."

My heart beat with machine gun speed. I assessed my situation and it wasn't good. I couldn't tell if he had a weapon, but I wouldn't put it past him. Being behind me, he had the situational advantage. He could attack and I wouldn't see it coming. *Think, think. You're smart, use those brains.*

"This is illegal, you know." It was a stupid thing but I wanted to keep him talking. His silence was more intimidating than his words.

"Do you think I care? This is about my daughter, and no one is going to keep me from seeing her."

My cell phone! I couldn't just make a call; Truccoli would never allow that. But if I could sneak it out of my purse, I could activate it without his knowledge—I hoped. I had to keep him preoccupied.

"What if I don't do as you say?"

"That would be a bad move, Mayor. A real bad move."

Slowly I lowered my right hand and moved it toward my purse, which rested on the seat next to me.

"Did you abduct your, wife, Mr. Truccoli? Did you kidnap Elizabeth Stout and Allen Dayton?"

"Don't be stupid. Why would I kidnap my former wife? She was a nothing—less than nothing. No ambition. No goals. She was just another waste of flesh. I don't know the others. They're of no concern to me."

I pulled the purse a few inches closer and slipped open the latch. Again I checked the rearview mirror. Truccoli sat in the center of the rear seat. He was looking from side to side and occasionally behind him. Nervous.

"Then why did you marry her?"

"I was young and poor, not that it's any of your business. I thought she could make me happy, but she failed."

"You're unhappy and it's her fault?"

He leaned forward and placed his mouth next to my ear. I snapped my hand back from the purse. His breath was sweet. "You're dancing on thin ice, lady. Don't try to psychoanalyze me. You're not qualified. Now shut up and drive." He leaned back again.

"I'm just making conversation," I managed to choke out. "We have some time before we get to Santa Rita." My breathing was ragged. Feeling oxygen-deprived, I calmed myself and focused on my inhalations. I reached for the purse again and fingered the cell phone. My heart skipped a beat and I felt I would lose control of my bladder any minute. I needed a distraction, something to get Truccoli to look away.

I glanced at the rearview mirror and let my eyes linger, looking away just long enough to make sure I wasn't about to drive my SUV up someone's tailpipe. Truccoli caught the glance and turned around in his seat to look out the back window. I slipped the phone from the purse, hit send, and set it on the seat. I wondered who I had last called, but couldn't recall. Like most cell phones, mine automatically dials the last number called unless the user enters another phone number. I prayed that someone would be there to hear.

"What? What did you see?"

"Nothing. I'm just scared. You're a frightening man."

"Most women find me attractive." He sneered.

"Yeah, I'll bet. Any of them out of prison?"

"You got a smart mouth, lady."

A tiny voice emanated from the phone. Someone had answered.

"What are you going to do to me, Mr. Truccoli?" I asked, sounding as desperate as I could. "I'm just a small-city mayor; I can't make your daughter love you."

"No, but you can make her hate me, can't you?"

"I didn't do that!" I shouted. I wanted to be sure that whomever I called heard. "You sneak in my car, hide in the back, and make me drive south to Santa Rita. How did you find me, anyway?"

"Easy enough. I parked on the street across from your office and waited for you to drive from the parking lot. Then I followed in my own car. I almost lost you in the traffic but I was able to keep you in sight. These big SUVs are easy to spot."

"So you snuck in while I was at Allen Dayton's house?"

"I was going to confront you in the backyard but then the exterminator guy showed up. I had just left my car. We even said hi to each other. I was going to follow you again, but then you pulled back to the curb and went in that other house. Do you know how maddening that is? I checked your car. You were careless and left it unlocked. I thought you'd never come out."

"You don't see how wrong this is?"

He laughed. "Wrong is a subjective term, lady. I have the right to see my daughter."

"She doesn't want to see you."

"Because you've poisoned her mind. This is your fault."

"I took her in so she'd have a place to stay."

"Who asked you to?"

"Some people do the right thing for no reason at all, but you wouldn't understand that."

He swore. "Take me to your house!"

"No!" I screamed back. I glanced in the mirror and saw him sweating. His eyes were wide and wild. His jaw was clamped so tight that I expected to hear his teeth break. He took several deep breaths, and another glance showed me that he had calmed himself a little. I felt a moment's relief.

He spoke again, but this time his voice lacked the heat of fury. His words iced me over. He recited Randi's home address. "She recuperating there, isn't she? That's what my hired man says."

Hired man? The implication was clear. "You leave her alone. One of your men has already injured her."

"That was nothing. As PIs go, he was an upstanding citizen. My new friend doesn't much care about the law." Suddenly he pulled himself forward and stuck his mouth by my ear again. I fought the urge to gag. "The conversation is over. You will drive me to your home and let me talk to Celeste alone, or bad things will begin to happen. Do you understand—" He stopped abruptly. "What is this?" He reached over the seat and snatched up the cell phone. A second later I heard the rear window open and felt the air rush in. Through the side mirror, I saw Truccoli hold the phone out the window and drop it. It bounced off the freeway surface, skipping along until it tumbled under the tires of an eighteen-wheeler one lane over.

"I'll make you pay for that," he said through clenched teeth.

Waiting was over. Things had gone from bad to worse. I couldn't know if the message got through the cell phone, but I did know I wasn't going to take this madman to my home, where Celeste and my parents waited. I had no way of knowing if there really was a hired bruiser perched at Randi's home. It might be real; it might be a bluff. All I knew was that this would be a good time for Paul Shedd's God to get involved. In my terror-saturated mind I heard my voice saying, "And Peter's God."

I knew one other thing: enough was enough.

I glanced in the mirror once again and saw that traffic behind me had slowed a little. There was some distance between me and the cars behind. I took a deep breath, braced myself, and slammed the brake pedal down. The SUV decelerated rapidly. I waited for the tires to lock up but they didn't. The term *antilock brakes* flashed in my brain. But the vehicle came to a quick stop in the middle of the freeway—sharply enough to throw Truccoli into the back of my seat.

The squeal of tires, the blaring of horns, filled the air. Traffic behind me came to a clamorous stop. Several cars in the outer lanes shot past.

"What are you—"

I didn't wait for him to finish the sentence. I grabbed my keys and reached for the door handle, but he pulled me back by the hair.

"No, you don't."

Pain scorched my scalp as he yanked my head back. I reached to the top of my head, groping for his hand. It was easy enough to find and so was the thing I was looking for—his little finger. Seizing it, I yanked it back as hard as I could. Something snapped and a scream that made my skin tingle filled the vehicle. Truccoli released me and I bolted from the SUV.

The rear door opened. Truccoli was climbing out of the back, a half second behind me. My instinct was to run, but I needed a bigger lead if I was going to have any hope of escaping. Instead I charged the door with my hands in front of me. I hit it with all my weight and the heavy metal door closed on Truccoli.

There was more screaming.

I turned. I ran.

I fumbled with my keys, looking for the remote lock. Locking the car was out of the question—the doors were open. I was interested in something else: the panic button. I found it just as a car screamed past, its driver leaning on the horn. I pressed the red button and heard the SUV's alarm go off. I wanted attention—as much attention as I could get. I had Truccoli's; I wanted someone else's, someone who could help.

Turning back, I saw Truccoli exit, his face red and his posture menacing. He started toward me, holding his injured hand and limping. He was picking up speed.

Another car zoomed past, the wind from it reminding me I was on a freeway; although I had been successful in stopping some cars behind me, impatient drivers were zipping around the congestion. California drivers are impatience.

"I ... want ... my ... *daughter!*" Truccoli screamed. From the first phone call to each dramatic meeting I'd had with him, he had struck me as a man teetering on the edge. The cliff had given way.

The music of shrill sirens began to fill the air. They sounded beautiful.

"Get out of the road, you stupid ..." The driver's voice faded as he sped by, but his hand gesture was memorable.

A glance over the shoulder made my stomach twist. Truccoli was closing the distance. I veered right, into oncoming traffic. More tires squealed. More horns blared. The lead car in the lane banked right and missed me by a foot. I continued forward, toward the white metal guardrail that lined the western edge of the freeway.

The rail was about thirty inches high. I climbed over and stopped short. I was looking down an embankment that dropped twenty or twenty-five feet to a dirt path that bordered the sandy beach. The slope was steep. Walking down was impossible, let alone running.

I heard footsteps behind me. I didn't, couldn't, look back. I jumped.

As I did, I felt something brush by my hair, and I knew that Truccoli had just missed latching on to me.

My feet dug into the foliage and soft soil, and then I began to roll. The thick blanket of ice plants cushioned my fall, but it was a fall nonetheless. It did nothing to slow my descent.

I landed at the bottom of the slope, flat on my back. Pain was firing through my body in every direction. My neck hurt as if someone had twisted it. Truccoli had tried. The fall had done the rest.

I pushed to my feet and scuttled forward along the dirt path. Ten steps later I heard a thud, followed by hot obscenities. I glanced over my shoulder and saw Truccoli lying in a heap. He had landed harder than I. Good. I pressed on. A few steps later I noticed a new pain, a lightning jab of agony in my hip. Terror urged me on.

The noises from the freeway above and to my right seemed a light-year away. I began to question my choice. At least on the freeway there was a slim chance someone would come to my aid. Down by the beach I was isolated. I had hoped the cars would frighten Truccoli off or that he would fail to follow me. I was wrong.

I pressed forward, willing one painful step to follow the other, but my legs moved slower than my demands. My heart was a trip-hammer and I thought my lungs would combust. The aches crescendoed in a cacophony of misery.

Another pain joined the mix. A hand grabbed my blouse and pulled. My feet went out from under me and I stumbled back into Truccoli. I didn't wait for words. I found my footing and spun toward him, my elbow aimed at his head. It connected with a thud, sending a coruscating, hot pain through my arm. His grip released and I started forward, but not fast enough. He snatched me again. This time he spun me around and backhanded me across the cheek. Flashes of light filled my eyes and my knees folded. He yanked me up and gave me another shot.

My vision narrowed to tunnels and my stomach turned with nausea. I couldn't tell if I was going to vomit or pass out. Instead I brought a knee up as hard as I could, connecting with his kneecap. I did it again and again but Truccoli wouldn't let go.

"You ... will ... do ... as ... I ... say." He drew his fist back and I covered my face, waiting for the blow to land.

It never came.

He let go and I melted to the ground. Parting my hands, I looked up to see Truccoli changing directions. There was someone with him. No, not with him—behind him. I heard a thud, then another and finally a third.

Truccoli fell backward like a redwood cut at the roots.

My gaze switched from the unconscious Truccoli to the man who had come to my rescue. His face was red as a beet, his breathing ragged, and his fists still wadded into fleshy hammers. He took several deep breaths, then said, "I told you to be careful."

Chief Webb never looked so good.

chapter 22

"Are you sure you don't want to rest in your bed?" my mother asked. She looked on the verge of tears. For the third time in as many minutes, she adjusted the cold compress on my head.

"No, I'm comfortable here." It wasn't a lie but it was a well-stretched truth. I wouldn't be comfortable anyplace. I had spent the last three hours in the ER. The doctor who treated Randi treated me. He listened to the story, shook his head, then ordered X-rays. A painful "Does it hurt when I do this?" exam followed. When it was all over, I had a slightly strained hip and a dozen bruises. Not bad, considering Truccoli had looked insane enough to kill me.

The ER doctor had taken it upon himself to inform Jerry of my condition, as a matter of "professional courtesy." Jerry arrived soon afterward and insisted on driving me home. I wanted to pick up my car, which had been towed to the Police Station for safekeeping. Jerry refused to listen to my logic. He wasn't going to let me drive.

Once home, I had to tell the whole story. My mother puddled up, my father paced in anger, and Jerry listened sympathetically. Celeste was morose. At times she shook. I tried to comfort everyone and they were working overtime to comfort me.

"Come here, Celeste." I held out a hand.

She did and tears brimmed in her eyes as she knelt by the sofa. I could tell she was looking at my swollen and bruised cheeks. "I'm so, so, so sorry," she said and began to cry.

I ran my hand through her hair. "It's not your fault, kiddo. I'm fine. You father is—"

"Nuts. He's insane. No wonder my mother divorced him."

I couldn't argue with her. "Just remember, he's the one who's nuts, not you. None of this is your fault. We're both victims. I don't want you to feel guilty. I don't like it when my friends feel guilty."

She smiled. I was about to say something witty when the doorbell rang. Jerry was on his feet in an instant and my father spun on his heels.

"Easy boys," I said. "It's just a doorbell. Remember, there's still a guard out there."

Dad went to the door and peered through the peephole. "It's Detective West. He has a surprise with him."

"I hope it's a good surprise," I said. "Don't leave him standing outside."

I propped myself up to see over the arm of the sofa. West entered and stepped to the side. Randi tottered in, swaying on her crutches.

"Ta-da!" she said with a big smile.

I was glad to see her. Surprised but very happy. Before Webb could ask if I was injured, I had told him what Truccoli had said about a hired man at Randi's home. A cell phone call later, men were on their way—including, I was later told, Judson West. Because he had been in Santa Barbara, he arrived long after the street cops.

"What are you doing here?" I asked Randi. "You're supposed to stay off your feet."

"That's what I said," West offered. "She's a little headstrong." Then to Randi he added, "No offense meant."

"None taken," she said cheerfully. "I gave him a choice: he could drive me here or I could hobble the ten miles on crutches. One way or the other, I was getting here."

"Don't just stand there." I raised myself to a sitting position. Mom protested but I waved her off with a smile. "I've been lying down too long. I need to sit." I patted the seat next to me and Randi worked her way into position. We looked at each other, then laughed. Dad brought in chairs from the dining room so everyone could sit.

"We're a pair, aren't we," Randi said. "I win; I have a cast. You only have cuts and bruises."

"Fine by me. You'll envy me the first time you try to shower with that thing on."

"I envy you in more ways than you know," she said softly. "I guess you heard: no bogeyman at my place."

"Yeah, West was kind enough to call. I guess Truccoli was bluffing—about that at least."

"He's lied about everything else," Celeste said bitterly. That cooled the room. "What will happen to him?" All eyes shifted to West.

"He's in pretty deep, Celeste. When he entered the mayor's car and forced, or I should say, tried to force, her to go someplace she didn't want to go, well, that makes it kidnapping. There are assault charges and more. He won't be getting out of jail on easy bail this time. He's being held for a bail hearing rather than someone looking at a chart and saying, 'Pay this.' The district attorney is pretty upset. I hear he's going to lower the boom."

"Good," Celeste said. "Maybe they can lower it several times."

I studied her for a moment. Over the last few days she had changed. The harshness of evil had evicted her teenager quality. Life had forced her to grow up faster than someone her age should. I felt something breaking inside me.

Turning to West, I asked, "How is the chief doing? He looked pretty worn-out when I last saw him."

"He's fine. I called the office a little while ago. One of the other detectives told me that the chief is having to repeat the story over and over—and is loving every minute of it. It's been a while since he's made a collar all on his own. Cops like him live for that stuff. Nothing rings their bell more than interrupting a crime and putting a quick end to it."

"I owe him big-time."

West just nodded. "You should know . . ." He looked at Celeste. "We shouldn't make too much of this, but I've finally gotten word from the SI people. That's where I was when you came by the station, Mayor. The blood on your business card does match Lisa Truccoli's DNA. We got a match between Elizabeth Stout's DNA and the blood left on the photo. I expect we'll get the same kind of result from Dayton's DNA and the file folder."

Celeste gasped.

"Now, hold on," West said. "We assumed that from the beginning, and it must be remembered that that is the only blood we found."

"It's still hard to hear," I said.

"I know. I stopped by the coroner's office and had Egan look at Mrs. Stout's body again. He found a small puncture mark on the end of her left thumb. It's odd in a way. I would have expected more violence."

The room fell silent. A moment later I heard Celeste sniffle.

"I have some questions for you, Mayor," West said as if he hadn't just dropped a ton of bricks on us. His tone had darkened.

"I think I know what's coming."

"What were you doing at Dayton's house? I know what you told me at Nat Sanders' but I think you're holding back."

"Nat Sanders?" Dad said. "She was the best news anchor ever. I used to watch her all the time. Cute too."

"Contain the libido, Greg," my mom said.

"It has nothing to do with libido," he countered. "I just admire her reportorial skill. You really met her?"

"Yes," I said, then told the whole story again. I looked around the room. West had just asked the question no one else dared ask. I took a deep breath and let it out slowly. "The ant thing bothers me. Randi got stung at Dayton's house. Lizzy died from a reaction to a fire ant sting. The coincidence is too much."

"I wouldn't put too much in the ant thing," West said. "I've done a little research of my own. Those ants are all over the Southwest and are making new inroads into California every day. Mrs. Stout may have had the misfortune of being kept near an ant infestation."

"That's the point. The exterminator told me the ants weren't that prevalent in our county. There had only been a few outbreaks."

"Wait a minute," Randi said. "How widespread?"

"The entire Southwest, as I said," West replied.

"No," she insisted. "How widespread in our county?"

"I don't know," West admitted.

"That would be California Department of Agriculture, right?" Randi asked.

"California Department of Food and Agriculture," I agreed.

Randi asked for a phone and called information. She made another call and we sat in silence while she did what she did best. A few minutes later she hung up. "There are less than a dozen places or so that have reported infestations in our county."

"But the abductor may be holding them outside the county," Jerry said. "They could be many miles from here."

"No," I said. "Lizzy's body was tied to the pier. She couldn't have died too far from that location. Surely the abductor wouldn't travel fifty or a hundred miles just to tie her to that particular pier. There are too many other, more convenient places to dispose of a body."

"Maybe he was trying to deliver a message," Jerry said.

West shook his head. "Mrs. Stout's death seems unintentional. I doubt that the abductor used a red imported fire ant to kill his victim. He would've had to have known of the hypersensitivity to insect venom. The mayor is right." He fell into silent thought. "I want those locations. Who did you talk to, Randi?"

"I anticipated that," she replied. "We should hear a ringing from Maddy's upstairs office any minute. I asked that they fax the locations."

"You're good," West said. "Ever thought of a career in law enforcement?"

"Leave her alone," I said. "She has a career."

He winked at her and mouthed, "We'll talk."

"Did you see anything more on the video?" I asked West.

He shook his head. "I viewed a little more after you left. Dayton came and went several times, but that's to be expected. If someone had been taping my home, they would have seen the same thing. The key point is that Dayton left but didn't come back, and there's no sign of someone making entrance into the house."

"She could see the whole house through her cameras?" Randi asked.

"No," West answered. "The cameras are set to cover her backyard, which means that because of the angles, they cover about a third of Dayton's rear yard. Several other cameras cover the street directly in front of her home. Again, the angles allow her to see a portion of Dayton's front yard and his front door. The rest of the house and the far side yard are out of view."

"So someone could have broken into the house through the side yard?" Randi pressed.

"True," West admitted. "We can't dismiss that idea. There are windows on that side of the house, but they were all locked. I checked for signs of forced entry and found none. It still appears that the abductor was let in."

"But that's the rub, isn't it?" I said. "The video doesn't show anyone entering the house after Dayton left alone—not even Dayton."

"Yeah," West said. "That's the problem."

I had started to say something else when the fax machine in my office rang.

"I'll get it." Celeste darted up the stairs. Moments later she came down with a piece of paper in her hand. "Is this it?" She handed it to Randi, who glanced at it and nodded. Randi passed it to West.

"It looks like I have some work to do."

The house was quiet—blissfully quiet. The week's pressure had all but squeezed the life out of me. The pains, bumps, and bruises from the afternoon's attack had drained me. I felt more raisin than grape. I let the hush embrace me like a warm coat. Mom and Dad had gone to bed. West had left a few hours earlier.

Jerry wanted to stay and play guardian again but this time I refused. After a couple of objections I put my foot down. "This is a girls' party now. No boys allowed." He chuckled, then rose from his seat, gave me a polite kiss on the cheek, and walked to the door. Celeste locked it behind him, then came back to the living room and sat on the hearth. She looked at Randi and Randi returned the gaze. I saw my assistant's eyebrows shoot up and down.

"What?" I asked her.

"I didn't say anything," Randi said.

"Me neither," Celeste chimed.

"You don't need to. I know that cute did-you-see-that look." I shifted my stiff body on the sofa. Each hour seemed to lock up another joint.

"I think he's sweet on you," Celeste said with a grin that only young women can manage.

"Who? Jerry? There's nothing between us."

"That's not what she said," Randi countered. "She said he was sweet on you, not that you were sweet on him."

"Are you?" Celeste asked.

"Are I what—I mean, am I what?"

"You have her flustered," Randi said. "I've never seen her flustered."

"I am not flustered," I insisted. "Jerry and I are friends. He had an interest at one time, but things have changed over the years."

Randi gave me a smug look. "Things have changed," she parroted. "We understand."

"All right, you two, you're taking advantage of a battered woman."

"And then there's the yummy Detective Judson West." Randi wasn't letting up. Celeste allowed a smile to settle where only a frown had been. "Don't you just love the name? Judson."

"He is so totally sweet on you," Celeste said.

"Oh, stop," I said. "I'm starting to regret inviting you to stay the night."

"I can see it," Celeste pressed.

"Me too," Randi added. "That's two against one. Or maybe it's unanimous and you're just playing dumb."

"We don't know each other well enough for him to be interested in me."

Randi guffawed. "Oh, come on. You think men sit down and reason this through? Male hormones and brain cells don't work at the same time. It's one or the other, like a light switch: on or off; off or on."

"Definitely on," Celeste said.

"Definitely on," Randi repeated. "Tell us, if dashing and debonair Detective Judson West were to ask out the powerful, influential, knockdown-gorgeous Mayor Maddy Glenn, would she go?"

"No," I said quickly.

"And why not?" Randi asked.

"It would be unprofessional. He's working a case in which I am involved. It wouldn't look right."

"Uh-huh, and if there weren't a case, what then?" Randi pressed.

"Not much sense in answering hypothetical questions."

Randi and Celeste looked at each other. "She'd go," they said in unison, then laughed. I couldn't help joining them. The laughter stemmed less from the comment than from too many days of oppressive thoughts and fears. To have a break, even a momentary one, was welcome. The fears weren't gone. All was not well. Lisa Truccoli and Allen Dayton were still missing, Lizzy was still dead, and we were no closer to finding an answer than when it all began. Randi and I had endured injury. Celeste was still a hollow shell, gutted by fear and imaginations of the worst. Her half-crazed father was in jail. But for a few seconds there was laughter, cleansing and cathartic laughter.

Then it stopped. Reality began to settle in once again, poisoning our moment.

After a few seconds of uncomfortable silence, Celeste said, "I think I'll go to bed."

We said good night and watched as she made her way up the stairs. I heard the door to the guest room open and close.

"My heart breaks for her," I admitted.

"She's a trooper," Randi said. "I don't know if I could be that strong."

"If anyone could, you could."

"I don't know." Her gaze went distant. "Things bother me more than I let on. I've been worried about you and everything else."

"And I've been worried about you. You've been a rock through all this, but I can tell it's getting to you."

She nodded. "It shows that much, huh?"

"Not to others, but it does to me." I stared at the dark fireplace and wished a flame were blazing there. A fire brings more than heat; it brings a place of quiet reflection. My mind ran back to when Celeste and I sat before a roaring fire the day someone abducted her mother. "We're closer than most. We know each other better than most in our working relationship."

"Perhaps," Randi whispered. She too was gazing into the empty fireplace.

"What's wrong?" There was darkness, a sadness, veiling her face. "Did I say something?"

Her head snapped around. "No. You've done everything right. As always, you surprise me with your insight and courage. It's almost frightening."

"Frightening? How so?"

She shook her head. "I don't know. Sometimes . . . sometimes it seems that the best course of action is to step back and let things happen. Things have a way of working themselves out."

"Not in my experience. Horses don't break themselves; some-one has to tame them. Life is that way."

Randi blinked several times. "Did you just use a ranch metaphor?"

I grinned. "I'm tired and on painkillers. I'm not at my best. I think I heard it in a movie."

She nodded. "I understand about the meds. I'm a little fuzzy-headed myself."

"Perhaps we should call it a night. I'll get you a blanket."

"No need. I'll be fine. The sofa is comfy and the room warm. Don't worry about me."

"You sure?"

"Yeah." Her gaze returned to the fireplace. "Who do you think is doing all this?"

"I wish I knew. The more I know, the more confused I become. The whole thing is out of kilter. Why abduct people associated with me but never make contact, never ask for ransom? What kind of person does that? Why leave clues like the drops of blood on my card, a photo of me, and a file you prepared? I'm no detective, but I doubt that many criminals do those kinds of things. Then there's Lizzy's death—an ant bite, of all things."

"An accidental death," Randi mumbled.

"That's what West thinks, not that it makes any difference. Lizzy is dead and died because of a felony. It's murder no matter how you look at it."

Randi nodded slowly, still staring at the cold hearth.

A light at the front window caught my attention. The light traced the window, then moved away. It was the security guard. He walked around the house from time to time, checking windows and doors. I had seen the light many times. In one way it was a comfort; in another, a reminder that a guard was needed to protect me and my own.

I turned back to Randi. She seemed thin and frail, as if half her weight had evaporated while I looked away. "Are you okay?"

She looked at me. Her eyes were red and puffy. "Yeah, I'm all right. Just a little tired and sore. I think the meds are making me sleepy."

"I'll leave you alone so you can sleep." I rose to my feet, a painful effort, but at least I didn't have a cast on my foot. "Are you sure you'll be okay down here? I don't mind sharing my bed for a night."

"I don't want to attempt the stairs. My ankle is killing me. I'll be more comfortable on the sofa."

"Okay. I'm going to bring the blanket down anyway. You can use it if you want."

I went upstairs, trying to ignore each ache and pain, pulled a spare blanket from the hall closet, and returned to the living room. Randi had stretched out on the couch, lying on her back, the wounded ankle resting on the padded arm. Her eyes were closed and her face was turned to the side. She appeared to be asleep. I spread the blanket out along the back of the sofa to make it easy for her to reach.

I felt blessed to have a friend like Randi. Well over a decade separated us in age, but at heart we were the same. I studied her still form for a moment, then noticed that a small tear had trickled down her cheek. My heart broke.

Fighting back my own tears, I climbed the stairs and went to bed.

chapter 23

It was probably the meds. I seldom take anything more powerful than ibuprofen, so my tolerance for stronger medication is low. The doctor had given me Tylenol with codeine to take the edge off the cuts, bruises, and hip pain. I had taken my second dose and it wasn't sitting well. The codeine was upsetting my stomach and unsettling, nonsensical dreams disrupted my sleep. I fought the bed for a while, then surrendered to the knowledge that sleep was out of reach.

I sat up and looked at the clock: 2:00 a.m. It was a miserable hour to be awake. Sitting in the dark had no appeal to me. I clicked on my bedside lamp. The light from it fell on a novel I had started two weeks before. I hadn't touched it since. I picked the book up, then returned it to the nightstand. I had no desire to read.

Normally I sleep well, but there are nights when my mind won't settle. In those times, I go down the hall and work for an hour or two. That usually helps. I rose, slipped into a terry cloth robe, and quietly made the short journey to my home office. I settled into my chair and turned on the desk light, leaving the overhead off. Too much light would do nothing to help me feel sleepy again.

I sat there listening to the silence for a few moments. I didn't know what the future held, but for now there was peace and quiet. I savored it, luxuriated in it, then turned my attention to my desk. I had spent very little time in here over the last week. A thin layer of dust covered the glossy wood surface. I ran my finger through it and looked forward to the day Maria would be able to return to housecleaning. Since Mom and Dad started staying over, I gave Maria time off. Mom was compulsively clean but never came into my office. She knew I could be territorial, especially about business matters—something I picked up from my father. She never touched his home office, either.

On the desk was the file Randi had prepared. I opened the folder and studied the material. Previously I had looked through the pages, impressed by her thoroughness and detail. I had not studied it at length, not truly studied it as it deserved. So now I carefully reviewed the proposal, the demographics, estimated expenditures, key issues, and likely opponents. The last one caught my eye. Every politician has two primary concerns when running for office: money and opponents. I had noticed the list before but had not taken in the names.

It was a short list. Congressman Martin Roth had yet to announce his retirement, so all this was based on inside information Randi had gleaned from friends who worked for the congressman. The list would grow once word was out. Roth was a Republican, and several from that party would vie for the spot. Robert Till, the county supervisor, whose district closely matched Roth's, was a natural assumption and would be a tough challenger. He had money, name recognition, and was as ambitious as they come. I watched his last campaign, and his speaking ability and natural charisma had shredded the other three candidates. He won his seat with fifty-eight percent of the vote. In a four-person race, that was an enormous number. Randi had him at the top of the list.

Another Republican would come from the business sector. Scott Elliot was the owner of two car dealerships. He could finance a congressional campaign out of his own pocket, but he'd had some bad publicity the year before. One of his managers had been playing games with lending institutions that loaned money for car purchases. Still, the memory of voters could be short about such things.

The list of Democratic contenders was longer. Not unusual, when an office is held so long by the opposite party. I was familiar with the name Wilma Easton. She was an assemblywoman in the state legislature. Although she had high name ID, she tended to self-destruct and came across as brash. She was also extremely liberal—too liberal even for her own party. Her acidic personality might cost her in a long and more visible campaign.

I didn't recognize the next name: Garret Kinsley. Randi listed him as an outsider but a possible dark horse. A former diplomat to Argentina, he was handsome, well spoken, and well connected. To date he had shown little interest in the seat, but that could change once Roth announced his retirement.

The next name yanked me back as if I were a dog on a leash: Tess Lawrence—the perpetual speck of dirt in my eye. I had never heard her mention an interest in seeking a congressional seat, but then why would I? We had never been pals. In fact, we had always been poles apart on just about everything. An asterisk appeared by her name. I looked to the bottom of the page and found a footnote: "Inside information from Lawrence's aide. Ninety percent probability for a run. She's been stashing money in her war chest and taking more speaking requests. Has contacted LA consulting firm. Most likely will announce late."

Randi didn't name the aide. Tess had gone through three in the last two years. Most likely, the last one fired had spilled the beans, although the current aide was still a possibility. I let the revelation percolate in my mind. I wondered why Randi hadn't brought it up in conversation, although she had asked several times if I had read the file. Perhaps she was waiting for me to react—her way of determining if I had actually put eyeball to page.

Tess could be a problem. She was shrewd, an excellent campaigner, and ruthless. I stopped myself. I had made no decision to run for the seat; why was I worried about Tess taking a shot at it? It was her right. Any citizen of age who hadn't committed a felony could run for office.

Who was I kidding? Tess would be a disaster in the office. The thought of having to call her Congresswoman was too much to think about. If I chose to be honest with myself, I'd run just to keep her from settling in on Capitol Hill. That was a lousy motive but it was nonetheless real. Regardless of what I told Randi and others, I've always wanted to make a run for Congress. Now was as good a time as any.

I had begun to imagine what it would be like to walk the hallowed halls of Congress, when my mind chose a different path. I tried to focus on the excitement of such a large campaign and to imagine myself seated in a joint session while listening to the State of the Union address, but my thoughts remained untamable. Instead of images of Capitol Hill, my brain was flooded by the dream of Peter and the cardboard box. This time the image came with an audio track of Paul Shedd's words on the pier. Was the Bible he gave Peter in the box?

I shook my head. It didn't matter if it was. It had been there eight years; another night, another week, another month or year would make no difference to the here-and-now. I returned my attention to the file folder but my eyes refused to suck up the words. All I could see was dream-Peter's sad countenance. All I could hear was the sincerity in Paul Shedd's voice. Faith was important to Paul;

there was no doubt of that. It had become important to Peter in the hours before he died.

Peter had not shared with me the true goings-on during the fishing trips. Perhaps he didn't know how. And after his ... what did Paul call it? Decision? Yes, his "decision." I'm sure he would have shared everything after returning from Los Angeles. That was the kind of relationship we had. We communicated well without suffocating each other. Peter never came back from LA. The conversation never happened. And now it was too late.

I took a deep breath and let it out slowly, as if the act would purge the smoky emotions. It didn't.

I turned my chair and looked toward the closet. It was long and covered by mirrored doors. I hate mirrored closet doors in general, but I hated them even more at that moment. Staring back at me was the worn, wearied, confused woman I had become. Beyond the doors was the box.

This was a waste of time. I hadn't been able to open the silly thing in eight years; I certainly didn't have enough courage to do it in the wee hours. Not much thinking happened over the next few moments. Somewhere between the time when I told myself the box was going to stay right where I put it almost a decade ago and the instant when I became conscious that I was seated on the floor with the cardboard container in front of me, I had crossed the room, opened the closet, and pulled out the fearful thing.

There was dust on the lid. It felt grimy to touch, and indescribable images of horror bobbed around in my brain. Eight years those things had sat in the black of the box. I realized my hands were shaking. I felt silly. I was a grown woman. There was nothing to fear. I was only doing what I should have done the moment the box crossed my threshold.

Tears began to run. The items in the box were just inanimate objects. That's all. The only connection to my husband was that he had owned them. People are not defined by what they own, I told myself. My logical mind was working overtime, but like a car on ice, it was spinning its wheels and going somewhere I didn't want it to go.

"This is stupid," I whispered and resolved to rise from my place on the floor and put the box back. It was late. I should be asleep. I had big issues to address tomorrow and needed my rest. That was the sensible thing to do.

I opened the box.

My breathing stopped. My heart hesitated.

The only light in the room came from my desk lamp. I had to tilt the box to see inside. I reached in and removed a set of keys. A leather tag with the BMW logo on it hung from the ring. I smiled. I had once accused Peter of loving the car more than me. I asked if it were true. He told me he'd think about it and let me know. Then he laughed and said I had better "wheels" than the car. I set the keys to the side.

Reaching in again, I removed his electronic Palm Pilot 5000. Again I had to smile. He had just bought the PDA and had spent two evenings inputting his address book. It was one of Palm's first products, antiquated by today's standards. In eight years it had become a museum piece. Peter thought it was the greatest invention ever. I wish he could see the handheld computer I carry today. I ran my hand along the black case, reminding myself that my husband had once held this. Like the keys, it was clean of any blood. For that I was thankful.

There were other things. A tie rested neatly in one corner. It bore dark stains that made me feel sick. I dropped it to the floor by the keys and Palm Pilot. There was the fountain pen I had given him the Christmas before. I found his checkbook, untouched since the day the police removed it from his body. I also found a Bible.

Slowly I removed the volume. I was surprised. For some reason I was expecting a black, leather-bound book, but this was a hard-back. I held it up to the light. The cover called it a "Study Bible." There were rust-colored stains on it. I fought off a shudder.

My back and hips ached. I was getting too old to sit on the floor for very long, especially after the day I had. I rose, crossed to my desk, and set the Bible down. I reseated myself and looked at the cover, staring at the stains for long minutes. No thoughts occurred to me. I was numb. "You've come this far," I said to myself. "Don't quit now."

I opened the book to the middle. It seemed like a good place to start. The title read, "Psalms." I knew what the Psalms were. They were songs, poetry. I turned the page, then another. A few moments later I began to flip through the pages, moving forward. I remembered that Paul had said he marked his Bibles, then gave them away. I was looking for the marks. Soon I was in the New Testament. Sure enough, passages were underlined and notes filled the margins.

I paused in the first chapter of the gospel of John. The words "All things came into being through Him, and apart from Him nothing came into being that has come into being" were underscored, and there was a handwritten comment in the margin: "Jesus the agent of Creation, Col. 1:16." I assumed that the reference related to another Bible passage. I flipped through the Bible until I came to a dog-eared page. "Romans 10" was printed at the top. Again a passage had been marked off: "But what does it say? 'The Word is near you, in your mouth and in your heart'—that is, the word of faith which we are preaching, that if you confess with your mouth Jesus as Lord, and believe in your heart that God raised Him from the dead, you will be saved; for with the heart a person believes, resulting in righteousness, and with the mouth he confesses, resulting in salvation." And again Paul had etched another note: "The bottom line of faith." *Paul takes his belief seriously.*

Then I noticed another note, different in ink and hand: "I believe this." The words were in a slant used by left-handers. Peter was left-handed. It was also written in a script I was familiar with, one made by a fountain pen. I was sure it was the very pen I had given Peter for Christmas, the pen that was resting on the floor behind me, next to the box I had avoided so long.

I couldn't tear my eyes from the comment. I couldn't turn any more pages. Those three words marked a huge decision by Peter. My eyes fell out of focus.

I had opened them again, ready to tackle the meaning of Peter's note and to see if I could find more, when a sound caught my attention. At first it was indistinct—something just outside the boundaries of recognition.

A voice.

Two voices.

In the house.

Was someone else having trouble sleeping? An unsettled feeling welled up. I turned off my desk light and moved through the dark room and opened the door an inch. I put my ear by the opening. I was right; I had heard voices. The first was easy to recognize. It was Randi. The second voice was male. Dad? He was the only male in the house. I started to exit the office, then drew up short. There was intensity in the voices.

". . . this is as stupid as it gets," Randi said in hot but hushed tones. "You'll ruin everything."

"Everything has already been ruined. It can't get worse."

"Yes, it can, you moron. You're making it worse right now. Give it time."

"Time? I don't think you understand how truly deep the trouble is."

The voice was familiar but one I hadn't heard for some time. I strained to pull the name out of the air—Dayton! Allen Dayton was in my living room talking to Randi. No, not talking, arguing. I opened the door wider and slipped from the office. I approached the stairs but didn't descend.

"I can't go home," Dayton said. "Not the way things are. You said you had all this figured out."

"I did. How was I to anticipate her death?"

I peeked over the rail. Randi was standing on one foot, leaning on her crutches. The only light in the room came from the street-lights as their illumination pressed through the sheer drapes. Dayton stood to one side.

What was he doing here? Had he escaped? That was wonderful news. Maybe Lisa had as well. I wanted to bolt down the stairs, but something wasn't right. Randi's voice and words were not welcoming.

"How does this help?" she demanded. "Coming here was the worst idea ever. Do you know what happens if you get caught?"

"What? I go to jail? I'm jail-bound as it is—for murder. So are you."

"Not if no one finds out—and keep your voice down. What did you do to the guard?"

"He's unconscious. I came up the beach side of the property and watched him circle the house. The guy is as regular as clockwork. When he came back around the corner, I hit him with this." He held up a handgun.

Randi lowered her head. "I don't believe this. You don't know how to use a gun."

"I used it well enough to put your plan into motion."

"Against two unsuspecting women," Randi shot back, her voice still a whisper. "You're lucky the guard didn't pound you to pâté."

"I can take care of myself."

"Really? That's a laugh. I must have been insane to hook up with you. Are you sure you didn't kill the guy? You've got one murder on you already."

"He was breathing when I bound and gagged him. I haven't murdered anyone. You're as much to blame as me."

"I didn't strap her body to the pier."

"We had to do something. We had to throw the police off our trail."

"You watch too much television," Randi said. "That just made things worse. Tell me Lisa is still alive and well."

"She's alive but I don't know how well. She refuses to eat. She's looking bad."

"You've got to get away from here. This is crazy. I'll figure something out."

"You've said that before. You haven't called. I think you're about to turn me in."

"Nonsense. I'd just be implicating myself."

My mind was racing. *I must be dreaming. The stress, the codeine have combined to give me the worst dream possible.* But although I desperately wanted to believe in the nightmare theory, my heart sank. My mind began to shut down. This was truth I didn't want to hear. The image of the bound guard, his head bleeding from a blow, tore at my soul.

Other realizations came pouring into my mind like floodwaters from a broken dam. My parents were in the house, and Celeste. Dayton sounded desperate enough to do anything.

"You're the one with the gun," Randi said. "What's your grand idea?"

"Only you can link me to all this. You're the only one who knows what happened. If you're gone, if Lisa Truccoli is gone, then I will be the only abducted person left. I can spin a story about escaping and going for help. They'd believe me. I'm a respectable member of society, a businessman, not a crook."

"It won't work, Allen," Randi said.

Keep him talking. I needed to do something. The alarm system had a panic button on it. I could push that and alert the police, and the noise might drive Dayton away. *The alarm system.* It was set before I went to bed. How did Dayton disarm it? It hit me like a bus. More than once I had forgotten something at home and sent Randi to retrieve it. She had to have the code to keep the alarm from sounding when she entered the house. She must have disarmed the system to let Dayton in. Still, the panic button would work, but it might send Dayton into a frightened frenzy. He already sounded fragile.

I slipped back into my office and made a call to 911. I told the emergency operator that there was a man in the house with a gun. She tried to keep me on the line. That is their training but it was out of the question. I was firm but quiet. "I'm hanging up now. Make sure Detective West knows . . . and do not ring the phone. If you do, you'll set the man off and someone may die." The operator protested but I rang off and left the office again. I hoped the operator had enough sense to take me seriously.

This time I didn't wait at the top of the stairs. I took a deep breath, screwed up my courage, and started down. "Mr. Dayton," I said as casually as I could muster. "I see that you are well. We've been worried."

He spun and aimed the gun at me. I don't know guns but it looked big and bad. His hand was shaking. Not a good sign.

"What are you doing here?"

I smiled. "I live here, remember?"

"I mean, what are you . . . Come down here and be quiet."

"That's bad manners, Dayton." My nerves fired a thousand impulses. "I'll speak in whatever tone I choose. It is my home." That caught him off guard.

"Maddy!" Randi said. "Go upstairs—"

"No!" Dayton barked, then lowered his voice. "I'm calling the shots now. Get down here or I'll put a bullet in your head."

The words sounded ludicrous, coming from this middle-aged executive who had probably never fired a gun in his life. Nonetheless, he was desperate. I finished my descent, then looked at Randi. She seemed to melt under my gaze.

"How long—"

"Long enough, Randi." My words were soft. I wanted to be furious but I was too hurt, too betrayed to react. That would come later—if there was a later. I turned back to Dayton. Behind him I could see that the glass doors off the dining room were open. Randi must have let him in through those doors. A few yards beyond the deck lay a moonlit ocean. Normally it would have been a beautiful sight. "Why, Allen?"

"That's none of your business."

"You're in my house with a gun pointed at me. You've threatened my life and apparently you've set yourself to destroy my career. I think I have a right to ask a few questions." My fear melted like candle wax, which surprised me.

"Ruin your career?" Dayton said with astonishment. "We were trying to save it, trying to make sure you made it to Washington."

"You call this helping me?" The void left by fear was filled with anger. "You kidnap two of my friends and pretend to be abducted yourself, you kill Lizzy, and you consider this good politics?"

"It wasn't meant to be that way. No one was supposed to be hurt." His voice cracked. "It got out of hand. It was supposed to last only a couple of days; then everyone would be found and your name would be in the papers for a week. A few months later you would announce your intention to run for higher office. The papers would naturally speak of the brave mayor who stood by her post despite the threat on her health and life."

Unbelievable! "This is how your firm works these days? What happened to polls, direct mail, and phone banks?"

"The competition is too tough," Dayton said. "We did preliminary polls. Your name ID is abysmal. Less than a third of the people in Santa Rita could call you by name or select your name out of a list of ten. Robert Till was in the eighty percentile, and even Tess Lawrence was double your numbers. You're not controversial enough to get people's attention. You're a great mayor but you need more if you want to move up."

"I'm just one person on your client list, Allen. This is too extreme for you."

He shook his head. "You're the *only* name on my client list. My partners are pushing me out. I should be working the statewide elections, not the chicken-feed local stuff, but they think I've lost my edge. I'm one of the founders of the firm—one of the founders! But that gets me nothing. My partner has positioned himself for a takeover. I needed a loan because of my debt, and my partner agreed to give it to me in exchange for a controlling interest. I was a fool. I gave it to him. I needed a success and soon. I was on the verge of losing everything."

"But the election isn't for nearly two years."

"I know that, Mayor. I'm not an idiot." He waved the gun. "That's when Ms. Portman approached me. I went over the file. We had drinks and then this stupid idea comes out of her mouth. 'Let's make the mayor a hero,' she says. 'It will be easy and no one will get hurt.' I thought she was joking, so I went along with the planning. It was fun, but then it began to make sense."

"I can't believe this ever made sense," I said.

"Shut up!" Dayton snapped. "Besides, you should be directing your criticism at your faithful aide. The whole thing was her idea."

I looked at Randi. Her head was down and she leaned heavily on the crutches.

"There's something you don't know," Randi said to Dayton.

"I think I know enough already."

Randi grimaced. "No, you don't. Not by half. I need to sit down. My leg feels like it's on fire." She hobbled to a chair.

"I don't care how you feel," Dayton said. "You're the only one who can link me to this whole stupid plot."

"And me," I said.

"Yeah, I guess now that's true." He raised the gun. "It appears I'm not the only one who makes colossal blunders."

I had hoped to hear sirens by now, but the night air was silent except for the sound of waves crashing on the shore, their gentle roar rolling through the open glass doors.

A motion. A man staggered into view. In the moonlight, I could see his hands bound in front of him. Tape covered his mouth and blood trickled down the side of his head. A trail of tape dangled from his right cuff. Somehow he had freed his feet. He tottered and I was certain he would fall.

"I said there's something you should know," Randi repeated. "They know about you."

"Not possible, unless you've told them something."

I spoke up. "She's hasn't told anyone anything. Something she'll have to deal with."

"The police have video of you leaving the house but never returning. Right now it's a puzzle to them, but they'll figure out that you faked . . . that we faked your abduction."

"I don't believe you," Dayton said, but his hand began to shake. I began to fear that the gun would go off by itself.

"It's true, Allen," I said and then told him about Nat Sanders. It clicked with him.

"It still doesn't prove anything."

"It will," I assured him. "I think it's time you gave me the gun."

"You're crazy."

"You know I'm the only sane one in the room. I overheard you say that Lisa was still alive. Lizzy died by accident. You're not a killer, Allen. You're a political consultant. It's time to put this campaign to bed." I held out my hand. "The police are on their way. I called before I came down."

"You're lying."

"I'm not good at lying, Allen. The whole sordid affair is over. You know it. Randi knows it. I know it."

Tears began to run down his cheeks. "It was all meant to help. No one was supposed to get hurt. You said so, Randi. No one was supposed to get hurt." He raised his tremulous hand and pointed the gun at his head. "There's no way out. No other way."

"Don't do it, Allen."

The guard charged. He hit Dayton in the lower back and both men plummeted forward. I heard the impact, I heard Dayton's breath forced from his lungs, and I saw the gun tumble to the floor.

The guard's taped wrists made his struggle with Dayton difficult; still he was able to climb on Dayton's back and pin him to the floor. He made a muffled sound through the gray tape over his mouth. I tried to strip the tape from his wrists. He shook his head and made motions to something behind me. Yanking his hands away, he reached for the tape on his mouth and pulled viciously.

"Don't!"

He wasn't looking at me. Before I could turn there was sharp, loud crack and something wet hit me on the back of the head. It began to rain red. I turned as fast as I could. I wasn't fast enough to change anything, but I was quick enough to see Randi drop the gun, then fall to her knees.

Half of her head was gone.

She dropped to the carpet.

A siren cut the night.

epilogue

In the movies, the heroine saves the day and then runs into the arms of her great love. In my case, I crawled into the kitchen and vomited. Seconds later my father appeared, then used words I had never heard him use. "Maddy? Maddy!" He found me, sat on the floor, and took me in his arms. I dissolved into a quivering hysteria.

Celeste was the next to arrive, followed by my mother. We became a heaving mass of tears. No one asked what happened. No one asked who was to blame; we just held each other until there was no longer enough strength to express emotion.

The police arrived minutes later and took Allen Dayton into custody. They moved me and my family outside. Under the canopy of a peaceful sky, draped in ivory moon glow, they asked questions. I answered as best I could. An ambulance arrived and I marveled at the irony. I knew it was standard operating procedure, but there was nothing they could do for Randi. They examined me, seeing the blood in my hair. I assured them I was fine, but they made their examination anyway. I no longer cared.

West arrived five minutes later, surveyed the scene, then took charge. We sat around the large glass-and-iron deck table. The color had bleached from my mother's face. My father was furious, with no one to vent upon. Celeste sat like a statue.

I explained everything I had heard and seen. I shook. I couldn't stop. *So this is a nervous breakdown.*

West listened patiently and asked few questions. "I'll be back." He rose from his seat and walked around the house. I did my best not to look inside but unexplainable inner pressure made me direct my eyes that way. A lump covered by a black tarp lay between my dining room and living room—a lump that had teased me about men just a few hours before. My sadness was profound. Even though Randi had been part of the stupid scheme, she was still one of the few people I had allowed close to me. A very large piece of me lay under that tarp.

More police showed. Some took photographs while others strung yellow tape around my house. Fifteen minutes after West left, the Coroner's Office showed: two men pulling a gurney behind them. They had to wait for Detective West to return. One lit a cigarette and gazed out at the ocean. Just another day's work for him.

Minutes passed like eons. It seemed as if the sun should have risen hours before. Conversation was minimal. We each sat in our own bubbling vat of shock and fear. Strength came from the proximity of loved ones, not in words.

Another person emerged from the side yard. Chief Bill Webb walked through the crowd of police, which parted like water before the prow of a ship. The fire in my belly broke into an inferno. I wanted none his snide remarks, no "I told you so," none of his down-the-nose glances. He stepped to my bench and sat down. At first he stared at the table, and then he let his eyes rise to mine. They were soft, the flint having morphed into cotton. He held out a hand and I took it. We sat that way for the next ten minutes. Occasionally an officer would approach with a question, but Webb would drive the man back with a look.

Nearly an hour had passed since West left. Then I heard his voice echoing down the side yard. "Make room, gentlemen." I turned and West appeared. He smiled, then stepped to the side.

Lisa Truccoli emerged from the darkness.

Two days later we buried Elizabeth Stout. Her husband stood unflinching through the graveside service. Tears rolled off his cheeks in silence. I laid a red rose on her dark coffin. Three days after that I stood next to the open grave of Randi Portman. The crowd was small; most were there to support me. Randi's parents huddled close to each other, exchanging strength through an umbilical shared only by those who measure their married life in decades. Detective Judson West stood to my left, Dr. Jerry Thomas to my right—bookends to my worn and tattered tome. It was good to have them there. My parents stood by, eyes shiny with tears.

After the funeral, beneath the boughs of a large oak tree, West filled us in on what he had learned over the past few days.

Once in police custody, Allen Dayton had held nothing back. He made no pretense of innocence, nor did he claim to be a victim. He had been within a second of pulling the trigger that would end his existence. That changed a person.

According to West, Dayton's rendition had been concise. The plan, which originated with Randi, had been to abduct Lisa and Lizzy, then release them after there was enough press coverage. The abductions were simple enough. Dayton explained and Lisa confirmed that the abductions didn't take place in the homes but near a restaurant close to the Santa Rita Yacht Club. Randi had called both women and asked for a meeting, stating that she was working on a proposed congressional campaign for me. Since they had been instrumental in my previous elections, she wanted them involved early. In turn, they met with Randi at the Crow's Nest, the yacht club's public restaurant. It is a high-class place with a reputation that extends as far north as San Francisco. I had held a thank-you dinner there after I was elected mayor, so Lisa and Lizzy had been there before.

It tore at my heart to realize that each had walked into danger out of loyalty to me. Lisa explained that she met with Randi, who described the congressional campaign she was envisioning and wanted to know if Lisa would participate. She also said that Lisa had to keep it a secret because Randi wanted to spring it on me.

Randi excused herself early, pleading another meeting, paid for the lunch, and left Lisa to finish her meal. As Lisa left the restaurant, she was accosted by a skinny man who said, "If you want to see your daughter alive again, then come with me." Lisa did what any mother would do—she followed. The man led her to a boat, telling her that Celeste was waiting for her. Once below deck, the man pulled a gun and bound Lisa, locking her in one of the small staterooms.

She would stay there for nearly a week.

The boat returned to shore twice during the following week. The first time was the next day, when they brought Lizzy on board. Dayton admitted that Randi had used the same ploy with her. It returned one other time, in the early-morning hours when Lizzy's lifeless body had been removed. Anytime they came close to shore or another boat, Lisa was gagged and locked in the stateroom. It had been in that room where she had helplessly watched Lizzy die. Lisa had no way of knowing why the death occurred.

The third party in the abductions was a surprise to me. Dayton, feeling no compulsion to save himself, felt none to save the other man—a man I had met. Randi and Dayton had recruited a private detective who was well down on his luck. A drug addict with expensive tastes, he was susceptible to cash. His name was Ned Blair, and he was the same Ned Blair who accosted us in the coffee shop. I had felt that Randi was overreacting, but bought into the suggestion that she was trying to make amends for showing Dayton the file without my permission. The truth was, she had arranged the conflict to heighten the deception. What she hadn't planned was interference from a Good Samaritan, interference that led to a scuffle and a broken ankle for her.

I still had trouble believing it—a conspiracy between an ambitious assistant, a washed-up consultant, and a drugged-out PI. If it had worked, Lisa and Lizzy would have been put ashore one night, the boat would have been abandoned, and Blair would have disappeared into the night with a few thousand dollars in his pocket.

Lizzy's death changed everything. The PI panicked, Dayton cracked, and Randi was left holding a fistful of trouble and a future lived out in prison, not on Capitol Hill.

When West finished, he shook my hand and said, "You are an amazing woman." Then he turned to Jerry. "Take good care of her." Jerry said he would and put his arm around me. I watched West walk across the carpet of grass and enter his car.

I hated to see him go.

The call came a month after the tragedy in my home. I was back on the job, seated in my office. The house had been professionally cleaned, the carpet replaced, and I was learning to live in the home of a suicide—a difficult task. If my home were not so closely associated with my husband, I would have left it immediately, but it was his pride and joy, as well as mine. For now I'd try to live there.

It was just after eight when the ringing drew my attention from the paper I was reading. I answered. It was Nat Sanders.

"I've been thinking about you," she said.

"Good thoughts, I hope."

"Yes, good thoughts. I hope this isn't too soon, but such things shouldn't wait too long. I've been doing research. You'll remember that's what I do."

"I remember." I could picture her at her computer, her ever vigilant video cameras scanning the area around her house.

"I've been following the news and the trial. I asked some questions and ran some numbers. I think it's time you started planning your run for Congress."

"That's what started this whole thing," I said with disgust.

"No, greed started this whole thing. Your aide was correct. Now is the time you should run. I want you to know that I'm here for you. I've prepared a file for you to look at . . ."

It was early, and the parking lot at the foot of the pier was nearly as empty as the freeway was full. That was fine with me. I had gone to the office for an hour, then come here, drawn by an invisible cord. I carried only my purse and one other item. I strode quickly with my head down, watching the scene between the slats change from asphalt to sand to water churned by small waves. Halfway along I came to the Fish Kettle restaurant. Locked tighter than a drum, as I knew it would be. I'd come prepared. I removed a quarter from the change purse in my bag and began to tap the window with it. Paul Shedd had been right; it was an annoying sound.

Peering through the glass, I watched as he emerged from the kitchen, his face marred by a scowl. He saw me and his expression changed to one of puzzlement. I grinned broadly, tapped the glass two more times, then held up the Bible he had given my husband so long ago.

Paul blinked several times, then quickstepped my way. He opened the door.

"The last time someone banged on your window with a quarter, you invited him in and gave him coffee and conversation."

"That I did, Mayor." He stepped aside. "Find a comfy seat. I'll get the coffee."

I chose the closest booth, sat down, and set the Bible on the table. Paul reappeared with two steaming cups of coffee.

"Do you have a few minutes?" I asked.

"I'll make the time for you."

I opened the Bible to the passage in Romans. "I've been reading the New Testament over the last few days. There's much of it I don't understand."

"That takes time, Mayor."

I nodded, then pointed at the passage that had been underlined in the book of Romans. "Peter wrote, 'I believe this.'" I took a deep breath. "After a lot of thought and mental wrestling ... well ... I believe it, too."

Paul bit his lip but the smile escaped anyway. "In the gospel of Luke it says that the angels in heaven rejoice over decisions like these. I've got a feeling Peter is putting them all to shame."

Peter in heaven. I liked the thought.

We want to hear from you. Please send your comments about this book to us in care of zreview@zondervan.com. Thank you.

GRAND RAPIDS, MICHIGAN 49530 USA

WWW.ZONDERVAN.COM